Purity's Ecstasy

Janette Seymour

A KANGAROO BOOK
PUBLISHED BY POCKET BOOKS NEW YORK

Another *Original* publication of POCKET BOOKS

POCKET BOOKS, a Simon & Schuster division of
GULF & WESTERN CORPORATION
1230 Avenue of the Americas, New York, N.Y. 10020

ISBN: 0-671-81943-7

First Pocket Books printing February, 1978

Trademarks registered in the United States and other countries.

Printed in the U.S.A.

PURITY

Once the ruggedly handsome Mark Landless rescued her from the horrors of the French Revolution, found her a place in England's highest aristocracy, and claimed her trembling heart as his own. Now he was held captive by Mediterranean pirates—and only Purity could set him free!

PASSION

But the villainous masked pirate, El Diablo, had other plans, as did the sultry Azizza, the Corsair queen of the Mediterranean. Though their treachery and debauchery threatened unending peril for Purity, she would gladly risk their worst—to be reunited with the one man whose touch set her world asunder and her soul aflame!

ECSTASY

Enthralling! Enticing! Exploring the heights and depths of love!

Books by Janette Seymour

Purity's Ecstasy
Purity's Passion

Published by POCKET BOOKS

Chapter One

It came out of the south like a white bird skimming the wavetops: a three-masted vessel of the sort known along the Barbary Coast—from Rabat to Algiers, from Algiers to Tunis—as a *xebec*. Viewed in the sunlight of a Mediterranean afternoon, from the quarterdeck of the lumbering Spanish merchantman, the approaching vessel was a thing of almost inexpressible beauty: straining white sails, sleek hull slicing the blue waters, a banner streaming at every masthead, and a great black flag abaft. But the Spanish captain knew that the *xebec* brought enslavement, rape, slaughter, and horrors unmentionable.

His first instinct—to crowd on studding sails and flee to the northward—he dismissed as a futile protracting of his fate. The lean three-master could run rings around his old tub. The Corsairs would bide their time and come alongside at full speed when the opportunity presented itself. Boarders would leap from her shrouds. A dozen would suffice—a dozen brown-skinned killers with their razor-edged scimitars that could take off a head as easy as breathing. They would be enough to subdue his men, already kneeling and praying for deliverance at the mere sight of the oncoming *xebec*. *Madre de Dios!* Well might they pray. There were not many among the middle-aged crew who would meet the Corsairs' stern requirements of age and fitness: the slave market of Algiers for a few of them, perhaps; for the rest . . .

The Spanish captain looked down into the waist of his ship to the passengers who had come crowding on deck at the news of the Corsair galley. There were men and women, children also. Also present was a nice young pair of newlyweds from Cadiz; well, it was to be hoped that they had made the most of their time together. There was a brawny Dominican monk; you will not be needing your breviary or your beads when you are chained to a galley bench or a treadmill, Brother! There was he, himself: lame from one of Nelson's cannonballs that had taken off the leg below the knee in the bloody shambles of Trafalgar. What hope for him? No chance of life—not even a few hellish years as a galley slave.

His mind was made up. He would fight.

The merchantman carried six long-nosed twelve-pounders, three on each side. They had not been fired for a year, and never in anger. Somehow, he managed to persuade his terrified crewmen that it was better to fight and die than to submit. Somehow, two of the cannons were loaded and trained. One of them was actually made to fire. The twelve-pound sphere of rusty iron struck blue water halfway between the Spaniard and the heeling *xebec*. It bounced high, struck water again, and again; it sank well short of its mark. That was the end of the merchantman's resistance.

The *xebec* cut close in under the Spaniard's stern,

so close that they could see the Corsair captain on the high poop deck, wrapped in a scarlet cloak and burnous, entirely hiding his face and figure. A whip-crack of sound, a blossoming of white smoke, and a death hail of grapeshot swept across the merchant-man's upper deck, slicing flesh and bone, severing vein and artery, tearing cloth and leather, killing and maiming. The Spanish captain died across his wheel. His mate, living, dragged him clear and then put the wheel hard over, bringing the ship into the wind. The sails flapped impotently. The old merchantman slowed to a halt and lay wallowing in the gentle swell.

The *xebec* turned likewise, white sails spilling, and slid neatly alongside its captive.

And the Corsairs leaped aboard, scimitars swinging.

There had been no resistance. The token slaying of one more Spanish crewman had been merely to over-awe the others. This unfortunate lay in a bloody heap by the bulwarks, while the pirates marshaled their prisoners in four groups on the deck. Women. Fit men. Children. The rest. This preliminary sorting-out was supervised by a grinning, black-bearded giant in a Turkish helmet surmounted by nodding peacock plumes. He strode down the lines of terrified pas-sengers and crewmen with two half-naked brutes pad-ding at his heels to do his bidding. An infant was dragged from its screaming mother and put with the other children. The Dominican monk had his cassock ripped from his shoulders to the waist, and appreci-ative hands ran over his white skin, probing the firm muscles. Ten years of hard work in him.

They came to the newlyweds from Cadiz, huddled together, their dark eyes staring. He was as slight and delicate as she, but protective to a fault. He fought them when they dragged her from him and cried like a child when the grinning giant ripped aside her bodice and kneaded her barely formed young breasts. He had to be lifted on high and hurled over the ship's side when they sought to discover if she was a virgin or not. His drowning screams soon faded, for he was a weakling and could not swim a stroke.

The task of sorting out was soon done. Depending on age and looks, the women were either for harem and brothel or for slavery. Children—girls and boys alike—would pleasure pashas and beys from Rabat to Constantinople, and many of the boys would be turned into eunuchs. The fit and strong among the menfolk—such as the Dominican—had before them a lifetime, long or short, of total and unremitting slavery in the galleys, the fields, and the silver mines. These three groups were shepherded aboard the *xebec*.

A dozen or so remained, mostly men, but there was a trembling old woman and a crippled child. The Corsairs, whose fearful reputation was greatly enhanced by the fact that so little was known about their methods, had a golden rule: dead men tell no tales. The unwanted were swiftly decapitated, and their remains were left where they lay. As the *xebec* sailed away, back to the south, from whence it had come, tongues of flame were already licking the bulwarks of the useless old merchantman, and by the time the Corsair vessel was hull-down on the horizon, a tall funeral pyre marked the scene of outrage.

The *reis,* or captain, of the Corsair had watched it all from the high poop deck of the *xebec,* as if scorning to play any menial part of the sorting and disposing of the captives, but he never missed any part of the proceedings. The bearded giant bowed low to his captain when all were safely below and the *xebec* was pointing its long stem toward Algiers. The salute was returned with a brief nod.

"Bring the monk to my cabin."

"At once, Noble One," said the giant, bowing again. He snapped the order to his brutish henchmen. "Fetch the infidel priest!"

The young Dominican came meekly enough. His coarse cassock hung in tatters from his waist, bound there by its knotted cord. An hour of standing in the broiling afternoon sun had already turned the smooth white flesh of his shoulders and chest to an unaccustomed pinkness. His wrists were manacled behind him, and he stumbled over the threshold of the captain's cabin and would have fallen but for the supporting hands of his escort.

"The infidel priest, as you ordered, Noble One," said the black-bearded giant.

The cloaked figure over by the wide stern windows turned to regard the prisoner. The darkness of the cabin, coupled with the glaring light beyond the windows, confused the Dominican's eyes. It was some moments before he could bring into focus the silhouetted figure in the scarlet cloak. When he had done so, he exclaimed, "Holy Mother of God! Is it you— *a woman*—who have done this horror today?"

The captain of the *xebec* had thrown the cloak high over each shoulder and lowered the concealing hood. Woman she was—and of a quality that inspired poets and drove some men mad.

She had hair of a flaming red that outshines the sun, gathered into one thick plait that hung below her waist. Her eyes were like a she-cat's: green and slanting, thick-lashed, and with a high arch of eyebrow. Her skin was a dusky olive, and the total perfection of her countenance was subtly announced by the minor defect of a small mole on her right cheekbone. But it was her mouth that so disturbed the Dominican

and sent his mind scurrying to his solemn vows. It
was a mouth of utter sensuality, molded by a dark
genius for the enslavement of men; full-lipped, rich
in color, framing white teeth, between which slid the
pointed tip of a tiny pink tongue that briefly moistened
the lips. The young monk swallowed hard and lowered
his eyes from her face to her body. He had little comfort to find there. . . .

Under the drawn-back cloak, she wore Turkish
pantaloons of cloth-of-gold, fastened just below the
navel with a jeweled clasp. Above that, she was clad
in a brief, sleeveless jacket heavily embroidered with
gold and sewn with pearls, rubies, and diamonds.
Stunningly, the garment was unfastened, rendering to
the eyes of the captive and his guards her bared
breasts, shamelessly outthrust, long-nippled, and in-
solent.

She pointed to the monk.

"Strip him naked!" she ordered in a voice like the
ripping of fine velvet.

Chapter Two

"Later, Josh, later! No, don't tear my clothes. Mistress will be up here in a moment to say good night to the little maid."

Nancy Shaw gently pulled herself away from her lover's grasp, and he, releasing her, allowed her skirts to fall. She leaned back against the paneling, her cheeks flaming. Really, Josh's attentions had become pressing, indeed dangerous, and could well cost both of them their positions in the household, for all that the mistress was tolerant and easygoing in matters of morals (being French), and particularly indulgent to poor working girls, possibly on account of having herself had a particularly hard youth in the terrible French Revolution.

Josh straightened his powdered wig and cast a self-consciously approving glance at himself in a pier glass outside the nursery door. He really did look fine, he told himself, in his footman's livery of Lincoln-green and old gold, with the silk stockings that so well set off his quite excellent calves.

He picked at a pimple that irritated his chin. "When shall you be free this eve?" he demanded petulantly.

Nancy regarded her lover, so handsome, quite the handsomest swain for miles around, but demanding. Let her play the minx with Josh, let her deny him his pleasure, be it so much as a squeeze of her breasts when the spirit moved him, or a five-minute consummation standing up on the back stairs, and he would be off with that lustful mare, Cecily, the upstairs maid, who even took tinkers to her bed above the stables and was almost certainly of the pox. No, best to placate him, to give of what one was able.

"Later," she said, "later, when the little maid is asleep, when the folks are at their dinner downstairs. Then I'll be ready for you. Come then, Josh, my darling lad."

He smirked and leaned to kiss her on the lips, her breasts. Nancy tucked herself back into her bodice as the sound of her mistress's footsteps mounted the winding stairs to the nursery. Josh made himself scarce.

"Is my little Chastity asleep, Nancy, or am I still in time to bid her good night?"

"Drifted off, she has, ma'am," replied the young nursemaid. "Sleeping like a cherub, she be."

"And she has had her drops of laudanum? Her cough has abated?"

"Much better, ma'am," said the nursemaid assuringly.

"But, if no great improvement shows tomorrow, we must get Dr. Withers to come in and bleed the poor little darling."

"Indeed we must, ma'am."

"I will go in and see her."

"Yes, ma'am."

Nancy followed her mistress into the darkened nursery, wondering as she did so how it felt to be chate-

laine of Clumber Grange and wife of Colonel Mark
Landless, a hero of Waterloo and confidant of the
great Duke of Wellington himself, not to mention being one of the acknowledged beauties of the land, if
not the supreme of them all. A prickle of unchristian
envy was kindled in the not inconsiderable bosom of
the young child's nursemaid as she regarded how Mrs.
Landless, following the mode of the time—and en-
hancing it as only a woman of supremely perfect figure and posture could—was dressed for a formal
dinner party in the simplest of white silk gowns in the
Grecian style, bereft of any ornament save a diamond
pendant that rested at the deep cleft of her magnificent bosom. And the hair—bless me! How did that
gleaming blonde mane stay in such studied placidity,
lightly bound in a fillet of silver, in a Greek chignon?

Purity Landless stooped over the high side of the
child's cot and, reaching down, lightly touched the
feverish cheek of the little girl who lay asleep there.

"Dorme-tu, ma mignon," she whispered.

"Like a cherub from heaven," said the nursemaid
fondly. "And I swear, ma'am, that the fever be nearly
left her."

"Yes, I'm sure you are right, Nancy," replied the
other, "but I am also sure that we should bring in Dr.
Withers tomorrow. You will be careful to keep close
watch over my darling tonight, will you not?"

"As if the little angel were child of my own womb,
ma'am," whispered Nancy piously. "Be not afeared
of that, ma'am."

"Very good. I will go and receive my guests," said
Purity Landless. "Good night to you, Nancy."

"Good night, ma'am," said the nursemaid, making
a curtsy.

The frou-frou of her mistress's skirts having faded
away at the head of the stair, Nancy wrinkled her nose

and put out her tongue in that direction. Fiddle-dee-dee to you, my lady, and I don't care at all about your silks, satins, fine breasts, and all. Go charm the gentlemen out of their heads and drive their pampered womenfolk out of their minds with jealousy. Have your pleasures. I'll not be deprived of mine. The little maid will sleep soundly till morn (thanks to the laudanum). I'll have my beloved lad, my lusty, sulky lad who half drives me out of my mind with his wicked, winning ways.

She quietly closed the door of the nursery.

"Be you there, Josh, lad?" she whispered into the darkness of the upstairs landing. "Come to your Nancy, my lusty Josh."

The coaches and carriages were ascending the long, curving driveway, past the silvery lake. Roe deer lifted their antlered heads haughtily to regard the intruders, then returned to their cropping of the smooth grassland. The great house stood on the hillcrest, its magnificent portico colored by the dying sun. There was a groom for every vehicle, a footman for every guest. And the beautiful and distinguished Mrs. Landless, a breathtaking vision in white silk, was there to greet her guests in the hallway.

"Mrs. Landless, so nice, such a pleasure, ma'am. Have you heard from the colonel, pray?"

"Not since Easter, Reverend Mauleverer. The last time was from Gibraltar, immediately prior to his departure for the North African coast."

"We must all pray for his safe and speedy return." The Reverend Honorable Bevis Mauleverer, son of a viscount and a cleric in holy orders, was not a frequent visitor at the great house, being a bookish man, fellow of an Oxford college, who left the working of his living and the care of the souls within it to the charge of his curates. He bowed low over his hostess's hand and implanted the customary kiss with his pale, ascetic lips. Purity looked down at the smooth brow, the prematurely graying hair, and, not for the first time, decided that she must, she really must, try a little matchmaking and get him married off to some nice girl in the shire. He could not be a day over thirty-five but was already going to seed through lack of human nourishment.

"Good evening, Mrs. Harker-Marlowe. How do you do, Squire Harker-Marlowe?" She turned dutifully to the next arrivals, mother and son.

"So beautiful, my dear Mrs. Landless." Old Mrs. Harker-Marlowe, widowed these twenty years, was half deaf and more than half blind, but she had been a great beauty herself in her day. She patted Purity's cheek indulgently. "How that wretched husband of yours can think to go running off to China, leaving you and that adorable little gel to languish alone, is beyond all belief. Did you remember to bring my wind pills, Hubert?"

"Yes, Mama," responded her son. Hubert Harker-Marlowe was hereditary squire of the parish, as well as being joint Master of the Clumber Foxhounds with the absent Colonel Landless. He was wearing a tailcoat of hunting scarlet, and his foolish, handsome face was blessed with a pair of baby-blue eyes of transparent innocence. "Not China, Mama. North Africa is where the colonel has gone."

"All foreign parts are as one to me," declared his mother, "and all are alike in their dissimilarity to England." She went on her way, a small and upright figure in black lace, smelling of mothballs and patchouli, with her big son in her wake.

"Hello, Purity. Bless me, but you look like an angel tonight."

"Robbie, how nice," said Purity, and meant it, giving the newest arrival both her hands.

Robert Gladwyn, like her husband a veteran of the Duke of Wellington's campaigns in the Peninsula and France, was a relative newcomer to that corner of Wiltshire, and he had succeeded to lands that bordered on Clumber's wide acres. Tall, sandy haired, with a pleasant, rather than a handsome, countenance that was enlivened by a quirky grin and a pair of candid, self-mocking eyes, he had early won himself a niche in Purity's heart as an amusing and undemanding friend.

"How's my godchild? How's my little Chastity?" he asked.

"The fever has nearly left her, Robbie," said Purity, "and she's sleeping peacefully with the nursemaid watching at her side. But, if she's no better tomorrow, I shall call in the doctor."

"I myself will call upon the young miss tomorrow," said Gladwyn, "with a few goodies and a plaything or two to while away the tedium of lying in bed."

"You spoil that child abominably, my dear," said Purity. "It's no wonder that she dotes on you."

The lord lieutenant of the county and his lady having arrived, and they being the last of Purity's guests, the chatelaine of Clumber Grange herself escorted them into the anteroom of the great dining hall, where obsequious servitors in the Clumber livery of Lincoln green and old gold were serving tall glasses of sparkling champagne. Fifteen minutes after, on receiving a nod from his mistress, the butler announced that dinner was served, and the assembled guests—numbering thirty in all—trooped, two by two, into the vast, high-ceilinged hall, where, in a sweep of silver, porcelain, and sheer white napery, a refectory table was set down the center, with two footmen behind every guest's chair.

The dinner that followed was as elaborate and varied as regards bill of fare, being comprised of the traditional three courses and entrées. The first course: asparagus soup followed by crimped salmon, filets of curnets, vermicelli soup followed by whitebait, and sole aux fines herbes. For entrées: lamb cutlets and peas, scallops of chicken, lobster curry *en casserole,* and chicken patties. The second course was announced by haunch of venison, with a choice of pigeon pie, braised ham, boiled capons, saddle of lamb, and spring chicken. For hardy campaigners of the gastronomic persuasion, the third course offered the temptation of roast duck followed by vanilla soufflé or green goose followed by an iced pudding. And for the glutton—as opposed to the gourmet—the table was liberally sprinkled with dishes of lobster salad, raspberry tartlets, *vol-au-vent* of pears, larded pea hens, custards, prawns, cheesecakes, and so on.

"Mrs. Landless, ma'am, I confess myself puzzled that Colonel Landless should betake himself to foreign parts," said the lord lieutenant of the county, which worthy gentleman was seated on Purity's right, in the place of honor. "I confess myself baffled as to how the colonel can bear to exchange his rural richness for the arid deserts of North Africa."

"It is to China that Colonel Landless has gone," interposed old Mrs. Harker-Marlowe through a mouthful of boiled capon. "I am assured by my son, here, that it is to China that the colonel has gone."

"North Africa, Mama," said her son wearily.

"I, in my turn, am surprised that Mark Landless ever settled down to be a gentleman farmer," said Robert Gladwyn, who was placed close by his hostess's left, a position that was higher than his rank and station deserved, and subtly announcing his close intimacy with the family. "I would have sworn that he would have stayed in the army and become a general."

"Mark is a born farmer," said Purity. She smiled, and memories of past, golden days came flooding back to her. "I detected it in him from the first. We once had a farm, you know, in Spain. We grew the most delicious grapes."

"I am not partial to the grape," declared Mrs. Harker-Marlowe. "Wines I find abominable for the wind; likewise, some sweet cordials. I have whiskey sent to me from our estate in County Wicklow. The Irish do it so well. My boy Hubert, here, is departing for Ireland next week, and I will get him to send you a dozen bottles, Mrs. Landless. You will find it a tremendous comfort, taken in wintertime in hot coffee with a dash of cream and sugar."

"You are very kind, Mrs. Harker-Marlowe," responded Purity gravely.

"But, why North Africa, ma'am?" asked the Reverend Honorable Mr. Bevis Mauleverer, who was seated beyond the lord lieutenant, with Mrs. Harker-Marlowe between them. The clergyman's ascetic and world-weary eyes played thoughtfully upon his hostess's hair, her chin, and her hands, but they shyly avoided her gaze. "You will forgive my ignorance of the circumstances, but, as you are aware, I do not mingle much in society."

"My husband," said Purity, "was approached by Professor James of Trinity College, Cambridge, to accompany him on an expedition to search for the remains of early Phoenician and Carthaginian settlements on the North African littoral. The expedition, which has been financed by the Royal Society, will take them to various sites on the Algerian and

Tripolitanian coasts. They will be subjected to certain hardships, but, I trust, nothing worse than my husband experienced while campaigning in Spain and France—and without the attendant hazards."

"But, I understand, ma'am," said the clergyman, "that there are very real hazards to be encountered in those parts. One has heard of the Corsairs, the Barbary pirates."

"My husband will be safe from those people," said Purity. "He and his companions will be traveling under the protection of a *firman,* or passport, from the Turkish authorities who govern the provinces."

"And this . . . *firman* . . . it will give your husband protection from the activities of the Corsairs?" persisted Mauleverer.

"But of course," replied Purity. She gave the clergyman a sharp sidelong glance, and for no reason she experienced an alien sense of unease.

"Yet he must inevitably come into contact with them if he visits Algiers and other cities of the littoral," said Mauleverer. "He must inevitably be witness to sights that would cause the greatest revulsion in the mind of any Christian gentleman."

While Mauleverer was speaking, a hush had settled down over the long table. The individual pockets of conversation flagged and faded away, and all eyes were turned to the figure in clerical black and twice-round collar.

"To what . . . sights . . . are you referring, sir?" asked Purity faintly.

"Ma'am, I speak of slave-trading," responded Mauleverer. "It is the abomination of the region, and it has been so since the Ottoman sultans expelled the Spaniards from Algeria in the mid-sixteenth century. Algiers, as it stands today, ma'am, is founded, almost literally, upon the trade in human flesh."

"How perfectly appalling!" commented the wife of the lord lieutenant. "Please continue. I am agog to hear the details."

"Men, women, and children are sold in the market-places like cattle," said Mauleverer. "Of the fate of the women—most of the women—it is not right and proper to discuss in mixed company."

"Oh, dear," said the wife of the lord lieutenant, disappointed. "Is it not?"

"The children, reared in the heathen faith, suffer a like fate as their elders," continued the clergyman. "Unremitting toil and degradation is their lot. No, Mrs. Landless, I think that your husband will find much that will cause him revulsion in North Africa."

"I am extremely disturbed to hear it, sir," said Purity.

"I think you are tending to exaggerate the position, sir," said Robert Gladwyn, who had been noting, with some concern, that the clergyman's argument had been causing his hostess increasing unease. "The slave trade is not what it was, and it will speedily be wiped out. The four allied powers that won the war against Napoleon Bonaparte—Great Britain, Austria, Prussia, and Russia—intend to suppress the trade and the Barbary pirates with it. I do not doubt that the mere threat of a British naval squadron bombarding Algiers will be sufficient to make those fellows give up their fiendish traffic—if it has not done so already."

"I sincerely hope so, Robert," said Purity feelingly. And she flashed him a grateful smile.

"That is also my profound wish," said Mauleverer, but he gave the impression of a man unconvinced.

The remainder of the meal was enlivened by general conversation of the lighter sort, in which the Reverend Honorable Mr. Mauleverer took little part. At the end of the meal, the last plates of the final course having been removed, Mrs. Harker-Marlowe sat back in her chair, cut wind noisily, and said, "Mrs. Landless, that was a delightful dinner. If you will excuse me, I will now take my departure. Hubert, you may remain till midnight, and then walk home. The exercise will clear your head."

"Yes, Mama," replied her son dutifully. Hubert Harker-Marlowe, who had been exchanging covert glances with an extremely attractive young woman halfway down the table, seemed greatly relieved at the imminent departure of his formidable mother.

It was in the hallway, after Purity had seen Mrs. Harker-Marlowe to her carriage, and was returning to her guests, that she was brought up short by a faint cry from the upper part of the great house. It was immediately followed by a scream, then the sound of a falling body.

"Oh, my God! Chastity!"

She took the stairs two at a time, and the guests streamed out of the dining hall after her, the menfolk leading and the shocked women trailing behind. All went up the winding stairs to the upper floor, and the nursery that lay above. Halfway to the nursery, on a small landing, Purity came upon the crumpled form of the child. With a howl of anguish, she picked Chastity up and held her to her bosom, keening like a mad thing and rocking back and forth in her anguish. Nor did she stop till the child herself began to wail in dismay. It was then that Robert Gladwyn managed to pry loose Purity's beloved burden, run his hands over the tiny limbs, and examine the tender flesh for lacerations.

"She is as right as rain, Purity," he said. "Not a bone broken, nor a cut anywhere."

"Likely the little mite toppled down the stairs unharmed and went straight back to sleep where she lay," commented someone. "The very young have a truly remarkable capacity for evading injury."

"Thank God!" breathed Purity, her eyes closed in the intensity of her feelings. All at once they snapped open, ablaze with fury. "Where is that wretched girl? Where is Nancy Shaw?"

Leaving the now-sleeping child in the arms of Robert Gladwyn, she ran like an avenging angel to the top landing and wrenched open the nursery door. A single taper dimly illuminated the room, disclosing the abandoned cot and the empty chair beside it. Of the nursemaid—nothing.

"Where is she? Where is that bitch?" screamed Purity.

She reached the door to the nursemaid's room in half a dozen swift strides and threw it open.

The couple sprawled upon the narrow bed turned dismayed countenances toward the splendid, blonde-haired woman in white who stood regarding them in towering fury from the doorway. Nancy Shaw was crouched atop her lover, and he with the flap of his breeches wide open and his powdered wig hanging over one ear. The better to enchant her paramour, Nancy had seen fit to divest herself of almost all her clothing. Save for a black ribbon around her neck and a pair of purple-and-white striped stockings with garters, she was nude. She screamed and covered her breasts when she saw the cluster of faces gathering behind that of her mistress. But it was her mistress's fury that most engaged her fears.

"Ma'am! Ma'am!" she wailed. "We . . . we wasn't doing anything wrong. We just came over tired, that's all."

"You could have killed my darling with your neglect, you slut!" cried Purity. And, reverting to her mother tongue as she was wont to do in moments of anguish, she added, *"Sale putain! Prostituée!"*

"Come away, my dear," Robert Gladwyn urged her. He had laid the child back on her cot. "Compose yourself."

"Mon Dieu! I have not finished with that bitch!" shouted Purity. "Get out of my way, Robbie. Stand aside, all of you!" Thrusting her way through the throng of wide-eyed guests, she stormed out of the nursery and returned soon after with a riding whip.

"Purity, I beg of you . . . " began Robert Gladwyn.

"Get out of my way!" blazed Purity savagely. "I will mark that bitch for whoring while my darling's life was in danger!"

"No, ma'am! No!" screamed Nancy, leaping from the bed, an action that permitted her lover to escape from the other side and address his trembling, hasty fingers to the task of buttoning up the flap of his breeches. The nursemaid, disregarding the display of nakedness that she was presenting to the staring guests in the doorway—most of them male—threw herself on her knees before her mistress, and, twining her plump arms around Purity's skirts, fell to a most heart-rending sobbing.

Staring down at the girl's well-formed back and shapely buttocks, Purity felt a sudden knot of compassion. Casting aside the whip, she untangled herself from Nancy's grasp.

"Get out of my house!" she said flatly. "Pack your things and get out—this very night, now. If you are not gone within the hour, I'll have the grooms flog you from here to the gatehouse, for I'll not soil my husband's whip on a whore."

Ice-cold and composed, now she turned to meet the concerted gaze of her guests.

"I apologize for the unfortunate diversion, ladies

and gentlemen," she said coolly and with a small smile. "Shall we now return to the table and enjoy a glass of port wine?"

She walked past them, her head erect, looking neither to the left nor right, but pausing for a moment to lay a hand. like a blessing, upon the cheek of the sleeping child on the cot. "Send for two of the upstairs maids to watch over Miss Chastity tonight," she instructed one of the footmen.

"By jove, but Mrs. Landless has a temper on her like a pantheress!" murmured the lord lieutenant. "I swear she was within an inch of flogging the hide off that wench."

Hubert Harker-Marlowe, dragging his gaze from the nude girl crouched on the floor, muttered that he was of the same opinion.

Nancy Shaw had her few belongings packed by midnight in a single carpetbag. Cloaked and bonneted, she issued forth from the kitchen entrance of the great house and took the winding driveway that led to the gatehouse. There was a slight hoarfrost on the well-tended grass, and she shivered with the sudden cold that assaulted her. From the far copse beyond the ornamental lake, an owl hooted, and it was answered by its mate in the distance. The moon was full.

Her bag was heavy, and the girl was obliged to rest from time to time, taking the opportunity to wipe her nose on her sleeve and curse the fate that had brought her so low. This was coupled with a curse for the woman who had shamed her before the ogling eyes of all those men, who had cast her out to starve in the streets.

"Damn you, my fine Mrs. Landless!" she whispered, looking back at the noble pile on the hillcrest behind her. "I'd give a year of my life to bring *you* to your knees and begging for mercy, so I would."

The long traipse to the gatehouse brought her to the main road beyond. To go left or right was scarcely of any consequence, for Nancy, orphaned and friendless, had nowhere to go. Her only prospect was to sell her young body, and one place was as good as another for that. She hefted her carpetbag and was about to set off down the road to the right when she perceived a coach standing in the deep shadows of a clump of trees opposite. Its lanterns were not lit, but she could see a muffled figure up in the driver's box.

"Come here, girl!" a voice called to her from the interior of the coach. Wonderingly, she obeyed. The door was open from the inside, and a hand reached out to take her arm. "Get inside."

"Sir, I . . . " faltered Nancy.

"Get in, Nancy. You'll come to no harm."

Nancy peered into the darkness of the coach, tried to make out the shape of the speaker's face, but she could not. With a shrug, she mounted the step, for what did she have to lose? The door slammed. The coachman clicked his tongue and shook his reins, and the vehicle moved off down the road. Once out of the shadow of the trees, the moonlight came streaming in through the coach windows and she saw her companion plainly.

"Why, 'tis . . . *you,* sir!" she exclaimed.

"I have been waiting for you, Nancy," came the answer. "What happened to the spotty-faced stripling who was having his way with you? Has he been discharged also?"

She made a grimace. "Not he. A man can get away with anything. 'Tis always the woman who suffers. Oh, he'll not work in the house again. They've sent him to be a field hand on the house farm. This time next week, he'll be bedded with a milkmaid."

"And did he kiss you good-bye, Nancy?"

"Not he, sir," she said. "He'd as likely have hit me."

"Then I shall do the honors for him," said the other, and, leaning toward her, he kissed her soft mouth, laughing quietly when she shuddered at the intensity of the embrace.

"I saw—and greatly admired—your charms tonight, Nancy," he said. And he whispered an obscenity into her ear.

"Mercy me!" exclaimed Nancy. "That's a fine way for a gentleman to talk." She giggled. "So that's why you were waiting for me, eh? You're after a good roll in the hay. Men! You're all alike!"

"I had in mind something of a more permanent nature, Nancy," was his reply.

"Pull the other leg; it's got bells on!" she scoffed. "Believe it or not, sir, I've known enough fine gentlemen not to be taken in by that yarn. Permanent, indeed! As soon as you've had your way with me, I'll be left by the roadside with a couple of guineas in my hand. And God bless you for the couple of guineas, for I've naught but five shillings betwixt me and starvation, and no one's going to employ a discharged nursemaid without a reference. It's whoring for me. Come, sir, let's get started."

"What I am offering you, Nancy," he said evenly, "is my protection, opportunity to travel to far-off, exotic places, and—shall we say?—a thousand guineas a year as an allowance."

"A thou——" She stared at him in the moonlight, but his face betrayed nothing. "Did you say a thousand *guineas?*"

"Fifteen hundred," he responded.

"Sir, you're mocking me!"

"It will be effected tomorrow. My coachman is driving us directly to London. We shall arrive there in time for luncheon at my town house. There you will be ensconced, and I will send to my bank for fifteen hundred guineas in gold. Will you *then* be convinced?"

She shook her head in puzzlement. "But, why *me?*"

He reached and tugged at the bow that secured her cloak, which fell apart, disclosing the generous structure of her bosom. Despite herself, despite the many men who had used—and abused—her since childhood in a parish orphanage, Nancy shuddered before the piercing intensity of his gaze.

"I have viewed your charms," he said, "and I wish to possess those charms for—shall we say?—*delicious* reasons, and not merely for tonight, but for an eternity." He smiled. "Or, at any rate, till those tender, soft, and delectable young charms have lost their bloom. Come now, my Nancy, why do you hesitate? A minute ago, you were mine for the pittance of a measly couple of guineas."

She put on a brave smile, but her fingers trembled when they fumbled with the lacing of her bodice. And, as he embraced her, she was strangely aware that she was in the presence of an evil so real that it could be seen, and touched, and smelled.

One thing alone had marred the Landlesses' return to Clumber Grange after the war, and that was Purity's seeming inability to conceive a child. The best medical opinions assured the couple that there was no reason why the state of affairs should continue. She was normal in every way.

Purity and Mark were content to wait, for she was still young. Meanwhile, into their lives came an ador-

able eighteen-month-old girl—an orphan who had
been brought to their attention by a friend in
London. They saw her and were conquered. They
went through the formalities of adopting her as their
own. They named her Chastity.

The night of the dinner party, the last of her guests
having departed, Purity instantly ran upstairs to the
nursery, there to reassure herself that little Chastity
was sleeping peacefully, was indeed unharmed after
her fall, and that the two surrogate nursemaids were
awake and alert. All three conditions prevailed.
Chastity's slight fever appeared to have abated and
she was seemingly not one bit the worse for her tum-
ble. The two young upstairs maids, who knew, chapter
and verse, what had befallen their former colleague,
were suitably terrified. Not for all the tea in China
would either have closed her eyes for more than an
instant. Purity went to her own bedchamber and undressed.

She had behaved abominably before her guests;
that much was certain. It was her Latin blood—that,
and the rude and early introduction to violence and
brutality she had encountered during the horrors of
the French Revolution. But for the last-minute revulsion against the desecration of that tender young
body, would she have found it in her to flog the girl?
She thought so. And the thought made her shudder.

Tomorrow she would send grooms riding in all di-
rections to bring back the erring nursemaid. She was
never to be a nursemaid again, of course. Purity had
been a fool to have entrusted darling Chastity to that
wild little slut, who was quite obviously at the beck
and call of any man who laid a caressing hand upon
her. But let her be brought back and given a task in
the sewing room.

The white silk gown slid to a pool around her feet.

She was entirely naked beneath, for the sheerness of the fabric was such that any undergarment would have shown. Naked, she regarded herself critically in the tall pier glass. With detachment, she acknowledged that her body was still quite flawless—a body made for loving, that was loved. . . .

"Oh, Mark, my darling, why did you have to leave me?" she asked aloud. "Oh, if only you were with me now, tonight."

Still nude, she slipped between the silken sheets and tried to compose herself for slumber, but straight to her mind came the words of the clergyman: "There are very real hazards to be encountered in those parts . . . the Barbary pirates . . . sights that would cause the greatest revulsion . . . "

Oh, my Mark, why did you have to leave me to go into all that peril? And for what? To help a dried-up old professor dig up a few relics and bits of bent bronze?

I almost hated you, my Mark, on the day you came back from London to tell me that you had accepted the offer to accompany Professor James to the Mediterranean. And it was so soon after the war, when we had had only a few short months together, when darling Chastity had just begun to call you Papa. We had our first quarrel then—at least, the first quarrel of no account. Before that, we had only quarreled about matters of love and life and death.

I let you go, heaven help me. Not by so much as a word or gesture have I revealed to anyone that I disapproved of your going, nor would I—not to Robert, the Harker-Marlowes, the parson, or anyone.

Oh, my darling, come back safely to me, and come back soon. . . .

As she lay and soliloquized, it seemed to her that

he came to her out of the darkness, from on high, descending upon her bed and gathering her up.

And then it began, as it had done from the first, with him: a slow, grand rhythm, like an ancient song, or the best of mighty breakers on some forgotten shore. She was carried up on high on an ecstasy of movement and sound. Joyful and yet weeping, she was carried up into the blinding sunlight of a new morning.

Still drifting in an ecstasy that had no end, she fell asleep. And in her dream she saw Mark Landless standing on a desert shore. He was nude, nude as she knew him——every part of him, every promontory and declivity, every inch of his beloved flesh, every mole and scar, the feel and the male scent of him. All of it was as familiar as her own body.

And as she watched, a shadow closed in around Mark Landless, a cloud that cast a darkness over him. He turned, looked up, and raised his hands as if to shield himself. But he could do nothing against the approaching danger; nor was he able to determine from which direction it was coming. He looked to left and right, and around him, ever more frantically, waving his arms around and calling to his unseen enemy to declare himself.

Purity joined her voice with his, screaming aloud to the thing that menaced her lover, entreating it to spare him, to leave him be. . . .

Still screaming, and slippery with her own sweat, she woke up.

It was on a fine spring evening, the time of the Angelus, a month or more after the events of the dinner party, that Purity was working in the fields with her people, as she and Mark had always done: barefoot like a peasant, her head protected from the weather by a broad-brimmed straw. She and a line of women were plucking weeds from among the young corn. In another hour, the tolling of a bell in the stable block would announce the end of another working day. There would be beer for all, meat pasties, and boiled potatoes. Rest.

"Here come the parson," announced the woman on her left. "He's on his little donkey. What a sight he do make, to be sure."

Purity straightened up and wiped her brow, drawing back a wayward lock of her blonde hair. She narrowed her eyes against the dying sun.

He came out of the sun, a black-clad figure in his shovel hat, mounted upon a trotting donkey. The donkey's hooves kicked up the dust of the dry earth in its passing.

Upon the instant, Purity experienced a most pressing premonition of disaster. Her heart pounded in her breast and her breathing quickened. Without waiting for the clergyman to draw nearer, she dropped her bundle of weeds and ran through the young corn to meet him, heedless of how she trod it down in her mighty haste.

The clergyman's eyes were upon her. Beneath the shade of the wide-brimmed shovel hat, she saw that they held an expression of deep concern, and she knew that her instinct had not been at fault. Something—something very dreadful—had happened.

"Reverend Mauleverer!"

"Mrs. Landless . . . "

Panting, she drew to a halt beside him, and the donkey began to crop at the hedgerow.

"It's my husband," she said dully. It was not a question.

"Mrs. Landless, I have to tell you. . . ." The man was clearly not liking his task.

"Is he . . . dead?"

There was immediate relief in his eyes. "Oh, no, you must not think that, ma'am," he said. "Why, there is every hope, every hope in the world, that Colonel Landless is alive and well. Only . . . "

"Only what, Reverend Mauleverer?" demanded Purity. "You say he is alive; you think he is alive. But there is some impediment. Is he, then, wounded? Ill?"

"Not as my best information has it, ma'am," said Mauleverer. "My best information—and I have it from the Royal Society at Somerset House—is that Colonel Landless, your husband, ma'am, has been . . . has been . . . "

"Has been what, man?" shouted Purity in his face. "Tell me, for pity's sake! You are driving me insane with your prevarications."

"He has been taken, ma'am," said the clergyman evenly, "by the Corsairs."

"By the Corsairs?"

She recoiled a pace, her eyes wide with horror, mouth agape, fingers clutching convulsively at her breasts.

"I fear so, ma'am," said Mauleverer.

"Captured by the Barbary pirates!" she cried. "Taken by those fiends! For *slavery,* you mean?"

The clergyman avoided her gaze. "That is the information I have, ma'am," he said. "It is their invariable custom. The males, the young and the vigorous, are always spared. The old, the useless . . . I fear, the Royal Society fears . . . that Professor James would almost certainly not have been spared."

"Spared!" she cried bitterly. "Spared for a life of slavery under the whip!"

"At least, ma'am, he lives," said the other simply.

"Yes, you are right, Reverend Mauleverer," said

Purity, a surge of passionate resolve breaking through her blinding misery. "He is alive. I know it. And, alive, he will be freed. Every penny we possess, all the influence the Landless family can wield, Mark's connections with the Duke of Wellington, his acquaintance with the prince regent—all these I shall exploit to have him freed."

"Oh, yes, I am sure there is much that can be done," said Mauleverer, but without much conviction.

Disregarding his lack of enthusiasm, she said, "Tell me, when did this thing happen, Reverend Mauleverer? When did the information reach you, and how?"

"It was this afternoon that a member of the society arrived here, ma'am," he replied. "In view of my cloth, it was deemed that I should be the one to bear you the tragic news. As to details, the society has little, save that the crew of an Arab fishing craft brought information to Malta that the ship, later identified as that bearing Professor James and his expedition, had been boarded and taken by a Corsair."

"And when was this? When did it happen, Reverend Mauleverer?"

"It was about a month ago, ma'am," he replied, "perhaps a little more."

"A month ago!" cried Purity. "A month ago! Yes, I was there! I saw it happen in the night!"

"Mrs. Landless," murmured the clergyman, looking around him for help and support, and from any quarter, "you have suffered a very terrible shock, ma'am. Will you not sit down in the shade and rest a while?"

"But, Robbie, I was told that they were to travel

to the North African coast under the protection of a Turkish passport of some kind."

"It appears that they waited a month in Gibraltar for the *firman,* but that, with the typical and grotesque inefficiency of the Sublime Porte, they waited in vain," said Robert Gladwyn. "The Turkish consul in Gibraltar was full of assurances, but the weeks drifted past. With the season advancing, Mark and the professor were faced with a decision: to wait, or to take the chance and travel without the *firman.* I think, Purity, that we may assume that it was largely Mark's influence that brought them to choose the latter option."

She nodded. "It would be just like him."

Three weeks had passed. She and Gladwyn were in her sitting room, which overlooked the ornamental gardens of Clumber Grange, which stretched, terrace after terrace, to the horizon of memorial oaks. Upon the leather-topped writing desk, by her elbow, lay a pile of opened letters, letters from the distinguished Fellows of the Royal Society of London for Improving Natural Knowledge giving condolences for her sad loss. There was a typically reserved, yet curiously affectionate, note from the Iron Duke, speaking of his bitter regrets at the loss of so fine a comrade, but nothing more—no hint of help. Finally, there was a missive, penned by a private secretary upon the crested writing paper of the Royal Pavilion, Brighton: "His Royal Highness the Regent deeply regrets . . . " But there was nothing more, no mention of assistance.

"Purity, my dear, what are you going to do?" Gladwyn reached out across the desk and laid a hand on hers. "You must face up to the stern fact that the government will do nothing about Mark, and the prince regent is powerless to do anything, even if he chose to try."

Purity rose, swept across the room, and whirled around to face him when she reached the window. Her eyes flaring, bosom heaving, she cried out in bitter fury, "So, it has come to this! Britannia rules the waves. but a British ship can be taken . . . "

"Portuguese, my dear," said Gladwyn soberly. "It was a Portuguese ship in which they were sailing."

"What matter?" she blazed. "A ship was taken. British subjects were murdered, enslaved. And you tell me that the government will do nothing to punish the criminals and rescue those who still live?"

"The position is very delicate," said Gladwyn. "When next the Congress of the Allies convenes, the Corsair question. the slavery question, will be high on the agenda for discussion. . . ."

"Discussion!" exclaimed Purity. "They discuss while my husband slaves under the whip!"

Gladwyn waited for her to finish, then continued mildly: "It is felt, in government circles, that any precipitate action against the Corsairs may prejudice the eventual outcome of the discussions. I am sorry, Purity. It sounds unfeeling—brutal, even. But that is how it is."

He bowed his head. With a small cry of compassion, Purity swiftly crossed to him and took his hands in hers.

"My dear friend," she said, "how wrong of me to speak to you so, you, who have done so much to help."

"I have done little enough," he said. "I merely sounded out a cousin in the House of Lords and dined with a few highly placed acquaintances in Whitehall. But the answer came back quite clearly from all quarters. They are not going to do anything about Mark, my dear. You will have to face up to that and shape your future life accordingly."

Her eyes flared. "Shape my future life?" she said.
"What can you mean, Robbie? I am a married woman
who is deeply in love with her husband. That is how
it will remain for me, be it a lifetime. If the congress
acts against the Corsairs, how long will it be before
I can expect Mark to be freed?"

His candid eyes searched her face. "I think you
are brave enough to hear the truth, Purity," he said.
"It is likely to be two years before the congress meets
again. Supposing that they arrive at a decision to
crush the Corsairs. Then it might be another year
before the machinery of government puts the decision
into action. Then the navy would move."

"Three years!"

"Or more."

"Three years under the lash! Worked like an animal. Beaten. Branded. Starved, perhaps. Robert, what
sort of man will be returned to me after three years
of that kind of treatment?"

He said, "That is why I advised you to face up to
reality and look to your own future. It is possible
that only a wreck of the man we knew will return,
if return he does. Another, and equally likely, possibility is that he will not survive three years of the
treatment he is likely to receive. Mark is a strong and
vigorous man in the prime of his life. He is also of a
will and temperament that would not submit easily.
Such men make bad slaves. There is only one way
to treat such men, to get the best out of them: *chain
them and work them to death!*"

She would have fainted and fallen then had not his
arms taken her. When she recovered, the tears came,
and he made no attempt to check them. He stood
and held her till the tempest had abated. Then, leading her to a sofa, he laid her down and, placing a

cushion behind her head, lifting her slippered feet onto the sofa, composed her comfortably.

"Sleep," he said. "You have suffered enough to-day."

"Robbie, I am grateful to you for telling me the truth," she said.

"I regret it," he said. "I regret the necessity. But I have too much regard for you, and for Mark, to let you live in a fool's paradise. Mark would not wish it. That I know well."

"No fool's paradise for me," she said. "I will learn to accept that my life with Mark is ended, so that, if the miracle happens and he comes back to me, it will be like being reborn."

"And meanwhile," said Robert Gladwyn, "I am your true and faithful friend, Purity. And you may lean on me as hard as you please."

"Thank you, Robbie."

He stooped and kissed her cheek and squeezed her hand. He went over and closed the window shutters against the daylight, then tiptoed to the door and left her.

For another week, the chatelaine of Clumber Grange moved like a silent wraith through the great house and grounds, receiving no one, addressing no one.

Purity's extraordinary beauty, which was the subject of comment by all who beheld her, seemed to take on a new refinement, as if suffering, like a cleansing fire, had hardened her perfection. Her body, a vessel shaped for love, took upon itself an added voluptuousness, and her face, softened by melancholy, a fresh allure.

It was openly argued in the shire that the chatelaine of Clumber Grange was a widow in all but name, that it was only a matter of time—and a short

time, at that—before further news from the Mediterranean would confirm that widowhood as fact.

So it was that, within so short a time of her receiving news of Mark's disappearance, untimely suitors
began knocking at her door. First came Hubert
Harker-Marlowe's younger brother, Roger. He called
three times and left flowers. She received him on the
fourth time. Roger's approach was simple, sincere, and
inoffensive. He pledged his undying love and devotion
and begged her to call upon him for anything she
needed. Without directly alluding to marriage, he had
her understand that, if the time was ever ripe, he
would be happy to lay his life at her feet. Purity thanked him gravely, and out of consideration for
his honesty and naïveté, she did not scream the truth
into his pink, good-natured countenance, which was
that, while she lived, be Mark Landless alive or dead,
she would not—could not—bring herself to share the
bed of any other man. The ecstasy she had enjoyed
with Mark was of a perfection that could not be
counterfeited or replaced. If a widow, then she would
remain a widow to the grave. Not hearing this, young
Harker-Marlowe departed, quite pleased with the interview.

Others came. Some were more subtle than Harker-
Marlowe; they wrapped up their intentions in more
devious ways. Purity saw through them all and sent
them on their way with smiles and good wishes. Only
one would-be suitor received the rough edge of her
tongue. He was the son of a neighboring landlord and
a well-known local stud who, so it was reputed, had
fathered a score of bastards from the time he was at
Harrow School. This sprig arrived at Clumber with
his breeches metaphorically unbuttoned, a pair of
bedroom slippers in his hand, and a contraceptive of
the thinnest possible goatskin in his pocket. Straddle-

legged on the bear rug before the fireplace in Purity's
sitting room, he looked around him and put a mental
price tag on the pictures and furnishings. Next, he regarded the object of his desires: a pretty woman with
an exceedingly handsome figure, and breasts unmatched in his wide experience. She was a farm
widow, furthermore, and, by definition, aching to
have a man in her bed. How could she do better than
he, himself, the finest stud in Wiltshire? And so,
without too much beating around the bush, he proposed as much to Purity. She, summoning her grooms,
had him marched down the driveway to the gatehouse and kicked out into the road. His horse was
given a sharp slap across the rump and sent high-
tailing in the opposite direction.

It was this incident that shocked Purity out of her
lethargy and indecision.

*"Damn them! Damn them all! I will go and rescue
Mark myself!"*

Faithful Robert Gladwyn was sent for. He came,
despite the fact that he was due to travel to London
that night and had coach and horses waiting. She received him in her sitting room, and he remarked that
she was quite changed. She was the Purity he had
known of old.

She told him briefly of her intention.

"Purity, it is out of the question for you, a woman,
to journey to Algiers!" he exclaimed.

"The Royal Society had considered it safe enough
for my husband and his companions," she retorted.
"Their only mistake was to neglect to get the *firman*.
I shall make no such mistake. I will hound the
Turkish consul in Gibraltar till he produces the *firman*. I am told that officials of the Sublime Porte are
not averse to taking bribes in order to facilitate their
transactions. I will bribe that man. I will give him

jewels. I will choke him with bright gold. Armed with that *firman,* I will go to Algiers and negotiate Mark's freedom. My God, Robbie, do you think I would hesitate for one instant to offer every penny Mark and I possess in the world, Clumber and all, to secure his release?"

"I will not attempt to dissuade you, Purity," he said simply, "for I know it would be a waste of time. So, what do you want of me? How can I further your enterprise?"

"First," she said, "you will promise me something, unconditionally."

"And what is that?"

"First, the promise."

"I promise."

"You will not offer to accompany me on the voyage of rescue. No, Robbie, hear me out. I know the hazards, and I would not have your life on my conscience. Agreed? You gave your promise."

"You are too clever for me, Purity," he said. "So, what else can I do?"

"My dear," said Purity, "there is so much you can do." Now she was all organizer, completely the mistress of the situation, so that Gladwyn stared at her in admiration. "First, I want you to go to Deptford, on the Thames River, and inspect Mark's old yacht, the *Minerva.* She has not put to sea for all of ten years, to my knowledge, and may well be a rotten hulk by now. On the other hand, she may be in condition to take me to the Mediterranean."

"A small yacht?" he said quizzically. "Is that wise? Would it not be best to take passage in a merchantman?"

She shook her head. "The *Minerva,* being smaller and seemingly insignificant, will offer less of a prize for the Corsairs to snatch," she said. "Besides, if the old yacht is still in the condition it once was, it may run rings around any Corsair."

"That is good thinking," he said, making a note in his pocket diary.

"Next, you must find me a captain and crew," she said. "I want the best, and I am willing to pay the highest wages. Make it clear to officers and men that we are not going on a pleasure cruise. But I think we should not tell them that I am planning to put my head into the hornets' nest."

"Captain and crew," said Gladwyn. "Then you will also need charts of the North African coast. These I can obtain from the Admiralty Hydrographic Department, where I have connections. I will attend to it as soon as I reach London tomorrow. Is there anything else?"

She smiled a secret smile. "There is one other thing, Robert. Will you pour yourself some wine while I leave you for a short while and then return? I have something to show you, and when you have seen what is to be seen, you will be called upon to make a decision."

"But, of course," he replied, puzzled.

Purity, still with her secret smile, left the room. She was longer that she had implied. Robert Gladwyn had downed one glass of port wine and was halfway through a second one before the door opened again.

He looked around, a smile of greeting already forming on his lips; it was washed away with surprise.

"Good day to you, sir," he said. And then he added, "Oh, it's *you,* Purity!"

She wore a man's curly-brimmed top hat, a caped coat, breeches, and Hessian boots. Her luxuriant blonde hair was drawn back in a club and fastened with a bow at the nape, after the style of the previous century, a style that still persisted, even among some of the young blades. Amused at his reaction, she lifted a magnifying glass and regarded him archly.

"Well," she said, "will I pass as a man in North Africa?"

He folded his arms and regarded her critically.

"Turn around."

She did so.

"Walk to the window and back."

She did so, swaggering in her Hessian boots and swinging the silver-knobbed cane that she carried.

"Well?" she asked.

"Very good," said Gladwyn. "Most convincing. You even have the walk right. You would pass for a more than usually handsome young buck from a Pall Mall club. And now . . . "

"Yes?"

"Take off that overcoat."

She frowned. "I thought you would ask me to do that."

He shrugged. "That caped coat, my dear, while admirable for Pall Mall in the rigors of a London winter, would be *quite* out of place in the searing heat of the Mediterranean summer."

"Oh, well." She sighed and inched out of the voluminous coat. Under it, she wore a short-tailed coat of light worsted, matching the breeches. Beneath that was an embroidered waistcoat and a ruffled shirt that admirably described the curving swell of her bosom.

Despite himself, Gladwyn could not refrain from laughing. He changed it into a cough when he saw that his mirth was not well received.

"I'm sorry, Purity," he said.

She stamped her small, neatly booted foot, setting her bosom bouncing.

"Damn it!" she cried. "It's my blasted breasts that give the game away, isn't it?"

He smiled his quirky, lopsided smile. "And all the rest of you, Purity," he said. "Every inch of your quite delightful body, my dear, announces you to be a woman. For myself, I would not have it any other way. If you were successfully to turn yourself into the counterfeit of a man, the very gods in Parnassus would weep."

And then they were both laughing. And she ran to him, embraced him, and kissed his cheek.

"Oh, and I wanted so much to travel as a man," she said. "Taken all in all, it would have been so very much more convenient. A woman is so *vulnerable*."

Over her shoulder, Robert Gladwyn saw his own reflection in a looking glass on the opposite wall. He caught the expression that flitted across his countenance when the thought of her vulnerability crossed his mind—taken in conjunction with the place she was going, and the bestial creatures to whom she would be placing her beautiful body in danger.

Reverend Mauleverer made the final attempt to stop her. This he did while her trunks were being loaded into the coach that was to follow hers to London. If anything, the clergyman's futile entreaties hardened her resolve all the more.

"You cannot throw yourself away on such a wild venture, ma'am," he declared. "I beseech you to reconsider, even at this late hour. Come with me to the church. Let us kneel and pray together, that wiser counsels may prevail in your mind, and that you see the folly of the course upon which you are set."

"Good-bye, Reverend Mauleverer," she said, offering her hand to the clergyman. "I shall be grateful for your prayers, but nothing will stop me now. I shall return with my husband or I shall not return. The issue is as simple as that. Good-bye."

She had given Chastity a parting embrace. The child was asleep in the nursery. She got into the coach and waved to the files of servants gathered under the portico to see her off: the men, in Lincoln-green livery; the women and girls, in their neat caps and aprons. All of them waved or curtsied, and there was scarcely a cheek that was not running with tears. Mauleverer raised his shovel hat and gazed after her. And so she was swept away from the home where she had known the greatest happiness of her life.

Her journey to London, going by way of Newbury and Reading, was uneventful and speedily accomplished. She and Mark owned a town house on Half Moon Street, and it was there that the coach deposited her and her baggage. Robert Gladwyn was waiting to greet her, and he was full of news.

"The *Minerva* has completed her refitting, and is as sound as she ever was. Captain and crew are aboard and await your orders. Purity, it still isn't too late to change your mind and let me accompany you."

"Robbie, my dear, remember your promise."

"As you say," he replied.

"Tell me about the crew," she said. "Tell me, particularly, about the captain."

"Hmm. Well, to be frank, the captain is my only disappointment. I hasten to add that there's nothing amiss with either him or his attainments. He has never held a command, but he has been a master's mate on an East India ship for over five years. A small craft like the *Minerva* will be child's play for him to handle. It's just that . . . well . . . he looks too damned good to be true. And he knows it."

"Robbie, Robbie," she said lightly, "do I detect a whiff of male jealousy? And the members of your sex are forever accusing us women of being catty."

He grinned. "I expect you are right, Purity. You

usually are. He's a handsome, swashbuckling devil, and full of his own importance. Makes me feel six inches shorter than I am, and despise myself for it. By the way, when do you intend to set sail?"

"Without delay," she said. "Tomorrow, if possible."

"Tomorrow!" he echoed. "My dear, you really are in earnest, aren't you?"

"Never more so in my life," she replied.

The next day, Robert Gladwyn drove her to Deptford in his smart town phaeton and pair, her baggage having been sent on ahead to the *Minerva*. The Surrey shore of the Thames, lush with meadows and pretty hamlets under the summer sun, accorded well with her mood, for the river, never far distant from the road, and the tall masts of ships rising over roof and treetop, gave a constant reminder that only blue-green water separated her from the man who was all her life, and that she would soon be consuming the distance that lay between them.

The *Minerva* lay in the Deptford creek, and the sight of her raking, schooner masts and sleek white hull had the power to turn her heart over. It was on the *Minerva*, so many years ago, that Mark Landless had taken her from Revolutionary France to be his ward in England—and afterward his wife. She could remember the first morning of that unforgettable voyage across the Channel when, on rising and looking out onto the deck, she had seen the nude figure of the yacht's owner, laughing in the sunshine while one of his sailors threw buckets of water over him. In that breath-robbing moment, she had fallen in love with Mark Landless and had worshipped that self-same body, had known it in innumerable nights of loving ever since.

The crew that Gladwyn had appointed—the cap-

tain, mate, and six men—was lining the rails to welcome her. The former swaggered forward and doffed
his cocked hat as she stepped on the deck, bowed low,
and took her proffered hand.

"Captain Hugo Sheriffs, ma'am, at your service."

"How do you do, Captain?"

She smiled to herself. He was everything that Robert Gladwyn had implied: tall and brawny, with the
most slender of waists and widest of shoulders; hair
the color of fresh butter and curly all over like a
young bull's; cornflower-blue eyes that crinkled at the
corners when he smiled, which was often. He looked
to be about twenty-nine or thirty.

"It is your wish, as I understand, ma'am, to sail on
the evening tide," said Sheriffs.

"That is so, Captain," responded Purity, "if that is
convenient for you."

He was standing close to her, closer than was necessary for the conversation. With his greater height,
he was constrained to look down on her, which he did
with an air of masterful condescension mixed with mild
amusement, as if she—a mere woman, plaything of
the superior sex—was owner of the *Minerva* only in
make-believe, and it was he, with his well-turned
calves and skin-tight pantaloons, his straight-nosed
profile and his lean flanks and flat belly, who was
really master.

"I am yours to command, ma'am," he said huskily,
adding, with seeming irrelevance, "in everything,
ma'am."

Sheriffs accompanied Purity and Gladwyn to her
cabin, under the poop deck. While little bigger than
one of the clothes closets back at Clumber, it was a
light and airy compartment, with lattice windows looking out over the stern and a comfortable cot set into
the bulkhead. The whole cabin was newly paneled in

unvarnished pine, with soft furnishings of royal blue trimmed with old gold.

"You have done marvels, Robbie," she said. "It is quite delightful."

Gladwyn looked pleased and said, "I was lucky to secure the best ship's carpenter on the Thames."

"And, if I may be so bold as to say so, you've also secured the best captain and crew on the Thames, ma'am," interposed Sheriffs, giving her a smoldering glance.

"I am quite convinced of that already, Captain," replied Purity sweetly. You, my fine fellow, are going to give me trouble before we are both very much older, she said to herself.

Gladwyn dined her that evening at a riverside tavern in Greenwich at a lamplit table on a balcony overhanging the water. It was a constrained meal, for her companion seemed sunk in melancholy, for all that he summoned every effort to conceal it. Purity was glad when the meal was over, for protracted farewells were not to her taste. When they rose from the table, the tide was just on the ebb. Later, when they kissed good-bye at the *Minerva*'s gangway, the old Thames was fit to carry the yacht out into midstream with scarcely a rag of sail. She stood on the poop deck and watched Robert Gladwyn waving till they were out of sight. The yacht's mainsail was spread like a white wing in the darkness above her head, and the waters whispered past the sharp prow. Her odyssey had begun.

"I will bid you good night, Captain Sheriffs," said Purity to the tall figure by her side.

For an answer, he swept off his cocked hat and bowed low. He made no reply, and it was too dark to see his face, but she wagered with herself that his cornflower-blue eyes were crinkled at the corners with amusement.

She entered her little cabin, which was lit by a single lantern. It was then she discovered that, either by oversight or by design, there was neither lock nor bolt on the inside of the door. She shrugged and told herself that it was something that she would have rectified by the ship's carpenter on the morrow. Then she stripped, washed herself in the handbasin, put on her nightdress, and climbed into the narrow cot.

She had brought with her a volume about travels in North Africa, written by a French Jesuit in the early part of the previous century. It was a work of almost intolerable tedium, and it provided little or no information of the type she sought. Purity struggled with the crabbed French type for fifteen minutes, then put the book aside. She had scarcely done so when there came a knock on the door, and before she could reply it opened to admit the captain of the *Minerva*.

One glance was sufficient to assure herself about his intentions. Captain Sheriffs was dressed—or, more nearly, undressed—for seduction. He was stripped to his shirtsleeves and pantaloons, the shirt unbuttoned to the waist and opened out to reveal the thick down of blond hair upon his chest and descending below his navel. In the dim light of the lantern, the skintight pantaloons showed scandalously taut across the sharply defined protuberance of his loins. He swaggered the few paces from the door to her cot and stood over her, one hand resting on the bulkhead to steady himself against the slight heel of the yacht. He was very close to her and looking down.

"And to what do I owe this intrusion, Captain?" asked Purity flatly. "Is anything amiss on deck that I must know about?"

"All is well on deck, ma'am," he replied smoothly.

"I have come to inquire if I can be of any further . . . service." He emphasized the last word.

You are looking down at me, said Purity to herself, and can almost certainly see my nipples under this absurd cambric nightgown. You would be amused if I covered myself with my hands in a flurry of embarrassment, but, damn you, I will not! Look to your heart's delight—they are not for you!

"I am obliged to you, Captain," she replied. "There is one service that you can perform."

"And what is that, ma'am?" He shifted from one leg to the other, an action that brought his taut loins to within an inch of her bare shoulder.

"Go straight away and inform your carpenter, or whoever is competent to perform the task, that I require a bolt on my door first thing tomorrow morning. Good night to you, Captain Sheriffs. Be careful not to bang your head on the way out."

He left her without a word.

His lady-killing proclivities apart, Captain Hugo Sheriffs was a good skipper who ran a tight ship and sailed her true. The crew was clean, orderly, and respectful. The men went about their tasks cheerfully and never complained, even when they were turned out of their hammocks to shorten sail in the dark hours and the worst of weather—and there was plenty of that.

Purity was an excellent sailor. On the run down to the Pillars of Hercules and the Rock of Gibraltar, she had need to be. The yacht was struck by gales in the Bay of Biscay. Off Cape Trafalgar, where Nelson had died in the arms of victory one October eve twelve years previously, the *Minerva* was laid over on her beam ends, and her foresail was stripped to rags. Morning brought peace, as if the tempest had never been, and in the afternoon watch, Purity looked through Sheriffs's telescope and saw the rock rising like the hump of a camel's back out of the blue horizon. They dropped anchor in the crowded harbor at nightfall.

Immediately upon arrival, she heard the tremendous news that a squadron of the Royal Navy under Admiral Sir Edward Pellow had been to Algiers and had negotiated the release of nearly two thousand Christian slaves. Frantic with anticipation, she went straight to the governor's residence, and, despite the lateness of the hour, demanded an interview with His Excellency.

Her hopes were dashed by the governor's first words: Colonel Landless had not been among the released. Indeed, said he, the Corsairs had played false; less than half their captives had been set free, and those were only the sick and the weak.

First thing the next morning, Purity went to the consulate of the Sublime Porte, where, in a bare anteroom embellished only with three hard chairs and a flyblown engraving of His Serene Majesty Mahmud II, Sultan of the Turkish Empire, she awaited the pleasure of the consul-resident for two hours, till that dignitary, having kept an infidel member of the inferior sex cooling her heels for a suitable time, condescended to see her.

The consul-resident proved to be a porcine young man in a heavily braided frock coat and a tasseled fez. He avoided Purity's eyes throughout the entire interview and sat with his hand extended toward a small boy who crouched at his feet and filed and polished his fingernails.

What did she require? Purity told him. He gave a sharp intake of breath and shook his head. A *firman* to travel to the cities of the North African littoral was rarely granted and took time. The purpose of her visit? Purity told him. Another sharp intake of breath. Yes, of course he had heard of the unfortunate incident of Colonel Landless and Professor James. Turkish Algeria, while theoretically governed by a *dey,* who ruled over three provinces controlled by *beys,* who were overseers to *caids,* who ruled . . .

He rambled on, pausing occasionally to draw at the ivory stem of a hookah pipe and once to admonish the boy in Turkish for some minor neglect of his duty. The burden of his argument, as Purity gleaned it, was that, though Turkey nominally ruled the North African littoral, it was the Barbary pirates who lorded it in Algiers and the other cities of the coastal plain. And only a *firman* gave any protection from their depredations. And, as aforestated, *firmans* were rarely granted and took time.

It was at this juncture that Purity drew from her reticule an emerald-and-diamond brooch that had been a Landless heirloom since the seventeenth century. She pushed it across the desk.

How much time would a *firman* take?

The pouched eyes of the consul-resident opened wide.

Perhaps, under the special circumstances, not quite so long as all that. . . .

Purity and the *Minerva* stayed three more days in Gibraltar, during which time her beauty and distinction made her the toast of such ships of the Mediterranean fleet as were assembled in the harbor. From their officers, she learned more about Admiral Pellow's recent mission to Algiers. The Turkish ruler, or *dey,* had refused to give an undertaking that no more Christians would be captured and enslaved by the Corsairs, and Pellow had given him three months to reconsider.

Purity asked them if they thought that the *dey* would finally agree. No, they did not, for the *dey* was not master in his own city. It was the Brotherhood of the Corsairs who had the real power in Algiers, and they would neither give Pellow his undertaking nor permit the release of any more slaves.

The well-meaning officers vociferously advised her against any attempt to venture into the Corsairs' domain to try to free her husband. Best to wait till the Congress of the Allies had made up their minds that the devils must be smashed. Then the fleet would move against Algiers, not to negotiate, but to destroy.

As for the *firman* she awaited, they laughed at its very mention, for it was well known that the sublime incompetence of Turkish officialdom was totally incapable of producing anything but delay and confusion.

On the third day, the consul-resident appeared at the hotel where Purity was staying. He came in an open carriage drawn by a pair of jaded hacks, driven by an enormous Negro in a feathered bicorne. Admitted to Purity's suite, he avoided her eyes, as before, and presented her with a thick envelope containing a sheet of parchment entirely covered with Arabic script and heavily embellished with seals and ribbons. It was the *firman,* permitting her to travel without hindrance within the domains of the Sublime Porte. He departed, taking the emerald-and-diamond heirloom with him.

From the time of their departure from England, Purity had been less than frank with her captain about their destination. With the passport in her possession, she invited him to take a glass of brandy in the sitting room of her hotel suite, and, when that personable lady-killer had downed his drink, she let slip her bombshell.

Sheriffs flatly refused to take the *Minerva* into Algiers, and he immediately resigned his command. This he withdrew when Purity offered him five hundred guineas, plus a hundred guineas a head for each of the crewmen. She also showed him the *firman,* which, taken in conjunction with a second glass of brandy, greatly reassured him. With a last, hot glance down Purity's bodice, he went back to the yacht to make preparations for sailing.

The tideless Mediterranean offering no hindrance to their departure, the *Minerva* put out that very night, and by morning it was making fine headway with a southerly breeze, with the coast of Spain on the left side, with the snow-capped peaks of the Sierra Nevada sharply engraved against the limpid blue sky. By the afternoon, it was stiflingly hot below decks, and Purity stripped herself nude—after carefully bolting her cabin door—and lay upon her cot with a cool breeze blowing over her from the open windows.

On the morning of the third day, the lookout sighted land to starboard, and Purity gazed upon the coastal plain of Algeria, with the mountains massed beyond. She was nearing her destination, and with the thought of it came doubts and fears.

Would Mark still be alive, after all? She had never considered it before, but what if he had resisted capture? Knowing him, it was entirely possible that he had gone down fighting, sword in hand.

Her mind, frantically switching from one doleful possibility to the other, seized upon the thought of the Corsairs refusing to ransom their prisoner, even though she was prepared to offer all she had. Might they not, indeed, accept delivery of the ransom money and never hand him over?

It was while she was tormenting herself with this

thought that there came a cry from the deck: "Sails in sight—dead ahead!"

She joined the others on the high poop, which commanded the best view of the horizon, and she was immediately aware that Captain Sheriffs was uneasy. He was pacing up and down and snapping unnecessary orders to his perfectly willing crew, pausing from time to time to peer through his telescope toward the sails ahead.

There were two craft shaping course toward them and coming on fast. Within minutes, Purity could see with the naked eye that they were three-masters, with banners at each masthead, and one of them had a large black flag at the stern.

"Corsairs!" said Sheriffs in a tight voice, snapping shut his telescope. "I trust you've got that passport safe, ma'am, for I think we're going to need it—and soon."

"I have it with me, Captain," said Purity calmly.

So intent were they in watching the approaching Corsairs that they did not spot the third craft—a *xebec,* like the others—till it had slid behind them, having come out from the shore. Sheriffs was now in a quandary, and it showed on his face. The oncoming Corsairs would be upon them in a matter of minutes. The one following effectively cut off any chance of retreat. To the right lay the inhospitable shore.

One option remained. . . .

"By God " snapped Sheriffs. "I tell you that we've sailed right into a trap! Those fellows were waiting for us, and I'm not staying here to be taken. Port your helm! Let fly your sheets! We're going to run!"

The speedy yacht turned sharply, presenting its trim stern to the land. The sails billowed before the wind. The wake hissed and bubbled all around the *Minerva.*

"They're turning with us, Cap'n!"

"By heaven, so they are!"

Purity's heart missed a beat to see that the *xebecs* were now on the same course as the *Minerva*. One was on the left side, two on the right, and almost abreast of her.

"Are we gaining on them?" cried Sheriffs.

"I think so, Cap'n!" replied his mate. "Yes, we're drawing ahead. The old *Minerva*'s showing those devils a clean pair of heels, all right! Hoorah!"

The men were cheering now, waving mockingly to the figures that could be seen on the decks of the three *xebecs*, calling to the *Minerva* to put on more speed, whistling for the wind, laying bets as to how long it would be before they lost their pursuers, hull down below the horizon.

Then came a puff of white smoke from the bows of the Corsair with the black flag, followed by a sharp report. Almost immediately after, something roared past Purity's head, and the billowing mainsail was ripped halfway up, as if by a giant hand.

"They're using chain-shot!"

"We're done for!"

Even as the *Minerva*, bereft of her most effective sail, slowed her pace to a mere crawl, the *xebec* that had fired the shot turned sharply toward the yacht, sliced through the water that separated them, and came close alongside.

There was not the slightest attempt at resistance from Sheriffs and his men. Unarmed, they could only stand and stare when the swarthy pirates leaped over the yacht's bulwarks, bright scimitars in their hands, wide grins on their bearded faces.

A giant in a peacock-plumed helmet came at Purity, his hand outstretched to grab. She turned to run—anywhere, perhaps to her cabin, to close and bolt the door, to delay, even for a few moments, the horror of violation. He was quicker than she. With one muscular arm around her waist, he raised his scimitar and brought the heavy brass hilt down upon her head.

Purity's world dissolved in a blinding flash of pain.

Her first waking impression was through her nostrils. the slow, heady odor of a voluptuous perfume —not a floral scent, like jasmine, or attar of roses, nor yet one of the more eastern blooms, but a musky, animal odor of the sort that makes civet cats howl to the moon.

Purity opened her eyes and found herself reclining on a sofa that was covered with a leopard skin. Her head throbbed intolerably, but apart from that she seemed to be unharmed. Her clothing was undisturbed.

A movement just outside her vision made her start. Turning her head, she saw that the same black-bearded giant in the plumed helmet who had assaulted her was standing guard behind the sofa, his arms folded. grinning down at her. Beyond him were two others. brutish-looking creatures, naked to the waist and gleaming with sweat.

She was in the cabin of a vessel, presumably the pirate ship. The compartment was in the stern, with carved and gilded windows that looked out over the tossing sea. The furnishings were of a barbaric splendor, in peacock blues, hot crimsons, gold, silver, and bronze. Apart from the sofa on which she lay, there was a canopied bed standing upon a dais. This, like the sofa. was covered with a leopard skin. In the center of the cabin, whose floor was strewn with silk rugs of oriental patterns, stood a throne-like chair.

Purity turned her head at the sound of an opening door.

"Ah, so you have recovered, Mrs. Landless. I was afraid that Ugo had been too heavy-handed with you."

A cloaked woman entered, and Purity knew the source of the strange and disturbing scent. The newcomer was the physical embodiment of the odor that permeated the cabin. Herself a woman of a passionate and headstrong temperament, Purity recognized in the other the same qualities. She was . . . all woman.

"Who are you?" demanded Purity.

The woman threw back the hood of her cloak and shook out her flame colored hair, which, unbound, hung around her shoulders like a mane.

"I am Azizza," she replied. "I have been awaiting your arrival with considerable impatience, Mrs. Landless."

"You know my name," said Purity, puzzled.

"I know everything about you," said Azizza, taking off her cloak and revealing the voluptuous form beneath. She wore Turkish pantaloons and a brief jacket of cloth of gold. "I was told that you were on your way."

"And you attacked my yacht!" blazed Purity, rising from the couch and confronting the woman. "The *Minerva* was going about its lawful business, and I was under the protection of a Turkish *firman*."

"You mean this," said Azizza, holding up her hand. The sheet of parchment was there, seals, ribbons, and all. "The thing is quite useless, since the consul in Gibraltar is not permitted to issue a *firman* without approval from Constantinople. How much did you bribe him to concoct this rubbish?"

"I gave him a very valuable piece of jewelry," said Purity.

The other woman laughed, then, turning, she sat down in the throne-like chair in the center of the cabin and draped a slender arm over the backrest, an action that caused the unbuttoned jacket to part and bare her right breast.

"Not only did he cheat you," said Azizza, "but he also sent word ahead to us that you were on your way. Turkish officials, you see, are to be bought by the highest bidder. We could not exist without them. Our way of life—the slave trade—exists under the mantle of their avarice and their incompetence. So, Mrs. Landless, you have come to rescue or ransom your husband?"

Purity took a deep breath and said, "Do you know where he is—my husband?"

"I do."

"Will you take me to him?"

"No. Next question." She smiled a feline smile of a creature that enjoys playing cat-and-mouse.

"Is he . . . well?"

"When I last saw him, he was . . . quite well."

"When shall you see him again?"

Azizza shifted in her seat. She pretended to notice for the first time her bared right breast. She drew the edges of her jacket together with a tight, mock-modest smile.

"I shall see him in Algiers," she said. And, after a pause, she added: "When next he comes to my bed."

"Liar!"

Purity screamed the word. She covered the few steps that separated her from her tormentor. And before Azizza could raise an arm to ward off the blow, Purity brought her hand across that painted, mocking mouth.

"Seize her!" snapped Azizza, and the two half-naked brutes took Purity by both arms. Her bosom heaving, she stared in fury at the woman in the chair, and the look was returned.

"That was a lie!" panted Purity. "My husband would never enter your bed, or any other woman's bed. Our bodies are for each other, alone."

Azizza wiped her lips with the back of her long-fingered hand and looked down to see the streak of blood that lay upon it.

"You will pay for that blow, Mrs. Landless," she said. "And you will pay now. Ugo, strip the infidel woman and hoist her up for a flogging!"

The grinning Ugo came up behind Purity, held as she was by his henchmen, and, seizing two handfuls of her light summer gown at the back of the neck, he ripped and rent it to the hem, rendering her nude on the instant, save for her gartered silk stockings. This done, he grunted an order to one of his men, who, turning his bare back and raising his arms, stood ready to receive the victim.

They picked her up—with her screaming and fruitlessly pummeling their grinning faces—and hung her, with breasts and belly in contact with the man's bent back, while he supported her by the wrists, with her feet dangling clear of the floor. She was helpless, her body displayed for their vile attentions.

Azizza came close and took hold of a thick knot of Purity's blonde tresses, dragging her head back.

"Know me for who I am, woman," she hissed. "I am Azizza the Corsair. I have lain with a thousand men and watched them writhe in torment of pleasure upon me. I have taken a hundred ships and slain with my own hands. I am not to be called a liar by a pale vixen of an infidel, nor does anyone lay a hand upon Azizza and live. Regrettably, I cannot have the flesh flogged from your bones, for I have made a promise to bring you alive and unmarked to Algiers, and that I will do. Ugo, show her the lash."

The giant came into her view. In his hand he held a long silken scarf that dripped water.

"You will be flogged with wet silk," said Azizza. "It inflicts the most exquisite agony, but it leaves no permanent marks upon the skin. Set to, Ugo!"

Her arms straining almost out of their sockets, her wrists tightly clamped in her captor's hands, her bare breasts and belly slippery with his sweat, Purity closed her eyes and waited for the first touch of the silken whip, while frantically striving to assemble, in her mind's eye, the vision of Mark's beloved face. By a hideous quirk of the imagination, she saw that face stooping over Azizza, and she saw his lips—the lips she knew so well—plant a kiss upon the peak of Azizza's breast. She screamed, and the image shattered in her mind like a broken looking glass.

An instant later, the first kiss of the wet silk descended upon her buttocks.

The *xebec* was shaping course through the starlit Mediterranean night to Algiers. After it came the two consorts, and the wounded *Minerva* wallowed far behind, with a prize crew aboard.

In Azizza's barbaric cabin, they had finished with Purity. She lay naked, still, and unconscious in Ugo's arms. Forty lashes of the silk whip had carried her through indescribable agony to blessed insensibility.

"Take her away, Ugo," said Azizza, "and have the infidel captain brought to me. By the way, Ugo . . . "

"Yes, Noble One?" The giant paused by the door.

"You may take her to your cabin and have your way with her tonight."

The grin broadened. "I thank you, Noble One."

"She is no virgin, but use her carefully, Ugo. I have made certain promises regarding her. None of your . . . extravagances. If there are teeth marks upon her body, I will have you flogged at the mast. Understood?"

He nodded vigorously, eager to be gone.

"Off with you, then. And tell them to bring the infidel captain."

When Hugo Sheriffs was bundled unceremoniously in through the door, Azizza was reclining upon the canopied bed. Sheriffs, his shirt hung about him in rags, and his eyes blinded by long hours in a dark and stinking hold, blinked and looked around him in puzzlement. When at last he discerned the figure upon the bed, a practiced grin spread across his handsome features. The tautness slid from his tensed frame. He straightened up, relaxed. Here was a situation in which, through long experience, he was entirely at his ease. Here was a woman—and a mighty fine-looking wench at that, though dusky of skin, and a heathen to boot—lying on a bed and awaiting his attentions.

The lamplight illuminated the subtle lights in the wealth of hair that cascaded across her pillow. When she raised one arm to smooth a lock from her cheek, one pointed breast emerged briefly from the opening of the jacket. Sheriffs swallowed hard.

"Good evening to you, ma'am," he said in a deep, purring voice.

"Do not come any closer," replied Azizza. "Stay where you are."

"As you say, ma'am," said Sheriffs, and he felt some of his assurance slip away from him.

"Remove your shirt—what there is of it," she commanded.

With an uneasy sense of having slipped into the wrong role, Sheriffs did as he was bidden. He dropped the shredded shirt to the floor and, remembering to puff out his brawny chest and draw in his belly to best advantage, he looked again to the woman on the bed.

"Now, take off the breeches," she said flatly.

"See here, ma'am," blustered Sheriffs, hastening to retrieve the situation, to put himself in the advantage vis-à-vis this extraordinarily domineering woman, "where I come from, a little amorous dalliance is usually in order. Supposing I come over there and . . . "

"The breeches!" commanded Azizza.

With a shrug, he unfastened the flap and slid the buckskin breeches over his hips. This was a devil of a way to be treated by a damned bitch of a blackie-white. This was more like being a stud bull on display in a show ring at a cattle fair than took his fancy. One consolation: he had nothing to be ashamed of; the bitch would find him well hung.

He stepped out of the garment, nude. There was a long silence, and Hugo Sheriffs knew that the game had irretrievably passed out of his hands. No easy seduction for him, this; it was she who was the seducer, and likely to be his rapist.

"Come here," she said at length. "No! Don't *dare* to lie upon my bed! Stand by me. Reach out your hand and touch me—*there*."

The *xebec* changed course on the fickle wind, her timbers, ropes, and panelings sighing with the movement. It was the first thing that Purity heard on slipping back to consciousness, and she found herself lying upon a narrow cot, with the light of a lantern glaring in her eyes and the hideous, grinning face of the giant Ugo looking down at her nudity. With a whimper of alarm, she covered herself with her hands and shrank away from him, only to cry out with pain as the rough blanket upon which she lay was dragged in harsh contact with the bruised and throbbing flesh of her back and buttocks.

The bearded giant's grin disappeared. His brutish face took on an expression of concern.

"Lady, you are hurt," he said. "Ugo flog you. Now Ugo make better. You see." From a dark cupboard in the narrow cabin, he took out a stoppered flask, out of which he poured a palmful of oily substance. "Turn over, lady," he said. "Ugo make better."

"No, please," pleaded Purity, and she drew a shuddering breath when her entreaty brought an angry narrowing of his close-set eyes.

"Ugo make better. Turn over."

"Yes, all right." She did as he demanded.

He was gentle with her beyond belief. The horny hands that had wielded the silken whip took on a tenderness of their own. He massaged her outraged body, beginning at the nape of the neck, then across her shoulder blades and down to the deep declivity at her waist, then to her hips and rounded buttocks.

Purity lay, face-downward, eyes closed. The gentle rhythm of his movements lulled her almost to sleep, and the smooth gliding of his oil-soaked hands soothed away the pain. For over an hour he worked upon her body, constantly smoothing and cosseting the tortured fibers, soothing the outraged skin, till all her pain had gone and with it her fears. Surely, she thought, no harm would come to her from this man who could be as gentle as a mother to a child.

When he had finished, she half-rolled over and, being careful to cover her breasts with her hands, smiled up at him.

"That was very kind of you, Ugo," she said. "And now I think I could go to sleep. Will you leave me now, please? I really am very tired."

The grinning giant unfastened the crimson sash that sustained his wide-bottomed Turkish pantaloons.

"No, please!" whispered Purity in horror.

"Lady be nice to Ugo, and Ugo not hurt lady," said the looming figure above her, naked now in the lamplight. He reached out a massive hand and kneaded her breast.

She continued to plead, but she did not dare to

resist him for fear of the violence she knew he would
wreak upon her. Eyes closed, she lay back upon the
narrow cot and tried to shut out the impressions that
assaulted her senses: the animal stink of him; the
hard and brutish mass of him that descended upon
her and crushed her down; the harsh, grunted, bestial
sounds he was making close by her ear.

And then, almost without noticing the transition,
she was being caught up in an alien rhythm; she was
mounting skyward in the grip of sensations from which
there was no escaping. She was high among thunder and
lightning in the night sky, with storm clouds all around
her and wild voices clamoring in her ears. . . .

The *xebec* was on a slanting course that brought
it ever closer to the shore. Ahead lay the humped
mass that was Algiers: white buildings just visible in
the early dawn, a few lights glittering like pearls.

In Azizza's stern cabin, Hugo Sheriffs stretched
himself and yawned. The woman was by his side,
though whether awake or asleep he had no way of
telling. They were both mother-naked, and a pearly
dew lay upon the slopes of her breasts. He glanced
along her olive-skinned body in a proprietorial manner. It had ended well, after an unpromising beginning. Sheriffs prided himself that he had come up to
the mark, as usual. Her demands had been heavy,
outrageously so. Only a practiced stud of a very high
order could possibly have satisfied her many and
varied pleasures. But he had done so. Clever fellow.
He chuckled.

Prisoner of the Corsairs. Well, it sounded pretty
bad, but, a couple of hours in that stinking hold aside,
it had begun promisingly well for him. He supposed
that his blackie-white bitch was of high standing
among her own folk. He was her personal prisoner,

and he had given a good account of himself in the Courts of Hymen. She was almost certain to keep him on as permanent stud. A man could pass a worse existence.

Stud to a Corsair queen. Who'd have thought it of Hugo Sheriffs, the butcher's son from Woolwich? The wheel of fate had certainly borne him up to a giddy height. He yawned and stretched again.

The movement made her long-lashed eyelids flicker open.

He drew himself up on one elbow and looked down into her smooth, beautiful, and impassive face. He traced a fingertip across her left breast, circling the taut nipple tantalizingly.

"How was I?" he asked smugly.

"Excellent," said Azizza.

"May I be so bold as to apply for a permanent position?" he asked, careful to smile in such a way that the attractive puckering of boyish good humor appeared at the corners of his cornflower-blue eyes.

"It is not possible," said Azizza. "By the rules of our Corsair brotherhood, all captives must be offered for sale to all comers at the slave market. No exceptions are made."

Slave market! Hugo Sheriffs's tantalizing finger paused irresolutely. Then his confident smile broke through again.

"Ah, but you can surely bid for me and buy me," he said. "Since you will, in effect, be paying yourself, I will cost you nothing."

"No," she said.

"But, why?"

She said, "When I have once brought a man to my bed, that is the end of it. No man knows Azizza twice. And take your hand off me!"

He stared down at her in dismay and growing alarm.

"But what's to happen to me?" he demanded.

She gazed up and down his blond-pelted body with detachment.

"A man of your appearance would be in great demand in a harem," she said. "The women like having personable-looking slaves to attend them."

"Well, that sounds promising," said Sheriffs. "I can see myself pleasuring a whole harem full of women. One might almost say that I was born to the trade."

"There will be no pleasuring for you," said Azizza. "You surely do not imagine that any *bey* or *caid* would permit a stud bull like you to roam his harem. You will serve the ladies of the harem with nothing but mint tea and sweetmeats—atfer you have been gelded!"

He screamed into her face, slack-mouthed, staring with horror. . . .

And now the sun was high in the east, and muezzins in the tall minarets of the Casbah were calling the faithful to prayer. The sound reached the deck of the *xebec* as it nosed into the ancient harbor. But it called in vain to the snoring giant who slept in the narrow cot by Purity's side, one massive arm circling her slender middle, one hairy paw clasping her left breast. And she, fearful that her slightest move might awaken him and bring a repetition of his brutish attentions, lay in the crook of his arm, her cheek against his hairy chest, her tears of bitter self-recrimination wetting both of them. She told herself over and over again that she was no better than a whore and a street woman; she had lost control of herself in the night of tumbled coupling upon that sordid couch, and she had taken vile and perverse pleasure from the brute by her side.

Chapter Three

When Purity was dragged out on deck to join her fellow captives under the searing noonday sun, Azizza's *xebec* lay alongside the jetty that had been created by the legendary Barbarossa—the original Barbary pirate of the sixteenth century—when he joined the mainland to the islets of Al Jazair. All around, along the jetty and anchored in its protective arm, was the Corsair fleet, *xebecs* and galleys, some three score in number: a feast of streaming banners and bright paintwork, teeming with bronzed killers, as deadly as a nest of scorpions.

They had given Purity a pair of ragged Turkish pantaloons and a short jacket which, blessedly, buttoned across her bosom. She was shoved into line beside Hugo Sheriffs. The swashbuckling ex-skipper of the *Minerva* had greatly changed overnight. He gave no sign of her presence, but stared, unseeing, at the deck, his nether lip trembling, eyes lackluster, cheeks ashen.

Narrowing her eyes against the glare, Purity gazed

up at the lines of dazzling white terraces that rose,
tier upon tier, to the crest of green-capped hills. The
highest part of the city, the Casbah, or citadel, was
immediately opposite and above the quay. And it was
up a winding road to the Casbah that she and her
companions were marched shortly after, watched by
the teeming crowds that thronged the route, and by
veiled women from secret balconies and jalousied windows all above and about. Purity's appearance—the
streaming mane of blonde hair, her dazzling complexion, splendid figure—and queenly carriage, and the
fact that her face was unveiled to the gaze of men,
excited much comment. Who was this infidel noble-
woman whom Azizza had captured? Surely such a
creature must fetch a thousand dinars in the slave
market tomorrow—and none but the very richest
could pay such a sum. But what a jewel for any
harem!

They were brought through a great archway and into an enclosed courtyard. From there, armed guards
herded them into a long building that resembled a
stone-built stable. Vast it was, like the nave of a cathe-
dral, and with alcoves and alleyways leading off on
both sides. There, upon the straw-covered floor, sat or
lay perhaps a hundred captives. Most were light-
skinned Europeans, though there were several extremely handsome blacks, and their clothing was, for
the most part, in rags. But it was the utter hopelessness of their looks, the expressions of total dejection,
that betrayed their state. Here were people for whom
the present had become a constant dread of what the
morrow might bring.

The guards left, shutting and barring the doors of
the building. Weary after the long climb to the Casbah,
Purity sank down upon the straw and leaned her head
against the cool stonework.

"Have you only just been taken, my dear?"

The speaker was a pleasant-faced woman next to her, with a plump and comely figure and dark hair streaked with gray. She would have been in her late thirties, and she spoke with the lilting brogue of the Irish.

"Last evening," said Purity, grateful to have met an agreeable fellow sufferer of her own sex. "My name is Purity Landless. And you?"

"I'm Meg O'Grady," said the other. "Five years this midsummer I've been taken, and five hellish years as I would not wish upon any Christian woman, so help me."

"What happened to you?" asked Purity, observing that her companion was dressed, like herself, in pantaloons and a short jacket, both of coarse material, and ragged.

"Why, it's in a harem I've been," said Meg O'Grady. "Not as a wife, I must add—'tis only women of real beauty, such as yourself, my dear, whom they eventually take for their wives—but as a concubine. Five years I've had to give my body to a heathen brute who used me like an animal . . . and worse. I'll not sicken you with tales of the indignities that brute has heaped upon me, nor of the times when I resisted his foul attentions and he would give me to his guards to make what sport of me took their fancy. Now I'm thought to be too old for a concubine, and tomorrow I'll be put up on the block and sold as a work slave. They'll burn a brand on my shoulder and chain my legs, and I'll be put upon a treadmill or a waterwheel and made to labor till I die. But I tell you, Purity Landless, 'twill be heaven compared to the harem!"

Purity, who had been listening to the Irish woman's account of her experiences with growing horror, had a thousand questions teeming in her mind. But, out of consideration for the other's feelings, she forbore to put them forward. Instead, she asked, "What about the other people here? Are many of them newly captured? And what will happen to them?"

Meg O'Grady looked around her. "Half and half," she said. "There was a Greek ship taken last week, and many of 'em are still here, awaiting the slave market tomorrow. There's your people. The rest, like me, are to be resold, either on account of age or because their masters and mistresses have tired of 'em. When a man, or a woman, has power of life and death over another, and can use that power according to fancy—like the way a child will pull the wings off a fly for his amusement—he or she will soon tire and seek new pleasures, new faces, new bodies. That's the way of it."

"I see," said Purity, who saw very clearly, and shuddered.

" 'Tis the children I most pity," said Meg O'Grady, "lads and lassies, both. When you have seen a bloated old pasha mauling a frightened child, you thank God to be of an age when such things could happen to you without destroying the soul within you. Yes, it is the children I most pity—them, and the poor, pretty fellers who're to have their manhood taken away from them."

Purity stared at her, wide-eyed.

"Meg, you don't mean . . . ?"

Meg nodded. "There's some here today," she said, "who will not be whole men by tomorrow's eve. They're sold off to be harem eunuchs. They're fellers of good face and figure who will wait on the harem wives and grow fat and smooth-chinned as eunuchs do. Them I grieve for. There's one such lad over there. A young Greek he is, taken on the ship they captured last week. See him?"

Purity followed with her eyes in the direction which Meg O'Grady had indicated. A dozen paces distant, a dark-haired young man—he could not have been a day over nineteen—sat with his back to the wall, staring before him. With a tug at her heart, she recognized the straight-nosed profile as being of the classic mold. Such a nose, such a profile, had the sculptors of ancient Greece given Adonis and Hermes. Praxiteles had seen that profile in the streets all around him. The Greek warriors who had combed out their curls before their glorious stand at Thermopylae had looked like that boy. Nude to the waist, with only a pair of ragged, knee-length breeches, barefoot and unkempt, he had the air of a young god fallen from Olympus.

"And they are going to do . . . *that* . . . to him?" asked Purity. "And does he *know?*"

"He's been told," said Meg. "The guards always tell those who're to be offered as harem eunuchs. They make a great sport of it. There's a word and a gesture for it. 'Twould make your heart sick to see the way it breaks some of the young fellers."

"It's awful—awful!" whispered Purity, and a lump came into her throat and her tears fell unchecked.

At that moment, the double doors of the building were opened and two guards staggered in under the weight of a large iron caldron. Immediately, most of the captives stirred themselves and leaped forward to surround the guards and their burden.

" 'Tis the midday meal," said Meg O'Grady. "Bean soup, and not much of it. Hasten, if you've an appetite on you. Me, I'm not much in the mood for eating."

No food had passed Purity's lips since the previous

midday, and, despite the searing experiences since
then, she had all the appetite that comes with youth
and a perfect constitution. Rising, she went to join
the food line.

The guards were scooping up the soup, which
looked thin and unappetizing and certainly almost
cold, into wooden porringers and handing them to the
captives, two by two. Some of the wretched creatures
looked half-starved, and there was a great deal of
pushing and elbowing aside to be next at the caldron.
The guards made no attempt to restore order; indeed,
it appeared to cause them much amusement that the
despised infidels should fight among themselves for a
few mouthfuls of bad soup. The guards' greatest delight came when, there being still a dozen or so people
waiting hungrily, Purity included, they grinned and
showed that the caldron was empty. Defeated, the
hungry ones turned silently away. Purity returned to
her place by the wall.

Meg O'Grady's head being bowed on her breast in
sleep, Purity was left to her own thoughts. They
turned, inevitably, to the horrors of the previous
night. First, she thought of Azizza's appalling declaration—which Purity knew to be false, did she not?—
that she had taken Mark to her bed. Next, she thought
of the cruel flogging, and then the humiliation that followed. Instinctively, her hands sought her defiled
body, as if to wipe away the memory of what had
been done to it. But how to cleanse away her guilt?
How would she ever be able to meet her face in a
looking glass—the face of a creature who had found a
depraved ecstasy in the arms of a male animal?

"Pardon me, *madame.* . . ."

Purity looked up, surprised to hear herself addressed in French, her native tongue. It was the

Greek youth. He stood over her, a porringer of soup in his hand.

"What is it, *monsieur?*" she asked.

"I saw . . . I saw that you did not get any soup, *madame,*" he said. "And, finding myself not very hungry . . . " He lowered his gaze, shyly.

"Are you offering your soup to *me?*" she asked.

"It will give me great pleasure, *madame,*" he said.

It was on the tip of Purity's tongue to refuse him with grateful thanks. But a strange impulse prompted her to another course of action. She smiled and, patting the straw beside her, she said, "I could not possibly deprive you of all your soup, but, since you are so kind, I am willing to compromise. Sit here, and let us share it. How do you like that?"

A rare smile broke across his well-chiseled lips, and his dark eyes widened with pleasure.

"That will be very agreeable," he murmured and sat down.

"You first," said Purity.

He took a sip, and his eyes never left her from over the rim of the porringer. He then passed it to Purity, who did likewise, one small sip. In this manner, passing it from one to the other, in silent regard, they drained the porringer. This being done, he turned the receptacle upside down for a moment.

"All finished," he said. "Everything must have an end—like life itself."

She caught her breath. "But you must not say that!" she exclaimed. "You are not going to die. . . ." She broke off, wishing that she could have blotted out the words.

He smiled and nodded. "That is true," he said. "There is all life before me. And I can tell you, *madame*, that these devils will not hold me for long. I am a seaman, you understand, from Piraeus, and it is to there that I shall return. I have a girl in Piraeus who is waiting for me."

Oh, my God, she thought. He's playing make-believe with me. Tomorrow he'll no longer be a man, and he knows it. But he's playing out the last day of his manhood by making believe that he's going to escape and go back to his girl in Greece.

"You must love her very much, this girl," she said. It was probably the wrong thing to say, but she had never had any experience to arm her for such an agonizing conversation.

"Indeed, I do," he said. "Mind you, I have not had the opportunity to tell her so. In Greece, you see, the girls are very heavily chaperoned. So far, I have only been allowed to pay court to her on Sunday evenings, with her family present. We sit on the balcony of her father's house, overlooking the harbor and the ships. Her mother and father, her grandmother, and her three younger sisters are there. Her father offers me a glass of retsina, and we drink together, he and I, with the womenfolk looking on. We do not talk very much."

He's never touched her hand, thought Purity. He's never kissed her. He's almost certainly a virgin, as she is.

"When I return to Piraeus," he went on, "it will be very different. I shall go to her father and I shall say, 'Look, I have come back from hell, and I now know what is important in life and what is not. I will not spend a year, two years, of Sunday afternoons drinking a glass of retsina on your balcony while you accustom yourself to the idea of my marrying her. We will go to the priest today, and you will not stop us!" He looked steadfastly down into the empty porringer, and then he added, "That is what I would do if I were back in Piraeus at this moment."

And a slow tear ran down his cheek and fell into the bowl.

It was nighttime in the great stone-built prison vault. There were no sounds but that of someone snoring at the far end and of the muffled sobs of some young girl haunted by the horrors that tomorrow would bring.

Purity raised her head fom the straw and looked around her. Meg O'Grady was fast asleep nearby, her bosom rising and falling steadily. It was dark, with only slivers of moonlight coming from a line of semi-circular windows that spanned the length of the nave-like chamber, high up. Close by, six paces distant, in a shadowed archway, the Greek boy was slumped against the wall. One bare arm and one leg emerged from the blackness into the dim light. Perhaps he was asleep, perhaps not.

Purity's resolve was quite unshaken when it came to the act of rising up, for she had turned it over in her mind all through the long afternoon and evening. Unhesitatingly, she tiptoed across to the archway, ducked into the concealing darkness, and crouched down beside the young Greek. Instantly, his hand came out and groped for her arm.

"You!" he exclaimed.

"Ssh!" She felt for his lips, placed her forefinger against them.

"You have come," he whispered. "I prayed against all hope that you would come, and I had just thought that hope was dead."

"You knew I would come," she whispered against his ear.

"Perhaps I knew," he said. "I think that I knew while we were drinking the soup together."

"I feel very wicked," she said lightly. "But I have

to tell you that I have never before allowed a man to entice me with a bowl of soup."

His bare arm was against her shoulder. She felt him tremble.

"What do we do now?" he whispered.

"Give me your hand."

His hand was scarcely bigger than hers, long and slender. Unfastening her short jacket, she slid his smooth fingers inside till they cupped first one of her breasts, then the other.

"You are so beautiful," he said. "As soon as I set eyes on you, when you first came in here . . . "

"You talk too much," she said against his lips. "Now, you must kiss me."

"I never kissed a girl before."

"It isn't difficult. See?"

Still kissing, she guided him till they both lay in the straw. The warmth and smoothness of his young body, as she let her hands glide over his back and shoulders, made her almost cry out for anguish and compassion. The warmth of her heart opened out to him when, his ardor roused and his nervousness overcome, he essayed gently to mold her breasts and rain kisses upon them. Then, with hasty hands, and each helping the other, they rid themselves of their few rags of clothing and lay, breast to breast, flank to flank, mouth to mouth, in the dark vault of the archway, safe from all eyes.

She surrendered without hesitation to the sweetness of the rhythm set up within her. She yielded to the first surge of ecstasy that lifted her skyward and bore her above the dark clouds of night, into the everlasting sunshine. Laughing and crying together, she let the benison of the sun wash over her, cleansing her every part and making her whole again. Then she drifted earthward, with the echoes of sweet music still ringing in her ears.

They lay together in the darkness, arms entwined, his head upon her breast. He was asleep.

She had an impulse to awaken him, to entice him, with her whispers and her body's softness, to at least one more transport of ecstasy—perhaps his last. But she resisted the temptation, and for entirely unselfish reasons. He was safe now in her arms, dreaming, perhaps, of the delicious satiety that they had shared. He was safe from the coming dawn. To wake him might be to destroy his peace. What if terror drove out passion? The night was far advanced. What if, his lips upon her breast and the desires mounting within him, he saw the first thin, gray light coming in through the high windows? She shuddered at the thought. No . . . she would let him sleep in peace.

What she had given this boy had been a gift shared. It was entirely possible, she thought, that the enjoyment of her body would only add to the bitterness of his future existence, for it was often said that what one has never had, one never misses. Did that apply in his own hideous circumstances? She hoped not.

For her part, the giving of her body had brought an unconsidered blessing. She felt—again. By willingly giving herself out of compassion, she had gained peace of mind. The vileness that had been wrought upon her the previous night might never have happened. One single act of loving kindness had set her free from the torments of conscience. She had learned more that night than the shape and feel of a Greek boy's body—she had learned an eternal truth about life and loving.

He stirred in her arms and nuzzled her breast like

a sucking infant. He gave a start when he realized who she was and where they were.

"Is it nearly morning?" he whispered.

"I think so," she replied. "I think I heard a cock crow a little while ago."

"Are you frightened?" he asked.

"A little," said Purity. "And you?"

He did not answer for a while, and then he said, "Less than I was."

"I'm glad," she said.

"I have a confession to make," he said.

"You have no call to confess anything to me," said Purity. "What there is between us calls for no confession, no explanation."

"It's a very small thing," he said. "When you said last night that you had never before been enticed by a bowl of soup, you said it in jest. I want you to know that I offered you the soup for just that reason. I wanted you—I wanted you more than anything in the world. And that bowl of soup was all I had."

She bowed her head and kissed his lips. Her mouth still close to his, she whispered, "And now I have a confession to make. I accepted your gift, shared it with you, so that I should be obliged to give you something in return. And that was very wicked and forward of me, because I had nothing to give you but my body."

He whispered, "I can see daylight. Look! You can pick out the shape of the high building beyond the windows."

"Don't look!" she said urgently, pulling his head down between her breasts. "Close your eyes. Forget. Think only of me. Hold me tightly. Do you find my waist slender? They say—my dressmaker says—that I have the slenderest waist in London. Can you feel my nipple brushing your cheek? Ah, that's quite heavenly. Do it again. And now the other. Oh, the things you have learned since last night."

"It was my first time," he whispered.

"But," she replied with an urgent, anguished glance over his shoulder to the new dawn that slowly lightened the window, "it shall not be your last. There is still a little time left to us. . . ."

It was over. A final cleansing. And she felt more pure than ever before in her life, so much so that, if Mark Landless had come before her then and there, she could have made her declaration with eyes open and no fear.

They were stirring all around them. People were sitting up in the straw, looking around, remembering where they were and what was to happen to them that morning. The girl who had wept in the early part of the night began to weep anew.

"Good-bye," Purity said. "One last kiss."

"Good-bye. Do you know . . . ?"

"What?"

"If I lived to be a hundred, if I possessed a thousand women, if I became the greatest lover in the world—I would never again recapture the perfection of knowing you. You have given me a whole lifetime in one perfect night."

She clung to him, blinded by the tears that she was grateful he could not see. And then she was gone.

Meg O'Grady rolled over, grunted, opened one eye, and looked at her. The Irish woman grinned. "The best night's sleep I've had for five long years. It was the first time, you see, that I haven't slept with the dread that I might be aroused to pleasure that dirty old goat who owned me. I tell you, Purity, the treadmill and the waterwheel are going to be a blessed release from that."

The sun rose above the building across the court-yard and came streaming in the high windows. A man shouted something outside. The Arabic phrasing sounded harsh and alien.

"Prison noises," said Meg. "It seems to me that I've been listening to the shouts of jailers all my life. My mother, you know, was feeding me at the breast in Newgate prison right up till the time they dragged her away and hanged her from the three-legged oaken horse outside the gates. She died well, they told me in later years, as well she might have. 'Twould be a poor Christian who wouldn't have the grace to die well for stealing a sack of flour to feed her starving family. Are you scared, lass?"

"A little," said Purity.

"You have no need to be," said Meg. "With your looks, you're one of the lucky ones. At the end of the day, you'll be in clover. Mind you, Purity, you must be careful at the slave market. Mark this well: do not resist, do not struggle with them, no matter what they do with you. There'll be the slave master and his men, and them who come to buy, and them who just come to ogle. They'll pry open your mouth to see your teeth. On the slightest pretext, they'll strip you naked where you stand. Before the eyes of all, they'll handle you as none but a lover should. There's no shame in those men, no pity. But don't resist. Be like a patient mare brought to market. Suffer in silence."

"Who is likely to . . . buy me?" faltered Purity, conscious of the strangeness and unfamiliarity of the phrase.

"Not my old master, for sure," said Meg. That miserly goat wouldn't pay the sort of money you're likely to fetch at the slave block—even if he had it. A lass of your looks and figure will fetch . . . oh . . . a thousand and more. You'll be looked on with favor by the rich sheikhs and *beys* who come from Tripoli and Oran, maybe from as far afield as Cairo and Constantinople, Baghdad, and Damascus."

"You mean I might be taken from Algiers?" cried Purity. "But that must never happen! I *mustn't* be taken from here!"

When the kindly Irish woman asked her why, Purity told her. Meg shook her head.

"I never heard tell of a slave in Algiers name of Mark Landless," she said. "He was not a slave of my master, but then the only males who ever came near the harem were eunuchs, and he was not one of them."

"The Corsair captain who took us, the woman called Azizza, claimed that he is in Algiers," said Purity.

"That she-wolf!" exclaimed Meg. "She's notorious all over the Barbary Coast, that one. Pray to heaven that your man does not fall into her clutches, for she has destroyed more men than could ever be counted."

Purity shied away from any further speculation about Mark and Azizza by interposing another question: "If I were bought by someone in Algiers, someone with the money to pay what you said I might fetch, who might it be? Can you name any names?"

"I can name some," said Meg. "There's him they call Omar Manzur. He's one of the Corsair captains, with six *xebecs* of his own to command, and as cruel as he's handsome. You might appeal to him, for he looks for nothing but the best in woman flesh. They say one of his concubines was unfaithful to him with a work slave and he had her buried alive in the sand. Then there's the *dey* himself, Abu Mikhnaf, though 'tis whispered that boys are more to his taste. And then there's El Diablo."

"El Diablo—but that's Spanish for 'The Devil,'"
said Purity.

"I know not where he took his name," said Meg,
"but it fits him like a glove, by all accounts. He's no
Corsair captain, but he owns a great fleet of *xebecs*
and rowing galleys—more than Omar Manzur, even.
Lives in a great palace on the hill above the old
Casbah fortress and is seldom seen, and when he is,
he walks abroad veiled, like one of the desert Tuaregs.
I've heard things muttered out of the corners of
mouths about El Diablo—things I can't repeat to a
woman gently reared, like yourself. No, I wouldn't
like to think of you in El Diablo's hands, lass."

"I think," said Purity reflectively, "that, from what
you've told me, Meg, my plans can best be served by
being bought by Omar Manzur."

"Like as not," said Meg, adding shrewdly, "but
don't let your gaze linger on any field slave, Purity,
or you're likely to end up trying to claw your way
out of a sandy grave!"

They sat in silence. Purity stole a glance across at
the Greek youth, who flashed her a shy smile. Soon
after, the doors were unbolted and thrown wide open,
and a trio of armed and helmeted guards commenced
to usher the captives out into the sunlight with the
butts of their spears.

"The slave market has begun, Purity," said Meg.
"Soon we'll know our fates. Good-bye, lass, if I
never see you again, as is likely."

"Good-bye, Meg," said Purity, squeezing her hand.
"Thank you for your advice. And I hope that . . . that
everything turns out for the best for you."

The Irish woman's comely, good-natured face was
illuminated by a smile. "Good, bad, or indifferent,
'tis going to be an improvement on the last five
years," she declared. One of the guards gave her a

rough shove toward the door, and she was lost to Purity's sight in the sea of bobbing heads.

Outside, she looked around for the young Greek, and she saw him from afar, in profile. He looked calm and resigned. She tried to edge her way through the crowd of captives to reach him, but she was dragged to one side by one of the guards and thrust into line with a small party of young women, comely women, with good bodies and faces—women for the harems.

The slave market, which took place weekly in the shadow of the old Casbah fortress, was attended by would-be buyers from all over the Middle East and beyond—even from as far away as Persia and cities of the Arabian gulf. Nomadic traders—dark-skinned travelers of the desert wastes—came from the far oases of the hinterland, from Chenachane, from Taoudenni, from In-Zizi, and from distant Timbuktu. They bought women—strong women, capable of withstanding the rigors of months-long journeys through some of the worst terrain on earth—and they bought cheaply. These women, if they survived, were sold at high prices to the black potentates of the lower Niger. Close to a thousand buyers and idle onlookers crowded the shady end of the great square below the fortress. And the captives were crammed together at the opposite end, in the sun. A flat slab of stone stood in the center, between them. This was the slave block upon which, for centuries, uncounted wretches had been bid for and bought like cattle.

The business was conducted in Arabic, the language spoken and understood in every part of Africa north of the Niger and as far to the east as the Black Sea and the valley of the Indus. It was conducted by a certain fellow named El-talib, "The Beggar," whose

father had been a slave master before him and his
grandfather before that. El-talib had a reputation as
something of a comedian, and he was in especially
good form the morning that they brought Purity
Landless to the block.

"Come, my lords and masters," called El-talib,
cracking the long horsewhip that was his symbol of
office. "Dip deeply into your purses, for the Beggar is
calling for alms. I bring you good slaves: strong fellows who will labor for you till they drop; pretty boys,
who, with a little snipping here and there"—like the
good comedian he was, he waited for the laughter to
subside—"with a little snipping here and there, will
nobly grace your harems. And then—the women.
Lords and masters, I have women who will drive you
to write poetry: French women, as pale as ivory, with
rumps like melons and breasts like ripe pomegran-
ates." He cracked the whip. "Dig deeply into your
purses, my lords and masters. First—the work slaves!
Bring them forth!"

El-talib's assistants drove a mass of men and women
into the middle of the square to the foot of the block,
using their long whips to control the movement. Almost the first to mount the block was Meg O'Grady.
She stood with her head bowed, meek as a lamb in the
burning sun.

"This infidel woman has done good service as a concubine and still has years of debauchery left in her,"
said El-talib, who believed in squeezing the best bargain he could. "Any bids? Any lord and master care
to come forward and handle the goods? Very well. Let
me have your bids for her as a work slave. Do you call
thirty dinars? Thirty-five over there. Any more?"

A black trader from the hinterland paid forty dinars
for Meg O'Grady. She was brought down from the
block and manhandled to a brazier by the fortress

wall. There they stripped her to the waist, and, while one grinning brute held her arms, another burned a red-hot brand into her plump shoulder. She screamed out in agony, and Purity Landless, hearing it, put her hands over her ears in the hope of shutting out the sounds.

The work slaves were quickly disposed of, for the value of such wretches was not a matter of much dispute. A strong-looking man or woman capable of five years of backbreaking labor went for between thirty and fifty dinars. The rest were knocked down for a few coppers; they were doomed to the mines, where, in the fierce heat and choking dust, their lives would be measured in weeks, if not days.

Next, El-talib brought forth house slaves, both male and female, including those who were to be offered as harem eunuchs-elect. Here, the bidding was keener, for a woman house slave with a good body might serve also for her master's bed, and for the beds of his guests. Also, fashion and fancy played an important part. Socially, it was perfectly permissible for a widowed woman to have uncastrated male slaves around her house, and the present fancy ran to coal-black Nubians of good figure and height. One such man was set up on the block that day, was stripped naked to display his maleness, and was keenly bid for by two middle-aged widows—plump and pampered ladies, veiled within silken palanquins borne on the shoulders of tall Nubians—who vied with each other to the tune of three hundred dinars before the hammer fell.

It was to the loser in this bidding that Hugo Sheriffs owed his salvation. The ex-captain of the *Minerva* produced a very agreeable impression upon the block, where his height and fairness excited much admiring comment among the matrons present. She who had lost in the bidding for the Nubian conceived the con-

ceit of the blond Adonis as a contrasting pair with her
present, favorite Nubian to carry her in her palanquin,
assist her in the bath, and share her couch. Scarcely
able to contain his utter relief—for he spoke a little
Arabic, and he was able to understand the assurance
that one of El-talib's assistants muttered in his ear—
Sheriffs came down from the block and departed to
begin a new life as servant and stud to a rich widow.

No such reprieve lay in store for the tragic young
Greek. His appearance on the block—so slender and
perfect of proportion, his demeanor so grave—brought
applause from keepers of harems, chief wives, and
such who had come to purchase young males to be
eunuchs in the seraglios. A lively bidding ensued, and
the Greek was bought for the record price of four hundred fifty dinars.

From afar, Purity Landless saw him brought down
from the block and taken across the square to a low
doorway leading into the fortress. He walked straight,
his head held high, a serene expression upon his perfect classical countenance. Just short of the doorway,
he half-turned his head and flashed a brief glance to
where the women captives stood, as if to catch one
last glimpse of she who would be the only lover of his
life. Blinded by tears, Purity never saw the gesture.
And the door closed.

The announcement that the last of the captives, the
comely women and girls, were about to be brought to
the block caused a palpable stir of excitement among
the watchers. Several richly attired personages stepped
forward closer to the block, the better to view the
goods on display, and, if the spirit moved them, to
taste and to try. Some of them, idlers with no intention
of buying, had merely come out of salaciousness. With
a sharp intake of breath, Purity picked out a slender
figure in a scarlet cloak and flame-red hair. Despite

the veil that covered the lower part of the face, she had no difficulty in recognizing Azizza. So the female Corsair had come to see her captive sold to the highest bidder!

For those women and girls awaiting their turn on the block, the proceedings were harrowing to the extreme. The first of their company to be offered was little more than a child, dark-eyed and raven-tressed, her nubile young body hidden in a long, ragged gown. She fought and screamed when they tore the gown from her, and she covered herself with her hands rather than submit herself to the close scrutiny of the men around the block. Then a lash of El-talib's horsewhip across her slender back brought her to submission. Two old satyrs, overweight pashas from Egypt, sweating with heat and lust, mounted the block and ran their hands over the trembling girl, plucking at her budding breasts and fondling the swelling roundness of her buttocks. They bid against each other for the possession of the child, and she went to the older and more raddled of the pair for over two hundred fifty dinars.

The process was repeated with every female who was set upon the block. For the prices they were being called upon to bid for a bedmate, no man was going to buy unseen. And, should that scoundrel El-talib, who would not tell the truth to save his own mother from being ravished by a Bashi-bazouk, lay claim that the female being offered was an attested virgin, why, that claim would be proved or disproved, there and then, before all. One by one, the line of women and girls mounted the block, were outraged with hand and eye, then went their separate, shameful ways.

Presently, it seemed to Purity that she must be next in line for the ordeal; but one of the guards held her back and pointed to the rear of the line. She—the high-breasted, blonde-tressed beauty—was to be offered last, as the choicest creature in the sale.

Sickened to the heart with the things they were doing to her fellow sufferers on the block, Purity closed her eyes and summoned up her fortitude for the coming ordeal. One name burned in her brain: Omar Manzur, Corsair captain and burier-alive of women. He would likely be present this day, and her best hope of remaining in Algiers and of finding Mark was for this Omar Manzur to buy her. To be taken to Cairo, Constantinople, or any such far-flung place would spell the end of everything. With Purity and Mark still alive in Algiers, there was always hope.

She opened her eyes and scanned the richly dressed men nearest the slave block. Which, she wondered, was Omar Manzur? There was a man standing next to Azizza. He was paunchy, old, and black, and surely not the swashbuckling Corsair whom poor Meg had described. She scanned the faces of the others. Most were old. She supposed that most very rich men were old. There was no one who remotely resembled the Omar Manzur who had been conjured up in her imagination by Meg's description. But he must be present, unless perhaps he was at sea. If in Algiers, would this man—this connoisseur of the best in women's flesh—absent himself from the slave market? She thought not.

A shove in the back and a harsh command roused her from her speculations. There were no more women and girls in front of her. Her time of trial had come.

An awed hush fell upon the onlookers as the beautiful blonde woman mounted the block. It was immediately followed by a flurry of excited talk, so that El-talib had to hammer, and continue to hammer for some time, to get silence.

"My lords and masters," shouted El-talib, "be prepared to dig deeply into your purses, for here, indeed, is the jewel of the collection! Taken only the day before yesterday by the illustrious Azizza"—he made a deep bow to the figure in the scarlet cloak, who inclined her head in acknowledgment—"this infidel aristocrat is fit to grace the harem of the highest personage present here today. Behold her, my lords and masters! Do I need to strip the clothing from that peerless body in order that you should behold the glories that announce themselves so clearly?" He paused for effect, and it was clear from the murmurs and imprecations that arose that this audience was of the opinion that the slave master should do that very thing. El-talib, who was not a salesman for nothing, and who knew that a pleasure delayed was a pleasure enhanced, merely raised his hand for silence, then resumed his discourse. "All in good time, my lords and masters, all in good time. May we first start the bidding? Later, if the high reserve that Azizza has placed upon this infidel aristocrat is not reached, I may be persuaded to unveil her charms in order to encourage the fainthearted. What am I bid?"

"Three hundred dinars!"

"Lord, you are jesting," declared El-talib.

"Three hundred fifty!"

"Master, is it your wish that my wives and children should starve?" demanded the slave master. "Do I hear four hundred?"

Purity stood in the broiling sunlight, her breasts rising and falling with emotion, the object of a thousand eyes, while the bidding rose steeply. And all the time she gazed covertly around her, seeking for the one who answered the description of the Corsair Omar Manzur. Each personage who raised his hand and called out a bid met her swift scrutiny; none fitted the picture she had in her mind. The bidding continued.

Presently, El-talib threw down his whip in a gesture of despair.

"It is of no use," he cried. "We are not within sight of the reserve price. My lords and masters, I fear that I shall be obliged to withdraw this merchandise from the sale."

"Why so?" A deep voice from the back made all eyes turn. Excited murmurs arose. The crowd parted, and out into the sunlight strode a tall figure in a black cape that swirled like a bat's wings around his broad shoulders. His swarthy face was illuminated by piercing, bright eyes that flashed beneath a jutting brow. Hawk-nosed and high-cheekboned, spare and muscular, with not an ounce of useless flesh upon him, he looked to be the perfect fighting animal. On his head was set a Moorish helmet chased with silver, and his breast was protected by a cuirass of the same workmanship. One lean hand rested lightly on the hilt of a curved scimitar worn on the left hip.

The newcomer halted, cocked a critical eye at the woman on the slave block, and repeated his remark: "Why so, El-talib, you slimy jackal? Where stands the bidding that you must withdraw the woman from the sale?"

"At nine hundred fifty dinars, my lord Omar Manzur," purred the slave master. "Does my lord wish to counter-bid?"

The piercing eyes swept Purity from head to foot.

"One thousand," he murmured sonorously.

"One thousand one hundred dinars!" This came from the paunchy black standing next to Azizza. It was he who had been leading the bidding from the first.

Purity held her breath. All eyes, her own included, were upon Omar Manzur, who unconcernedly stroked his firm jaw and shook his head.

"No woman is worth more than a little over a thousand dinars," he said, "be she a queen of beauty and a paragon of voluptuousness." He smiled, and it was a cruel smile. "And I have known women," he added.

This sally brought a chorus of amusement from the crowd. Purity, unable to understand a word of what was being said, was nevertheless aware that Omar Manzur was dismissing her—a knowledge that was confirmed by the smug grin on the face of the paunchy individual.

"So be it," declared El-talib. "My lord Omar Manzur retires from the bidding. The bid is with Abu Nuwas at one thousand one hundred dinars. Any further bids? Then, on the count of three, I declare Abu Nuwas to be the buyer." He raised his whip. "One . . . "

A concerted gasp rippled through the crowd. Someone swore an oath. Omar Manzur, who had turned to depart, checked his stride and looked back, his dark eyes suddenly flaring wide. The slave master, pausing with his whip raised, looked behind him to the figure on the block.

Her eyes fixed upon Omar Manzur, Purity, having unfastened the short coat that was her only upper garment, slowly peeled it from her shapely shoulders. Her breasts, freed of any encumbrance, stood revealed in the sunlight, proudly jutting out, unashamed.

She dropped the rag of material to her feet. The crowd sighed.

Omar Manzur's lips parted in a white-toothed, savage grin.

"One thousand two hundred dinars!" he said in a clear voice.

"And three hundred dinars!" From the man by Azizza's side.

"Four hundred."

"Five."

"Six."

It was Omar Manzur's turn to bid. He glanced up at Purity, grinned, and shrugged.

"Such a pity," he said, "but no woman is worth it."

Purity's hands hesitated on the way to the waist of the Turkish pantaloons that were her only remaining garment. In a silence of the grave that fell upon the huge concourse, her hands moved on and unfastened the knot of the waistband. Slowly, her eyes never leaving those of Omar Manzur, she slid the material over the round of her hips, held it there for a breathtaking moment, then allowed it to fall in a pool around her bare feet.

A long pause ensued, then Omar Manzur said slowly, "We will put an end to this charade. I bid two thousand dinars for this woman, and I will go no further. This I swear on my father's head."

All looked to the paunchy Abu Nuwas, who seemed not one bit put out; indeed, he appeared to savor the moment and drew it out for as long as he was able to, till El-talib hammered the butt of his whip on the ground and called out, "What is your answer, Abu Nuwas?"

"Two thousand one hundred dinars," replied the other.

If Abu Nuwas had hoped to spark anger and disappointment in his opponent, he was greatly disappointed, for not by the flicker of an eyelid did Omar Manzur display his emotions; instead, with one last, cool, and appraising glance toward the nude figure upon the slave block, he turned on his heel and walked away, the crowd parting to let him through. And Purity watched him go with despair.

Suddenly the slave market was dispersing, and it

was all over. El-talib handed Purity back her clothing and treated her to a black-toothed grin of approval.

"Well done, woman," he said to her in English. "By the Prophet, I wish I had a hundred such as you. Then I would buy me a palace and retire with a thousand concubines."

"We . . . who has bought me?" asked Purity with an anxious glance toward Abu Nuwas, who was counting money into the extended palms of one of the slave master's assistants.

"Not him," replied El-talib with a note of contempt. "Not Abu Nuwas, who is a servant and a eunuch. He was bidding for his master."

"And who is his master?"

"Him they call El Diablo—The Devil."

She was taken from the great square in a palanquin carried by two giant blacks, and the last thing she saw before they drew the silken curtains around her was the green-eyed gaze of Azizza. The woman Corsair was staring at her, but the veil hid her expression.

Purity lay back against the soft cushions, fastened her jacket, and breathed a sigh of relief.

Her stratagem, though misdirected, had not been entirely in vain. She had been bought by El Diablo—true. And poor Meg had spoken of him as being a monster. But, like Omar Manzur, he lived in Algiers. She was not to be carried off to Cairo or Constantinople, but would remain within reach of Mark. Next, she must find Mark. She must put forth every effort, overcome every obstacle, be prepared to make any sacrifice, or debase herself in any way (it was here that she recalled, with a shudder, how successfully she had counterfeited total shamelessness while stripping herself before the multitude).

Nothing mattered but to find Mark and effect his release. With that clear-cut resolve before her, she was able to speculate on her immediate future without shrinking with revulsion.

What manner of man was El Diablo? Well, she would find out soon enough. When night fell, or sooner, she would doubtless be subjected to his desires. He would wish to taste the pleasures that he had purchased at some considerable expense. Her body was his.

She must endure it. For Mark's sake, she had to put aside the scruples of a lifetime. Her body—she touched her breast—now belonged to someone else, although her mind, her soul, and her inner being were still her own, and utterly devoted to the man she loved. To resist El Diablo would surely be to bring punishment upon herself, perhaps imprisonment—perhaps even death. Imprisoned or dead, what use would she be to Mark?

This resolve set firmly in her mind, another stratagem suggested itself. Supposing that she so delighted El Diablo, supposing that, by her voluptuousness, she so besotted him that he was willing to grant her anything she asked, could that not be turned to great advantage? What if she was able to persuade her doting master to allow her to move freely around the city—with an escort, naturally? She would be able to seek out and find Mark and, given that El Diablo kept her supplied with money for her wants, perhaps be able to buy his freedom. After that—escape for them both. Yes, that was what she must do: make El Diablo her devoted slave. She smiled and, all unconsciously, her fingers unfastened all but one button of her tightly fitting jacket.

The journey in the covered palanquin, which, by the motions involved, appeared to be the ascent of a hill, presently came to an end. The curtains were drawn back to reveal Abu Nuwas, who motioned to follow him.

Purity alighted from the palanquin and stole an awesome look around her. Meg had spoken truly when she hinted of El Diablo's wealth. The surroundings were magnificent to the extreme. She was in a high-walled courtyard that was tiled in multicolored squares of highly glazed faïence. Tiled, also, were the walls, the slender columns, and a pretty dome that surmounted a fountain in the center, from which a single jet of water rose as high as the inside of the dome and made the air cool with its very sound.

Following the Negro, she passed through a maze of pavilions, each tiled in a different dominant color: pale lemon, azure, delicate grays, black and white, Nile green. Each pavilion was furnished with silken screens and low divans covered with opulent cushions. They presently came to an archway that was guarded by another Negro carrying a broad-bladed stabbing spear and a circular bronze shield.

Her guide gestured for her to go through the archway.

"Enter," he purred in a high-pitched voice. "The Excellent One will receive you now."

With one last glance down her front to reassure herself that she was showing a generous amount of her bosom, yet not too much, Purity took a deep breath and went in through the archway to a room that was tiled in pinks and blues and hung with diaphanous white silks of the sheerest and most transparent sort. A fountain splashed into a lapis lazuli basin, and, through the swaying hangings, she could discern an outside balcony and the rich green of cypress trees stirring in a slight breeze.

"So you've come at last! Well, I never would have believed it!"

Purity spun around at the sound of the voice.

Reclining upon a wide, low couch at the end of the room, opposite the coolness of the balcony, was a shapely young woman in Turkish trousers and jacket covered all over with fine pearls and brilliant jewels. Upon her head she wore a silken turban fastened with a spray of diamonds. She was veiled, but the eyes that regarded Purity were of disconcerting familiarity. Moreover, her skin was pink and white, and her hair was light brown.

"Who . . . who *are* you?" asked Purity.

The other woman laughed. "Don't recognize me, do you, dearie?" she said. "I'm not surprised at it, seeing as how I've changed me costume, not to mention me way of carrying on. Nice here, isn't it? Here, have a sweetmeat." Reaching out, she took up a carved ivory box from a side table and held it out to Purity. In it, upon a nest of vine leaves, were several sticky-looking sweets covered with dusted sugar and topped with glacé cherries. "Go on, have one, dearie," said the other. "I'm fair addicted to 'em, for all that they're making me as fat as a kitten."

"No, thank you," answered Purity faintly.

The other took one of the sweetmeats and brought it to her veiled lips. Then, with a mischievous twinkle, she unfastened the veil at one side so that it fell, revealing her pert, pretty face, that, save for a certain plumpness, had not changed since Purity had last seen her.

"*Mon dieu!*" exclaimed Purity. "Nancy Shaw!"

"That's right," said the ex-nursemaid cheerfully. "Her you discharged without a reference for having a bit of lustful pleasure while on duty. Heh! 'Tis a small world, and no mistake, ain't it? Mind you, dearie, there's no coincidence in you and me meeting up like this, no, definitely not. It was what you might call prearranged. But more of that later. Sit you down beside me, do. That's right. My! You've a fine figure, and no mistake. I always did envy you that figure—not that I've ever seen so much of it as you're showing now." She cocked an eye at the deep cleft of Purity's breasts. "Did they strip you in the slave market?" she asked cheerfully.

"I . . . was stripped," admitted Purity.

"Terrible the way they treat the women down there," said Nancy, reaching for another sweetmeat. "You get used to seeing it, of course, but the first time I watched from the palanquin—I was there to buy a matched pair of black eunuchs to be bath attendants; you'll see them before long—it made me feel quite . . . well, you know what I mean. To see those women being undressed and felt all over, I went all of a hot flush. I tell you, if I'd had a man with me in that palanquin, he'd have learned what life's pleasures were all about!" The ex-nursemaid lay back on the cushions and laughed till she nearly choked on her sweetmeat.

A score of questions flowed into Purity's mind, but some imp of caution told her to proceed slowly. So she asked, "How long have you been here, Nancy?"

"A month, maybe a little more," said Nancy. "And since we'll be living together, you'd best get used to me calling you Purity."

"As you please," said Purity mildly.

"I don't bear you no grudge, you know," said Nancy. "Mind you, I'd have torn your eyes out on that first night. But I never was one to bear a grudge. And you had good cause to discharge me, right enough."

"I sent the grooms after you the next morning,"

said Purity. "I'm afraid I'm not one for bearing grudges, either. But you weren't to be found."

"Ah! I was far away by then," said Nancy, looking slyly to one side. Then, she asked, "Tell me, how is the little maid—how's my darling Chastity?"

Purity looked down at her hands. "She was very well when I left," she said. "And she'll be well looked after by my husband's maiden aunt, who's moved into Clumber."

"Ah, yes, poor Colonel Landless," said Nancy. "I heard as how he'd been taken, poor gentleman."

Purity looked up sharply. "Nancy, do you know where he is?" she demanded. "If you do, if you have the slightest inkling, I beg you by all that's holy to tell me!"

The other's eyes flared with what could only have been fear, and she stole a glance toward the balcony, where, through the diaphanous draperies, could be seen the swaying tips of the cypress trees.

"Mrs. Landless, ma'am—Purity—I don't know," she said earnestly. "And, to be honest with you, if I knew, I wouldn't let on. Here it's best to know nothing, see nothing."

"But, Nancy, I've got to find him!" said Purity.

Nancy shook her head. "You'll never have a chance," she said flatly. "He'll never abide the idea of you being reunited with your husband."

"He? You mean . . . ?"

Nancy nodded.

"But, Nancy, this man—this El Diablo—how did he come to bring you here? And why am I here, and, as you implied, why and how was I expected? Who is this man, Nancy?"

Nancy shook her head. "It would cost me my tongue to tell you, dearie," she said. "But one thing I'll let slip." She leaned forward and whispered in

Purity's ear: *"You know him as well as he knows you!"*

At Nancy's suggestion, Purity was brought to the bath chambers, which occupied a whole block in the sprawling complex of buildings and secret gardens that housed the mysterious El Diablo and his vast entourage of majordomos, slaves, eunuchs, and concubines. The first of the chambers was a hot room, where Purity was divested of her skimpy clothing by a pair of brawny Negro eunuchs and laid down upon a tiled couch. There, in the sweltering, dry heat, while the attendants removed the exuding grease from her perspiring skin with ivory scrapers, she lay there and thought of what she had been told by Nancy. . . .

The man called El Diablo knew her, and she knew him!

She searched her mind for a clue. It was certain that he was not an Arab, a Turk, or any denizen of the East, for she knew only those with whom she had come into contact since her arrival off Algiers. And Nancy had quite clearly implied that she knew this man of old. Who, then, could he be?

There were so many possibilities: from her childhood in Revolutionary France, to her upbringing at Clumber and her school days in Bath; her marriages and her misfortunes; the time she lived in Spain; her journey back to the Seine château where it had all begun; life since the war, in London, Clumber, and Brighton. In all those years, she had met hundreds of men of all ages, classes, and nationalities. She had made scores of friends, and some enemies, though her worst enemies were dead. Who was this man?

One thing was clear . . . and she shuddered at the thought.

Whoever he was, he wanted Purity Landless with a

single-minded and forceful persistence, and he had gone through a great deal of trouble to get her!

Many things—scraps of conversation, dropped remarks—were now falling into place. She remembered almost the first words that Azizza had addressed to her aboard the *xebec:* "I have been awaiting your arrival." At the time, she had thought that the female Corsair had only been alluding to her betrayal by the Turkish consul, who had sent word ahead. In the light of what she knew, or guessed, now, the words also had a more sinister meaning. And then, when Azizza had ordered her to be flogged, she had stipulated a whip of wet silk, for, as she had said: "I have made a promise to bring you alive and unmarked to Algiers." She had forgotten the remark; it had been washed from her mind by the agony of the flogging that followed, but it came back to her now.

"Now the Excellent One will please advance to the steam room," purred one of the attendants, making a deep obeisance.

In the steam room was a black girl, nude save for a sash of scarlet muslin around her slender middle. She led Purity to a marble throne, where she sat and sweltered in the unbearable steam, relieved from time to time by a tin container of delicious, ice-cold water that the girl threw over her.

When Purity had had enough, she was directed to plunge into a richly tiled bath of cold water built into the center of the floor. She emerged, dripping and refreshed, and the black girl swathed her in luxuriant Turkish towels.

"Now the Excellent One will please advance to the massage chamber," murmured the girl.

The masseuse was a splendidly built, yellow-haired Caucasian who spoke barely a word of English, but who devoured Purity with hot, Magyar eyes. She was nude to her waist. Her bare breasts, when she bent over Purity to massage her back, trailed across Purity's shoulders and spine.

Relaxed, full of a glowing sense of physical well-being, Purity redirected her mind to the mysteries that surrounded her.

This man who had schemed and plotted to secure her for some reason—and that reason could only have been to own her body for himself—was not in Algiers at the moment. This, also, Nancy had let slip. He was at sea, but he was expected back at any time. They said that El Diablo always veiled himself like a desert Tuareg when he traveled abroad. When she, Purity, came face to face with him, doubtless in a bed-chamber, would he take off the Tuareg veil and show himself?

Would her surprise be very great?

That would greatly depend upon whom he turned out to be. There were some men of her acquaintance —not mild-mannered, gentleman-like, Robbie Glad-wyn, for instance—who might well lead double lives as English country gentlemen and owners of Corsair fleets in Algiers. It was an eccentric age, and the English upper classes bowed to no one when it came to eccentricities of the most extravagant sorts. She put her mind to producing a gallery of faces. . . .

"Please to turn over on back, Excellent One," said the masseuse in a heavily accented, husky voice.

Purity obeyed, and she luxuriated in the firm strokes the woman's capable hands made across her belly and flanks, her shoulders and breasts. A sense of splendid ease robbed her of coherent thought, and she was unable to concentrate upon the possible identity of El Diablo. She put it from her. It scarcely mattered. Better to lie and let one's mind wander through more pleasant pastures of contemplation, as, for instance,

Mark. She tried to make believe that it was he who was stroking and molding her body so excitingly. In such a manner, when they were lying together, nude to nude, did Mark draw his hands slowly from her throat to her belly in one long stroke, cupping her breasts along the way. She drew a sharp intake of breath to feel her right nipple taken gently between finger and thumb and lightly drawn out. An impulse to offer a mild reprimand to the woman was instantly dismissed from her mind; indeed, she experienced a few moments of anxious anticipation till the gesture was repeated with her other nipple, and she gave a pleasured sigh.

Only Mark knew how to massage her belly and her thighs so lovingly. It was a torment not to writhe with the pure ecstasy of it. So she relaxed and let herself writhe, eyes tightly closed, a blissful smile on her lips.

Almost unaware, she was caught up in a rhythm of her own making, moving in time to her own gasping breath. Caught, she was borne skyward.

Mark, oh, Mark!

And now she was mounting higher, borne upon no less than three separate rhythms, all in the most complex counterpoint, the beats weaving one among the other, advancing and retiring, growing stronger and stronger, till she thought her head would burst, then dying away into an infinite distance.

"Mark, Mark, I love you!" She screamed the words in the ultimate transport of her rapture, when she reached the vast height where it is impossible to breathe, to think, even to exist. And then she was tumbling earthward, satiated, blissful, fulfilled.

She stretched herself and pillowed her arms behind her head. The masseuse was unconcernedly donning a short linen jacket, covering up her generous breasts.

"Thank you so much," murmured Purity, thinking how trite it sounded.

The woman bowed her head in acknowledgment, but without meeting Purity's eyes.

After the Turkish bath, Nancy Shaw showed Purity to the suite of chambers that was to be hers. It occupied the same floor of the harem block as her own. Like Nancy's, Purity's sitting room possessed a balcony that commanded a view of the harem garden: a place of cool fountains and well-trimmed bushes and trees, of elaborate paths and flowerbeds marked out with tiles and pieces of colored faïence. It was a most un-English garden, exceedingly prim and formal.

The bedroom was hung with swags of diaphanous material in chocolate and pale lemon-yellow, and the bed, wide enough to accommodate half a dozen people, had a canopy over it. Glancing up at the underside of the canopy, Purity saw that it was set with small pieces of looking glass, reflecting her face a hundred times.

Nancy gave a prim cough. "Ahem! It's the same with my bed, and with the rest of the harem. He—the master—likes to watch himself, and you, when he's doing his lovemaking. Each to his taste, I say, though I likes a bit of privacy myself. What do you fancy to wear, dearie? There's plenty to choose from."

She drew back a curtain, revealing a wardrobe that was hung with clothing of all description, and there was more neatly piled on perfumed shelves. The costumes were all Eastern in style, and all were of diaphanous quality. After some choosing and trying on, Purity settled for a pair of Turkish pantaloons of cloth of gold, a silk blouse of total transparence, and a caftan of the same material as the pantaloons. At Nancy's suggestion, she wound a white silk turban around her piled-up tresses and secured it with a gold clasp from a considerable collection of bijouterie contained in a Moorish chest. She then regarded herself gravely in a pier glass.

"I look," she said, "like a right, regular concubine."

"That you do, Purity," said Nancy. "And I tell you, dearie, it's an occupation that's not to be sneezed at. Mayhap it's not for the likes of yourself, who's had everything the heart desires. But for a poor working lass like me, reared in a parish orphanage, risen from kitchen slut to nursemaid, and then thrown into the gutter . . . "

"Nancy, I'm sorry about that, I really am," interposed Purity.

"No cause for you to be sorry, dearie," said the other, placing a reassuring hand on her arm. "I deserved it, and it led me to higher things, so, in a manner of speaking, I should be grateful to you, as, indeed, I am." Whereupon, she kissed her former mistress on the cheek, and Purity willingly responded by returning the embrace.

The muffled notes of a gong resounded through the building.

"That is the midday meal," said Nancy. "Come, Purity. 'Tis your first opportunity to meet your new sisters."

Purity took a last glance at herself in the pier glass. The ensemble really looked quite enchanting; she supposed that, considering its origin, a wardrobe in a harem, it was also greatly attractive to men. When she and Mark were free, when they returned together to England, she must obtain such garments, lots of them, to wear in their intimate moments together. Oh, Mark, Mark, how I do love you!

"Are you coming, dearie?" asked Nancy from the

door. "My, you're a one for going off into daydreams, and no mistake!"

"Coming, Nancy."

Nancy guided her through silent, arcaded corridors, down winding staircases, across the harem garden, past the splashing fountains, where a peacock stiffened out its tail and displayed its hundred eyes in defiance, to an archway that led into a long room with a large Oriental carpet set down in the middle. The carpet was laid with bowls and dishes of various foods and crystal pitchers of colored drinks. Seated cross-legged around the four sides of the carpet were—Purity made a swift count—twelve women and girls who eyed the newcomer with a revealing disparity of expressions. The youngest ones—and a couple of them, at least, were no more than sixteen or seventeen—gazed at her with frank interest, as if she were a new girl at a school. The more mature ones of her own age mixed interest with a critical eye, taking stock of her hair, her complexion, hands, bosom, and stature. All save two, a very young black girl and a doll-like Chinese woman—were Caucasians.

"Ladies, this is Purity, who's just joined us," said Nancy cheerfully, adding, *sotto voce,* in Purity's ear, "I don't know all their names, so there's no point in introducing you. Find your own way around. Some of 'em speak English, and some of 'em speak French, so you shouldn't be stuck for conversation. Sit down, dearie, and let's eat. Mercy me, I'm quite famished. What have we got? Not mutton again!"

Purity sat down on the edge of the carpet next to Nancy, with the young black girl on her other side. In the act of doing this, the full force of her bizarre situation struck her for the first time. Here was she, a respectable married woman of aristocratic lineage, joined in a ring of concubines, all of whom owed au-

thority to one man who had their lives in his hands, a
man who could order any one of them to be whipped,
branded, tortured, or decapitated at his whim, all of
whom, furthermore, were obliged to give their bodies
to him without the slightest hesitation. And here they
all were, herself included, sitting in a ring, eating—
she peered into the nearest bowl—what looked like
cold mutton stew!

"When I first came here," murmured Nancy, "they
all ate out of the same bowl with their fingers, which
is the heathen way things are done in these parts.
Thanks to my influence, we now have plates and
forks. Help yourself, dearie. It's a lot more wholesome
than it looks."

The conversations, which had clearly been interrupted by the new arrival, broke out again. All about
her, Purity heard Arabic, French, and some English.
The young black girl was carrying on a loud and jab-
bering monologue to her neighbor in some unidentifi-
able tongue. Under cover of this sound, she and Nancy
were able to have a private conversation.

"They all look very . . . content," said Purity, glancing around her. It seemed a very odd comment to
make. The very idea of all those women and girls being owned by one man, sharing one man, seemed so
alien. And now she, too, was one of them.

Speaking with her mouth full, Nancy replied:
"They've got plenty to be content about, dearie.
They're waited on hand and foot, well provided for in
every way—and particularly in bed."

"Oh," said Purity.

The other nudged her and winked. "When it comes
to the pleasuring of a woman, there's none to touch
him," she said.

"Indeed?" asked Purity faintly.

Her companion nodded, then took another mouthful of stew. "There's some fellers," she said, "and I expect you've had 'em in your time, Purity, whose idea of pleasuring a wench is to throw a leg astride her and rut like a ram till they've taken their pleasure, be it sooner or later, and let her underneath fend for herself. There's some so-called gallants—and women of the world like us know 'em well—whose idea of pleasuring a wench is to emulate a stallion at stud, and with about as much feeling. You know what I mean?"

"Er . . . quite," said Purity.

"Now, him," said Nancy, "he's a feller who knows what a woman needs. For a start, she needs to be wooed. And he's a great one for wooing, that El Diablo. And after the wooing comes the teasing, gentle teasing, as would drive any woman wild with lusty joy. I expect you know the feeling."

"Well, I . . . "

"And after the teasing comes the pleasuring, and such pleasuring as you'd not forget in a long time. And there's none of your wild, selfish rutting, as the kind that leaves a lass high and dry and wanting. That's not his way."

"You must miss him very much," said Purity for want of a better comment upon Nancy's engaging frankness.

"That I do," replied the other. "It's been too long, and there's times when I'm like a bitch in heat. But even in this place, there's ways and means."

Purity gazed at her in puzzlement. "Nancy, you don't mean . . . ?"

"A harem ain't a nunnery, dearie," said Nancy with a wink. "There's ways and means."

"You mean *men?*"

"That I do." Nancy looked around her and pitched

her voice in a whisper. "Mark you, it'd mean a flogging, or worse, if he ever found out."

On her first day as a concubine, Purity learned the
prime lesson of harem life: the great enemy is inactivity.

The midday meal over, the women returned to their
separate quarters. Purity spent the long, lonely, perfumed afternoon on her couch, turning over in her
mind the plan she had devised for accomplishing
Mark's rescue.

According to Nancy, he who called himself El
Diablo was a practiced sensualist. So much the better;
he would be all the more vulnerable to her voluptuousness. A man who took the trouble to woo and
win a woman was the sort who was himself easy prey
to a woman's wiles. This man, who knew her and
whom she was supposed to know, would find his
match in Purity Landless. For Mark's sake, she would
ensnare El Diablo and win freedom for them both.
With this thought in her mind, she drifted off to sleep.

It was dusk when she awakened, and a heavy lan-
guorousness lay upon the subtropical air. Rising, she
went to the balcony and looked down into the garden,
which looked so cool and inviting that she was
prompted to go down and walk in its shaded paths. A
second prompting made her decide to take Nancy as a
companion.

She crossed the corridor to the other woman's suite.
"Nancy, are you there?" she called.

Her voice drew a startled exclamation from behind
the hangings that surrounded the couch. In the half
darkness, she saw a figure rise up and look toward
her. With a start of alarm she saw, from the breadth
of shoulder and the thickness of neck, that it was a
man!

"Lawks! Is that you, Purity? My, you did give me a scare!" cried Nancy from the couch.

He, whoever he was, came bustling through the curtains, a bundle of clothing held in front of his total nudity. Purity barely had time to realize that he was young, pale skinned, and well formed before he was gone in haste.

A candle flame blossomed behind the flimsy hangings, revealing Nancy lying like a pink-and-white nymph upon the cushions. Like her departed companion, she was entirely nude.

"Nancy, I'm sorry," faltered Purity.

"Don't upset yourself, dearie," Nancy said in a good-natured response. "Mark you, had you come a little while back, I might well have thrown a chamber pot at your head. Come to think of it, I should have thrown a chamber pot at your head the last time you caught me in the act, for that was the most inopportune moment I can think of." She laughed.

"Your . . . friend . . . is one for whom you risk a flogging, or worse, I presume?" asked Purity.

"Yes, he's one of the palace guards who defend the outer walls. They're all whole men, and they're not allowed inside the harem on pain of death. But there's many a lusty lad who'll take the risk for a bit of hanky-panky, and there's eunuchs who'll look the other way for a handful of dinars."

"And you, too, are willing to take the risk!" Purity shook her head. "Really, Nancy, you are incorrigible."

"You know little Nancy," said the other with high good humor. "She never was a one for misbehaving." And she slapped her plump thigh.

"I am going to get a breath of fresh air," said Purity. "I don't suppose I can persuade you to accompany me."

"Little Nancy has had all the exercise she needs for one day," said the other.

"Then I'll say good night." Purity paused at the door. "Do you think . . . is it likely that El Diablo will be here tomorrow?"

"Mayhap," responded the other. "We'll have to wait and see, won't we?"

Purity found her way through the arcaded corridors and winding staircases to the harem garden, where she was immediately assaulted by the heady odor of the night-scented honeysuckle that hung in abundance from the walls of the seraglio. The peacock and its own harem had taken to the lower branches of a cedar tree, from which roost they gazed in haughty disdain upon the woman who disturbed their rest. She paused by the fountain, reaching out her hands to catch some of the cool droplets. There were many different-colored fish moving in the dark shadows of the tiled basin.

Something else moved just within the scope of her vision. She half-turned her head to see what it was and was immediately taken from behind by a brawny forearm that was wrapped, chokingly, around her throat, cutting off her breath and all sound. Another arm around her waist lifted her up as if she had been a rag doll. Struggling, silent, fighting for breath, she was carried the length of the garden, through an archway, to the edge of a balustraded terrace. Far below the terrace, at the foot of a sheer sweep of stone wall, the lights of the Casbah winked in the gloaming of the subtropical night.

A rope was hastily knotted around her chest and tightened under her arms. The choking arm was replaced by a gag of silk, which, crammed into her mouth with brutal force, was then held in place by a handkerchief. She barely had time to make out the

face of her assailant—he was a black-bearded Arab—
before she was unceremoniously bundled over the balustrade. She toppled her own length, sickeningly, until
all the air was driven from her lungs as the noose
tightened with a jolt and she was brought up short.

Then she was being lowered, down, down the dizzy
height of the sheer wall, spinning around and around
as she went, like a marionette on a string, till she
reached a small vineyard at the foot of the wall, from
out of whose concealing bushes came more men, who
took hold of her and cut her free.

Far above, he who had lowered her looped the rope
around one of the supports of the balustrade and then
descended the wall.

It was neatly done. Purity's disappearance was not
discovered till midnight, when the captain of the palace guards came upon the body of one of his sentinels
on the terrace behind the garden. The man had had
his throat cut as cleanly as a melon.

Chapter Four

There were six of them: desert Arabs, bearded and dark-visaged, dressed in flowing robes. They were big fellows, who said nothing, but moved quickly through the dark alleyways of the Casbah with their captive. Two were in front, two behind, and one held each of her arms. When the streets straggled away to nothing and cobblestone gave way to thorn scrub and palm, one of them put his forefinger in his mouth and gave a whistle. Two more of them came out of the darkness. They were horse holders, with wild-eyed stallions at rein.

The leader of the party, the one who had given the signal, leaped to his high-cantled saddle, and another lifted up Purity for him to take. He draped her across his front, one arm around her waist. His chest was bare under his caftan, and she could feel the warmth and smell the musky odor of him.

"*Bismillah!*" He gave a wave of his arm, then set his sleek-necked stallion into a standing gallop. The others followed behind.

The going was hard almost at once, a steep climb that searched out the mounts' staminas. After reaching the top of the first hill, they descended into a valley, with the horses' hindquarters set down hard and trailing long plumes of sand in the moonlight.

No one had thought to ungag the prisoner. With difficulty, Purity contrived to drag the scarf from around her mouth and spit out the bundle of silk. The rigors of the long day then overwhelmed her, and, to the jolting rhythm of the gallop, with a stranger's arm around her lightly clad middle, she fell asleep.

That part of the Algerian littoral is called the Tell, and it is formed of wrinkled hills with valleys and basins between. Beyond lies the desert, and beyond that are the Atlas Mountains, whose high passes are the gateways to the great beating heart of inner Africa. Riding hard, with frequent stops for brief rests, the party was deep into the Tell by midnight and proceeding along a steep-sided valley that grew narrower with every turn, until, rounding a bluff, they came to its end. And there, rising from the valley floor, and set, story upon story, till its battlements and pinnacled towers reached the lip of the escarpment, was a castle. Hewn half out of the rock, with massive outworks whose stones had been laid by armies of slaves long dead, it was a relic of bygone ages. Carthaginians had caused it to be built as protection from the warring tribes of the south. It had outlived the Roman Empire, the Vandals, and the Mauritanians. It would likely outlast time.

Purity, who had awakened from her uneasy slumbers at every halt, opened her eyes when the leader drew rein beneath the lowering mass of stonework and shouted an order. There was a heavy rumbling, and a heavy drawbridge descended from the portals, coming to rest across a deep ditch that fronted the fortress, revealing a dark arch that lay beyond. She caught her breath with anticipation as they clattered over the bridge, under the arch, and into a courtyard lit with flaming torches set in the high walls all around.

The leader dismounted, pulling Purity after him and setting her on her feet, where she would have swayed and fallen from sheer weariness had he not taken her in his arms again. He called an order to one of his men, and, gathering up her inert form, he carried her through an arch and into the castle, up a flight of steep steps set against the wall of a four-sided keep. Torchlight threw his giant shadow on the undressed stone walls, and his footfalls sounded hollowly in the vast space.

He came at last to an apartment on the second floor, a simple room paneled in fine woods and smelling of jasmine flowers and sandalwood. And there, upon a wide divan covered in silk shawls and soft cushions, he laid his burden. Purity gave a small sigh, stirred, raised a faltering hand to her cheek, let it fall, and returned to the profound sleep of the utterly jaded in mind and body.

The Arab stood over her, his arms folded, till presently there came the sound of footfalls down the corridor outside the room. He turned and made a low *salaam*—as Omar Manzur entered.

"Ah, you have the French woman?" asked the Corsair.

"Yes, *reis*. She sleeps."

Omar Manzur crossed over to the divan and looked down into the sleeping face.

"Did the capture go well?" he asked. "Was the alarm raised?"

"Our man killed one of the guards. There was no alarm," replied the other.

"It is good," said Omar Manzur.

Stooping, he reached out, and, taking the edges of the cloth-of-gold caftan, he drew them aside, revealing the sleeping woman's perfect breasts, steadily rising and falling under the transparent shirt.

"By the beard of the Prophet!" breathed the man who had brought her there. "Never have my eyes beheld such a woman. Does the *reis* wish her to be awakened and carried to his bed?"

Glittering-eyed, Omar Manzur stared down at his captive. He shook his head.

"Tonight, she will sleep," he murmured. "It will bring her strength and inspiration for the night that will follow. For I tell you, Achmed, that will be a night that will set the stars aflame and make the moon halt in its course across the sky!"

Purity slept through the night and the morning that followed. She woke up at midday and found herself being fanned by a young slave girl who was perched on the edge of the divan beside her. The girl—she was only a child, and she spoke neither English nor French—led Purity by the hand to an adjoining bath area where she stripped and washed her new mistress, afterward scenting her with jasmine oil, dressing her hair, and robing her in a new blouse, pantaloons, and caftan, all of rose-colored silk, and setting on her braided hair a round Turkish cap decorated with pearls.

The girl stayed with her all that day, declining to respond to Purity's attempts to communicate with her, in sign language, with the intent of finding out where she was and who her captors were. The girl remained obdurate but respectful. She brought Purity a simple selection of kabobs served on vine leaves, some pilaf, sweet halvah made of crushed sesame seeds and sugar, and a tiny cup of bitter Turkish coffee.

At sundown, she again took her charge by the hand, bathed her from head to foot once more, oiled her smooth body with jasmine, and attired her in filmy pantaloons, a short jacket of net sewn with brilliants that left no secrets around the structure of her bosom, a silk turban, and a veil. Purity was puzzled about the latter, and she made questioning signs to the girl, who only shook her head and signified that the veil must remain. Then, taking her by the hand again, she led her mistress out of the room.

A spiral, stone-cut staircase led to the floors above. Purity counted three, till her guide opened an iron-barred door, and they stepped out into the warm desert night, smelling of sage and the million small flowers of the desert.

On the roof of the castle, a Moorish-style garden had been laid out. Where long-dead Carthaginian archers had stood and shot their arrows down upon besiegers, there were now tiled fish ponds and cool fountains. Where vats of molten lead had once been overturned to run along gullies and out upon the enemy, there now were neat rows of jasmine and magnolia, bougainvillaea, and scarlet hibiscus blooming in abundance. And the entire garden was roofed in by a canopy of purple silk that stirred gently in the light airs of the night.

The girl guided her past a line of potted magnolia trees and into an open, tiled space that was overlooked by a stepped dais, upon which was set a wide couch covered in the skins of wild animals: leopard and lion, zebra and antelope. Seated there, his dark eyes glittering upon her, was her captor. She knew him at once.

"Sit by me," commanded Omar Manzur, addressing her in perfect French.

Her guide had vanished, as if she had never existed. Purity walked across the open space that separated her from the Corsair, disturbingly conscious that he was regarding every movement of her body and devouring every part of her with those disconcerting eyes.

When she reached the dais, she took two steps up and seated herself at a prudent distance from him. He glanced at her sidelong, his hawk-like nose held high, a thin smile of mocking amusement on his cruel lips.

"So," he said, "your heart's wish has come to pass."

"I do not understand you," replied Purity.

"Oh, come, *madame,* it is not so difficult," he said. "Have you forgotten the slave market? Where is the beautiful French woman who divested herself for the enticement of Omar Manzur?"

Purity ignored the question. "And divested herself to no avail," she countered tartly. "Omar Manzur did not consider her worth the price."

The Corsair threw back his head and laughed, revealing the muscles of his strong throat and shoulders. Freed of his gaze, she eyed him covertly. He wore pantaloons, with an open caftan over his upper torso. A white turban was wound around his neatly shaped head and fastened with a jeweled dagger. His feet were bare, and the toenails were well shaped, neatly cut, and polished.

Presently, he said, "When I saw you naked, I bid two thousand dinars and swore a binding oath that I would go no further. I was not to know that that jackal Abu Nuwas had been given orders from his master to purchase you at any price."

"You learned that afterward?" asked Purity with great interest. "From whom?"

"It was common knowledge," said the Corsair. "If I had not come straight from my *xebec* to the slave market, having just put into the harbor, I would have heard it gossiped about in every coffeehouse in the Casbah that El Diablo desired the infidel woman with the wondrous hair and would pay any price to possess her."

Despite the warmth of the night air, Purity shuddered, as if someone had just walked over her grave.

"Do you know why he desires me so strongly?" she demanded.

Omar Manzur raised one dark eyebrow and stared pointedly at her half-nude torso. "Need you ask?" he replied.

"But, surely, he has women to spare," said Purity. "He could take any woman he desired, slave or free. Why me?"

The Corsair shrugged. "I have already answered that question," he said. "Look into your mirror. You will see there why that dog will give the earth for you."

"And now—*you* have taken me," said Purity.

"Indeed I have," replied the other.

"Have you not put yourself in some danger on that account?"

He nodded. "El Diablo would have me slain if he could, or, if taken alive, I should then die in protracted agony in his torture chamber. Did you know that your former master has a torture chamber in his palace above the Casbah?"

"Who *is* he?" she demanded.

"Do you not know?" he replied. "He is an infidel, like yourself. We have been rivals for years. It is only a matter of time before one of us kills the other. It is written in the stars. But now, if I may return to my original declaration, which you so neatly ignored. You disrobed before a thousand pairs of eyes for the sake of Omar Manzur. Now your heart's wish has come to pass. You are his."

Purity lowered her gaze before his searching eyes.

"There . . . there is something I must tell you," she said in a voice that was scarcely above a whisper.

"Tell me," he murmured.

"It . . . it cost me a very great deal to shame myself like that," she said. "And I did it for a very particular reason."

"That I know," he said.

"But not for the reason that you supposed," she said.

"That also I know," he said.

She looked up, her eyes flaring with surprise.

"You *know?*"

"It is not widely known—but I learned without very much difficulty—that the beautiful Mrs. Landless had come here under the supposed protection of a useless *firman* to secure the release of her husband. The husband is in Algiers, but I do not think that Mrs. Landless knows precisely where. Obviously, the worst thing that can happen to her is to be sent away from the city, so she decided that she must be bought by Omar Manzur. Do I have it correctly?"

"Yes," she whispered.

He shifted his posture and leaned over toward her till their shoulders were nearly touching. He looked closely into her eyes.

"What would the beautiful Mrs. Landless give to know the whereabouts of her husband?" he asked.

"I would give anything!" she exclaimed. *"Anything!"*

"That is a very enticing prospect," said Omar Manzur. He reached up and, taking the side-fastening of her veil, let it fall from her face. "Can you enlarge upon that declaration with a little more precision? What, for instance, would you do for me?"

"I would give myself—my body—to you," she said.

"How?" he asked. "Tell me how, and in how many ways."

A shiver ran through Purity's frame.

"Is it your wish to shame and humiliate me beyond bearing?" she whispered.

"Is it your wish to learn the whereabouts of your husband?" he countered.

"Yes! Oh, yes!"

"Then let me hear, from your own lips, what you are willing to offer in return. Answer me. And look at me when you speak."

Her nether lip trembled as she met his gaze. "You may use my body as you wish," she said. "I will deny you nothing."

"And?"

Purity said, "And I will pleasure your body in any way you demand, withholding nothing, shrinking from nothing."

His fingertips were resting on her right shoulder; they scurried like a spider across her bosom and unfastened the tiny pearl buttons of her brief jacket.

"The bargain is struck," he said. "I will take the first part of your payment this night. And in order to inspire you to achieve the more esoteric refinements of passion, I have arranged a brief diversion."

He clapped his hands.

To one side of the dais was a carved screen, like the jalousies that covered the windows of harems. Scarcely had the reverberation of the Corsair's handclap died away when the unearthly wail of a flute issued from behind the screen. At the same time, lamplight blossomed through the intricate patterning, revealing two slave girls, one playing the flute and the other tapping out a complex rhythm on a pair of hand drums. Both were nude to the waist.

"See what follows," murmured Omar Manzur in Purity's ear.

From out of the shadows beyond the masses of

flame-headed hibiscus stole two figures, hand in hand, male and female: she had skin as pale as ivory and waist-length hair the color of ripe wheat; he was as black as night and towered head and shoulders above the woman, for all that she had the stature of a goddess. Save for a loop of beads across her brow and a matching necklace, she was nude. Her companion's total nakedness was accented by a scarlet turban wound around his head. They moved into the center of the open space with hesitant, complex steps, advancing and retiring in time to the flute and drums.

"The woman is a Circassian, from the Kuban province of Russia," murmured Purity's interlocutor. "They are highly prized as both concubines and dancers, since they make no distinction between total surrender and total fulfillment—to them the terms are synonymous. He is a Nubian, of course. Algiers matrons of experience and discrimination will have no others for their bed slaves, and one can see the point of their argument."

The couple having reached the center of the floor, the music abruptly ceased, and the two figures stood as still as statues, white counterpointed with black. There was no movement but the slight rise and fall of their breasts.

"Now begins the dance," said Omar Manzur. "It is a very ancient, traditional harem dance called 'The Capture.' As you might suppose, it is frankly erotic, a ritual of arousal. I hope you will find it to your taste."

He had drawn Purity close to him, his arm around her, her shoulder against his bare chest, her buttocks pillowed in his lap. Mrs. Mark Landless, high-born wife and mother, chatelaine of Clumber Grange, in the county of Wiltshire, now was the plaything of a Corsair who was capable of burying a woman alive.

She was promised to him in the most unequivocal terms, her body bared to his hands and eyes. She watched the two nude mummers as they turned and gyrated in a protracted mime of amorous dalliance.

She closed her eyes. For you, my darling Mark, and for you, my sweet, my baby Chastity. And pray that, when this nightmare is over, I shall be able to shut my mind to the humiliation and be whole again. . . .

"You are sleeping, my lady?" murmured Omar Manzur, caressing her possessively. "But you must not miss the next part of the dance. It is more . . . instructive."

Obediently, she opened her eyes. The music had taken on a strident ululation, to the rhythm of which the couple were joined in an act of sensuality; the Circassian was lying supine, with the Nubian kneeling over her.

Purity caught her breath. The music was seductive, and so was the sweet-scented desert air. She felt warm, cosseted, cared for. Before her eyes, like a colored fragment of an erotic dream, two beautiful creatures were engaged upon what she and Mark had long regarded as one of the most tender and loving offerings that one body can bestow upon another. Why, then, close one's eyes against the sight of it?

Omar Manzur's caresses were becoming more explicit, and Purity found herself responding to the rhythm of the music, and she was writhing gently in his lap. Yet, of the man into whose hands she had agreed to deliver herself, she gave not a thought. Mark's beloved face and body were fixed in her mind's eye to the exclusion of all else. Even the naked mummers were distanced by the reality of her communion with the man she loved. They were no more than pasteboard figures in a shadow theater, playing out familiar, sweet themes of abandonment that she had learned in her tumbled bed back in dull Wiltshire.

The flute piped one last, long trill. The drums fell silent. The two nude slaves, their dance done, backed into the shadows, hand in hand, bowing as they went.

"Was that to your liking?" asked the Corsair.

"It was very charming," said Purity.

Omar Manzur rose, and, reaching down, drew her to her feet. With one arm around her waist, he led her to the dancing floor.

"And now, my lady," he murmured in her ear, "we will dance 'The Capture.'"

The flute sketched out the first portion of the dance, and the drums took up the rhythm. Slowly, languorously, Purity swayed her hips and advanced toward her partner.

She awoke when the first light of dawn tinted the pinnacles of the castle a rosy pink. There was a light frosting of morning dew on the supports of the great purple canopy, and the desert air stuck coldly to her skin, being covered only with a sheepskin, sharing it with the man who lay sleeping at her side on the couch, nude like herself.

Her thoughts returned to the events of the previous night. She had danced "The Capture" with Omar Manzur. In keeping with her promise, she had performed every portion of that protracted homage to sensuality. It had been easy, for, seduced by the music and by her own inner cravings, she had only needed to imagine that it was Mark who joined her in the unashamed excesses demanded by the dance. And, later, when her partner had carried her to the couch and consummated the promises that her body had made upon the dancing floor, she had continued self-deception. It was Mark who had gathered her up and

carried her into the realm of the stars, Mark who had
surrounded her head with glory and who brought her
earthward again, breathless and fulfilled.

A prickling of unease caused her to glance sidelong
at her companion. She gave a start to see that his
dark and regarding eyes were wide open and fixed
upon her.

"How long have you been watching me?" she asked.

"You were thinking of last night," he said. And it
was not a question.

"Yes."

"You kept your side of the bargain, Purity," he
said. "You made your first payment in rich coin."

"And now you will fulfil your part of the bargain?"

His brow furrowed. "To do that, it is necessary that
we make a long journey."

"To Algiers?" she asked. "Is it so far to Algiers,
where my husband is?"

He shook his head. "There is a saying of our people:
'The fruit of the tree is only a hair's breadth from the
reach of my hand, but it is a day's ride to fetch a lad-
der.' To determine the exact whereabouts of your husband, it will be necessary to travel far in the opposite
direction—far into the desert."

She said, "Then you yourself do not know where
he is, but you know someone who does?"

"Precisely. Your quick wit is exceeded only by your
beauty."

His gaze fell reflectively upon her bare shoulder.
With a sudden pang of alarm, Purity sat up, and,
reaching for her skimpy jacket, she inched into it and
buttoned the material across her bosom. He watched
her with a thin smile of amusement.

"When do we leave?" she asked.

"Today, as soon as the sun has gone down. It is

madness to ride in the desert when the sun is high. Do you ride well, Purity?"

"Yes."

"I have an albino palfrey that will suit you very well. She needs to be handled with firmness—as do many women."

There was no mistaking the insinuation in his voice, and his eyes were feasting upon her. Desperately wishing that she had more clothes to put on, Purity, remaining seated in an upright position and gathering around her as much of the sheepskin as she could, sought for a fresh topic of conversation.

"You speak excellent French," she said at length. "Where did you learn it?"

"In Egypt," he said. "My father, who was Albanian, spoke fluent French and was military governor of Alexandria under the Turkish administration. When Napoleon Bonaparte invaded Egypt, we fled to join my mother's people, the Bedouins."

"It is to them—the Bedouins—that you refer when you speak about 'our people'?" she asked.

"Yes," he said. "And it is with them that I shall end my days, wandering with my camel herds, out into the wide desert in the rainy season, moving from oasis to oasis in the dry summer months."

"A life of peace?" she commented. "Will that suit you, a Corsair?"

"The day of the Corsair is nearly spent," said Omar Manzur. "One year, three years at the most, and they will send ships to destroy us, for we have been a thorn in the side of the infidel since the days of Khair ed-Din, the one you call Barbarossa. For three hundred years we have been the terror of the Mediterranean. We have robbed, burned, and enslaved. We have extorted protection money from those who wish to pass on their way unharmed, and we have cheated them.

The Sublime Porte, which calls itself the ruler of
the Barbary Coast, shuts its eyes to our activities,
and Turkish officials grow fat on our bribes. But it
cannot go on much longer. The world is changing.
What the Americans did at Tripoli, the British will do
against Algiers. There are those alive today who will
see the last *xebec* and galley burned to the waterline
and the last Corsair *reis* garrotted on the jetty of Al
Jazair. But I shall not stay to see it. By then I shall
have returned to my people."

He paused, glancing at her quizzically, raising one
eyebrow in what she had already come to recognize
as a familiar quirk of his. "I am talking too much,"
he said. "And I could be forgiven for thinking that
you are leading me on in order to evade another payment of your bargain. But that could not be so,
of course."

He reached out his hand, placed it around her waist,
and drew her to him. She came, unresisting.

Omar Manzur himself supervised Purity's preparations for the journey into the desert. He was seated,
cross-legged, on the divan in her bedchamber, while
the young slave girl, whose name was Leya, bathed
her mistress and helped her into the pantaloons and
the transparent blouse that she had been wearing on
her arrival at the castle. Over these went a more ro-
bust garment: a mantle of coarse camel's hair, cut in
the shape of a sack, with holes for arms and head.
This was the *aba,* which, so the Bible tells us, was
worn by the prophets. Her hair, made into long plaits
and wound around her head, was then covered with
the characteristic Arab *haik,* a piece of patterned cloth
folded in a triangle and held in place with an ornamental cord. Over all went the heavy burnous, the
hooded cloak that is the Arab's protection against the

heat of the sun and the cutting winds of driven sand, his covering in sleep, and his grave cloth in death. Somewhere they found boots of soft deerskin that were small enough for her delicate feet. Omar Manzur himself drew them on and laced them up to her calves. He showed her how to wind the ends of the *haik* across the lower half of her face so that her mouth and nostrils would be shielded from the sun and sand—and her sex hidden from prying eyes.

"You will pass for a young Bedouin warrior," he said approvingly.

The men were waiting down in the castle courtyard: the eight who had brought her from Algiers, all mounted and ready. The white palfrey was held by a grinning lad who assisted her into the saddle and gave her the reins. Omar Manzur bestrode a wild-eyed black stallion whose distant ancestors must surely have borne their masters against the Crusader knights.

The remainder of the cattle garrison, womenfolk and slaves, gathered to witness their departure. Omar Manzur gave a piercing whistle, and a great wolfhound bounded from the kitchen quarters and crouched by the black stallion, its tongue wagging, eyes fixed in unswerving adoration at the tall figure up in the saddle.

"Bismillah!" the Corsair shouted and then led them across the drawbridge, into the dying sunlight of the desert.

He took them the length of the valley at a full gallop. Purity, her eyes fixed on the black stallion ahead, quickly discovered that the palfrey was responsive to the slightest touch of the knee and rein and was a natural racehorse. One by one, the others were overtaken by the little white mare, till only Omar Manzur's black stallion remained to be beaten. A wild exhilaration seized Purity's spirit. With the night breeze streaming through her loose robes, she hunched herself low over the palfrey's neck, urging the animal on, calling it to give of its best. Purity was lost to all sensation save that of the chase.

Omar Manzur drew rein at the end of the valley and stared in surprise to see Purity flash past him almost immediately. She checked the palfrey's gallop, turned, and came back, smiling to herself.

He turned in the saddle to look back. His men had not yet come into sight around the last bend of the valley.

"Where did you learn to ride like that?" he demanded.

"As a little girl in France, I rode cart horses before I could even walk," she said. "And I learned more advanced equitation every Thursday at Lady Crawley's Seminary for the Daughters of Gentlemen, which is in Bath."

"You never cease to astonish me, Purity," he said. "See! Even Sharib applauds you."

The wolfhound came running toward them, its ears and tail streaming, tongue wagging wildly, giving its deep-throated trumpeting bark. The rest of the party trailed behind.

There was admiration in their eyes when they came up to her, and some muttering and pointing, for an Arab admires fearless horsemanship above almost any other attribute, even in a man of a lowly caste, or even in a woman.

They went at a walking pace. The moon rose above the hills to their right. Something howled out in the darkness ahead, causing the wolfhound, Sharib, to give a hoarse growl and the hairs at its nape to stiffen and stand up.

Purity rode, stirrup to stirrup and boot to boot, with Omar Manzur. They proceeded in silence for a while, and then he said, "We will make camp before

dawn and sleep for a while. After that, we will lie in
the shade till the sun is down."

"When do we reach our destination?" she asked.

"At sunset of the second day."

"Who is the person we seek—the one who knows
where my husband is being kept?"

He did not reply for a while. He just stared ahead
into the darkness, as if weighing his reply. And then
he said, "I will explain everything when we reach
camp. There is much to tell. You will make one more
payment in the rich, golden coin that I have come
to cherish so highly, and then I will explain all. By
this time tomorrow, you will know where to find the
one whom you seek, and you will never willingly lie
with Omar Manzur again, nor will he force his attentions upon you. That is a promise. Are we agreed?"

She felt his hand brush against her thigh; he was
holding it out to her palm uppermost. She took it in
hers and looked into his eyes, pinpointed with desert
starlight.

"We are agreed, Omar Manzur," she said.

"Ayeeee!" With a wild whoop, he dug his heels into his mount's flanks and went streaking off into the
velvet darkness. She set her mount in pursuit, and the
others followed. They proceeded over the long, curving
crest of a dune, silhouetted against the rising moon,
with sprays of sand kicked high above them, trailing
like a ship's wake, and Sharib, the wolfhound, was
baying all the while.

He drew rein at a clump of lonely palm trees,
standing like forlorn sentinels over a clump of rocks
and a pool of muddy water. The horses and the
hound drank it readily enough, and the men passed
around a goatskin of clear water, from which Purity
took a delicious, cooling drink, handing it then to
Omar Manzur. It was then, concealed as they were

from their companions by the bulk of his black stallion, that the Corsair bent and kissed her full on the lips. It was a kiss of surprising tenderness, from which she found it impossible to turn away.

He then said something in Arabic.

"What does that mean?" murmured Purity.

For an answer, he merely smiled and placed a finger across her soft lips.

They mounted and rode on. Throughout that long night, as she journeyed at his side, not one more word passed between them. He gazed steadfastly ahead, his hawk-like profile set and expressionless. She was lost in her own, new, and strangely disturbing thoughts.

His kiss, unexpected, disarmingly gentle, and of obvious sincerity, had pierced her defenses and confounded the careful fiction that she had woven about herself and him.

This man—she looked sidelong at him, but he made no response—had made the most outrageous demands upon her body, in fact, not only her body, but upon her self-respect, her pride, and everything that she held dear. With him, body to body, she had performed acts of erotic imagery, improvisations of shameless intimacy, such as she had only before granted to one man in her whole life. And she had emerged unscathed, simply by willing Mark into his place: making his kisses Mark's kisses, his embraces Mark's embraces, and substituting his lustfulness for Mark's. By this device, she had been able to soar to the rare heights of ecstasy that she had only known with Mark, and with none other, though the lovers in her past had been many, and she had been used by some whom it would have been a mockery to call by the name of lover.

She had sincerely believed that, in giving herself to Omar Manzur, and by achieving perfect fulfillment in the climax of their coupling, she had in reality made a mystical communion with her absent husband. It was a belief that the Corsair had struck at and destroyed with a single kiss.

His kiss, by its unexpectedness, by its tenderness, and by its sincerity, had aroused her spirit—and fired her body.

She shuddered at the thought, all peace of mind shattered in the instant.

Tonight, under the desert stars, with a new day beginning to dawn just over the eastern horizon, he would lie with her—perhaps, as he had said, for the last time. There would begin the slow, protracted preliminaries to fulfillment that they had first performed in the dance of "The Capture." Her spirit would rise on the crest of a joyous abandonment of her own body. She would reach the shattering heights and return with glory ringing in her ears. But it would not be because she had imagined herself to be with Mark. That she would never be able to do again.

With one unexpected kiss, Omar Manzur had placed himself between herself and the image of the man she loved. When he made love to her at dawn, it would be he whom she would follow up into the tumbled clouds of delight. The kiss had destroyed her; her loins ached for him.

Abandoned bitch! Worse than a whore!

What to do? Refuse him her favors? Impossible, for to do that would be to break her solemn promise. And he, a man of stern and implacable principles—one who believed in the Arab law of an eye for an eye and a tooth for a tooth—would sever his part of the bargain, also. Because of her scruples—and because of her abandoned lust—she would condemn Mark to perpetual slavery.

Her only course was to receive him, as she had

promised, to risk the almost certain consequence of
finding with him an ecstasy as rare as that she had
enjoyed on the previous occasions, when she had been
able to deceive herself that she was with Mark.

A tear coursed down her cheek unregarded. They
rode on through the night in silence.

High moonrise picked out the wrinkled crests of the
Atlas Mountains ahead. Their destination lay somewhere in the wilderness at the foothills of the mountains, where there was water and scrubland for the
camel herds. In the winter season, so he had told her,
his people would cross the mountains by one of the
high passes and descend into the land of their delight
—the vast Sahara, the Garden of Allah, put there by
God so that He would have one place on Earth where
He could walk in peace and solitude.

She must have half-dozed in the saddle, for she
reacted with a start to Omar Manzur's harsh order
that brought his men to a halt by a huge outcropping
of rock resembling an upturned wreck of a ship.
There they dismounted. A tremor ran through her at
the touch of his hands around her waist as he lifted
her down.

"It will be two hours till dawn," he murmured
against her cheek, in a voice of unaccustomed gentleness, as if . . . as if he *knew* that he had breached
the defenses of her chastity, that she was his for the
taking, promises or no promises.

The men lit a fire of thorn scrub and prepared tea
in a curiously shaped brass vessel with a curling
spout, sprinkling into the infusion some dried petals
of jasmine flowers. Omar Manzur handed Purity her
share in a tiny porcelain bowl that had somehow
survived the rigors of the ride. She sat, cross-legged
like the rest, in front of the fire and sipped the aro-
matic brew. Then, one by one, the men rose to their

feet, murmured good night to each other, and each
went to find a sheltered corner at the foot of the
outcropping in which to cover himself with his burnous
and sleep.

Presently, she was alone with Omar Manzur. He
murmured that he was going to look to the horses,
and he walked away out of the firelight with Sharib
padding at his heels. She waited a while, then got to
her feet, unlatched the fastening of her burnous, and
trailed it through the soft sand to the base of the rock
where a slight declivity suggested a place of rest, and
there she spread out the coarse square of gray cloth
and lay down.

She never heard his soft-footed return, nothing, till
his urgent, hissed warning: *"Be still! Move, and you
are dead!"*

She held her breath, staring up at his looming shape
three paces from her, dark against the dying firelight.
An eternity passed, during which time he seemed to
be gathering himself to spring. When he moved, it was
in one swift, stooping rush, his hand outstretched to
grab something.

The something was close by her elbow, a hand's
breadth from the edge of the laid-out burnous. He
seized and dragged. A short length of threshing, writhing coils hung for an instant from his hand. He
cracked the coils like a whiplash. He threw them on
high toward the patch of scrub, then dropped to his
knees and exhaled loudly.

"It was . . . a poisonous snake?" she asked.

He nodded. "A horned viper. They lie in the sand,
buried up to their eyes, waiting for their prey—small
animals, mice, rats, and such that come out at night.
You had frightened that viper, and it was coming out
for a bite—just to make sure. Their bite is by no means
always fatal, but I would never take a chance."

"But you did take a chance," she said, "a very great chance. It might have been you!"

Suddenly, she was overcome with a most violent fit of trembling, so that her shoulders shook, and she lost control of her lips. Added to that, the tears poured down her cheeks and she was racked with sobs.

"Purity, little flower, what is the matter?" He put his arms around her shoulders and drew her to him. In that moment, the terrors to which she had been subjected in the past months—the news of Mark's disappearance and the agonies of grief and indecision that followed; the seizing of the *Minerva* and her flogging and brutal rape; the events of the slave market and what had come after—all came crowding into her mind and overcame her. Clinging to the Corsair, as the only safe haven in a mad world, she sobbed her heart out and then began to feel better in consequence.

When she was quieter, he gently laid her down. This done, he unlaced her deerskin boots and drew them off. He massaged her feet between his fingers till they tingled. He then took off the headdress and drew the coarse mantle over her head, afterward unplaiting her lustrous tresses and laying them out around head and shoulders. Purity herself slid the pantaloons over her hips and kicked them off her feet. Nude beneath the transparent blouse, she lay with her arms pillowed behind her head looking up at him, her mind quietened, calm, and submissive.

Swiftly disrobing himself, he lay down beside her, drawing his own burnous over them both.

The moon had gone down. The myriads of stars remained, and dawn was still only a promise, as, without recourse to blandishments and erotic play, Omar Manzur tenderly took her, and she received him.

"If you are so happy, why are you crying?"

He touched the tear that lay upon her cheek. The morning sun was high up in the sky at the far side of the rocky bluff. The spot where they lay was in cool, deep shadows, and it would remain so till the afternoon.

"Only a man could ask a question like that," she said fondly. "Don't you know the workings of a woman's heart and mind? For a woman, joy and misery are two sides of the same coin, and they are sometimes interchangeable. I rejoice that my husband is still alive; yet, at the same time, I am in an agony of despair in case I shall never see him again. I grieve to be away from my child; but I look forward with joyous expectation to see how much she will have grown while I have been away. And what we did together, you and I, before the dawn came—that is both a cause for joy and sadness, some sadness."

"Explain that to me more fully," he said.

She touched his cheek gently. "No, Omar Manzur," she said. "That is something I shall never tell you— nor anyone else."

"Not even him—your husband?"

"Not even my husband."

"Hmm!" He frowned and lightly stroked the slope of her bare breast. She made no attempt to stop him, but gazed down at him reflectively.

"Omar Manzur, I want to ask you something," she said.

"Yes?"

"When was it that you buried a woman alive for being faithless to you?"

He frowned. "A man has his pride," he said. "As a Corsair captain, a *reis* of some standing among the brotherhood, I have a reputation to maintain."

"That, Omar Manzur, is no answer to my question,"

said Purity, firmly removing his hand from her breast.

"What was your question?" he asked sulkily.

"When did you bury that woman alive? And, for that matter, who was she?"

He raised himself up on one elbow. Close by was the declivity that marked the spot from which he had plucked the snake. Sullenly, he began to scoop up handfuls of sand and fill it in. She watched him, amused.

"Well?" she said.

"I have never buried anyone alive," he said. "Did you think I was capable of it?"

"No," she said, "not since last night."

He sighed. "I have failed with you, woman."

"You have succeeded admirably," she said. "And now, would you make us both some tea?"

He got to his feet and gathered his burnous around his nakedness.

"I have become a servant to a slave woman," he said.

She watched him stride over to the embers of the fire, squat down, and begin blowing on them, feeding the new flames with pieces of brushwood, building a fresh blaze. She wrapped her burnous around her and lay regarding him.

All is well, she thought. Last night I gave myself to a good man. The fact that I had no choice makes no difference. I gave myself, in truth.

In tranquility, she remembered their lovemaking. He had been inexpressibly tender with her for the first time—an echo of the unexpected kiss that he had given her earlier. Tenderly, gently, he had borne her to a high mountaintop and had shown her the delights of heaven and earth, laid out for her gaze. And all the time it was his face that loomed around her, not the face of Mark. With her hand in his, trustingly, she

had gazed upon the delights of heaven and earth, and
she had found them to be good. Still hand in hand,
they had descended the mountain in quiet serenity.
No explosions of sound. No choirs of heavenly angels.
No exquisite agony that reaches beyond the threshold
of pain and touches the fringe of perfect bliss. Just
tranquility.

Small wonder she had wept and laughed at the
same time. It had been laughter for the joy of realiz-
ing that she had been right, after all. It had in truth
been Mark, and not Omar Manzur, with whom she
had earlier soared to the heights of divine ecstasy.
Tears of relief, for release. And there had been a tear
for Omar himself—he who had been so gentle and
giving. It was he who—it had to be faced—had possibly fallen in love with her.

"How is the tea coming?" she called.

He looked around, scowling. "Free a slave and win
a slave driver," he growled. "It is ready. Shall I bring
it to you, or will you sit by the fire?"

"I will come there," she said, getting up and winding the burnous around her.

Sitting cross-legged, facing each other across the
pine-scented flames, their hands cupped around the
bowls of tea, they sipped in silence for a while.
Presently, Sharib came toward them with its ungainly
stride. First came a noisy lick for its master, and then
Sharib sat down by the fire, panting heavily.

"He has been chasing hares since sunrise, I do not
doubt," said Omar Manzur.

"He loves you," said Purity. "Your men, also, love
you and respect you. I can see it in their eyes and in
the way they respond to you. And it is not because of
your fearsome reputation for cruelty."

He cast a guilty glance over his shoulder, then addressed her in a voice that was scarcely more than a

whisper: "You will never speak of . . . you know . . ."

"The woman never buried alive? Of course not. What do you take me for? A man is entitled to his pretenses, his illusions."

He nodded. "Purity, I think that you are perhaps the most understanding person I have ever known. Because of that, I have hopes that you will show understanding, and not revile me, when I tell you what must now be told."

She looked at him over the rim of her tea bowl.

"Go on," she murmured. "Try me."

He said, "Purity, I have used you."

She shrugged. "We all use someone, sometime, Omar," she said. "I have used you in order to get from you the whereabouts of my husband, and I would do it again."

"Has it ever crossed your mind," he asked, "that I have never known of his whereabouts, nor had any hope of finding anyone who could enlighten me, but that I only offered you promises in order to take you to my bed?"

"Many times," she said. "But I told myself that I must trust you, for only by trusting you did I have any chance of finding him. And, indeed, I have been proved right. You have found someone who knows where he is. You have promised me that tonight your friend will tell me."

"My mother," said Omar Manzur. "It is my mother who will reveal his whereabouts—I hope."

"You hope—you only *hope?*" She stared at him across the dancing flames of the fire. At the sharp note in her voice, the wolfhound raised its head and pricked up its ears.

"My mother," he said, "has never set foot within sight of Algiers, knows nothing of the ways of the Corsairs, greatly disapproves of my activities, and has cer-

tainly not come into contact with your husband, nor
with those who hold him captive. But tonight she will,
I hope, tell all."

"And how will she do that, pray?" demanded Purity.

"She is a soothsayer," responded Omar Manzur.

"A *soothsayer!*" Incredulity, bitter disappointment,
contempt, the confronting of an upper-class English
upbringing with Eastern mysticism—they were all contained in the manner in which Purity mouthed the unfamiliar word.

He silenced her with a brusque gesture of his
bronzed hand.

"Give me a hearing," he said. "I deserve it of you,
Purity, for, though it was lust for your body that first
drove me to make the compact with you, I am now
sincere. I tell you that, if your husband is alive, my
mother will be able to describe exactly where he is.
When I say 'hope,' I mean that, if she is unable to tell,
it can mean only one thing. . . ."

"That he is dead?" Her anger and disappointment
were all gone.

"Yes, Purity. But if he is alive—and you have Azizza's word that he is alive, and of what benefit would
it be for her to lie to you?—I tell you that my mother
will declare his whereabouts in great detail. Perhaps
Azizza was lying when she told you that he is in Algiers; my mother will confound the lie. I tell you that,
by her necromancy, she has found many lost people,
children gone astray in sandstorms, and missing herds
of camels and goats. I have never known her to be
wrong. She foretold that Bonaparte would lose his fleet
and be forced to abandon Egypt. She named the hour
of his final defeat and the year when he will surely
die. Last winter, when news was brought to her that
my *xebec* had foundered and sunk in a gale, she did

not trouble to look up from her weaving loom, but merely said, 'My son Omar Manzur is safe and well in Tripoli.' This was true, Purity. The *xebec* that was our consort, that had seen us dismasted and heading for a lee shore, and that brought back the news to Algiers was not to know that, thanks to Allah and the skill of my seamen, we brought the dismasted hull safely ashore on a sandy beach near Tripoli. Are you convinced, Purity? I would never deceive you—not now."

She looked across the flickering flames. This man— this good and wayward man, this violent but curiously gentle man—loves me, she thought. Of that, I am no longer in any doubt.

"I am convinced, Omar," she whispered.

Before setting off again in mid-afternoon, they ate a frugal meal: a morsel of bread, a few dried dates, and tea. The men were in a light-hearted mood. Seeming to sense their nearness to the Bedouin camp and their kinsfolk, they laughed and joked a lot, playing tricks on each other. Some of the tricks were barbed with an edge of cruelty, for the desert is a hard school, where softness is equated to effeminacy, and kindness is a luxury. All the more wonder, then, that just before mounting up one of the men found a desert flower—a tiny yellow bloom growing amidst the thicket, having by a small miracle struggled to life in the arid wilderness—and presented it to Purity with an air of serious courtesy. She accepted the flower with like seriousness and tucked it into the fastening of her headdress. It was dead and withered within the hour.

With the low-cast sun sending long shadows across the sand and rocks, they made good distance, alternately walking and cantering toward the distant line of mountains. During a short rest, one of the men caught sight of a hare. It bounded from behind a small rock at his feet and streaked across the sand, as if it had wings. Sharib gave chase, baying wildly as he went. The hare weaved and dodged, but it was not able to shake off its oversized but nimble pursuer. Purity, whose sympathies were all with the hare, was dismayed to see the men placing bets on the outcome, tossing coins on the ground and challenging their fellows to match them. Most of the money must have been wagered on Sharib, for there was a loud chorus of disappointment when the hare, reaching a mound of scree at the foot of a rocky outcropping, ducked out of sight into a hole. Sharib searched and snuffled for a while, then returned to face the scornful abuse of his backers.

They rode on. In the half light, they came within sight of the Bedouin encampment: a dozen or so large black tents with winking fires and a long line of tethered camels and horses. As they drew closer, a group of horsemen came out of the camp and thundered to meet them. Omar Manzur urged his black stallion into a wild gallop, and Purity and the others did likewise. The two parties surged toward each other, yelling with a frenzy. Those who carried guns—long-barreled muskets, highly chased and ornamented—fired them in the air, while the rest brandished their glittering scimitars on high. The two tightly massed bunches of riders met, then passed through each other, stirrup to stirrup, with clashes of steel against steel as blades met in the air. When Purity drew rein and turned her palfrey, Omar Manzur was reaching out in the saddle and exchanging embraces with a grinning giant of a man with a livid scar across one cheek.

"Purity, this is my brother Jamal," he said in French.

The brother's eyes narrowed in puzzlement as, Purity having unwrapped the *haik* from the lower part of her face, he perceived her to be a woman. He saluted her, at the same time casting a quizzical glance at Omar.

"*Madame,* you are welcome to cross our humble threshold," he said.

They rode together into the camp. Next to come and greet them were dogs, mostly of the mongrel variety, mean looking and seemingly half-starved. Afterward came the children, boys and girls both. They were handsome, brown-skinned little creatures with dazzling eyes and unbelievably shrill voices. On the edge of the camp were gathered the womenfolk, all heavily veiled and dressed from head to foot in voluminous black.

Omar Manzur leaned across and murmured in her ear, so that his brother should not hear: "Purity, I am afraid that our brief idyll is now over. While we remain in my brother's encampment, we shall have to part. You will eat and sleep with the women and girls."

"When shall we see your mother?" she asked.

"Tonight, after the evening meal," he said. "At that hour my mother holds court in her tent, receiving all comers, giving her counsel in matters great and small. She is the veritable ruler of our tribe, for all that my brother is sheikh. It is because she possesses the all-seeing eye. Women count for little among the Bedouins, but my mother is different."

He delivered Purity into the care of his brother's wives, none of whom spoke a word of French or English. They regarded Purity over the top of their heavy veils with schoolgirlish awe. Indeed, they were little more than children, though one had a baby at her breast and two others were heavily pregnant. The womenfolk of the tribe ate in a communal meal tent, and they were served by black slave girls, wretched-looking creatures, half nude, who wore heavy iron

collars around their necks and were treated by their
mistresses with less concern than if they had been
dogs.

The meal was taken from a communal pot by hand,
with the assistance of large pieces of bread. Having
eaten frugally on the journey, Purity now had a good
appetite, and she put aside any doubts she may have
had about the contents of the pot, which looked like
stewed mutton, but could well have been goat. The
other women ate voraciously, scooping up large
amounts of the food and slipping it beneath their veils
with great dexterity, chattering away like parakeets all
the while. It was quite clear, from their gestures and
glances, that the blonde-haired, unveiled infidel woman
in their midst was their sole topic of conversation.

The communal pot having been emptied, the slaves
brought washbowls filled with jasmine-scented water
and soft towels for the diners to rid their mouths and
fingers of grease.

Sweetmeats were then passed around. Purity was
charmed by a little girl who brought her a platter of
dried figs and then ran back to hide her face in her
mother's skirts. Purity and the woman exchanged
nods, and by that trivial incident the ice was broken
and the strange newcomer was accepted. Another of
the women offered her a cup of Turkish coffee. The
children, who had been watching her shyly from afar,
came forward to examine her at close range, and one,
greatly daring, reached up to touch her hair. In no
time, Purity had a child sitting on each side of her and
a baby on her lap, while the fond mother beamed
sloe-eyed approval over the top of her veil. And then,
coffee and sweetmeats having been consumed, Sheikh
Jamal's wives showed Purity, by sign language, that
they were all to attend upon the woman with the all-
seeing eye. They all proceeded to another of the large

tents made of black goat hair, where the menfolk were
already assembled.

The women and the young children sat cross-legged
at one end, the menfolk and the older boys at the
other end. Purity exchanged a glance with Omar
Manzur, and he gave her a reassuring smile.

All chattering faded away into an oppressive silence.
Somewhere outside, a horse whinnied and a dog
barked. A night zephyr gently stirred the swagged folds
of the great tent. It was intolerably hot inside, and it
smelled of packed humanity and mutton fat. Purity
felt her stomach begin to turn.

After what seemed an eternity of waiting—it may
have been as much as an hour, and one of the infants
was whining petulantly—a curtain in the center wall
of the tent was drawn back and Omar Manzur's
brother entered, leading by the elbow a little woman
clad, like all the others, in a black robe, black headdress, and a concealing veil. Sheikh Jamal *salaam*ed
deferentially to his mother. Then, taking her hand, he
assisted her stiffly to seat herself upon a pile of cushions in the center of the tent, between the menfolk
and the women.

There followed a ritual whose details were lost on
Purity, though the implications were quite plain. In a
series of exchanges conducted in Arabic, several of the
men and women came forward and addressed what
seemed to be either complaints or questions to the
sheikh, who, in turn, repeated them to his mother. In
no case was the old woman—Purity could see white
hair emerging from her head covering, and her hands
were gnarled with rheumatism and covered with a
lacework of swollen veins—slow to give a reply; she
answered directly. The supplicants or complainants listened in every case with undivided attention and
appeared satisfied with the old woman's answers. The

process was continued till no more people came forward. A slave then brought the old woman a bowl of coffee, which she drank beneath her veil while the assemblage looked on in respectful silence.

It was then that Omar Manzur stood up. Advancing to the center, he pointed to Purity and addressed his mother in the French language: "All-Seeing One, a guest has crossed our humble threshold seeking counsel. She is French by birth and married to an Englishman. He, taken by Corsairs—I am not implicated in his taking—is a prisoner somewhere, perhaps in Algiers. It is possible that there is a conspiracy to prevent this woman from finding, and securing the release of, her husband. She humbly begs you to look beyond the veil that is no barrier to your all-seeing eye and tell her where he is."

The old woman glanced at Purity, who was acutely conscious of a tremendous power being directed toward her.

"Is the bond between this man and this woman hallowed by religion?" The question, delivered in perfect French, was clearly addressed to her son, though her eyes never left Purity.

"They were married according to the rites of their faith," replied Omar Manzur.

"Is there issue to the marriage?"

"I understand there is an adopted infant, a girl-child."

"Is this woman chaste?"

Omar Manzur's gaze shifted uneasily to Purity, and when he replied, his voice was scarcely above a whisper. "She has suffered rape, but she has not given herself of her own free will," he said.

"That is not true!" Purity's voice rang out clearly in the hot and breathless tent. She drew a shuddering breath. "I have been raped, certainly, but I have also given myself out of compassion. And on one occasion, though I had no choice but to accept, I gave myself willingly." She looked straight at Omar Manzur as she spoke the words.

A long silence ensued. Then the All-Seeing One said, "I detect no evil in this woman. If it is within my power to discover the whereabouts of her man, I will do so."

"Thank you," whispered Purity, and she realized that she was trembling.

In an awesome silence, the old woman stretched her gnarled hands before her and closed her eyes. The vast tent, lit only by a single lantern, seemed suddenly to be possessed by myriads of shifting shadows, and Purity became aware of the immensity of space that lay just outside its frail walls: the vast stretches of sand and scrub that began at the threshold; the high mountains beyond; the trackless wastes of the Garden of Allah at the far side of the mountains; all above, the vast vault of the sky.

Still with her hands extended before her, the old woman began a low, keening dirge that sounded like a lament for the dead, at the same time rocking herself back and forth. Purity distinctly felt the hairs at the nape of her neck stiffen and stand erect, and her skin crawled till she was aware of her own shape from head to foot. The realization came to her that the hot, airless, and stuffy tent was becoming colder and colder. Moreover, the lantern's flame was flickering and growing smaller, and the shadows were increasing in number and complexity of shape.

The woman fell silent. The lantern flame gave a last flicker, then died.

Biting back an impulse to scream aloud, Purity clasped her hands together and tried to cling tightly to her fleeing sanity. By now it was bitterly cold in the tent, so cold that, by the thin moonlight seeping in through the raised sides, she could see the clouds of breath issuing from the mouth and nostrils of the woman crouched next to her.

Presently from out of the desert there arose a wind, faint at first, then greatly increasing, till the black vault above their heads swayed and billowed like the sail of a great ship. Some of the children were wailing with terror, and their mothers could not silence them. The wind increased in fury until it seemed that the heavy tent posts would be ripped from their moorings and the whole edifice would be carried away. And, in the midst of it all—in the fury of sound, in the near-darkness, and in the biting cold—the old woman in the center rose to her feet, and, arms still extended, threw back her head and screamed a single word: *"Mort!"*

At the sound of that word—the French word for "dead"—Purity Landless toppled forward on her face in a profound swoon.

They left in the early dawn, before the camp was aroused. Only a barking dog watched them go. She supposed that Omar Manzur had said his farewells to his mother, brother, and other relations the night before. Without a word, they mounted and rode off back the way they had come, back to the castle in the Tell, with their escort trailing behind and the wolfhound bringing up the rear.

Purity, upon recovery from the swoon, had spent the night dry-eyed and sleepless, staring up into the darkness of the tent that she had shared with Sheikh Jamal's wives.

Mark was dead. There was no doubting it for an instant. The circumstances in which the old woman had declared the dreadful tidings were of a sort that

permitted for no skepticism. She had seen, she had
heard, she had felt, and she had experienced things
that allowed for no rational explanation. Omar Manzur
had warned her of the circumstance in which his
mother would be unable to divulge her husband's
whereabouts—the circumstance of Mark being no
more. It had come to pass.

Dry-eyed, quiet, she rode at the Corsair's heels till
they came to the selfsame outcropping of rock like an
upturned ship, where they had camped on the outward journey, where she and Omar Manzur had made
love for the last time, where she had listened with
growing hope to his explanations of his mother's
prowess.

She sat with the men and sipped a brew of tea.
Then she went to lie in the shade, in a spot that Omar
Manzur had prepared for her, to rest through the midday heat. And when he had settled her down, he stole
quietly away, leaving her to her own bitter thoughts.

They set off again when the sun was low. They rode
through the night till nearly dawn, then made camp
again in a valley at the southern edge of the Tell.
Once more, true to his promise, the Corsair left her
alone to sleep in peace. Sleep she did—but not in
peace. Her dreams were haunted by visions of Mark
lying dead and bloody in some vile dungeon where
he had been struck down, or floating among the sea-
weed, white and bloated, with the crabs already at his
eyes. She woke up screaming, and Omar Manzur came
to her, put his arms around her, and tried to comfort
her.

His gentle ministrations succeeded, for she fell into
a quiet slumber. Still holding her in his arms, he laid
her down and himself with her. When dawn lit the
eastern horizon with its new pinkness, the Corsair was
still sleepless, and she was locked in his arms, asleep.

She awoke to find him crouching by her with a freshly made bowl of tea, which he solemnly presented to her.

"What are you going to do, Purity?" They were the first words he had spoken directly to her since they had arrived at the Bedouin camp two nights previously.

"I don't know," she said. "I . . . I haven't given it a thought. I never took it into consideration, you see . . . what I would do if he were dead, after all. There was always hope. But now . . . now that I know for certain . . ."

"You should return to England, to your child," said Omar Manzur. "In my *xebec,* I will take you as far as the Pillars of Hercules and put you aboard an English ship. You could be home by the next full moon."

She looked at him, knowing full well that there must have been other options in his mind. Wanting her as she believed he did, he could have taken advantage of her grief and confusion to suggest that she stay with him, whether as wife or concubine. Helpless as she was, he could keep her by force, use her as he willed. But he would do none of those things.

"You are generous and kind, Omar," she said. "I will give you my answer soon. At this moment, I have not yet come to terms with the reality of my loss. I can't accept that I must go through the rest of today, and tomorrow, and the remainder of my life in a world without Mark."

Her tea cold and neglected, she lay back in the sand, and he did likewise. Side by side, they remained in silence till the sun went down. And he never touched her.

The meal before departure was the customary handful of dried dates, a piece of bread, and tea. Though aware of the cloud of grief that lay upon their blonde female companion—and because of which, with true Bedouin courtesy, they treated her with politeness and consideration—the men, now that they were nearing their destination—their wives, and children—became like excited schoolboys among each other. They laughed and jested as they rode, sang bits of songs, and would willingly have remained at the gallop till the castle came in sight.

It was dusk when they entered the steep-sided, winding valley that ended with the Carthaginian castle, and it was almost dark when the battlements came into sight.

"They heard us from afar," said Omar Manzur. "See, the gatekeeper has already lowered the drawbridge."

They cantered the last stretch and clattered in single file over the drawbridge, calling out to their people inside to come and greet them, but the courtyard beyond was empty and unlit.

Omar Manzur drew rein and looked around him. Something in the Corsair's hawk-faced profile made Purity catch her breath. At that same moment, Sharib threw back his head and gave out with a loud and blood-chilling wail.

Then, one by one, they saw it.

Purity was almost the last to turn her head and stare in the direction of the gatehouse that housed the mechanism for raising and lowering the drawbridge. When she did so, she choked on a scream of horror.

Suspended from the high ramparts of the gatehouse, turning slowly around and around, so that the blackened, dead face appeared with every turn, was a hanged man: the gatekeeper.

Omar Manzur's scimitar hissed from its scabbard.

"Back across the drawbridge!" he shouted to his men.

Too late! With a creaking of primitive ropes and pulleys, the heavy drawbridge was already on its way up. Just as they realized that they were caught like rats in a trap, rows of heads appeared on the battlements all around the courtyard. A savage order from on high brought a ragged volley of musketry. Sharib's mournful wail was cut short, and the great animal fell dead. A horse screamed and reared up, throwing its rider. Purity saw Omar Manzur choke on a torrent of crimson and spin from his saddle. With an anguished cry, she slipped from her palfrey's back and ran to his side. Turning him over, she tore off her headdress and wiped his mouth.

He was fading fast. The piercing dark eyes had lost their power to command, and the splendor was ebbing from his powerful frame. This notwithstanding, he was able to smile up at her. He tried to speak. Bending low, she put her ear close to his lips, and, above the crash of the gunfire, she heard his whisper.

"Purity, we were . . . mistaken. Your Mark still lives. What my mother saw was . . . *my* death."

Then he was gone.

Chapter Five

It was all over in the time it takes for a man to fire a musket, reload, and fire again. No more than that was needed. At the end of it, Omar Manzur, his Bedouins, and his wolfhound lay dead, or dying, and a maddened horse careened around the courtyard. The other mounts huddled together in a corner, terrified by the sounds and by the smell of burned gunpowder and spilled blood.

Purity was unscathed: the killers had had their orders.

Presently, they swaggered out from the door of the keep, and Purity saw that they were led by the giant Ugo. He grinned and pointed to her, kneeling by the body of Omar Manzur. At his order, one of the men came over and dragged her roughly into the keep. She was spared the sight of them dispatching the wounded and dying with their scimitars.

When they had finished their bloody work, Ugo and his men came back into the keep, where a long table stretched the length of the great hall. It bore the marks of centuries of wear, and it had possibly seen service in the Crusades, when the knights of Christendom had swarmed in the lands of the Turks. Now it was laden with food: haunches of roast meat, steaming bowls of pilaf, and, because these men had no respect for the commandments of the Prophet, great pitchers of wine, which they had brought with them on the foray. It was wine that had been taken from captured ships, fine vintages that had been destined for the tables of prelates and ambassadors of the Mediterranean seaboard.

Purity was not to know it, but these men, Ugo included, were Bashi-bazouks, Turkish irregulars who had fought in Egypt against Napoleon Bonaparte, and who, seeing the easy spoils to be gained by piracy, had deserted and drifted to join the Corsair fleets in Algiers and Tripoli. Violent men, of unmatched cruelty and ferociousness, they were favored as crewmen by many of the Corsair *reises,* including Azizza. Held in contempt by the Bedouins because of their treachery and lack of any regard for religion, they loathed the Bedouins in return. It had been a labor of love to massacre Omar Manzur and his followers.

Some of the inhabitants had survived the capture of the castle: the womenfolk. It was they who had been obliged to prepare the feast with which Ugo and his killers were to celebrate the capture, a celebration that had been briefly postponed by the return and violent dispatch of the Corsairs, thereby adding a dark note to the rejoicing, at the thought of the corpses lying out in the courtyard.

Purity, struggling in the grip of the brute who held her and who was trying to rip her camel's hair mantle from her shoulders, was rescued by Ugo, who thrust the other man aside with a loud curse. Ugo had had his orders concerning Purity, and rape at his hands or those of his followers had been expressly excluded.

No matter, there were plenty of other women available in Omar Manzur's castle, and, meanwhile, the French woman with the unbelievable hair was available as a plaything. Ugo took his place at the center of the long table, dragged Purity down upon his lap, and poured himself a brimming cup of rich Spanish wine, which he proceeded to toss back in one long draft, afterward refilling the cup. Slaughter was thirst-producing work.

Shocked and confused by the abrupt and horrifying turn of events, Purity could only huddle on the giant's lap and try to shut out the clamor all around her. One thought, one brilliant ray of daylight, shone through the bewilderment and the terror: Omar Manzur's dying declaration had struck upon her ears with the ring of true coin. It was his death, and not Mark's death, that his mother had seen beyond her veil. . . .

She was dragged from her contemplations by Ugo, who was forcing the wine cup against her lips. Useless to refuse it; she drank as little as she was able to, and she allowed most of it to run down her chin and soak her breasts.

The Bashi-bazouks were now all seated and tearing at the meat, scooping up handfuls of the pilaf and washing both down with gulps of heady wine. Drunk with wine and glutted with bloodlust, they were clamoring, nevertheless, for fresh excesses, headier delights. On the pretext that there was perhaps a fortune in looted treasure hidden somewhere in Omar Manzur's castle, they picked out a young woman from among the cowering survivors of the massacre. She, lovely of face and figure, was tied up by her slender wrists against the rough stone wall, stripped naked, and interrogated by a grinning, unshaven oaf, who, with horsewhip in one hand and a leg of mutton in the other, took alternate bites from the one and energetic

strokes with the other. The cruel flogging provided a
background for the protracted feast.

I have trodden this path before, thought Purity,
appalled. Years before, in her early childhood, she
had witnessed such scenes when the French château
in which she had been reared had been assaulted by
a mob of Parisian revolutionaries. While still a girl,
she had seen her stepmother casually drowned in a
lake of spilled cognac, others led out to the slaughter,
women and young girls outraged by the score, and
people—men, women, and children—hanged like clus-
ters of fruit in a high tree.

The horror around her was, if anything, even more
intense. Here were men untouched by the most remote
contact with human decencies. They were not embit-
tered starvelings of the Paris gutters seeking vengeance
upon the aristocracy that was responsible for their mis-
eries, but half-animal brutes for whom cruelty for its
own enjoyment was second nature. Close to where she
was sitting, they had gotten hold of two females, a
woman and a girl, whom they had discovered to be
mother and daughter. What sport they contrived with
this terrified pair! With one of the men holding the
razor edge of a curved knife against the mother's
throat, what excesses of abandonment was the girl persuaded to perform, one by one, upon her tormentors!
The half-demented mother, when the roles were reversed, would have crawled to them—indeed, she
crawled to them—to save her child as she had herself
been saved, for a brief time.

As the hour grew late, and more wine had been
consumed, the excesses became more bizarre. How
can a creature that calls itself a man eat with one hand
and kill with the other, or eat and violate, or drink and
do both? Now they had a screaming girl stretched out
across the table among the half-eaten meats. When

they had taken her among them, they cut her throat, and her blood besplattered the food.

Purity closed her eyes and her mind, for nature provides such escapes when everything outside the mind becomes intolerable. The bearded brute who held her was not so far gone in his cups that he forgot his orders. She was not greatly molested, unless to be half-stripped and casually mauled was to be molested. And when Ugo, finally overcome with wine, slipped slowly to the floor, he dragged Purity with him. She spent the lifelong night upon the flagstones, with his massive arm imprisoning her, his snoring face pressed between her breasts, and horror upon horror going on all around her.

In the dawn, the Bashi-bazouks bestirred themselves and looked around them with half-ashamed grins at the disasters they had wrought. The whipped girl still was hanging, now lifeless, from the wall. Others lay in tormented postures on the floor of the hall. No survivors remained of what had been Omar Manzur's stronghold.

Released from Ugo's grasp at last, Purity struggled back into the rags of her clothing. She kept her eyes averted from the sights around her. She meekly followed when Ugo motioned her to come and tried not to see the corpses still lying in the courtyard. She mounted her palfrey and suffered it to be taken on a leading rein by Ugo when they rode out across the drawbridge. And during the entire journey back to Algiers, she held one thing clearly in the forefront of her mind: Mark lives, Mark lives, Mark lives, and nothing else matters in the whole wide world!

As she might have guessed, it was back to El Diablo's palace high above the Casbah that they brought her, for, as Nancy Shaw reminded her in horrified tones, they were Azizza's men, and Azizza was an ally of El Diablo.

"All Algiers knew that Omar Manzur had taken you," said Nancy, "for you're as likely to keep a secret in the Casbah as hide a virgin in a brothel. 'Twas all over the place by noon the next day that you'd gone with Omar Manzur to his castle in the Tell. Azizza swore to get you back, for had she not promised El Diablo that you'd be here and unmarked when he returned to Algiers?" Her eyes flared wide. "And here's news for you: he's back already, may God protect me!"

It had become obvious to Purity that, during her outburst, Nancy had displayed an anguish of mind that could scarcely have been brought on by her, Purity's, doings. There was a sick look in the ex-nursemaid's face, and her eyes were red-rimmed, as if from weeping. Her hair had not been dressed that morning, but hung in uncombed rats' tails. She was wearing a crumpled caftan with nothing beneath.

"Nancy, what is it, what ails you?"

"Oh, I don't want even to speak of it!" cried Nancy. "My only comfort is to pretend it isn't happening, that I dreamed it in the night, and that I shall soon forget it." She flung herself down upon the couch, face uppermost, staring at the ceiling, her hands convulsively clutching at the silken coverlet, moaning quietly to herself.

"Tell me, Nancy," pleaded Purity. "You'll feel better for sharing your misery. Tell me, do."

Presently, the other woman lowered her eyes and, fixing Purity with a frightened stare, said, "They found one of the palace guards lurking inside the harem last night!"

The significance of the statement did not at first

strike Purity, but when it did, she blurted out, "Nancy! You don't mean . . . ?"

"It was my lad," said Nancy. "He'd just left me, and he was caught red-handed by his own captain. They've been more careful with the patrols since you were taken."

"But surely he won't tell them about you, Nancy!"

"He . . . he's being put to the torture!"

"Oh, no!"

Nancy flung herself sidelong on the couch, drumming on the cushions with her impotent, small fists.

"He'll tell all!" she wailed. "They'll drag it out of him, for all that it will mean a worse death for him. They'll get from him the name of the woman he'd been visiting. And then I shall be done for!" She turned around to Purity, seizing her by the arm, screaming into her face. "Do you know what they did to the last woman who went with a feller? I'll tell you . . ."

"Nancy, calm yourself," said Purity. "It may never happen."

"I had it from one of the older concubines," persisted the other. "This wench—she was no more than a bit of a thing—was cast aside by El Diablo. First, the torturers had their sport with her, raped her among them, and God knows what else mischief. Then she was branded like an animal and put to work on a waterwheel, going around and around the livelong day, in the broiling sun, as naked as the day she was born. Chained to that wheel, waking and sleeping!"

"Hush, Nancy, hush!" said Purity. "You mustn't even think of such things. The man may never talk, for, as you say, it will only be the worse for him if it's found out that he actually went with one of the harem women."

"To lessen the torment, even for a brief moment,"

said Nancy dully, "a man will say anything, do anything. That's what I've heard."

Having unloaded her terrors upon Purity, she seemed calmer. But it was the calmness of an animal being led to the slaughter, an acceptance of the inevitable, a shutting off of the mind against the unthinkable. As Nancy crouched, staring at the blank wall, Purity crossed to a side table and poured her some water. She was turning to go back to the couch when she saw—them. The glass dropped from her nerveless hand and shattered to crystal shards at her feet.

Nancy perceived the newcomers the same instant and gave a cry of alarm.

There were three of them: half-naked brutes in leather skullcaps. One of them carried a whip coiled in his massive hand. He pointed to the figure on the couch and rasped a guttural order in Arabic, at which his companions went over, seized Nancy by the arms, and dragged her to her feet.

"Come with me, Purity!" begged Nancy. "Be with me for as long as you can. Let there be one decent, human face to look at, one hand to hold, before they ruin me!"

Purity followed the trio and their captive through the archway and into the corridor beyond. There she glanced interrogatively at he who was the leader, miming a gesture. Appearing to understand her meaning, he gave her a careless shrug. They went on their way, and she went with them.

There was an iron-barred door set low against the wall of a building in a quiet part of the garden where even the birds did not sing. Two steps down, through the door, and a winding stone staircase led into Stygian darkness beneath the building. They descended. At the second bend, they came upon a guttering torch set in a bracket against the stone wall.

Around the next bend, there was another. They passed no less than five torches before they reached the foot of the staircase, by which time the air was as cold and dank as in a crypt, and the roughly dressed stone walls ran with water and were streaked with green slime.

They emerged in a vast cellar with a vaulted roof swagged with cobwebs and ancient mold. A stench of burning hung in the chill air. There was a glowing brazier set under a rough chimney piece, with branding irons and other instruments glowing redly in its coals. By the flickering light of torches, Purity perceived many means of destruction furnishing that awful place. There was what she instantly recognized as a torture rack, with a massive spiked wheel for turning. Ropes and pulleys hung from iron rings in the vaulted roof. A whipping block, with manacles for wrists and ankles, stood against one wall. Ranged along another wall were rows of appliances: pliers, screws, curiously fashioned leather thongs, head pieces, masks of dull iron, and whips and lashes of all varieties devised by man. Nancy was sobbing quietly in her captors' grip.

With a sharp intake of breath, Purity saw two figures seated side by side on throne-like chairs set upon a raised dais at the end of the chamber. One she instantly recognized as Azizza, the woman Corsair. The other, shrouded in a black caftan and *haik,* with a heavy veil of dark blue cloth covering all the countenance, so that only the shadowed eyes were to be seen peering out at her, was—it could have been no other —El Diablo!

"I see we also have the pleasure of Mrs. Landless's presence," drawled Azizza. "Come forward and meet your master, Mrs. Landless."

Purity obeyed, and Nancy was dragged with her.

At the foot of the dais, she paused and looked up at the veiled figure, whose eyes continued to burn down upon her.

"Who are you?" she demanded.

A low laugh, muffled and unrecognizable behind the heavy veiling, answered her.

"Do I know you?"

The muffled head inclined in a nod. He then made a brusque gesture with a black-gloved hand, directing his gaze to the woman seated at his side.

"El Diablo will make himself known to you in his own good time," said Azizza. "In the meantime, it suits his . . . caprice . . . to keep you in ignorance."

The she-Corsair's upper body was covered in a polished breastplate of beaten silver, cunningly fashioned upon the shape of her own nude torso. The thin metal was hammered by some lewd artist-craftsman into the semblance of her own pointed breasts and erect nipples, her own flat belly and deeply indented navel. Her lower limbs were encased in pantaloons of cloth of silver to match the armor. On her flame-colored tresses she wore a scarlet turban set with a high plume of osprey feathers. She looked like a barbarian chieftainess.

After regarding Purity for some moments, she said, "So! You have returned from your brief sojourn with the handsome and devastating Omar Manzur! One presumes that he possessed you—by force, naturally. It would be out of the question for a well-bred lady from England to lie willingly with a half-caste Bedouin. You shared his couch? Answer me, woman!"

"Yes," replied Purity coolly.

"And with some enjoyment, I should imagine." Azizza smiled reminiscently, running a tiny, pointed tongue over her full lips. "He shared my couch on one occasion and I found him to be very . . . adequate. But now he is dead, so they tell me."

"Your brutes shot him down like a dog," said Purity.

Her riposte, delivered with a whiplash of contempt, caused Azizza's green cat's eyes to narrow with sudden fury, but it soon passed. Seeming to dismiss Purity from her mind, she turned her gaze toward Nancy, who was still pinioned by the two half-naked men.

"So, you have been a-whoring in your master's bed!" she said.

"It's not true!" cried Nancy. She turned her gaze to the figure seated beside Azizza. "Please believe me, *please!*"

Purity looked toward El Diablo to see what effect the woman's plea might have had upon him, and she was shocked to discover that the gaze of those shrouded eyes was not directed toward Nancy, but toward her! Furthermore, they continued to devour her for the remainder of that protracted and harrowing scene, additionally adding to Purity's unease.

"You're lying!" rasped Azizza. She gestured to the brute with the whip. "Show her the witness!"

Obedient to the order, the man crossed to a curtain that masked an alcove in the wall nearby. Drawing it aside, he revealed the figure of a man suspended by his thumbs from a rope attached to a ring in the roof. He was very young. His face, had it been washed clean of blood and the expression of agony, must have been pleasing to look upon. His newly matured body was shapely and strongly formed, as could be seen because he was entirely nude. The eyes were closed, but not in death, because his chest rose and fell in panting breath.

"Khalid!" cried Nancy. And she instantly pressed her knuckles against her lips, her eyes swiveling to

Azizza, knowing that by uttering the youth's name she had condemned herself out of her own mouth.

"Exactly," said Azizza. "He is called Khalid and is, or was, a member of the palace guard. After a considerable amount of . . . persuasion . . . the chief torturer here"—she gestured to the brute with the whip, who bowed his head in response—"managed to extract your name from his lips. If you still persist in denying your guilt, I am sure they will be delighted to make him repeat his evidence."

"No!" cried Nancy. "Not that, not that!"

"Khalid will be quite happy to oblige," said Azizza blandly. "Despite his unfortunate condition, he was most lucid a little while back, diverting us with a detailed account of your lovemaking together. You really are a most accomplished whore, are you not? Are you quite sure you don't wish to hear the evidence again? For my part, I should be delighted, and I am sure that *Mrs.* Landless"—she pronounced Purity's title with heavy scorn—"will find it most instructive."

"No!" said Nancy. "Please, please don't hurt him anymore!"

"His suffering is almost over," said Azizza with relish. "Yours has yet to begin. El Diablo has left it to me to devise your punishment, which I have done with considerable pleasure. You are accused, condemned, and now you will hear your punishment."

"Please," she whispered, "please . . . "

"The torturers will possess you this night," said Azizza. "It is their perquisite—which is never denied them—to have for one night any woman who passes through the torture chamber to do with her as they please. And I can assure you that these fellows—Bashi-bazouks, all three—know things to do to a woman that are undreamed of in your whore's reper-

toire. It is entirely possible that you will cease to exist
—as a woman—by tomorrow's dawn."

"Nooo!" cried Nancy.

"However," resumed Azizza implacably, "you will
still be alive, and you will still possess the outward
semblance of a woman, which will suffice for your
needs. Then will follow your punishment proper. Have
you heard of the mines?"

Nancy responded in a breathless whisper.

"Louder!" snapped her tormentor.

Falteringly, the wretched woman made it known
that she had never heard of the mines.

"They lie beneath a mountain deep in the Tell,"
said Azizza. "They are worked by slaves—all men,
for no woman could survive the back-breaking labor
in such conditions. Only the strongest survive for more
than a few weeks, and those who do—the creatures
who are more like animals than men—never see the
light of day. Their food and water is thrown down the
shaft to them and they fight over it like animals.
Again, the strongest take the lion's share and survive.
These brutes, these half-animals, hunger above all for
one thing. They hunger for women. They bay like
hounds to their guards to send them down a woman—
any woman."

"No!"

It was Purity who interrupted her, Purity who saw
clearly what was coming. Hideously aware that El
Diablo's gaze was upon her, as it had been upon her
throughout, she took a step toward Nancy and, disregarding the men who held her, laid her hand on the
woman's shoulder.

"They won't do it to you, Nancy," she said tenderly.

Nancy trembled under her touch, but she summoned up a tight smile for Purity.

"Don't carry on so, dearie," she said. "What better fate for a poor whore like me?"

"What better fate, indeed!" cried Azizza from the dais. "You will be lowered into that pit, whore, and they will fight over your body like animals. Like animals they will take you, one after the other, again and again, unceasingly. They will . . . "

"No!"

Purity turned on the woman Corsair, her eyes blazing. Azizza pretended not to notice her, but pointed to Nancy, addressing the chief torturer. "She is yours till dawn!" she cried. "Take her!"

The grinning brute stepped forward with alacrity and seized the neck of Nancy's caftan and rent it to the waistbelt.

"No!"

For the third time, Purity's cry rang out. This time it was directed to the veiled figure seated beside the she-Corsair. This time, mounting the dais, she regarded him closely, but she recognized nothing in the shrouded eyes that continued to regard her unwaveringly.

"I am told that you know me from the past," she said. "I am led to believe that you have contrived to have me made your captive because you desire my body. But, surely, this you can do to any woman in your harem. You can go down to the slave market and buy yourself a score of women—young, beautiful women, whores and virgins, both. Azizza, surely, is yours for the asking"—she threw a look of contempt at the woman Corsair, whose green eyes flashed with loathing—"for I am sure that she would be incapable of refusing any man, even the half-animals in the mines whom she has so eloquently described."

"I will have your tongue torn out for that!" cried Azizza, rising.

The veiled figure raised his hand in a gesture of admonition. Azizza sat down again.

Purity continued: "How will it profit you to possess me against my will, whether I come to your bed in a docile manner or screaming and raking with my fingernails? You, who have bought women as bed slaves, must know the emptiness of taking a woman who relinquishes herself because she has lost all hope. Rape, surely, must have lost its savor through sheer repetition. Do you not long to possess a woman whose ardor can match your own?"

She paused.

"Continue." The single word, muffled beyond recognition, emerged from behind the dark blue veil.

Purity took a deep breath. "Spare this woman," she said, pointing to Nancy. "Forgive her transgression and allow her to resume her place in your harem, a place which, I promise you, she greatly enjoys, for she regards you highly, and it was only because of your absence, because she missed your attentions, as she has told me many times, that she was tempted to take that callow boy to her couch. I say forgive her, and . . . " The words froze on her lips.

"And?"

Purity dropped her gaze before the shrouded eyes.

"I will come to your bed," she said. "I will come without any repining. You will find no cause for complaint against me, for I will give myself to you freely, without any reserve or any shame."

"Infidel whore!" hissed Azizza. "They are all alike!"

El Diablo silenced her with a gesture.

"Well?" asked Purity, her heart pounding.

"Free the woman!" El Diablo pointed to Nancy.

"You must be insane!" screamed Azizza. "She is a whore! They are both whores!"

El Diablo's black-gloved hand took the she-Corsair

full across the mouth, punctuating her protest with a scream of pain and shock. Thereafter, she said not a word, but sat and smoldered as the torturers let go of Nancy. Purity, drawing the other's garment back over her bare shoulders, guided her out of the place of pain.

They watched the departure of the two women: Azizza with cat-eyed fury; the torturers with wistful regret.

There was no telling what emotions reigned in the mind behind the dark blue veil. As for the naked youth who slowly revolved by his thumbs in the curtained alcove, he was past all emotion, all desire.

Purity was with Nancy, in the latter's suite, when the chief eunuch brought the order from his master that Purity was to come to him that night.

She received the news with inward calm—at first. It was only when the sun began to dip below the roof of the seraglio and the garden began to fill with shadows that the true realization came upon her—the quality of the promise that she had made to the man who called himself The Devil. And she began an uncontrollable trembling that she could not hide from Nancy.

"Oh, dearie, are you taken with the flu?" cried the ex-nursemaid solicitously, taking Purity's hand and stroking it between hers.

"I expect it's my bad conscience," said Purity. "I have made a promise, you see, that I can't possibly keep. How could I? How could I freely give myself to a man I have never seen? Worse, how can I surrender to someone who—as it may turn out—I know only too well, and loathe on that account. It would help me greatly, Nancy, if you were to tell me who he is." She looked questioningly at her companion.

"Dearie," said Nancy, "believe me, it will profit you nothing to know who he is. If he wants to reveal himself tonight, reveal himself he will. If not, he will not. Leave it be at that, I beg you. After what you have done for me, I could refuse you nothing, so I beg you not to ask me—for your own sake."

"Then I shall have to do whatever I can," said Purity. She smiled, despite herself. "You know, Nancy, I had great plans to bend El Diablo to my will in order to secure Mark's release and my own. Look at me now—trembling like a schoolgirl in anticipation of her first kiss."

"Get you ready for him, dearie," said Nancy. "Have a bath, change into your prettiest attire, and before you go to him I will give you a draft of something as will set all your fears to naught."

"A draft—of what?" asked Purity.

Nancy tapped the side of her nose and looked wise.

"'Tis a little something that the harem women use from time to time," she said. "From all I've heard, 'twill make you happier than ten jiggers of gin, and no headache will come after. No more questions, now. Off with you to the bath. And, Purity . . ."

"Yes?"

Nancy reached out and trailed her forefinger gently down Purity's smooth cheek.

"I don't have the words to say what's in my heart, dearie," she said, "for I'm an ignorant, untaught orphan lass. But this I will declare: I shall stand in your debt for what you did for me my whole life long. And if there be any mortal thing I can ever do in return—any service I can perform for you and yours —that I will do, so help me."

Her eyes brimming with tears, she kissed Purity on the lips.

Thrusting aside her fears as well as she was able to,

Purity was already formulating a plan by the time she reached the bath chambers and submitted herself to the attention of the Negroes in the hot room.

Tonight she would lie with El Diablo, the man who owned her body. He would make demands upon her that would be consistent with the promises she had made to him. It would take all her fortitude—inherited from her aristocratic French forebears, of the sort that had permitted them to mount to the guillotine with dignity—to which were added the peasant virtues of patience and cunning, derived from her early upbringing, to see her through her time of trial.

She passed into the steam room, the domain of the black girl. Between the stifling steam and the dousing of ice-cold water, Purity considered her course of action for the coming night. And when the thin edge of panic took her, as it did from time to time, she brought Mark's face into her mind's eye. This quenched her fears and trod down hard upon her shrinking scruples.

She went from the steam room to the massage chamber. The yellow-haired Caucasian's tawny eyes flared wide to see her, but one savage glare from Purity precluded intimacies. The capable hands skillfully punished her body without recourse to any familarity. Purity lay and relaxed, telling herself that all would be well. All *must* be well—for Mark's sake.

Back in her suite, she riffled through the entire wardrobe that was at her disposal. Nothing suited her mood; it was all too . . . blatant. She must employ subtlety and taste. She must extemporize.

Purity went through the wardrobe all over again till she came upon something that fired her imagination. It was a simple coat of the sheerest linen that buttoned high in the neck, with wide sleeves, and skirts that trailed on the floor. Quite devoid of ornamentation, it could only have been intended as some kind of bathrobe. She put it on over her nakedness and liked what she saw.

To her hair she gave the most meticulous attention, drawing its tresses into a high chignon at the crown of her head, and permitting a thick lock of it to fall from the center of the chignon to her shoulder.

Her *maquillage* was simplicity itself: a hint of eye liner at the corners of her eyes, a faint dusting of rice powder, and lips quite heavily rouged.

She stood back and examined the effect in a pier glass, and she approved. One thing remained to be done. . . .

Peeling off the delicate linen coat, she immersed it in the miniature fountain that splashed coolly in the center of her sitting room, afterward wringing it out. The chilliness of the damp cloth puckered her skin when she drew the garment on again, and the material adhered closely to her in parts, clinging to the firm protuberances, dramatically draping across the well-defined declivities. It was nothing blatant, but it subtly announced the fact of her total nudity underneath.

Ready at last, she crossed the corridor to Nancy's suite. Her former nursemaid was reclining upon the divan in her dishabille. Her eyes widened to see Purity's costume.

"Oh, God!" she cried. "Are you dressed for the night's pleasures, or are you off to take a bath? Mind you, now that I look closer, I can see what you're getting at."

Purity sank down upon the divan beside her.

"A short while ago, I was full of resolve," she said. "But now I'm frightened again. How can I go to him looking like this?"

"Ah, I've the very thing for you, dearie," said

Nancy, patting the other's hand comfortingly. She crossed to a carved chest, upon which stood a crystal flagon filled with a milky-colored liquid, from which she filled a tall glass and brought it over to Purity.

"Drink it down, dearie," she said encouragingly, "and I promise you that the whole world will light up for you."

Purity gazed dubiously into the milky depths of the glass, took a tentative sip, and grimaced.

"It's quite horrid," she said. "Must I drink it all?"

"The whole lot, so I am told," replied the other, "or you might as well not have any at all. Down with it, Purity. You'll be all the better for it."

And so Purity consumed the entire glassful.

The summons to El Diablo came soon after. Abu Nuwas entered—as by his office of chief eunuch he was entitled to enter—without knocking on the portals, and he informed her in mellifluous tones that the lord and master required her presence.

"Good luck, dearie," whispered Nancy. "I'll be thinking of you."

They parted with a squeeze of hands. Her heart pounding, dry-mouthed, she followed her guide through shadowy courts and secret gardens. It was quite dark, for the moon had not risen, and the myriads of stars served only to pick out the tiled paths along which she followed the eunuch. And as she went, Purity experienced a strange lightness in her tread, as if . . . as if she were walking on air, clear of the ground. Her mind, likewise, seemed to be detaching itself from within her brow and beginning to exist in a spot that was just out of reach above her head. It was very odd, and totally unaccountable.

They came to a white marble building, set among whispering cypress trees, that was onion-domed, shuttered against the night.

The man who was guiding her—it was very strange that she did not seem to have met him before, nor could she remember from whence he had brought her—tapped lightly on the carved door panel of the building, and, seeming to receive an answer from within, drew it open for her to enter. Whereupon, her guide closed the door behind her and departed.

She was now standing in a large, octagonal-shaped room that was colonnaded all around with pillars of veined marbles. The intricately tiled floor and the walls were scattered with priceless Persian rugs of woven silk. All the windows were heavily shuttered, and, there being only one small hanging lamp burning in the center of the ceiling, she did not at first see the dark-veiled figure reclining on a cushioned divan against the far wall.

Finally, she saw him—and without the slightest feeling of alarm.

An arm was raised, a finger crooked, gesturing her to approach. She obeyed without question, her mind directing her body from afar, as if it were someone else's body.

The stranger was dressed in a black robe striped with white. A black cloth entirely covered his head, and a dark blue veil masked all the remainder of his countenance. Only shadowed eyes were to be seen, peering out at her.

"Dance for me," he demanded.

"Of course." A woman's voice answered him quite readily. She supposed, and with only faint surprise, that it must have been her own voice.

He clapped his hands. Immediately, the sound of distant music drifted through the colonnaded chamber: airy, insubstantial music, like the breath of the wind through the strings of a harp. Instantly responding to its lure, she began to sway from the hips in time to its subtle rhythms, undulating her arms and hands in counterpoint to the sinuous motions of her torso. Her mind, while not inhabiting her body, directed its every motion with an impulse of sensuousness that had suddenly taken possession of it.

When the music quickened its tempo, so she, likewise, felt compelled to make her movements more abandoned. Now she was dancing in air. The formally patterned tiles had blossomed a multitude of flowers beneath her bare feet. The marble colonnade had become a circle of great palm trees reaching up into the night sky. The breath of a million flowers scented the air. With passion directing her hands, she undid the fastenings of her flimsy garment, peeled its clinging dampness from her heated skin, and stepped out of it nude. Nude, she danced before the impassive, veiled figure on the divan. Her mind, in its rhapsody of abandonment, directed her to enticement, so that she swayed close to him, so close that he had only to reach out his hand to lay brief caresses upon her flanks and her bosom.

The music then became a madness, clamoring in the mind and assaulting the senses with nameless promptings. Now her every movement was calculated for his delight, every gesture an invitation to seduction.

When the music finally died away, she walked joyfully through the field of flowers to kneel at his feet as he opened his flowing robe, revealing himself to be totally nude beneath it. And she embraced him intimately, giving without stint, without hesitation. She was driven on by the desires that crowded her overheated mind.

She supposed it must be morning. Awakening, she gazed up at the arcaded ceiling, whose subtle moldings were illuminated by thin shafts of daylight seeping in through the chinks in the window shutters.

Raising herself up, she saw, to her slight surprise, that she was naked. Her clothing—the linen coat that she remembered having put on the evening before—lay nearby on the tiled floor of the chamber.

Her hair was unbound and cascading in a blonde profusion around her shoulders and breasts. She shook it clear of her forehead, then experienced an unaccustomed lightness in her head, as if . . . as if she had drunk a glass of wine too many. And that was odd, for she had touched no wine for a very long time. How long, she could not quite remember.

Last night, surely, she had had a dream. In the maddening way that dreams have, it was already receding into the darkness of forgetfulness. She tried harder to retrieve something of it, clutching at inconsequential shadows and striving to give them some form. She had been . . . in a garden. Yes, that was it. She had stood barefoot in a field of flowers and had danced there.

Someone else had been with her. Mark—yes, it must have been Mark, for the quite tangible feeling of well-being that suffused her whole body and mind this morning was the same sensation that she always experienced after they had made love together through a long night. Last night, then, she must have dreamed that Mark and she had made love together, and that was why she felt so content and fulfilled . . . though strangely light-headed.

She lay back in the cushions, her arms pillowed behind her head, while the chinks of daylight grew stronger and the chamber was rid of even its most shadowy corners. And at the same time the realization of her present plight came back to Purity Landless, slowly at first, then increasing in sharpness and intensity.

She sat up with a start, instinctively covering her breasts with her hands.

"I lay with El Diablo last night—here!" She cried it out loud.

It had been no dream, but hard reality. The coat of dampened linen that she had contrived to seduce the desires of El Diablo must indeed have served its purpose, for by some means it had been taken off her. Nude as she now was, she must have spent the night with him. On the selfsame divan upon which she now lay, he must have possessed her.

Why, then, did she have no recollection of it? There was nothing but the few figments of a dream, now gone completely, vanished like snowflakes in sunlight. Surely, what may or may not have taken place between her and the creature in the veil could not have inspired such a dream, nor have left her feeling so contented.

Putting her mind to it, her last remembrance was of leaving Nancy's suite with Abu Nuwas walking in front of her. After that—nothing. And, just prior to that, she had drunk the noxious draft that Nancy had prescribed for her.

The draft!

That must account for it. The draft had clearly been some kind of drug, under whose influence she had passed a whole night in a limbo of total forgetfulness, as if in a dream. How, then, had she conducted herself? Had she slept? Had El Diablo been reduced to slaking his lusts upon her sleeping body? If so, then he must have been sorely disappointed with the bargain he had struck, and with she who had promised so much.

The uneasy thought was interrupted by the opening of a door, admitting a wide shaft of daylight into the chamber. Turning, she saw Abu Nuwas on the threshold. The chief eunuch bowed quite civilly, he who was accustomed to treating her with thinly veiled insolence.

"My lord and master conveys his good wishes, and he hopes that the Excellent One has slept well," he said, pronouncing the extravagant harem title with something approaching respect.

"Very well, I thank you," said Purity, endeavoring to spread her hair to cover as much of her nudity as possible. She need scarcely have troubled, for his shifty eyes avoided her.

"Then will the Excellent One be pleased to accompany me?" he said.

"Yes, of course," said Purity. "I wonder, would you please pass me my clothing?"

He stooped and handed her the linen coat, and she got into it. The warm night had dried out the dampness, but the material's transparency was still considerable. Purity took a fringed silk shawl from the divan and draped it around her shoulders.

"Where are you taking me?" she asked.

"The Excellent One has found favor with my lord and master," said the eunuch. "And so . . . "

"And so—what?"

"And so she is to be permitted to see her husband," murmured the other, his sly eyes meeting Purity's for the first time, revealing malice within them.

She was going to see Mark!

Purity stared uncomprehendingly at the dark visage before her, a hundred questions leaping to her mind. Did they have far to go? How was Mark? Would she be allowed to touch him? Would they be permitted to embrace? To stay with each other for any length of time?

The latter questions posed a practicality. . . .

"Will I have time to go to my suite and change into something more suitable?" she asked.

The eunuch treated her flimsy garment to a cursory glance and gave a disinterested shrug. He grunted that he had received no instructions except to escort her immediately to her husband.

Outside were two Nubian guards, eunuchs both, carrying broad-bladed stabbing spears and oxhide shields. They walked in procession to her tryst with the man she loved.

They came to one of the many gardens set amidst the palace complex. It was a place of high box hedges, like a maze. In the center was a fountain splashing cool water into a basin of goldfish. The chief eunuch bowed and left her, but two guards remained behind, standing stiffly to attention some distance away, their weapons held upright. Purity seated herself on the edge of the fountain and waited.

Some considerable time passed till she heard shuffling footsteps and the metallic clank of dragged chains. Her heart leaped. Rising, she made to run toward the source of the sounds, but one of the guards barred her way with the shaft of his spear. She waited, breathless with love and impatience.

There were two of them. As they came into sight around the side of the box hedge, she experienced a stab of disappointment. The first to appear, the one leading, wore a tattered monk's habit tied around with a knotted cord, and his tonsured skull was already half-grown with stubble. His hands were chained together, likewise his ankles, and he dragged a length of chain behind him.

His companion—she cried out with the horror of recognition—was Mark.

He was cruelly changed. His tallness was bowed,

as if with fatigue. Burned by the sun, his cheek barely
showed the old scar that ran from the corner of his
left eye. But a new and crueler wound—scarcely
healed, and showing signs of never having received
attention—lay across his forehead, near the hairline.

She ran to his side, the guard raising his spear to let
her pass.

"Mark, my darling! Oh, Mark!"

He raised his head, and she recoiled with the physical shock of meeting his eyes—those once-wondrous
eyes, still as blue as the ocean, but dead now, and
lackluster.

"Do . . . do I know you, *madame?*" he faltered
hoarsely.

"Mark!" she cried.

She flashed a glance toward the man in the monk's
habit, seeking some explanation. He was quite young,
younger than Mark, and his eyes were haunted.

"Madame, I am afraid he will not know you," he
said, speaking clear English, but with a Spanish-
sounding accent.

"Why . . . *why?*" she wailed despairingly, her eyes
flashing back to Mark, who had lowered his gaze and
had taken on a patient, ox-like appearance, as if he
had already dismissed her presence and had returned
to some private world inside his own head.

"Madame, he was gravely wounded during his capture," said the monk. "I, who was taken a few days
previously, heard it from his fellow captives. It seems
that when the Corsairs boarded his vessel, he snatched
a cutlass from one of the fallen sailors and fought
like a demon. They cut him down. You see the
wound. It was a blow that has destroyed his memory
and much else."

"Oh, my God!" Purity pressed her hands to her
eyes and rocked back and forth in a paroxysm of

grief. The monk waited patiently till she was done. Mark continued to stare at the ground in front of him.

Presently, she managed to compose herself. Drying her eyes with her fingertips, she lifted her chin and regarded the monk.

"You have been with him all the time since then?" she asked.

He nodded. "I am Brother Francisco, of the Dominican Order," he said. His handsome face clouded. "Or, rather, I *was* of the Dominican Order, for I fear that my body and soul are sullied almost beyond redemption. Yes, I have been his companion in adversity since we met at the slave market. We have eaten from the same bowl and performed the same labor. His name is Mark, you say? I never knew."

"He has even forgotten his name?" she cried.

"Yes, even that. You are his wife, *madame?*"

"Yes."

The mild eyes gazed reflectively at her, taking in the glory of her hair, her face, but discreetly avoiding the rest of her body.

"Your sufferings and your anguish must be very great," he said, "for I have seen with my own eyes what treatment is meted out to women captives here. Though I am beyond praying for myself, I will, nevertheless, pray for you, and for your Mark."

"Thank you, Brother Francisco," said Purity. "But, tell me"—she glanced at Mark again, but he was far away from her, behind his own dead eyes—"where are you kept?"

"That I have been forbidden to divulge," said the Dominican, glancing sidelong to where Abu Nuwas was now watching them closely and within hearing distance.

"Are you here, in the palace?" persisted Purity.

"I may not tell you," he replied.

"But is there anything I can do to help you?" she asked in anguish. "Supposing that I were able to."

"Anything to lighten our existence," he said, "be it merely a little more food, a brief rest from our interminable labors, a kind word—anything would be like manna from heaven."

It was at that moment that Abu Nuwas clapped his hands and gestured brusquely to the Dominican, signifying that the interview was finished.

"We must now go, *madame*," said Brother Francisco. "It has been a great pleasure to meet you. Would that it had taken place in happier circumstances."

She took his manacled hands in hers.

"I will do what I can for you," she said. "Look after him, I beg you, Brother Francisco, for I love him dearly, with all my heart and soul."

"That I will do, *madame*," he promised. He took Mark by the elbow, and the other looked up slowly, seemed to recognize the monk, and smiled vacantly at him. "Come, Mark," said Brother Francisco.

Purity had an impulse, instantly quenched, to throw her arms around Mark and rain kisses upon him. It was the certainty that such an action would only serve to puzzle and distress him that made her refrain. Biting upon the knuckle of her forefinger to prevent herself from crying out, she stood and watched through her tears as the two men shuffled away, dragging their chains after them, the Dominican gently leading Mark Landless by the elbow.

Abu Nuwas bowed and smiled, making no attempt to mask the malice in his pouched eyes.

"I am instructed to inform the Excellent One that she is to attend my lord and master again tonight," he said sibilantly.

"My husband!" cried Purity, pointing the way Mark

and his companion had gone. "Can't something be done to help him?"

"I will convey your words to my lord and master," said the chief eunuch.

"Can a doctor be brought to tend to his wound?"

"Perhaps that can be arranged."

"Some decent food for him and his friend?"

"I am sure that my lord and master will look with favor upon your requests," said the chief eunuch, "for, as I have intimated, you have pleased him greatly, and it is to be hoped that you continue to do so—for your husband's sake."

So that was it!

She told the whole story to Nancy, seated side by side with her on the balcony overlooking the harem garden, under a striped awning that had been lowered against the searing heat of the Mediterranean afternoon. Beyond the rooftops of the seraglio, far out in the horizon of startlingly blue sea, the white sails of a distant ship hinted at a freedom that seemed a whole world away.

"To my own bargain, the one I made on your account," said Purity, "El Diablo has now added new conditions. I am to give myself to him in order to provide the simple necessities of life for Mark. That was why he had Mark paraded before me. Nancy, you can't imagine the condition he's in—half-starved and hunched over from hard labor. He's emaciated, with flea bites all over his arms and chest. And he has a dreadful wound on his brow. God, I wish I had the means to kill El Diablo!"

"He's a swine, and no mistake," declared Nancy. "I've never held any other view. The first time he embraced me, I felt the evil in him spill out all over me.

But there's no denying, he's a master when it comes to sex."

"To hell with sexual pleasures!" snapped Purity. "I have no recollection of *that* part of it, thank the stars!"

Nancy glanced at her sidelong, smiling. "Ah! That would be due to the draft I gave you," she said. "It takes everyone in different sorts of ways. Some will sing like canaries, and others will dance till they fall down with sheer weariness. Many will remember nothing the day after."

"What is that liquid?" demanded Purity. "Heaven knows, if it's the most vile witches' brew concocted of things unmentionable, I shall continue to have need of it, and as soon as tonight, for I cannot face that creature's embraces with my mind clear and my every pore shrinking from his contact."

" 'Tis an old harem receipt," said Nancy. "There's this and that in the way of herbs and potions. And I fancy there's more than a touch of opium."

"Opium?" Purity shrugged. In an age where tincture of opium was readily available at any street-corner chemist's shop in England, where it was freely given to babies to halt their screams and to women for the agonies of childbirth, the word had no power to strike fear. "Well, if it's only opium, you'd best get me another draft before tonight."

"That I will, dearie," Nancy assured her, "that I will."

The day dragged past on leaden feet, but its sheer emptiness created a sense of timelessness, so that the yawning periods of the mid-afternoon were no sooner commented upon and deplored than the subtropical night was fast descending, and Purity's new time of trial was upon her.

She bathed and dressed herself for her ravishment. With no longer any conscious intent to please, she

picked out the first costume that her hand touched in
the wardrobe and dressed her hair in a single plait
over her right shoulder. It scarcely mattered one way
or the other. Every garment in the wardrobe was contrived to exploit the delights of a woman's body for
the delectation of a man, and Purity Landless would
have looked ravishing in a gunny sack with her hair
all awry.

"My goodness! You'll drive him clean out of his
mind!" Nancy commented when she saw her.

"Please!" cried Purity. "Spare me that! Do you suppose that they've done anything yet for Mark and that
young monk?"

"I was just about to tell you when you knocked me
all of a heap with envy at the sight of you," said
Nancy. "I sought out Abu Nuwas, who tells me that
your husband and his friend are now being better
looked after."

"That's a blessing," said Purity feelingly. "And his
wound?"

"A physician was brought in to see him this very
afternoon," said the other, "though, being no doubt a
black heathen, I wouldn't think he'd have the capacity to be of much help to poor Colonel Landless."

"I believe that Islamic physicians are highly competent," said Purity. "I am pleased that El Diablo has
responded to my request."

Nancy cast her a shrewd glance. "But I'm thinking
that you'll still be needing the draft, for all that," she
said.

"Oh, heavens, yes!" cried Purity. "After having seen
what he allowed to happen to Mark, I think I should
scream if I let that creature's hands so much as touch
the hem of my skirts. Where is the draft, Nancy?"

"Here, dearie," said the other, holding it out to her.
It was past midnight when Abu Nuwas came for

her, and she was reclining upon the divan in her own room, lost in a drugged world of her own imagining. The oddly obsequious stranger was inviting her to accompany him. Well, then, she would do so. The walk through the moonlit gardens was made on air, and the very trees were bending to whisper in her ear. This time she was brought to a small dining room with jalousied windows that overlooked the lit-up city far below. A small oval table was set with very English-looking napery and silverware, glasses and a candelabrum. English to a fault, also, was the appearance of the man who called himself The Devil. By some perverse quirk of fancy, he had taken off his Eastern costume and dressed himself in an evening frock coat of black silk, with a neckcloth of sheer white lawn whose immaculate folds might have been wound and tied by Beau Brummell's valet himself. His head and face were hidden in a hood of black silk.

Purity's drugged mind, directing the fickle movements of her body from somewhere out of reach above her head, decided that this veiled personage had just finished dinner and was being entertained by two young women of the terpsichorean persuasion. Two young women, one a Chinese and the other as black as night, were engaged in a complicated dance to the accompaniment of a girl who squatted in a corner with a flute-like instrument. The music, thin and reedy as it was, touched a chord of excitement in Purity's mind. When the veiled stranger motioned to her to sit beside him, she advanced with hips swaying to the tempo of the dance. When, she having sat down, he reached out and unfastened the buttons of her short Turkish jacket, it seemed not unreasonable to her, for the dancers were also bare-breasted.

She was not able for long to restrain herself from joining the dancers. Without any prompting from the man at her side, she presently rose and assumed the role of principal interpreter. At her guidance and following her example, their combined movements took on a shamelessness that was in no way prurient, but merely served to give accent to the music. And when, to achieve greater freedom of movement and a more intense level of voluptuousness, she stripped away her remaining garments, the black and the Chinese girls did likewise.

Three nude figures—one as dark as night, another the color of fine amber, the third with skin like magnolia—were entwined in the movements of the dance, their bodies sometimes touching, sometimes in postures of embrace. And the veiled man clapped his hands in applause of their efforts. Then, when the music died away, they sank to the floor, breathless, bosoms heaving, smooth skins bedewed with pearls of sweat.

At one end of the room was an alcove draped with diaphanous hangings, behind which was a large divan piled high with cushions. It was to this that El Diablo led his three women, one by one, with Purity going last. A silent-footed eunuch doused the lamps, all except one, which glowed faintly above the divan, providing enough light to pick out the three naked and entwined forms displayed for their lord and master's pleasure.

That night, as if in a dream, Purity experienced the manifold delights of four bodies: the muscular hardness of the male and the yielding softness of the females—including her own. Lost in the influence of the drug, she scaled heights of an alien ecstasy whose peaks she had formerly discerned only from afar, in the blue-gray mists of distance.

Morning found her awakening in her own bedchamber, to where she had been carried in the arms of a eunuch. As on the previous occasion, she had no recollection of what had taken place. There was nothing but a vague sense of attainment and well-being, though this was not so marked as it had been the first time. Furthermore, she was stricken with a headache, for which Nancy had the explanation.

"You've had two large doses of the draft in two days, dearie," she declared. "And that's overdoing it."

"But you told me there'd be no ill effects," complained Purity.

"Not from one draft now and again," replied the other. "That's the way the harem women use the opium. More often than that and you find yourself unable to live without it. And then you're in trouble, for it takes a strong hold on you."

Purity caught her own reflection in a pier glass. She looked pale and strained.

"If he sends for me again tonight, I shall have to have another draft," she said. "I know that I can never face him with my mind whole and awake. God only knows what I do under the influence of that drug, but I could not possibly counterfeit it in my waking state."

"Happily, you'll not be sent for this night," said Nancy. "Neither will I, nor any of us, for Abu Nuwas tells me that El Diablo left the palace early this morning and is not expected back for some days."

"Did he also give you any news about my husband?" asked Purity.

"That he did, dearie," said Nancy. "He told me that Colonel Landless and his friend, the monk, have been given extra food and certain privileges to make their lives easier."

"Thank heaven for that," said Purity fervently. "If I thought I could greatly improve their lot, I think I could face El Diablo without the aid of the drug. And how is Mark's wound? Did Abu Nuwas tell you if the physician has attended him again?"

"His wound is being dressed twice daily," said Nancy.

"Do you think I shall be able to see him again?" asked Purity. "Or speak to Brother Francisco and assure myself that we're not being told a pack of lies?"

"I think we can arrange something," said Nancy, and she threw Purity an arch glance.

"What do you mean, Nancy?" demanded Purity.

Strangely, the ex-nursemaid was not to be pressed further. She simply kept quiet, and Purity could only speculate about her companion's tantalizing remark.

Two days passed, and Purity experienced to the full the languid inactivity of harem life. She took most of her meals with Nancy in one or the other of their suites, but on one occasion only she ate with the other concubines, when she was somewhat put out by the, for her, puzzling, disconcerting glances that she received from two of the younger women—a Nubian and a Chinese.

On the morning of the third day following her encounter with El Diablo, Nancy gave Purity the news that Abu Nuwas, acting as master of the palace in his lord's absence, had declared that she and Purity could venture beyond the walls and into the city—under strict guard.

So it was that, heavily veiled and wearing voluminous caftans, they took their places together in a large palanquin borne by a quartet of giant Nubians. Six spearmen marched before and six after. And Abu Nuwas headed the party astride a little white donkey.

Down the winding, narrow streets of the Casbah they descended. Through the chinks in the palanquin's heavy curtains that hid the two women from the lustful eyes of men, they were able to see the teeming bazaars: the streets of the tinsmiths, the bakers, the gunsmiths, the sword makers, the tailors, and the sherbet vendors. They could smell the spices of the East, mingled with the odors of struggling humanity and the heady scents of rare perfumes. They came at last to the slave market, for the chief eunuch had a commission from his lord and master to purchase house slaves of suitably good appearance.

The palanquin came to rest in the shady end of the square, among several others, all containing veiled women from the harems and palaces of the city. Through partly drawn curtains, Purity gazed out upon the scene that was burned upon her mind as if with a hot iron.

Nothing had changed: the huddled groups of poor wretches who had just been brought out; the work slaves and the house slaves; the smaller groups of young women; the boisterous, jesting slave master, with his great whip.

Purity pressed her hands against her eyes and shuddered.

"Nancy, I can't bear to look upon those poor creatures," she said. "Do we have to stay?"

"Bide your patience, dearie," murmured the other. "Let Abu Nuwas complete his business here, and we shall move on. Before this morning's over, you'll be glad you came on this jaunt. I promise you."

Lowering her hands, Purity met Nancy's amused gaze.

"What do you mean?" she asked. But she received no reply, just a wink and a smile.

Purity kept her eyes averted from the proceedings in the square, and she was not kept in agony of mind for very long. El-talib, the slave master, dispatched his evil business with speed that morning, for they were a poor bunch on offer: the passengers and crew of a Spanish merchantman that the Corsairs had captured near the Balearic Islands a week or so previously. The men were dark, stocky, and unattractive, but suitable for hard work. The women, barring a handful, were built in the same mold. Abu Nuwas made some halfhearted bids and then threw up his hands in disgust. Turning to face the palanquin, he met Nancy's eyes, then gave her a nod.

Nancy squeezed Purity's hand in hers.

"Now comes your surprise, dearie," she whispered.

The Nubians took up the palanquin and set off after the eunuch on the white donkey. As they left, the work slaves were being branded. The stench of burning skin and flesh followed them all the way across the square.

"Where are we going, Nancy?" pleaded Purity. "Why do you keep me in suspense? Tell me, please do. Does it concern Mark?"

"That it does," said the other, smiling.

"Am I going to see him again?"

"In a manner of speaking, you are," Nancy replied cryptically. Nor was she to be persuaded to say more.

The narrow street that led down from the slave market to the harbor was the same one up which Purity had been driven in the company of her fellow captives. It had not been so long ago, but it seemed to her, that morning, as if half her lifetime had passed since then. Hidden from prying eyes inside the curtained palanquin, they came at length to Barbarossa's jetty, overlooking the Corsair fleet that lay in its protecting arm. And there they halted.

Nancy drew back the curtains. To one side was the towering mass of the Casbah, with the citadel on high, white-walled, dark-eyed with gun apertures, commanding the harbor. To the other side, at the end of the jetty, was the stone-built battery, with idle gunners lolling in the embrasures and with the crescent banner of the Turkish empire curling lazily in the zephyrs.

"See that galley?" said Nancy, pointing. "It's the red one."

Puzzled, Purity followed her finger. Anchored some distance from the jetty, no farther away than a boy could throw a stone, was a large galley whose tall sides were painted blood-red in contrast to its white, holystoned decks, upon which, by reason of the jetty's greater height, they could look down. A score of long oars protruded from portholes in the vessel's side and lay slack and still in the water. There was no one on the deck except a sentry with a halberd, lolling under an awning of the poop.

"Yes," said Purity. A premonition of joy quickened her breath and her heartbeat. "What of it?"

"Bide in patience for a while yet," said her companion. " 'Tis nearly noon."

They waited in silence. At the stroke of noon, a cannon on the ramparts of the citadel boomed out across the harbor, as was the custom every midday. There was a puff of white smoke against the dazzling blueness of the sky, a reverberating echo, and then a cloud of seagulls rose screeching. Abu Nuwas turned in his saddle and exchanged a nod and a glance with Nancy, who clutched at Purity's hand and squeezed it hard.

"Watch the galley!" she whispered.

Moments later, Purity gave a sharp intake of breath as a group of figures emerged from a companionway onto the main deck of the red-painted vessel. They comprised two swarthy Corsairs in white turbans. And two other men . . .

"Mark!" cried Purity. "Oh, my darling, my husband!"

He followed his two guards across the wide deck, and Brother Francisco came after him. Neither was manacled. Mark Landless walked straight and tall, his head erect, as Purity had always known him. There was a stark white bandage wound around his brow, and he looked to have been given a fresh, untorn shirt. Even at a distance, the improvement in his appearance and bearing was quite discernible. The monk, also, had lost his prison pallor.

Her heart was pounding, as if murmuring her love. Purity watched, clutching at Nancy's hand, as Mark threw himself down upon a pile of cordage and sails that lay at the base of the galley's mainmast. Brother Francisco did likewise, while their two guards lolled nearby.

"Taking the air and a bit o' sunshine," commented Nancy. "From now on, they're to be allowed up on deck for an hour from noon every day."

"Is he . . . are they kept aboard that galley?" asked Purity.

"Have been ever since they were taken," said Nancy. " 'Tis a terrible existence, being a galley slave. I've heard tell they're chained to their oars, and there they sit, night and day, rowing or sleeping, till they perish."

"Horrible, horrible!" said Purity. "Nancy, I've got to secure his release from that galley. For that, I'd give myself utterly to El Diablo, with or without the aid of opium."

"That's as may be," replied Nancy. She sounded doubtful. "But at least you'll be able to come down here every noontime and watch him. That I've arranged with Abu Nuwas."

Purity squeezed her hand. "Nancy, you are a true friend," she said. "But how did you persuade him to . . . ?"

Her companion laughed lightly and winked. "There's ways to pleasure any man," she said, "even one of his kind."

"Nancy, you don't mean . . . ?"

"They have memories," she said, "recollections of a woman's body. It takes them in different ways. Abu Nuwas . . . well, he wants to do no more than undress me and stroke me." She laughed good-naturedly. "You wouldn't have me deprive a poor eunuch of his pleasures, would you?"

"Nancy, I can't let you! If anyone has to bribe that disgusting old creature with her body . . . "

"Not you," said Nancy firmly. "He doesn't fancy you, and he has told me as much many times. He likes his women on the plump side, with breasts like dumplings, women of my sort. Fie on you for all this idle chatter! Look, Colonel Landless is getting up and moving about."

"Yes, yes!" cried Purity. "And he's coming in this direction. Oh, Mark, my darling. If only you could see me, recognize me, wave to me."

The tall figure with the bandaged brow strode slowly to the ship's side, where he remained for some time, his hands resting upon the bulwarks. He appeared to have some idle interest in the men up on the ramparts of the harbor battery. They were sponging out one of their long black cannons with a mop on the end of a pole. Not once did he so much as glance toward the palanquin on the jetty, where sat the woman who would have given her all for a word of love, or one touch of his lips.

They stayed for the full hour, till Mark and his companion were sent down below again. For the last half of the time, Abu Nuwas fretted and seemed anxious to go. Purity realized that, though Nancy had made light of the matter, her well-rounded body must have inspired powerful lusts in the mind of the chief eunuch, for it was clear from his manner that the ex-

pedition to the jetty had been conducted without the
knowledge or permission of his lord and master.

True to her word, Nancy arranged for Purity to
gaze upon Mark the following day, and each succeed-
ing day for nearly a week. Purity lived for that one
brief hour out of each twenty-four. The thunder of
the noon gun from the high citadel became a daily
signal for a voyage of delight. Distanced as she was
from Mark by a stretch of water, by the heavy veil
that covered her face, by the remembrance that lay
locked in his ruined mind, she had no recourse but to
place the tall figure on the sunlit deck in a passing
show of scenes lovingly recalled, scenes like the time
when she had peered out into the sunlight on another
deck to see him nude and laughing in a shower of
flung, diamond-spangled, rainbow-hued water, or the
preliminaries to the first occasion on which he had
possessed her completely—when he had held her face
downward over the arm of a sofa and slapped her
bare rump till she screamed for mercy. It had been
heart-searing at the time, but in recollection it seemed
infinitely rewarding. Lost in some such remembered
episode, and gazing all the while upon her distant
beloved, she became aware that Nancy's knowing eyes
were upon her and upon her hands, which she was
pressing tightly against the rapid rising and falling
of her bosom, so that her gaze faltered and she felt
her cheeks blush crimson.

On the sixth morning—it was a Tuesday, as she
was aware, for she had laboriously constructed a
calendar dating back to the fateful day of her capture—Purity awoke with the, by then, familiar sense
of delight and anticipation and ran to the balcony to
look out upon the new day. She was not able to see
the red galley from even her high vantage point, for
the palace wall blocked out the view of the harbor

as far as the battery at the end of the jetty. But what
she saw there that fateful Tuesday morning made her
reel back against the sun-warmed wall in dumb astonishment.

Stretching across the mouth of the harbor, as far as
she could see, and coming in from seaward in long
and purposeful lines, were a cloud of ships: high-walled
battleships with rows of gundecks; smaller vessels,
frigates and gunboats.

She raced to find Nancy, her flimsy nightshift flying
behind her. Nancy was also on her balcony, having
been aroused by one of the female attendant slaves.
Her face, when she turned to Purity, was white and
wild, her eyes staring with terror.

"They've come back!" she shrieked. "The British
are back! They've come to wipe out the Corsairs!"

Admiral Sir Edward Pellow, commanding the fleet
that sailed into Algiers harbor on August 27, 1816,
may indeed have had the ruthless intent to which the
hysterical Nancy Shaw had attributed to him, but his
orders were, firstly, to negotiate.

The outrages of the Corsairs having finally stirred
the British government to action, the admiral had been
returned to the Mediterranean, where, backed by the
powerful argument of twenty-five large and small
ships, to which was added, at Gibraltar, six frigates of
the allied Dutch Navy, he had come to make demands, not of the Brotherhood of Corsairs, but of the
dey—the puppet who misruled Algiers in the name of
the Sublime Porte.

Anchoring his flagship under the very guns of the
battery at the end of the jetty, and half a cannon
shot from the Corsair *xebecs* and galleys anchored between him and the shore, Sir Edward took counsel
with Dutch Admiral van Cappellan and then gave

instructions to his emissary, a senior lieutenant of his
staff who spoke Arabic, was known to be steady
under fire, and had a way of thumping a table in an
argument that commanded respect.

"All the remaining slaves are to be freed," said
Pellow. "That's the important item. Secure what you
can of all the other items on the list, but obtain the
immediate release of all the slaves."

"All the *Christian* slaves, Sir Edward," interposed
his Dutch colleague.

"Ahem! That is quite correct, Admiral," responded
the other. "My brief does not include any of the
heathen persuasion. See to it then, Popkess."

"Aye, aye, sir," said the lieutenant.

"It is now eleven o'clock," said Pellow. "I will have
that black devil's reply by"—he consulted a large
turnip watch, then cocked an interrogative eye at the
Dutchman—"shall we say one o'clock, hey?"

The other nodded assent.

The emissary's boat put out from the flagship's
gangway, bearing on its stern the white ensign of the
Royal Navy surmounted by a flag of truce. It was
rowed to the jetty by Jack Tars in blue-and-white
uniforms, with beribboned straw hats. It was watched
—from battery and from citadel, from the teeming
Casbah and from the heights above—by uncounted
pairs of dark and wondering eyes.

It was watched, till the top of the harem wall cut
it from view, by Purity and Nancy.

"You see, there's to be no violence, no bloodshed,"
said Purity reassuringly. "They've merely come to demand that we be set free, just like they arranged the
release of the other slaves in the spring. Think of it,
Nancy—to be set free! To be able to return home!
Mark. You. All of us. . . ." Her voice trailed off into

silence as she saw that her words were being received by her companion with less than enthusiasm.

"Home!" snorted Nancy. "You may speak of home, *Mrs.* Landless, you with your fine mansion, your deer park, your crested silver, your servants, and your well-behaved little girl in the nursery! What of me? What home for me? And don't you go offering to take me back as nursemaid, *Mrs.* High-and-Mighty Landless, or I'll scratch your eyes out, so help me!"

"Nancy," said Purity mildly, taking the other by the hand and gazing into her flaring eyes till the anger melted and tears came, "my dear, don't say hurtful things like that to me."

With a sob, Nancy stepped forward and, throwing her arms around Purity, buried her face against the other woman's shoulder.

"Oh, I don't want to be sent back to England!" she wailed. "What is there for me in England? My place is here with him. No matter how he's treated me, though he'd have had me raped to death if you hadn't saved me, I'm nothing without him."

"And stay you shall, if that's your wish, Nancy," Purity assured her. "No one has the right to force you to leave against your will."

"You're sure of that, dearie?" Nancy raised her ruined, powder-streaked face, staring up into Purity's face with tear-swollen eyes. "I want no other place but this. Truly, I'd wish to die and leave my bones here in Algiers."

"If there's any question of the navy freeing us," said Purity, "I will use all the influence I have, and all my husband's influence, to ensure that you are allowed to remain here."

Rumor—never so precise and well-informed as when facts are scanty—thrived mightily in the palace of El Diablo in the ensuing hours. From one of the serving slaves, Purity and Nancy—who kept a constant watch on the harbor from the balcony—learned the undoubted fact of El Diablo's return that morning. Their next visitor, Abu Nuwas, said that both El Diablo and Azizza were still at sea, and that—this delivered with a lustful glance at Nancy's ample and barely concealed charms—there was no cause for either of them to suppose that the infidel British had come to free slaves. No—they had come to bring presents for the *dey,* presents and peace with the Corsairs.

There was no firing of the noonday gun. Perhaps they were apprehensive that the men on the tall ships might fire back. Eschewing luncheon, Purity and Nancy remained on the balcony, sipping water against the heat and nibbling at peaches. They had no timepiece, but they were aware, from the distance that the shadow of the harem wall had crept across the garden paths below, that more than two hours had passed since midday, when into their sight slid the returning navy cutter, the two lines of straw hats bowing forward with every pull of the oars, trailing a mackerel wake across the glassy blue of the harbor.

"They're taking a message back from the *dey,*" whispered Purity. "Surely it won't be long now before we know our fate, for better or worse."

Oh, let us be freed, she prayed. Today. Now. Let me go down to the harbor, board that red galley, and unchain my darling with my own hands. I'll take him home, back home to Clumber, and to our darling Chastity. The best medical attention in the world will be brought to restore his memory. Loving care will . . .

"They're climbing aboard," said Nancy, shielding her eyes against the sun's glare. "There's an officer in a cocked hat. He's reached the deck and he's doffed his hat to the others standing there."

Love will restore him, thought Purity. And never
again will I let him go from my side. The quiet life
of Clumber, with occasional forays to London, a week
or so to take the sea air in Brighton, and a short stay
at Bath in the summer—that will be our life. No more
war. No more venturing to wild and dangerous places.
No more . . .

She broke off with a start, and her reaching hand
met Nancy's, already groping for hers, as from the
three-tiered wall of the British flagship there issued a
rippling line of orange flame that was quenched in a
rolling bank of dense white smoke, and was instantly
followed by a rolling thunderclap of awful sound.

It was two-thirty. Protracted argument and table-
thumping had achieved nothing.

Chapter Six

The first broadside from the flagship was aimed high,
toward the guns on the ramparts of the citadel. Several of the shots entered the embrasures, overturning
cannon and men in an appalling mess of slaughter.
One hurtling, thirty-six-pound sphere of iron struck the
high wall of El Diablo's white sandstone-and-marble
palace at a spot halfway down into the vineyard where
Omar Manzur's man had lowered her. The palace was
immediately above and beyond the citadel.

Scarcely had the gunsmoke of the first broadside
dispersed to reveal that the flagship had hoisted a long
string of signal flags before other ships of the fleet
commenced to fire. The crash of their broadsides, interspersed by the shrill, silvery blasts of trumpets, assaulted the two shocked and horrified women on the
harem balcony with almost physical force. They huddled together, their arms and bodies entwined, against
the wall. More gunfire—nearer, so that it caused the
balcony beneath their feet to tremble, as from an

earthquake—betokened that the cannons of the citadel were answering the British.

It was Purity who first recovered her balance.
Nancy was half-crazed with shock and terror, and incapable of coherent thought or movement. Purity cast
one last backward glance down into the harbor, which
was now entirely hidden in a pall of swirling white
gunsmoke interspersed with lurid orange flashes. She
half-lifted, half-dragged her trembling burden from the
balcony and into the shelter of the room. Almost immediately after, a random cannonball, striking the
balustrade of the palace terrace, bounded through the
wall beyond and scorched a swath of destruction
across the prim harem garden, shattering the fountain,
a cedar tree, a line of box hedge, and smashing
against the base of the building immediately beneath
Purity's quarters. She and Nancy did not hear the
ball's destructive passage above the din, nor, so great
was the agitation caused by the guns of the citadel,
did they feel the tremor when it came to its violent
rest.

Despite the noise outside, despite the constant jolts
and tremors, the coolness of Purity's room had the
power to calm. She closed the shutters. Some of the
din was lessened.

Nancy lay upon the divan. Nearly nude, with her
plump cheeks smeared with tears and powder, she
looked like a nymph gone curiously astray. But she
had recovered some of her composure.

"One thing's for sure," she declared. "The navy's
not going to take us back to England, not without flat-
tening all of Algiers first. Oh, Purity, my dearie, how
can I say such a thing?"

She leaped up and ran to Purity. Their roles had
become reversed in the time it took for the gunners on
Admiral Pellow's flagship to sponge out their reeking

barrels again and reload. Purity was crouched against the far wall, her face buried in her hands, the tears running through her fingers.

"He's down there!" she cried. "Down there in that holocaust! Aboard that galley! Chained to his oar! Helpless! Perhaps dying! Perhaps . . . "

"Dearie, you must be brave," said Nancy with all the ardor of someone who has recently passed from abject terror to a semblance of imperturbability.

"I must go to him!" cried Purity.

"That you must, my love," said Nancy, "but not now. You'll go later, when the fighting's over."

The time was two forty-five. In the quarter of an hour since Pellow's flagship had opened the bombardment, half the guns in the isolated battery at the end of the jetty had been silenced. The Corsair fleet, trapped in the arm of the harbor, prudently held its fire, since none of the ships carried more metal than the long-nosed twelve-pounders required to bring unarmed merchantmen to heel, and to have attracted the return fire of Pellow's battleships would have spelled suicide, for a single broadside from one of the great three-deckers could have reduced a frail-hulled *xebec* or galley to ruin. The battery having largely been rounded to rubble, twisted metal, and riven flesh, the allied fleet turned its attention to the citadel of the Casbah high above.

In the following hours, through the heat of the afternoon, and in the brief subtropical twilight, and when the velvet darkness fell, the Dutch and British gunners poured a hail of fire upon the embrasures of the citadel, causing the most terrible havoc within, while they, themselves, lying at anchor within their wooden walls, received the full burden of the return fire. Between the first shot and the end of the action, there were killed and wounded, among the allies, over nine hundred officers and men in ranks. The loss suffered by the Algerians was impossible to reckon.

With the coming of darkness, the firing became ever more wild and ill directed. Purity and Nancy, lying entwined, breast to breast, had lived through it all in agonies of dread. When the shots began to fall into the palace precincts, when the lurid glow of burning buildings, the stench of smoke, and screams of the wounded and dying reached their scented, silk-hung refuge, despair seized them both.

"We're done for, sure as fate!" cried Nancy.

"I don't want to die here," said Purity. "If there's any time left for me, even a few moments, I want to spend it within sight and sound of Mark."

"You'd never get out of the palace," said Nancy. "And if you did, you'd be cut down as soon as you reached the jetty."

Their eyes met in the gloaming. By a lurid flash of gunfire, Nancy saw the resolve in the other's countenance.

"If I reach that jetty, I will swim to the red galley," said Purity.

"My God, I think you will!"

"Help me, Nancy, I beg of you!"

"That I will, dearie."

Taking Purity by the hand, the ex-nursemaid led her former mistress to her wardrobe, where, from behind a pile of exotic raiments, she produced a long pistol that was decorated in the Moorish manner, with inlays of silver and ivory in the wooden furniture and Damascene work in the metal. From a curiously carved powder flask, she primed the pan and closed the frizzen, then pressed it into Purity's hand.

"You know how to cock and fire a pistol?"

"Yes," said Purity.

"Use it if you have need to," said Nancy. "I have

kept it by me these many months, having wheedled it away from that poor boy, my fancy lad, Khalid, heaven rest him. Come, I'll show you the way to the side door that the guards use. Maybe in all this hell it will be unguarded."

They stole out into the corridor. No one was in sight. The door at the end of the corridor hung drunkenly upon its hinges with a hole punched in its center panel by a cannonball. The missile itself was embedded in the wall opposite. Purity averted her gaze from two twisted bodies lying close by.

Outside, the flame-rent sky was as light as day. The courtyard of El Diablo's magnificent palace had suffered cruelly: the domed fountain was a heap of rubble, and the night-scented honeysuckle lay in sorry loops amidst broken faïence and mounds of tumbled masonry. Where the gate had once been—but which was now a wide gap in the palace wall—the body of Abu Nuwas lay like a cast-aside puppet, an expression of wide-eyed astonishment on his dead face.

"The way lies open, Purity," said Nancy. "Get you gone. There's no one around."

"Good-bye, Nancy. I shall never forget you."

"Away, lass, before you make me cry like a babe."

They kissed and clung to each other for a moment while a tremendous explosion rocked the very ground upon which they stood, and a cascade of blazing fragments rose high above them.

"Good-bye."

"Good-bye."

Only a low pile of rubble separated Purity from freedom. She clambered onto it. Beyond, where the gate had once been, a narrow street ran in tortuous bends and declivities down to the harbor.

She cast a last glance back to Nancy—and she saw

a massive, bearded figure in a peacock-plumed helmet looming up behind the ex-nursemaid.

"Nancy!" She screamed the warning.

But the giant Bashi-bazouk had no intentions toward Nancy. Brushing her aside, he began to follow Purity. His white teeth showed in a bestial grin. In his right hand he carried a curved scimitar whose polished blade redly reflected the flame-rent sky.

"He's been sent to fetch you!" screamed Nancy. "Use your pistol, Purity!"

Purity shuddered, cocked the weapon, and, holding it at arm's length, aimed it for the forehead of the Bashi-bazouk. Ugo's grin never wavered for an instant.

"Shoot, damn you, shoot!" Nancy's frantic cry was repeated. It detracted Ugo from his purpose, but only for a moment, only for as long as it took to thrust with the curved point of a scimitar, to drive it through the tender flesh and out the other side.

Closing her eyes, Purity pressed the trigger. The weapon bucked in her hand on the report. Her nostrils were briefly assaulted by the reek of burned powder. Then she was stumbling down the pile of rubble—past the staggering giant who was falling with his hands pressed to what was remaining of his face —to the plump, rounded figure in the bloodstained finery of a harem concubine.

Nancy still lived, but she was sinking fast. She smiled up weakly at Purity.

"There's no hurts," she said. "But I fear 'tis all over with poor Nancy. Lovie, I beg you to listen to what I have to say. . . ."

"Yes?" Purity held her close, looking down into the plump, pretty face that was being rapidly drained of life before her eyes. "Tell me if you must, dear, but don't fret yourself."

"I have lied to you," whispered the dying woman. "'Twas for your own sake, or so I pretended, that I wouldn't give you the real name of El Diablo. There was some truth in it, sure. But 'twas really to protect him that I said nothing. . . ." She coughed, and a thin trickle of bright blood issued from the corner of her mouth.

"Hush," said Purity. "It doesn't matter."

"Heaven help me, I have loved him in my own way," said Nancy. "But for your own sake, Purity, should you ever meet him again, now or later, you must know that he is . . . " A paroxysm of choking coughs racked her.

"Rest yourself," murmured Purity. "Don't try to talk anymore, my dear."

Nor did Nancy speak again. She lay with her head against Purity's breast, as if in sleep. It was her eternal sleep, and the secret of El Diablo remained locked within her dead brain.

It was said afterward by the Algerians that hell itself had opened its mouth upon them. Having reduced the citadel to a silent mass of pounded rubble, the fury of the allied guns was turned, not upon the lines of *xebecs* and galleys that lay at anchor, but upon the town itself—for the Corsair fleet, if taken intact, represented prize money that would greatly enrich Englishman and Dutchman from admiral to powder-monkey.

Purity descended to the harbor wall through a holocaust of sound, flame, and fury. The entire lower part of the Casbah was all but consumed. Most of the buildings in the poorer quarters were built of dried mud; these had turned into ovens in which the inmates had been roasted alive. The gutters ran with molten metals: lead, silver, even gold. Everywhere cowered the terror-stricken inhabitants. Some were carrying children, a few sticks of furniture, and bundles of treasured possessions. Women, regardless of being unveiled before the eyes of men, were calling out for their children and their husbands. None of them had the will to leave the narrow, blazing streets.

Purity reached the lowest level of the town and peered out across the harbor. The open space before her was dotted with sprawled forms that bore mute testimony to the flying hails of grapeshot and canister that swept the waterfront of all life. The jetty and the water's edge were perhaps a hundred paces from where she crouched behind the comparative safety of a stone pillar. But it was a hundred paces that she could never hope to tread—and live. The allied battleships were hidden by their own cannon smoke, their positions marked by the flashes of orange flame piercing the dense white clouds. They were still firing upon the lower part of the town, and Purity was able to see whirling spheres of iron bounding across the waterfront and smashing through walls and roofs.

The Corsair fleet was still intact. The allies were firing to each side of the packed galleys and *xebecs,* or over the top of them.

She saw the red galley, moored where it had been for the past week. There seemed to be not a mark upon it. The furled white sails were untouched by fire or shot, and lights burned in its stern cabin windows. Somewhere on the oar deck, huddled with his fellow unfortunates, the man she loved was listening to the inferno outside. It was possible that his poor, wounded mind was incapable of comprehending the very real peril in which he was, and that, she decided, was a blessing.

Her course was simple, being dictated by the hideous circumstances in which she found herself. She would remain where she was in the hope that the firing slackened so she would be able to risk the hazardous dash across the open space to the jetty, leap into the water, and swim to the red galley. She had no thought of anything beyond that—merely to reach Mark, to see him once more, perhaps for the last time, to hold him to her, perhaps even to reach inside his destroyed mind and make herself known to him. Her hopes went no further than that.

She waited—and was the horrified spectator to all that followed. . . .

It was probable that the first allied shot to fall upon the massed Corsair fleet was fired low in error. It struck the *xebec* nearest to where Purity was crouched. She clearly saw the shower of splintered woodwork rise above its deck. An instant later the craft burst into flame, and the panic-stricken crew poured over its sides and splashed into the water. By the light of the blazing *xebec,* she perceived new activity aboard the other ships: men running to and fro, grouping around their guns. Shouted orders came quite clearly to her across the water.

One of the Corsairs opened fire into the mass of billowing smoke that shrouded the allied battleships. Another followed. Winking lines of fire rippled along the low-slung sides of *xebecs* and tall galleys. Dry-mouthed with apprehension, Purity saw that the burning craft had become a hazard to its close-packed companions, so that they were casting free their anchor cables and drifting across the harbor, spreading sail as they went, firing their contemptibly light weight of metal at the Leviathans beyond the battle smoke.

And then the red galley was moving in the water, shaking free its furled sails. With a sob of anguish, she saw the idle oars suddenly stir to life, move in unison, dip into the water, drive the cumbersome vessel forward, and rise as one and dip again.

"No!" screamed Purity. "Please, God, no!"

The red galley was heading seaward, with others following after. But the way was blocked by the enemy. A chance clearing of battle smoke revealed the slab side of a huge British three-decker, every gun port clearly etched in the light of flames, white ensigns curling lazily from every masthead. The red galley was well within throwing distance of the British battleship, and moving slowly. Purity held her breath, suspended her mind in a limbo of agonized waiting, watched the long rows of oars slowly rise and fall, and prayed for a concealing cloud of smoke to drift across the galley and hide it from the English gunners.

The three-decker's broadside, when it came, drowned Purity's scream from her own ears. There came fifty great cannons speaking as one, fifty death-dealing balls of iron hurtling across the narrow space to the galley. Even at such close range, many of them missed, striking the water all around, sending columns of spray mast-high. It scarcely mattered; properly directed, one or two would have been sufficient. Most of the fifty-gun broadside tore into the galley's hub, ripping beams and planing into flying, razor-edged slivers that tore flesh, bone, and artery. Purity was still screaming when, with the long oars—some smashed like twigs—lying still, the red galley rolled slowly over on its beam ends, dipped its long prow, and plunged beneath the surface of the harbor.

It was over in less time than it takes to tell. The galley and the men within it—the slaves included, chained to their oars—were gone from sight. One minute it had been a seagoing vessel abounding with life and energy; the next minute it was a sunken coffin.

Purity watched the spot in the water where the red galley had disappeared, shaking her head in disbelief. "It can't be true. He can't have gone from me, not like that. It was a nightmare, and soon I shall wake up. . . ."

The firing ceased at nine o'clock, by which time the allied fleet had burned eighteen tons of gunpowder and hurled five hundred tons of shot and shell. No sooner had the firing ceased than a southerly wind sprang up from the desert and carried the attackers out of Algiers harbor, where they anchored offshore to await the morning.

Out at their anchorage, an awesome view of their grim handiwork was granted to Admiral Pellow and his men. Much of the town was one huge blaze, by whose light they could see that the battery on the end of the quay had been reduced to a mere heap of ruins, likewise most of the citadel. Stores and warehouses on the waterfront were burned-out shells of blackened stone. Of the Corsair fleet, nothing remained but floating wreckage.

Scarcely had the allies anchored when the wind increased to the proportions of a storm, and the sky was rent with jagged forks of lightning. The great ships pitched and tossed at their cables like toy boats in a fountain. But no rain came, no merciful rain that might have doused the fires in the town and spared so many homes and possessions.

With the end of the gunfire, it might have been thought that, the fires excepting, the agonies of the Algerines were over for one night. Not so. From out of their hiding places came the jackals of disaster who were to be found everywhere, in every age—those who thrived in times of calamity: the looters, the vandals, the despoilers.

Purity Landless, lying huddled in a heap of numb misery, where she had been since witnessing her loved one's end, raised her head at the sound of someone—

it sounded like a young woman—screaming with pain
and mortal terror. Some distance from where she lay,
two grinning oafs were manhandling a young girl. She,
not even of an age to be veiled, had her caftan torn
from her shoulders, and one of her assailants was
roughly kneading her half-formed breasts, laughing at
her screams. Without a second's thought or hesitation,
Purity leaped to her feet and ran to the girl's aid. She
snatched at the arm of the creature who was hurting
her, screaming to him to desist. The man's first reaction was to throw her off, but his second glance at
the newcomer revealed to him that a tastier prize than
the immature girl had delivered herself into their
hands. He shouted something in Arabic to his companion, who responded, pointing to Purity and grinning. The girl was released, and she ran away as fast
as her young legs could carry her. Purity was left alone
with the two jackals.

They were quite young, in their early twenties. And,
oddly enough, they were not bad looking, and their
caftans were clean and decent, their fingernails well
kept. One of them wore a gold ring set with a precious
stone. They were probably students and from good
families. Jackals were to be found in every walk of
life; it needed only calamity to bring their beastliness
to the surface.

They closed in on Purity, who backed away fear-
fully, suddenly aware that she had thrust herself into
disaster. They were discussing her as they came, pointing to her wonderful hair and her voluptuous body.
Looking down at herself, she realized for the first time
that day that she was still wearing no more than the
flimsy nightshift in which she had risen from her
couch that morning, and it was holed and rent in many
places.

A lightning flash immediately overhead illuminated

the eager faces, the flaring eyes of her would-be rav-
ishers. The accompanying thunderclap drowned her
screams when they rushed at her, and, each seizing one
of her arms, bore her back against a waist-high railing
that skirted the limit of the harbor. And there they
unbound the sashes from her own waists and tied her
wrists to the railing so that she stood with arms
stretched wide, helpless against their intentions.

They made some sport of stripping her, each taking
a handful of the fine linen of her nightshift and
wrenching in unison, rendering her nude. Together,
also, they took their pleasure of discovering her body,
embracing her with surprising tenderness, smoothing
their questing hands over her shoulders, waist, rump,
and thighs. They explored with their eager mouths her
lips, the glory of her breasts, and the firmness of her
dimpled belly. She endured it all, eyes wide, staring
up at the storm-rent sky, her blonde hair streaming in
the warm wind of the desert, her mind fixed upon her
recent and heartbreaking bereavement, beside which
her present ravishment was something almost without
meaning.

Half-uncaring, she was aware that they were argu-
ing as to which of them should first possess her, and
that, the question settled, the winner was opening his
robes and baring himself. He closed with her. Only
the shock of his eager intrusion made her cry out.
After that she was able to dissociate herself from his
labored breathing close by her ear and shut her mind
against his frenzied thrustings and scrabblings. Somewhere, she supposed, a woman named Purity Landless
was being outraged, spreadeagled in a night of tempest
on a far-off and alien shore. It could not be she. She
was high above and riding the storm clouds of an all-
consuming grief that made her inviolate to mere rav-

ishment. Her body, that was nothing—just a mere husk of mortality from which the spirit had departed.

Mark, oh, Mark, how shall I live without you?

The first ravisher having spent himself, the second took his place. She was no longer aware of it. Only when they had had their way with her—when they untied her arms and replaced their sashes around their waists, when they shamefacedly threw her the rags of her nightshift, jocularly kissed her and patted her cheek, then strode off into the night to find more mischief in the disaster-ridden city—did she sink to the ground and, burying her face in her hands, weep for shame and humiliation at what they had done to her.

There being nowhere for her to go, for it was out of the question to return to the shot-torn palace of El Diablo, she kept moving. In one of the narrow streets, where the flames had died down, leaving charred walls and darkness, she found a heap of belongings that some wretched creature must have dropped in flight. Among them was a woolen cloak, which she put on to cover her nakedness, pulling the hood well forward over her face to disguise her sex.

In the upper part of the town, where the buildings were larger and more substantially constructed, the fires were still raging, fanned by the storm wind. There, some of the inhabitants had recovered the will to survive and were striving to save their homes. There was a communal well, in a tiny square overhung with tall tenement buildings, from which they were raising water by the slow and laborious method of lowering buckets on ropes, from whence, in a living chain, they were passing the buckets from hand to hand to be thrown into the heart of the flames. Someone called to Purity, pointing to the living chain. She joined the line without hesitation. Next to her was a young, unveiled girl—she could have been the twin sister to the frightened child whom she had saved down by the harbor —who passed her the brimming bucket and flashed her an eager, heartening smile with every burden. They toiled together through the night, with the smoke and flames all around them, with the sound of crashing masonry and of roofs collapsing in rising showers of bright sparks that lit the scene as bright as day. Finally, Purity's hands and arms were blackened with soot, and—the hood of her cloak having fallen back —even the glory of her hair was hidden in blackness.

In the dawn light the storm abated, and the flames died down with the wind. Purity and the girl exchanged tired smiles and sank together to the ground. There they slept, hands entwined, till nearly noon, when the tramping of booted feet and the harsh barking of commands roused them up with the others.

"Prepare to halt! Halt! To your left hand, face! Order your muskets!"

Drawn up in the square were three lines of marines: red-coated, red-faced, heads kept erect by tall leather kerchiefs banding their necks, varnished black hats gleaming, bayonets winking. A six-foot sergeant saluted to a diminutive young lieutenant.

"Your orders, sir?"

"Commence the search, Sergeant. Question anyone who speaks English. Take all Christian slaves under your charge, and suffer no resistance. Carry on."

"Sir!"

Purity edged her way through the awed and watching throng of Algerines toward the marine officer, who turned at her approach, his hand falling to the hilt of his sword, to see the spectacle of the blackamoor woman with the mass of tousled hair and the wild eyes. He had heard, he had been told many times, that the blackamoor women were worse than their menfolk, and they committed unspeakable atrocities upon their prisoners.

"Stand back, you, there!" he cried. "Keep your distance, you virago!"

"Sir, I must speak with you," said Purity.

"By God! You speak English almost like one of us!" exclaimed the young officer.

"Sir, I am the wife of an Englishman," said Purity. "At least . . . at least . . . " Her voice broke.

A closer look had convinced the lieutenant that she was, indeed, a vastly different creature from that which he had at first supposed. Without more ado, he told two of his men to escort his find down to the harbor, where his major had set up a command post. This gentleman, upon questioning Purity and learning that she was not only what she claimed to be, but that she was also the wife of the missing Colonel Mark Landless, gave her his arm and escorted her personally to a waiting boat that took her straight to the flagship. The allied fleet had returned to the harbor. The *dey* of Algiers had capitulated to Admiral Pellow's demands. The day of the Corsairs was ended—as Omar Manzur had predicted.

Admiral Sir Edward Pellow greeted her in his comfortably appointed stern cabin with easy grace, as if receiving smoke-blackened wives of retired British officers of field rank—and this one, as far as he could discern, nearly naked under her ragged cloak—was part of the normal warp and weft of an admiral's daily life.

Pellow, a man approaching sixty, came from a naval family, and he had had a long and distinguished service career, to which the bombardment of Algiers was to be the crowning glory and earn him an earldom. He was pleasantly imperturbable after the manner of his class and calling. He rose, took her proffered hand, implanted a token kiss upon its sooted skin, and offered her his own chair.

"Mrs. Landless, ma'am, it is indeed a pleasure and a relief to see you safe. I have every hope that the colonel, your husband . . . "

"My husband, sir, is dead," said Purity flatly.

"Ma'am, I . . . "

"He was a galley slave," said Purity. "Your guns sank the galley and him in it. I saw it go down. I watched for a long time, but not a soul survived. And he, you see, would have been chained . . . down there . . . "

"Mrs. Landless, ma'am, what can I say? You have my deepest, my most profound, sympathy and sorrow at your sad loss. If there is anything . . . "

She drew in a deep breath and steadied herself. It was important, she felt, not to break down before this grave and courteous man, for Mark's sake.

"It is true that you are freeing the slaves, sir?" she asked.

"The Christian slaves only, ma'am," he replied. "My orders do not include any of the heathen sort."

"And how is this to be done?"

"By my orders, their former masters are to turn them loose and instruct them to make contact with our patrols of bluejackets and marines who are patrolling the town," said Pellow. "They will then be marshaled to a command post on the waterfront, where, after being given a meal, they will be sorted out into their various nationalities in preparation for being returned to their homelands. It will be a long and trying procedure, but I confide to you that it will be completed within three or four days."

"Sir, I should like to assist in the task," said Purity. "I speak both French and English, and I could be of

some help with the women and children. Add to that,
I should like to look out for some among them who
were kind to me when I was captured." She was
thinking of poor, branded Meg O'Grady and of the
tragic Greek boy.

Pellow seemed pleased and relieved at her request,
assuring her that her assistance would be most valuable. He glanced dubiously at her blackened hands
and then at her ragged clothing. Something would
have to be done about that, he ventured.

She bathed in the admiral's own bathtub, brought
into his great cabin by two grinning seamen. It was a
high-sided contraption of beaten copper, and it took
fifteen buckets of water that had been heated on the
ship's galley stove to fill it up. A generous cake of
good navy soap accompanied Purity into the cosseting
warmth, where she luxuriated for an hour and
emerged clean and refreshed in body, if still drained
in spirit.

She dried herself on one of the admiral's soft Turkish towels, watching herself dispassionately in the admiral's pier glass.

Mark had said many times that her body was made
for loving. Well, it had been loved—and used—many
times. Only Mark had had the touch to draw from
that body—that highly strung and complex instrument
—the ecstatic music that transcended earthly lust.
And now Mark was gone forever. And her body, now
with the master musician dead and gone, was no more
than a beautiful object whose purpose was finished,
something to be adorned and cared for in health and
sickness, a repository for her dead spirit, to be admired by some, coveted by some, perhaps even possessed by some—but never entirely, never again.

She would live. In the dark hours of the bitter
night, when the violators had left her, she had contem-

plated death, had half-resolved to walk into the harbor
and keep walking till the waters closed over her head,
to be joined with the man she loved in eternal rest.
Only one thing had stopped her: the love she bore for
their adopted child. For Chastity's sake, and for nothing else, she would stay alive and laboriously stoop
and build the pieces of her new existence without
Mark.

They had found her some clothing. A tall and slender young midshipman had provided a good lawn
shirt, a pair of buckskin breeches, and silk stockings.
The youngest and smallest middy aboard possessed a
spare pair of buckled shoes, which, when stuffed with
rags at the toes, would stay on her slender feet. Thus
attired, her hair combed and plaited back in a braid,
she looked to be what she was: a beautiful woman
dressed up as a man.

She returned ashore on the next boat that left. As
they rounded the flagship's towering sides, the evidence of the previous night's assault was plain to see.
Half a dozen gaping holes had been driven through
the thick planking, and the hideous pock-marking of
grapeshot was everywhere. The midshipman in charge
of the boat told her that they had suffered twenty-
seven in dead and wounded, and he pointed to a long
line of small boats proceeding seaward out of the harbor entrance, each carrying a doleful burden of still
forms wrapped in white ensigns: dead sailors being
returned to the everlasting deep.

Closing with the shore, she experienced the horrified realization that they were passing almost over the
very spot where the red galley had taken its last
plunge. Somewhere down in the pellucid blue depths
beneath her, a drowned figure was slumped in chains
across a broken oar.

"The Corsair ships that were sunk last night," she

said to the midshipman, "will any of them be raised up?"

"No, ma'am," he replied. "We carry no heavy lifting gear in the fleet."

"Is the water very deep there?" she asked and pointed.

The boy squinted toward the end of the jetty on his left, and away to a cluster of rocks that stood beyond a low headland to his right. When he had gotten his bearings, he replied, "Between eight and nine fathoms, ma'am. We took constant soundings when we first sailed in yesterday morning."

"How deep is that—in feet, I mean?"

"About fifty feet, give or take a few."

"Too deep for divers?" She knew the answer even before she asked the question.

"No man could get down to that depth and come up alive, ma'am," said the midshipman dismissively. He directed his attention to his oarsmen. "Smarten up your strokes, you dogs! We're in full view of every telescope in the fleet, and I'll not have you making a damned fool out of me! One, two! In, out! In, out!"

Upon arrival ashore, Purity again made the acquaintance of the marine major, who greeted her with markedly more interest than upon the previous occasion. He introduced himself as Major Gregg and presented his naval counterpart, Lieutenant Popkess— that same table-thumping Popkess who had been the admiral's emissary to the *dey*. Uncaring of their questing eyes upon the details of her figure that were so imperfectly concealed by the thin lawn shirt and the tightly fitting breeches, she pointed to a long line of people snaking across the jetty and asked what they were doing.

"They're the first batch of released slaves," said Gregg. "They have been fed and watered, and now our fellows are quizzing them. Trouble is, most of 'em are Eyetalians, Spaniols, or damned Froggies, and they don't speak our lingo."

"I am French by birth, and I naturally speak the language," said Purity mildly.

"Eh? Upon my word, I do apologize, ma'am," said the marine officer, greatly put out.

But Purity was already walking toward the line of forlorn men, women, and children who were filing past a row of makeshift tables at which sat navy clerks with pens, ink, and reams of paper.

There was little rejoicing among the freed slaves. They were too tired, too shocked by the long night of bombardment and fire, and too overcome by emotion to properly comprehend that they were at liberty. And then to be hustled into line by grinning men in scarlet and blue, to be questioned and probed by pinchbeck officialdom, was more than they could bear. Many were weeping, men included.

Purity took her place by one of the tables. She watched every face that came before her, on the lookout for a familiar countenance. She was soon caught up in the tide of human tragedy that flowed past her.

There was a French girl. Purity spoke with her. Aged nineteen, she had been a captive for two years. She still wore the shameful harem garb in which she had delighted the senses of her lord and master on the night before the holocaust. She carried in her arms a dark-skinned baby, obviously greatly loved by her. Back home in Périgord she had been an aspirant nun, a novice of the Ursuline Order.

There was a Sicilian girl. Purity was told that she had been captured while on passage from Palermo to Ragusa, a voyage made necessary by the appalling state of the island's roads in winter. She had been on her way to marry her childhood sweetheart when the Corsairs came out of the mist. Her mother and father, her grandparents, and her older brothers who accompanied her had been slaughtered out of hand. She had been a captive plaything for seven months. By the tally of those seven months, she was visibly with child. Purity's informant, speaking in fractured French, told how, upon hearing that she was to be freed and returned to her homeland, the girl had attempted to kill herself, and she was likely to try again at the first opportunity.

There was a young man. He spoke fluent French and directed his full attention to Purity. The fussy navy clerk, impatient of delays, demanded that she translate the burden of the man's account, but she ignored him. Through her tears, she listened to his story, simply told, and without any intent of soliciting her sympathy; it simply had to be unburdened. He was Portuguese, and he had served under Wellington's command against the French in the Peninsular war. Upon his discharge, he had married a wonderful girl from his own village in the Algarve and had settled down in the happy anticipation of raising a large family and tending his vineyard till such a time as he handed it over to his many sons. Now he was returning home—a eunuch.

Those who have suffered, and suffered greatly, are able to offer comfort, for what they have to offer rings out with the noble sound of true coin. Purity spoke from her heart, from her immediate experience of suffering. It was little enough, but it may have helped some of those tragic and bewildered people over the first shock of their release.

Nightfall came, and still the long lines of freed slaves continued to come. The sailors built fires on the beach, feeding the flames with charred woodwork from the burned-out habitations fronting the harbor. Over these fires, navy cooks boiled up great caldrons of salt meat: the staple diet of seamen the world over, salt pork or beef of antique origin, so durable that it could be fashioned into items of bric-a-brac, such as snuff boxes, that would take a high polish. With the salt meat went hardtack, a ship's biscuit with the consistency of brick, and riddled with weevils, most of which obligingly left their abode when the biscuit was tapped sharply on a tabletop. In this case, the hardtack was boiled up with the salt meat into a gray stew. Most of the freed slaves, who had had nothing but a bowl of soup since the beginning of the bombardment, ate the stew readily enough. And, outside the glowing circle of firelight, wide-eyed Algerine children looked on hungrily.

Declining an offer of the admiral's cabin, which Pellow sent ashore by messenger, Purity composed herself for sleep upon a boat cloak lent to her by Lieutenant Popkess. This she laid out in the circle of firelight upon the jetty. All around her lay the humped forms of the ex-slaves, men, women, and children, all sleeping in their first night of freedom.

Despite her weariness, Purity was wakeful for hours that night. Lying with her arms pillowed behind her head, staring up at the myriads of stars, she turned over and over in her mind the events of the previous weeks: her capture by Azizza and the cruel flogging that came after; the night she had lain with the tragic Greek boy and cleansed her soul of evil; her strange idyll with Omar Manzur, who had surely loved her; his death, and her meeting with El Diablo; Mark. . . .

Always her thoughts returned to Mark. His beloved face—strong and beautiful, as she would always remember it—was with her, in the forefront of her mind, when she presently drifted away into a profound sleep.

The dawn air struck her skin with a chill touch, and she awoke with a feeling of malaise that manifested itself in a slight headache and an aching of her limbs. Attributing it to the effects of sleeping out of doors and being subjected to the discomforts of the night, she merely dismissed it from her mind and threw herself into the task of succoring the unfortunates all around her.

More slaves had been freed overnight, some of whom had journeyed considerable distances and were weary and starving. They were fed upon the heated-up remains of the previous night's stew, and they rested where they lay.

"Mrs. Landless, ma'am, you are not looking well this morning, you really aren't." The homely, serious face of Lieutenant Popkess turned lugubriously toward her, regarding her with mournful eyes. "I beg you to return to the ship, ma'am, and let the surgeon have a look at you. 'Tis my belief you have a fever, for your cheeks are mightily flushed."

"You are kind, Lieutenant Popkess," said Purity, brushing back a stray lock of blonde hair that had fallen across her cheek, "but I assure you that it is nothing. And how can I abandon you when there is so much to be done?"

"Eight hundred seventy-five people so far," said Popkess, consulting a sheaf of papers that he had with him. "And more are on their way, so I have been informed. I don't know how we shall feed 'em all, let alone find room for them aboard the ships. By heaven, those damned Corsairs have much to answer for, if you will pardon the expression, ma'am."

A straggling line of people was coming out of the town and heading toward the jetty. Idly, Purity noticed that two of them were carrying a litter upon which lay a shrouded figure.

"Yes, they have much to answer for," she repeated. "Tell me, Lieutenant Popkess, have many of the Corsairs been taken prisoner?"

"Only a handful, ma'am," he replied. "And none of 'em are of any quality. Their captains went down with their ships. To give the devils their due, they perished bravely."

"You have no news of a Corsair who called himself El Diablo?" asked Purity. "Or of a woman named Azizza?"

"I have not heard either name spoken, ma'am," he replied. "And no women were taken."

And so, she thought, is El Diablo dead, and Azizza with him? Did they, then, sail out to destruction? The red galley had belonged to El Diablo. It was entirely likely that he and Azizza—his ally and undoubted *inamorata*—had been aboard it during the bombardment and had perished together with Mark. She looked out across the water, chill-looking and gray under the sunless morning sky, to the spot in which the galley had taken its plunge. And she shuddered—not from fever.

"Let's see what we have here," said Popkess, rousing her from her somber reverie. "Spaniols, by the look of 'em."

Purity followed him to the pathetic group of newcomers. They had laid the litter upon the ground. The figure upon it was at first masked from her sight, but as she drew closer, she saw that it was a man who lay there, and that he wore the habit of a monk.

She ran the last few paces, then fell on her knees beside the litter.

"Brother Francisco!" she cried.

The Dominican's eyes flickered open. Clouded

with puzzlement for a moment, recognition slowly dawned in their shadowy depths.

"Madame, it is you," he said weakly. And his hands sought hers, fumblingly. They felt hot and dry to her touch.

Between laughter and tears, she clung to his hands, trying to frame the question that meant her whole life.

"Have no fear, *madame,*" said the monk. "Mark is alive and well."

"Thank heaven!" The burden of empty years fell from her in the instant, and a vista of wonder opened up before her tear-blinded eyes. "Oh, thank heaven!"

"Heaven is indeed greatly to be blessed," said Brother Francisco, "for, though I have the fever only mildly, you can see how low I am laid. Some of the slaves have perished from it. Mark, however, has not been stricken."

"Not only free, but also well," said Purity gratefully. "Whatever have I done in my life to deserve such good fortune? Oh, Brother Francisco, you will not know him six months from now. Oh, how I shall tend and cherish him, make him whole again in mind and body."

"His mind is already mending, *madame,*" said the monk. "You would scarcely believe the change in him since—and I suppose by your influence—we were allowed some rest and fresh air away from those accursed oar benches. Why, when Mark and I parted company—the night I was taken ashore from the red galley—he said farewell and addressed me by name."

She stared down at the flushed, feverish countenance, a new horror mounting in her mind.

"What did you say?"

"I was taken ashore, *madame,*" said the monk, "on the night before the bombardment, at the insistence of the physician. Mark remained aboard. Has he not yet been freed?" The sick eyes looked tired and puzzled. "I do not understand why you are looking at me like that, madame."

One long, drawn-out scream rose to the gray overcast, and a trio of seagulls rose in terror at the sound, soaring away across the harbor.

Then she was running, wild-eyed and uncaring of life, toward the water's edge. Popkess and one of the sailors caught her before she was able to throw herself in, though she screamed to them to let her go, pleading with them, telling them that Mark had died twice in her mind and that she could endure no more.

They managed to restrain her. She lay wrapped in the boat cloak, close by the fire, shivering as with ague. By noon she was very ill with the fever.

Chapter Seven

Her whole world was bounded by the paneled ceiling above her head, as she lay, too sick to move even her head, and most of the time delirious. In her more lucid moments, she was able to comprehend that she was aboard a ship. The pattern of light upon the ceiling was made up of diamond shapes that betokened a leaded glass window. And whenever the ship was brought around upon another tack, the pattern shifted and she was able to follow it with her eyes till it went beyond their scope. And all the time she could hear the creaking of ropes and woodwork, and sometimes the dash of waves against the wooden walls that enclosed her.

Restless, hot, and uncomfortable, she lay through the night and day, tended from time to time by a stout gentleman in a gold-laced coat who took her pulse and shook his head gravely. One day he opened the neck of her shift and placed six leeches on her, three to the upper part of her chest, one in the cleft of her bosom, and one below each breast. This, as he explained to a pale young man who always accompanied him, and whom he addressed as Mr. Surgeon's Mate, was because the lungs of the patient were the palpable seat of the fever, and the removal of the morbid blood from the area of the chest wall was a sovereign specific in such cases. Some days after, the fever not yet having abated, the surgeon applied a small blister to the upper part of her chest by means of a heated silver spoon. This being done, the two of them raised Purity up in their arms and lowered her bare feet into a wooden vat of very hot, almost boiling, water. Her screams were terrible to hear and her agony was very great. Notwithstanding the severity of treatment, she continued in a state of high fever for twenty days, with only slight remissions toward the end of that time.

She was fed daily by a young cabin boy. He was Admiral Pellow's own servant, a decent youth with a sympathetic manner. Every noon he entered and, lifting her up against his broad shoulder, fed her nourishing broth by the spoonful, and with great patience. That, and an occasional sip of navy lime juice, was Purity's only intake throughout the severe part of her illness.

Later, in her more lucid state, when the fever abated for as much as a whole day, she was able to rouse herself to interest and inquire of the ship's whereabouts. They had passed Gibraltar, said the cabin boy, and they were heading straight for Biscay and home. The main part of the fleet was in company, he added. Some of the freed slaves—the Spaniols and Portugueses—had been put off at Gibraltar and Lisbon. Others, the Froggies and Eyetalians, had been taken to Marseilles and Genoa by fast frigates. Purity listened to him with half an ear, soon and easily tired by the effort of concentration. Also, the talk of slaves and journeys seemed to have so little connection with her small world, which was bounded by an eternity of waking and dozing, by idle hours spent staring up at the patch of sunlight on the ceiling. Only one word had the power to quicken her, and that was "home."

Home meant Clumber, and Clumber meant Mark and Chastity.

Mark was dead. She knew that. Even during the worst of the fever, she had been agonizingly aware of the loss. As her condition gradually improved, so did the sense of loss burn deeper into her mind. However, she was going home, and her darling little Chastity would be waiting for her. It was a thought that kept her sane.

On the twenty-third day of her illness, the surgeon took her pulse, listened to her chest, and declared to his assistant that the morbid condition of fever had, thanks to their symptomatic and supportive treatment, been banished from the patient. Purity was permitted to rise and take a bath in the admiral's copper tub. From then on, she sat for a few hours every day in the stern window and watched the gray waters of Biscay slide past. It was on the morning of a day in late September that, warmly wrapped in a boat cloak, she was carried up on deck by a brawny tar to see the shores of the Thames River slide slowly past in the early mist, with herons rising with ungainly grace from the reeds on the Essex shore, and topsail barges plying down to Silvertown and Limehouse.

She was home.

They put her ashore at Wapping Old Steps. The admiral saw her over the side, commented with compassion upon her pallor and thinness, enjoined her to take the greatest care of herself, and brushed aside

her halting, tired attempts to thank him for his many
kindnesses.

Lieutenant Popkess escorted her ashore, where a
hackney coach had been obtained to take her to 17A
Half Moon Street. He handed her into the coach,
then caught her around the waist when she all but
stumbled and fell in her weakness. They drove by way
of Fleet Street and the Strand, where the morning's
traffic was already a sea of bobbing tall hats and the
steaming hides of horses. Purity sat with her eyes
closed, her head back against the rest, half-waking,
half-sleeping.

And they came, at length, to her house in quiet
Mayfair.

A smart society doctor, summoned by Purity's
housekeeper from Wimpole Street, examined the patient and pursed his lips to see the evidence of the
rigorous treatment she had received at the hands of
the navy sawbones. His verdict was quite unequivocal:
one week's complete rest for Mrs. Landless, followed
by a further week confined to the house. And there
was no possibility of her journeying down to Clumber
for at least three weeks. No, Mrs. Landless, it was
quite out of the question. He could not guarantee her
future health if she further weakened her constitution
by traveling the road as far as Wiltshire.

That night Purity lay in bed and wrote a long letter
to Mark's maiden Aunt Julia at Clumber, telling her
that she was safely back in England, but she was the
bearer of the sad and tragic tidings of Mark's death.
She sent a thousand kisses for Chastity, and she said
she would be home in three weeks. Meanwhile, would
Aunt Julia please write to her with all haste and give
news of darling Chastity and Clumber?

The following morning, two letters arrived at 17A

Half Moon Street. The first, delivered by a pair of liveried grooms bearing the prince regent's coat of arms upon their sleeves, was brief almost to the point of extinction:

> St. James's Palace
> Friday, September 27, 1816

Madame,

His Royal Highness enjoins me to proffer his deepest solicitude and sympathy upon your sad loss, which has greatly detracted from his joy over the glory of our arms in the reduction of Algiers. Madame, I remain,

> Your obedient servant,
> Robert Henneck, Knight,
> Assistant Private Secretary

The second letter was brought by a lugubrious manservant in a tall hat, who insisted on waiting for a reply. The letter was from the victor of Waterloo, and it was as brief as that of the regent:

> Apsley House
> Friday, September 27, 1816

Madame,

I should like to have the honor of calling upon you at your earliest convenience. Please indicate a date and time to the bearer. The matter is of the utmost urgency.

> Your servant, Madame,
> Wellington

So eager was she to hear the urgent matter that the
duke wished to communicate to her—it could only
concern Mark, surely!—that Purity, disregarding her
physician's instructions, ordered the duke's manservant to be told that she would be happy to receive
His Grace at four o'clock that very day. She spent
the rest of the morning and afternoon in a state of
nervous excitement. Her head was aching intolerably,
and a recurrence of feverishness was imparting a
most becoming bloom to her satin cheeks when,
dressed in a simple hostess gown, and with her glorious blonde hair plaited in a chignon, she awaited the
arrival of her distinguished guest in the drawing room
on the upper floor. Punctually at four o'clock, a carriage drew up outside, the doorbell was rung, voices
rose from the hall, booted feet ascended the curving
staircase, and as the last chimes of the hour tinkled
thinly from the marble shepherdess clock on her
chimney piece, the great man was announced and entered the room.

"Your servant, Mrs. Landless, ma'am." He came
forward to where she sat, took her proffered hand,
and bowed low over it.

"Your Grace," murmured Purity, "such an honor."

Field Marshal Arthur Wellesley, First Duke of
Wellington, had made Purity's acquaintance on only
one previous occasion, in Spain during the war, and
then only briefly, for all that Mark Landless had been
his aide-de-camp for many years. He was taller than
she remembered him, of high color, and with a
generous mouth and an imperious beak of a nose. He
was dressed simply, in a bottle-green broadcloth coat
and white pantaloons. Fresh from his famous triumph at Waterloo and at the apogee of his military
career, the duke was a mere forty-seven years of
age. Despite grief and illness, Purity, a woman of

passion to her very fingertips, was instantly aware of the force and masculinity that emanated from the man.

"It goes without saying, ma'am." He had a clipped, staccato manner of speaking. "It goes without saying that I am desperately grieved at the news of your husband's death. Indeed, I could not feel more deprived if I had lost a son or a brother. We are all diminished, ma'am, all of us."

"You are very kind, sir," murmured Purity, close to tears. "Please be seated."

The footman brought a silver tray of tea, along with wafer-thin cucumber sandwiches, scones, and buttered muffins. Wellington accepted tea with milk and an inordinate amount of sugar. This he drank in one gulp and then accepted another.

"I will now touch upon the urgent matter to which I briefly referred in my letter," he said. "You will have anticipated that it concerns Colonel Landless."

"I had hoped as much, sir," said Purity. "Tidings of my late husband, tidings of any nature, are of the deepest concern to me."

Wellington nodded, placed his cup and saucer upon the table by his seat, and, rising, walked to the window. His next words—the shocking statement—came as he was gazing gloomily down onto Half Moon Street.

"I have to tell you, ma'am," he said, "that I am, in a sense, responsible for your husband's death."

"Sir!" Purity half-rose, the blood draining from her cheeks.

Wellington turned. "In the sense, ma'am, that he was acting under my orders. It was upon my orders that Colonel Landless went to North Africa."

"But, I don't understand," faltered Purity. "The ex-

pedition to search for early remains . . . Professor
James . . . the Royal Society . . . "

The duke made a brusque gesture of dismissal.
"That was merely a *ruse de guerre,* ma'am, to mask
our true intent. Neither Professor James nor the Royal
Society was in the least interested in early remains.
Poor James, God rest his soul, was an expert on mili-
tary fortifications."

"Military fortifications?" echoed Purity. "Then . . . "

"The departure of your husband and his party to
North Africa, ma'am, was in the nature of a military
operation carried out in conditions of great secrecy
in order to examine the defenses of the Corsair ports,
particularly Algiers, and to advise upon the best means
of attacking them. You are surprised, ma'am?"

Purity smiled; it was a sad, wry smile.

She said, "I confess that I was hurt beyond measure
when my dear husband—so recently reunited with me
after the war, and with a newly adopted child to cherish—should have departed with such haste to dig for
the remains of long-gone civilizations in the desert. I
should have known better. I should have known that
he had gone out of duty."

"Duty performed without hesitation or question,
ma'am," declared the duke, "and carried out with
brilliant success!"

Purity stared at him uncomprehendingly. "But . . .
I thought . . . I was given to understand that he was
captured before his ship ever reached Algiers," she
said.

"Not so, ma'am," replied the duke. "He and James
had landed in Algiers. *Firman* or no *firman,* they had
thoroughly tricked the authorities there into thinking
that they were what they purported to be. They secretly examined the fortifications. James wrote an excellent appreciation of the means by which the port

could be attacked from the sea. And that report was
on its way, by a friendly fishing craft, before they were
captured while sailing *away* from Algiers."

"But, are you saying that the Portuguese ship in
which they were captured had actually been *in*
Algiers?" asked Purity.

The duke nodded. "It was one of the many vessels
that paid the Corsairs for safe conduct through the
Mediterranean," he said. "And yet, for some reason,
the Corsairs came after that ship after it had departed
from their port. They boarded it, slew James out of
hand, I don't doubt, and took your husband captive."

In the long silence that afterward lay between them,
Purity could hear a lavender seller calling her wares
at the far end of the street.

Presently, she said, "They were betrayed!"

"Undoubtedly, ma'am," said the duke. "But by
whom?"

It was then that Purity told him of everything that
had happened to her since setting sail from Gibraltar
in quest of Mark. She omitted only those details which,
by reason of her shame, she could not bring herself
to utter.

"This fellow who called himself The Devil—you say
that he is known to you, ma'am?"

Wellington had listened to her account in silence,
with not so much as a twitch of a muscle in his aristocratic countenance. Characteristically, his first comment was a question that went to the heart of the
matter.

"I was informed that I knew him as well as he knew
me," said Purity.

"And you have no idea as to his identity?"

She shook her head. "None whatsoever."

"Because his face was hidden," said the duke, "and

because he spoke only a few words, which were muffled by reason of the heavy veil. On how many occasions did you meet him, ma'am?"

Purity felt her nether lip begin to flutter, and her hands were trembling.

"Three times," she murmured.

"And what took place on these three occasions, ma'am?"

What took place? Oh, my lord duke, do you imagine I could tell you that, even if I knew? How could you conceive what the genteel Mrs. Mark Landless had done in order to try to save the man she loved? Would you believe that the hostess who so primly pours tea and commends to you a cucumber sandwich had danced naked with a Corsair *reis* and slept with him in the desert sand? Could you begin to imagine what she might have done with El Diablo after she had taken opium?

She said, "At our first meeting, he spoke only briefly, as I have told you. Of our subsequent meetings I have no recollection whatever, for I was drugged on both occasions."

"Drugged!" exclaimed the duke.

"Drugged," said Purity.

"I see," said the duke, who clearly did not. He thought for a few moments, then said, "It is clear, from what you have told me, that this El Diablo and his female accomplice, this Az——"

"Azizza," supplied Purity.

"I am obliged to you, ma'am. This Azizza knew— or guessed—the true nature of your husband's expedition, and captured him, though fortunately not before he and poor James had successfully performed their task. Furthermore, as you have pointed out, they had prior knowledge of your own approach to Algiers, for the Turkish consul in Gibraltar had been alerted to send them news of your arrival there. It smacks, ma'am, of a conspiracy, yes, a conspiracy. And you have no idea, not the slightest notion or suspicion, of this fellow's identity?"

"Sir, I have not," said Purity in complete truth.

"Do you think he still lives, and the woman, also?"

Purity drew in a deep breath to steady herself, then said, "The galley in which my husband perished belonged to El Diablo. Some at the palace said that he and Azizza were in Algiers at the time of the bombardment, and it is not unlikely that they were aboard their ships. Yes, I think it probable that they may have perished. I can only say . . . " She broke off.

"Yes, ma'am?"

"I can only say that I hope both of them have met the fate they richly deserve!" She made the statement with vehemence, and she instantly received the impression that it had not been well received by the duke, who was looking at her askance, one well-bred eyebrow raised. Good God! He thought her vengeful utterance had been "unladylike"!

"Do you really?" he asked mildly. "Do you, now, ma'am?"

"Sir, you cannot imagine the horror and degradation that those two, along with their fellow Corsairs, visited upon their helpless victims!" cried Purity. "Unless you have witnessed it with your own eyes, you can only hear of it from the lips of another. And I have neither the talent to describe, nor the wish to offend your ears with, the things I have seen. Add to all that, sir"—she bowed her head, and a tear fell upon her hand—"add to all that the fact that they brought about the death of the only man I have loved, or will ever love, in the whole world."

Wellington let a few moments pass, then cleared his

throat and said, "I have seen war, ma'am, and what you have spoken of, what you have hinted at, is not war—it is an abomination. You are right to wish them dead. In the phrase of our national poet, it is a consummation devoutly to be wished. If you thought you detected disapproval in my glance, you were mistaken, ma'am. I was merely registering surprise that you should be so sanguine as to suppose that a pair of such thoroughgoing rogues would perish so easily. In my experience, the greater the rogue, the more tenaciously he clings to survival. And I include Napoleon Bonaparte amongst that company," he concluded dryly.

"You think they may still be alive?" asked Purity.

The Duke of Wellington looked down at his well-shod feet, seeming to admire the gleaming, highly honed half-boots to which he had given his name.

"I have always said, ma'am, that all the business of war, and, indeed, all the business of life, is to endeavor to find out what you don't know from what you do. We know that we have broken the power of the Corsairs in Algiers. Whether the Corsairs' power will be revived depends largely upon the survival of such leaders as El Diablo and Azizza. Till I have evidence of their deaths, I shall assume that, sooner or later, we shall have to go back into Algiers again with fire and sword."

Purity shuddered. "If I thought they had survived," she whispered, "if I thought that I should ever come face to face with either of them again, I could never rest easily while I lived."

"That I can well understand, ma'am," said the victor of Waterloo. And Purity knew that, though in her shame she had concealed much from him, the duke, with his great wisdom and insight, had comprehended the unspoken.

Shortly after Wellington's departure, the footman who came to clear away the tea tray found his mistress in a state of collapse. The physician was sent for, and upon being told that Purity had not only risen from her bed but had received a visitor (and *such* a visitor!), he was so incensed that he privately instructed the housekeeper to send word to him if her mistress so much as lifted her head from her pillow for a whole week.

The next day the feverishness died down. Too weak to protest, Purity allowed herself to be fed and cared for by others. A week passed, enlivened only by a letter from Aunt Julia at Clumber. The old lady expressed heartbreak over Mark's death—he had always been her favorite—but she did not unduly dwell upon the tragedy; instead, she diverted the young widow's grief by dashing off three pages of anecdotes concerning little Chastity, who had progressed from the toddling to the walking stage, and her talking was coming on famously. Smiling, tearful, Purity read of the child's escapades with her pony and cart, how they all adored her in the servants' hall, and how she remained quite unspoiled while being doted on by everyone.

Not much had happened at Clumber. A bit of news about Robert Gladwyn: Aunt Julia had met Gladwyn's estate manager while out riding, and the man had informed her that his master was abroad and was not expected back for a month or so. And it had been a good harvest in Wiltshire generally. . . .

Purity's strength improved with rest. Two weeks later she was up and around, fretting to set off back to Clumber. The physician examined her and gave his opinion that her remarkably fine constitution had entirely thrown off the evil effects of the fever. She had regained her lost weight; her figure had returned to its

habitual sleek voluptuousness, as evidenced by the
merest glance at her own nakedness in a pier glass;
her cheeks had recovered their wild rose coloring and
texture.

She was Purity once more.

It was late October and on a day of Indian summer
when she got into the coach that was to take her west-
ward. The servants gathered on the steps of 17A Half
Moon Street and waved farewell to her till the coach
swept out into Piccadilly and headed for the Great
West Road. Purity, snug in a traveling costume of
dark blue with black frogging, with collar, cuffs, and
muff of sable fur, leaned back against the cushions and
savored the passing scene, nursing the coming delight
of being reunited with her child and with the place on
earth where she had known the greatest happiness of
her life, with Mark.

Mark . . .

Somewhere beyond Reading, where the horses had
been changed, she closed her eyes and slipped into the
limbo between waking and sleeping, where images in
the mind can be at their sharpest and most real. And
then she was back in her bedchamber at Clumber,
lying in wait for her husband and lover, her scented
body lightly clad in silk and lace, her skin prickling
with desire and anticipation, and her senses straining
for the first indication of his approach. And then came
the tread on the stair, the footsteps in the passage beyond the door, her shrinking down beneath the silken
sheets, with one eye peering over the top of the
counterpane to see him enter and smile at her. The
pure delight of watching him undress before her, baring his lean, muscled body, his proud maleness . . .

The rattle of the coach wheels roused her from her
reverie. She sat up as they came to a stop in an inn
yard. It was quite dark. She had prudently instructed

her coachman to halt for the night in Newbury so that she could savor the full delight of arriving home in the daylight.

She ate a light supper, drank a small glass of wine, and retired early to a tolerably comfortable room with a four-poster bed. She snuffed out the candle, then closed her eyes and willed the interrupted daydream to return. Blessedly, her grief-stricken mind, eager for solace, embraced the delights of recollection.

Mark was with her, lying at her side.

The hands that were slipping the thin nightshift from her shoulders must surely be his—and not hers. With what loving care he drew aside the lace, exposing her eager breasts to his caressing fingertips, molding them gently in his palms. And that touch, so light, must have been his lips brushing her nipple. Moaning with sweet agony, she willed him to repeat the kiss, over and over again.

Trembling, helpless, her whole body opening like a flower to the summer sun, she felt his hands—they were surely not *her* hands—draw the wisp of silk and lace down to her waist and over her hips. And now the hands were smoothing her belly, and a loving fingertip was gently probing the declivity of her navel. How Mark always delighted in her navel and said it must have been carved by one of the Greek master sculptors of ancient times.

She caught her breath and shuddered with a sudden, sharp rapture as the fingertips quested her thighs. Blinded with bliss, she felt herself being gathered up to the high places where Mark, and only Mark, had the power to transport her, to regions uncharted and unheard of, ever-changing in color, sound, texture, scent, and feeling, peopled with great sounds that dinned in her ears and drowned out her own cries of ecstasy.

And then came the slow, dream-like return to reality: laughing and crying together; drained of passion; languid from a blissful contentment that stretched out in the darkness, unending. . . .

They were through Marlborough and skirting the rolling downlands, where the shadows of passing clouds chased each other across the sheep-clipped grass, and where copses of beech and oak stood sentinel on every hillcrest. The Clumber village church spire came into sight in the valley below. As yet, Long Barrow Hill hid the gates and carriage driveway from view, but the fringe of elm trees that marked its curving edge had been so denuded by the winds of autumn that the eye of faith could discern, through their spidery branches, the weathercock that topped the stable block of the great house.

Mercy! Look who's here! Around the next bend in the dusty road came a dark-clad figure on a slow-moving donkey. His shovel hat was bowed over a book of devotions that he was reading. Let the donkey find his own way! Eager to be home, Purity nevertheless could not find it in her to be so uncivil, so she called to the coachman to halt.

The clergyman's eyes narrowed short-sightedly to see the face that looked out at him from the coach window. He gave a start of surprise.

"Why, it's Mrs. Landless returned home!" he exclaimed. "What a blessing it is to see you, ma'am."

"Reverend Mauleverer, I hope you are well," said Purity.

"Indeed, I am, ma'am," replied the cleric. "Ah, but the sad news of Colonel Landless's passing has laid a blight upon us all. I give you my deepest condolences, ma'am, coupled with those of my flock. I hope you will give your assent to a memorial service that I have planned to hold two weeks from Sunday at three o'clock."

"I should like that very much," said Purity.

He ran a finger along his pale, ascetic lips, as if trying to conjure up words that would not find shape.

Presently, he said, "I think you have suffered greatly, Mrs. Landless—that is to say you carry with you the indefinable air of one who has known much travail."

"I have endured much, Reverend Mauleverer," said Purity simply.

"Endurance is all," he replied.

An awkward silence hung between them. The donkey snuffled and began to rub its head against the coach door. The clergyman fidgeted with his rein, and he seemed relieved when Purity bade him farewell. It had been a most inconclusive encounter.

The tall, wrought-iron gates of Clumber Grange came into sight at the bottom of the hill. Crighton, the gatekeeper, and his wife rushed out of the lodge to greet her, reaching up and touching her hands. The good woman was in tears. She had known Mark as a little boy who had called to see her on a fat Shetland pony, and to whom she had given oatcakes smothered in honey.

The mile-long carriage driveway led to the ornamental bridge over the landscaped lake, with its man-made island set with a bijou temple in the Grecian style, through the deer park, with oak trees that had been mature when Francis Drake had sailed around the world. And then came the sweeping majesty of the great house atop the hill.

"Clumber!" She pronounced the word like an incantation. How many times, and in how many varied circumstances, had she come home to this place! And now she was returning alone, and she would remain alone for all her lifetime.

They had seen her from afar. The small army of servants ran out of every door and flocked to surround her coach. Willing hands lowered the folding steps, strong arms were held out to help her down, and honest smiles and heartfelt tears were all around her.

Purity asked, "Where is Chastity? Where is my darling girl?"

There was a child, as dark as a gipsy girl, in a taffeta frock and button boots, with an ill-fitting straw bonnet topped with a butterfly bow. She gazed up at Purity with the gravity of all childhood and smiled to show two very white teeth set right in the middle.

"Mama!" she piped.

They all wept unashamedly to see the beautiful blonde woman fall on her knees before the child and fold her to her bosom, raining kisses upon her, calling her name over and over again.

"Chastity, my Chastity, how you have grown! I would never have known you. You are so changed. *Ma mignon. Ma chérie.*"

Aunt Julia was the last to arrive, for she was crippled with rheumatism and was too proud, too stubborn, to walk with the aid of a cane.

"Go about your business, all of you!" She dismissed the servants gruffly, then gave Purity one withered cheek to kiss. "You don't look too bad, my gel," she opined. "Come in and have a cup of tea. Nice to have you home."

Bless her, thought Purity. Bless this crotchety old spinster lady with a heart of gold. If I had been greeted in any other way, I would have broken down.

Aunt Julia never stopped talking throughout luncheon and far into the afternoon. She was an encyclope-

dia of opinions about the upbringing of Chastity. The
child was "chesty," and this necessitated a strict
regimen that excluded fatty foods like milk and butter,
which only served to encourage the bronchial condition. Likewise, she must always sleep with the nursery
window tightly closed, because it was well known that
the night air brought on the consumption.

Purity listened with half an ear, smiling across at
Chastity, who, as a great treat, had been allowed to
have luncheon with her elders. Purity interrupted
Aunt Julia only once, to tell her that the Reverend
Mauleverer had proposed to hold a memorial service
for Mark. It was a piece of news that the old woman
greeted with a sniff of contempt, being herself one of
the Norfolk Landlesses, which meant she was non-
conformist and very strictly "chapel."

At five o'clock, as was her custom, the old lady
went for a nap before dinner, leaving Purity with the
news that she would shortly be returning to Norfolk.

Aunt Julia departed home the following week, by
which time Purity had accustomed herself to a way of
existence that enabled her to live through most of the
day without being stricken at every turn by heart-
searing memories of Mark.

The secret, she quickly discovered, was not to run
away from the memories, but to face them squarely.
She and Mark had been accustomed to working in
the fields with the farmhands; then she must continue
to do so, and in the process come to terms with the
ghost that labored at her side. They had always gone
for a stroll together before dinner, in the orangery if
the weather was inclement, along the terrace if it was
fine. Purity resumed the custom alone, not as a slavish
indulgence of sentiment, but because she had always
enjoyed it and continued to do so. On the other

hand, Mark had greatly esteemed well-hung game and had insisted on venison, grouse, partridge, or pheasant in season. She could not abide the flavor of game, so she had it removed from the Clumber cuisine. So it was that, by retaining some of the ways and customs that she had shared with her dead husband, and by abandoning others, yet never ignoring them and blinding herself to their existence, she found herself able to live with memories and not be their slave.

It was a month after her return to Clumber, and two weeks after Mark Landless's memorial service in the parish church (when Purity had been obliged to sit and listen to a two-and-a-half-hour sermon from the Reverend Mauleverer on the totally irrelevant text of the parable of the talents) that The Cousins arrived— uninvited and unannounced.

Arthur Finch-Landless was a first cousin to Mark, the only son of his father's brother. It would have been difficult to imagine two men more unalike. It was said that Arthur favored his mother—the Finch half of the Finch-Landless—which could be taken as a curse upon that lady. Arthur was chinless, foppish, and had never in his life raised a finger to do more than play cards and toy with women's bodies. He stood before the vast open fireplace in the great hall of Clumber, warming his backside and gazing covertly at Purity's bosom, while his mousy, vindictive-looking wife, Alice, appraised Purity's hair, her *maquillage,* and put a price upon her hostess gown and her jewelry. They had with them a thin-faced individual whom Cousin Arthur had introduced as Mr. Shacklock, his lawyer, though why they should be accompanied by their lawyer had not been explained. Mr. Shacklock sat and said nothing.

Purity was busying herself with an embroidery frame, half-listening to Cousin Arthur's drawled pronouncements upon the weather, upon politics, and upon the prince regent's debts. The other half of her mind was directed toward the cousins' seven-year-old child: a stout and sly-looking youth who was presently engaged in amusing himself with Mark Landless's presentation sword, which hung under its late owner's portrait at the end of the hall. He had drawn the beautifully fashioned weapon and was stabbing it into a wooden beam. Soon she could stand it no longer.

"I think little Cyril had better put back the sword before he cuts himself," she said, breaking in on Cousin Arthur's peroration.

"My Cyril is quite capable of taking care of himself," said Alice Finch-Landless sharply. "But if it's your *property* you're worried about . . . "

"Cyril, my dear fellow, I think you should put back the sword," drawled his father with the air of a man who did not expect to be obeyed.

"Shan't!" responded the fruit of his loins, and he took another stab with the weapon.

Purity stole a glance toward the long-cased clock. "Will you be staying for dinner?" she asked. Then she added, with as much conviction as she could bring herself to assemble, "You will be very welcome, of course."

"A thousand regrets, my dear Purity," said Arthur, "but I must be in Bath by noon tomorrow, and we shall have to cover quite a distance tonight."

"Such a short visit," said Purity, relieved, "but it is very welcomed," she added.

"Long enough for the purpose," commented Alice Finch-Landless with a sharp glance toward her husband.

"Quite, quite," responded the latter. He coughed

and looked down at the toes of his highly polished Hessian boots.

Thinking that she had not heard right, Purity raised her eyes from her embroidery.

"Did you say 'long enough for the purpose'?" she asked. "What purpose, pray?"

Alice Finch-Landless drew herself up in her chair, puffed out her vestigial bosom, and, ignoring Purity's question, addressed herself to her husband. "I think we have heard enough of your prattle, Arthur," she said. "May we now get down to business?"

"Er . . . quite so, my dear," responded Arthur. He glanced toward the lawyer. "Be so good as to . . . um . . . do the honors, will you, Shacklock?"

"Yes, Mr. Finch-Landless," said the lawyer, taking a sheaf of papers from a briefcase that stood beside his chair.

"Will someone kindly tell me what is going on?" demanded Purity.

"All in good time, ma'am," said Shacklock, peering at her over the top of his spectacles. "The importance of this visit will speedily become apparent to you when I have quoted to you from various papers I have brought with me. First, a deposition . . . "

"A deposition?" echoed Purity.

"A deposition, ma'am, is a sworn affidavit, which, properly signed and witnessed, will stand the test of law in any court in the land. Such a deposition I have here, and I will now read it to you.

" 'I, Brother Francisco, of the Third Order of the Blessed St. Dominic . . . ' "

"Brother Francisco?" Purity rose to her feet, her embroidery frame skittering across the flagstoned floor. "What business can *you* possibly have had with Brother Francisco?"

The lawyer looked cunning and said, "The business,

ma'am, of obtaining firsthand evidence that will stand
the test of law. I have depositions, also, from Lieutenant Hubert Ryan Popkess, Royal Navy . . . "

"Lieutenant Popkess!" exclaimed Purity.

"And Major Andrew Alastair Gregg, Royal Marine
Artillery," continued Shacklock. "But the evidence of
neither of these officers and gentlemen will stand the
test of law, being only hearsay evidence, you see.
However, they were witnesses to a certain statement
delivered by the said Brother Francisco, upon hearing
which, I repaired to Cadiz and took a sworn affidavit
from the said Brother Francisco."

"You went to Spain to see *him?*" cried Purity. "In
heaven's name, why?"

"I think we would proceed more swiftly if you held
all your questions until the end, after you have heard
what Shacklock has to impart," said Alice Finch-
Landless.

"Quite, quite," agreed her spouse.

"Shut up, Arthur!"

"Yes, m'dear."

Purity resumed her seat, gazing steadily at the lawyer.

"Please continue, Mr. Shacklock," she said evenly.
"I will not interrupt you again."

"I thank you, ma'am." The lawyer cleared his
throat and resumed his reading of the document. Purity listened with growing puzzlement, mixed with
anguish, to hear the stilted and legal-sounding phrase-
ology, so unlike the halting, whispered words she had
heard by the side of the sick man's litter in far-off Algiers.

" 'Upon being taken ashore with the fever at ap-
proximately seven o'clock on the evening of Monday,
August 26, 1816 . . . I can positively state that the
man I knew to be Colonel Mark Landless remained

aboard . . . chained by the wrists to the oar, by the waist to the oar bench, by the ankles to the stretcher or footrest . . . ' "

"Of course Mark is dead!" Purity screamed the words. "I don't need any piece of paper to tell me that! I saw it happen with my own eyes! Why are you torturing me?"

The lawyer looked to Alice Finch-Landless, spread his hands, and smiled in triumph.

"Need more be said?" he commented.

"The matter is cut and dried," said Alice, turning to her spouse. "You have come into your inheritance, Arthur." And, gazing fondly down the hall to her offspring, who was busily testing the edge of the precious sword against a window molding, Alice added, "And likewise my darling Cyril."

"Your *inheritance?*" shouted Purity. "What do you mean—*inheritance?*"

"She doesn't know," said Alice Finch-Landless maliciously.

"Never crossed her mind. I shouldn't wonder," said Cousin Arthur.

"I understand you are a French lady by birth," said Shacklock to the astonished Purity. "Perhaps you are more accustomed to the Continental laws of inheritance. Here, in England, the law is based upon primogeniture—that is to say, the firstborn inherits the whole. Your husband is dead, and the entailed estate passes to the next in line—that is, to my client, Mr. Arthur Finch-Landless."

"It's a pity you never had a child to succeed," said Alice Finch-Landless. "Adopted children don't count under the law, of course."

But Purity only had eyes for Shacklock, who was now gazing at her with something like compassion.

"Not Clumber!" she shouted.

"Every stick and stone," he said. "The contents and appurtenances, without and within. Every messuage and outbuilding. All livestock and garnered harvest. Every acre of land and seed sown within same. Everything."

"Everything!" exclaimed Purity.

"We shall not turn you out into the street, my dear Purity," drawled Cousin Arthur reassuringly, taking her by the soft flesh of her upper arm and drawing close to her so that he could cast a sly glance down her bodice. "You and your dear child are welcome to remain at Clumber for as long as you choose." He licked his already moist lips.

"In the dower house!" added his wife sharply.

The dower house had always been a joke between Purity and Mark. It had not been occupied since the death of his grandmother in the early 1770s. The roof was half gone. Constant dampness, woodworms, and death-watch beetles had consumed most of the interior fabric, and it was the abode of bats, rats, and one particularly noisy owl.

"We . . . we will go and live in the London house," said Purity.

Shacklock pursed his lips and took from his briefcase another document.

"The residence known as number 17A Half Moon Street, Mayfair . . . " he began.

"Not that!" cried Purity. "They can't take that from me! My husband bought that property with his own money!"

"With money from the estate," said the lawyer. "And every penny is entailed."

"Mayfair is very smart," said Alice Finch-Landless to no one in particular. "I shall greatly enjoy having a town house."

"Is there nothing, Mr. Shacklock, nothing in the en-

tire estate that I may any longer call my own?" asked
Purity.

"Such as would be deemed to be your personal possessions, ma'am," said the lawyer, not unkindly. "Any
possession of your late husband that was his by way
of a gift. His immediate personal effects. That is all,
I'm afraid."

"Arthur," said Alice Finch-Landless, "I shall have
this room entirely redecorated in the new Chinese
manner. Arthur, you aren't listening to me!"

No one was listening to her, least of all Purity, who
had drawn herself up, straight-backed, like some
queen of the barbarians. Her head in the air, dry-eyed,
she kicked aside the train of her long hostess gown
and, turning, walked sedately down the hall to where
little Cyril Finch-Landless stood regarding her fool-
ishly. She gently disengaged the child's plump fingers
from the hilt of the sword.

"This sword, Cyril, dear, was presented to Uncle
Mark by the Duke of Wellington in appreciation for
his services in the Peninsular war. Do you see the
inscription on the blade? It says: 'To a valiant brother
in arms, *et cetera, et cetera.*' Can you not yet read,
Cyril? You must see to it that your deficiency is speedily rectified. If you are to inherit Clumber, it will be
necessary to know how many beans make five. Good-
bye, Cyril."

With a sweet smile on her peerless countenance,
keeping her head high, outwardly in perfect control of
her emotions, Purity walked the length of the hall,
graciously inclined her head to her three uninvited
guests and bade them good night, and went out of the
door at the end and closed it behind her.

"By God!" exclaimed Arthur Finch-Landless. "I'll

say one thing for that Froggie filly—she's damned
cool."

His wife turned on him.

"Shut up!" Alice screeched. "I know what's on your
mind, you dirty beast. Don't think I didn't see you
slavering over her boobs!"

"Mama!" wailed little Cyril. "Auntie's took my
sword! Why can't I have my sword?"

"And you can shut up, too!" retorted his mother
wildly, smacking him across the head.

The succession to the mansion and rolling acres
of Clumber Grange had commenced inauspiciously for
the Finch-Landlesses.

Purity's native fortitude saw her through the next
few days. She summoned Mark's old lawyer from
Marlborough. He confirmed the facts of the English
law of entail. Between copious pinches of snuff, he
droned away about estate tail, male tail, and female
tail. He touched upon the donor and the revisioner.
And it all added up to one conclusion: with Mark
dead without an heir, the estate passed to the next in
line, and the next in line was Arthur Finch-Landless.
All that was left for her, Purity, was the grace-and-
favor residence of the dower house, and such financial
provision as the Finch-Landlesses might, in their be-
nevolence, send her way.

"I would rather starve than take a penny from those
people!" cried Purity.

The old lawyer hunched his shoulders and took another pinch of snuff. There was a very slender chance,
he told her, that she could perhaps delay the execution
of the inheritance by challenging the presumption of
her husband's death. The evidence of the Dominican
monk, though strong, might be deemed to be a bit on
the circumstantial side; likewise, her own evidence.

"My husband is dead!" cried Purity. "Even after I saw him die, I had to endure the agony of having my hopes raised and dashed again. I will not go through that a second time. He is dead. Let him rest in peace."

The lawyer blew his nose loudly and put away his papers. He would make a last reading through the relevant passages of the laws, he told her. Perhaps he would consult Williams, K.C., who was very sound on entail. Would Mrs. Landless wish to go to the expense of learned counsel? Perhaps not. It was all very sad, very sad.

She and Chastity would have to leave Clumber!

It was as much her fault as Mark's that the thing had happened. Their wild and passionate courtship, with its background of war and revolution, had not been the emotional climate in which one puts aside money or draws up wills. In the few brief months they had spent together at the war's end and before he had departed for North Africa, they had been lost to everything but their mutual love—that and arranging for the adoption of little Chastity. If only she had thought to prompt him to make some provision, however small.

Steeling her courage against a breakdown, she took stock of her own position. She had a little money invested in the care of a merchant bank in London. That, and her personal jewelry (the Landless family heirlooms: the diamond parure, the pearl-and-emerald tiara, the collar of gold and topaz, not to mention innumerable rings and brooches—all those would, henceforth, be for the adornment of the unbearable Alice Finch-Landless) and Mark's personal belongings (the presentation sword would be the last thing she would sell, she vowed) might add up to enough to keep Chastity and herself in a decent state and provide a small dowry when the girl came of marrying age.

After that, for her, what? A lonely and poverty-stricken old age, with a golden fund of memories to carry to her grave?

That night, alone in her bedchamber, Purity gave way to grief and bitter misery. She walked through fire and plumbed depths of hopelessness from which it seemed there could be no escape. In the darkest hour, when the thought of putting an end to herself had a sweet and beckoning allure, she crept into the nursery and looked down upon the young life that she and Mark had together taken under their charge. She reached down and touched the soft cheek and smoothed back the dark tresses. And she emerged from darkness into light.

She would survive—for Chastity's sake, for the sake of Mark's memory. The decision having been made, nothing that came after was anything nearly as difficult. The ordeal of calling together the staff of the estate and informing them that they were to have a new master—to witness their obvious dismay and sorrow at her leaving—she found to be well within the boundaries of her fortitude. Supervising the packing of her possessions and Mark's (when it came down to it, there was so little: three medium-sized trunks) and of Chastity's few things, she was able to perform dry-eyed. Even the saying of good-byes did not test her as greatly as she had feared. One person alone she would have wished to be with her when the time came to leave Clumber, but Robert Gladwyn was still traveling on the Continent and had received no news of Mark's death or of her return.

The day of their departure arrived, and a hired coach came to take them to London, where Purity had decided to begin the new life. It would have been simplicity itself to have drawn the window blinds, so as not to see Clumber for the last time in all the heart-rending beauty of its winter raiments; she resisted the impulse as being unworthy of the love that she bore for the place where she had known her greatest happiness. Dry-eyed, still, with the child on her lap, she watched to the bitter end, till the great house was out of sight, and till the frozen lake, the mist-wraithed copses, and the wide sweep of frost-carpeted parkland were gone from her forever.

From an advertisement in the *Times,* Purity found a decent apartment on the third floor of a terrace house in Holborn that was kept by a Mrs. Whipple, the widow of a Peninsula veteran. The apartment comprised a large bedroom at the front, a smaller one that would serve admirably as Chastity's nursery, and a sitting room, all furnished. This, with half board of breakfast and supper, was cheap at forty pounds per annum.

Mrs. Whipple had a daughter, Susan, a girl of thirteen, who helped her mother to run the establishment and who was willing to act as an occasional nursemaid for a small amount of money. A mutual adoration was immediately kindled between Chastity and Susan, the latter sweeping the infant into her arms and declaring her to be an angel. The girl bore her precious find down to the kitchen to introduce her to the cook and the kitchen maids, leaving Purity alone to her sad task of unpacking and laying out her few possessions.

An early half-length portrait of Mark, painted in oils and showing him in regimentals as a young captain in the Life Guards, she hung in a vacant space over the sitting room chimney piece, and under it she placed his presentation sword. In her bedroom, she placed more mementos of Mark: his silver-mounted set of brushes and looking glass; crystal bottles of pomade and Macassar oil (how the male-like scents invoked memories of him!); his quilted dressing gown, which she used as a bed cover; his ivory-handled hunting whip.

At seven o'clock, after having supervised Susan in the routine of bathing Chastity and putting her to bed, Purity ate supper in her sitting room. This being done, she wrote a letter to Aunt Julia in Norfolk, briefly outlining her new misfortunes and giving the old woman her present address. She then retired and slept soundly.

So ended the first day of Purity Landless's new life.

The next morning, while setting out to visit her bankers in Threadneedle Street, she encountered on the stairs and made the slight acquaintance of the young woman who lived in the apartment beneath her. She looked to be in her late twenties, of attractive face, dark hair, and excellent figure. Her costume, while of good materials and finish, had a certain flimsiness that ill accorded with a cold winter's morning. Indeed, on second glance, Purity decided that she must be wearing an evening gown beneath her fur-trimmed velvet cloak, and her cheeks, lips, and eyes were quite noticeably painted. They exchanged good mornings, and the other let herself into her apartment. It then occurred to Purity that her neighbor might well have been returning home from a late-night ball. But what ball, or other celebration, could possibly have lasted till nine-thirty the following morning?

She took a carriage to her bankers, down Newgate Street, past the grim prison, where she averted her gaze from the tall, three-legged gallows that stood sentinel by the iron-bound doors—the place of public execution. The same newspaper from which she had learned of Mrs. Whipple's vacant apartment had also carried an account of the public hanging, on the previous day, of three malefactors at Newgate, one of them a female of eighteen. The law was not mocked or flouted in Regency England.

It was some years since Purity had driven into the commercial heart of the great city. Nothing had changed. Outward opulence masked a squalor that lay just behind the marble facades. Crested coaches rattled past gutters where barefoot children scrabbled in the mud for anything of the slightest value. In the financial capital of the civilized world, little girls huddled from the wind in dark alleys and offered their starveling bodies for pence. And the reeking miasma of open drains hung over all.

Threadneedle Street was all tall hats and grave faces, for there was nothing so serious as the amassing of money. A crossing sweeper obliged by pointing to the numbered doorway that housed her bankers, Messrs. Colfax and Reem. A steep flight of stone steps brought her to a set of double doors, the outer pair of which were open for business. She sought in vain for the names of Colfax and Reem. Painted in flowing copperplate on the inside door was the legend: STOKESLEY, JUPP, MEEKER AND MEEKER—MERCHANT BANKERS.

She knocked and went in. A pale young clerk looked up from a ledger behind a rolltop desk and inquired as to her business. When she said that she was seeking the whereabouts of Colfax and Reem's chambers, he looked put out. He laid down his pen, and, bidding Purity to take a seat, he knocked upon an inner door, and receiving an answer, he went in and closed it quietly behind him.

Purity waited, puzzled and not a little uneasy. She did not have long to wait.

"Mr. Jupp will see you, ma'am," said the clerk, reappearing.

Mr. Jupp proved to be a gentleman in his middle years who, presumably for reasons of baldness, affected the type of bag wig that had gone out of fashion thirty years previously. He rose from behind his desk and, waving Purity to a seat, asked her name.

"Not one of the Clumber Grange Landlesses, ma'am?" he inquired. "In the county of Wiltshire?"

"That was my late husband's property, sir," replied Purity.

"I see." Mr. Jupp's eyes avoided hers, and he pretended to busy himself with a ledger that lay on the desk before him. "Ah, touching upon your business with Colfax and Reem, if it be not impertinent, might one ask if you had any pecuniary connection with said firm?"

"I have a small amount of money in their charge, invested, as I understand, in shipping."

"In shipping. Ah, might one further inquire how much is this small amount to which you allude, ma'am?"

"Five hundred pounds."

"Five hundred. Ha!" Mr. Jupp inserted his finger up the side of his wig and scratched his head.

"Sir, why are you asking me these questions?" demanded Purity. "I came here with a simple inquiry. I understood this to be the address of Colfax and Reem, but I now find your firm occupying the chambers. Can you tell me their new address, please?"

Mr. Jupp continued to avoid her eyes, and also to remain evasive.

"Ah, you have not been here before—you did not yourself deposit the money with Colfax and Reem."

Holding her patience in check, Purity said, "No, the money, which I brought back from France at the end of the war, was deposited by my late husband's estate manager."

"And you have a receipt for same, of course?"

"Of course!" Purity's voice took on a note of alarm. "Sir, what is all this about?"

He met her eyes at last.

"Ma'am, I have to tell you," he said, "that the firm of Colfax and Reem, merchant bankers, no longer exists."

Purity stared at him, horrified. "You don't mean . . . ?"

"The end of the war has benefited some," said Mr. Jupp, glancing down at a remarkably fine onyx ring that he wore upon his signet finger, "and has ruined others. Upon cessation of hostilities, Colfax and Reem moved very strongly into shipping. It was an ill-advised move."

Purity could contain herself no longer. Leaping to her feet, she regarded him, arms akimbo.

"Sir, will you tell me where these gentlemen, Colfax and Reem, are to be found?" she demanded.

"There has not been a Reem these twenty years," replied the other. "Colfax resolved his problems, personal and financial, in this very room six months ago —when he put a pistol ball into his head."

"And my money?" She saw the answer in his face.

"The executors wound up the business," he said, "what there was remaining of it. You have lost your money, ma'am. There was not a farthing in the pound for creditors. Sit yourself down, I beg you, ma'am." He rose with concern and called out to his clerk in the outer office: "Giles, be so good as to bring the lady a cup of tea!"

Destroyed—she was destroyed!

With Chastity peacefully asleep in the next room,

Purity sat in candlelight and worked and reworked a
maze of figures that always brought her back to the
same conclusion: the lost five hundred pounds was
the major part of the bridge that should have joined
the present with a time when Chastity would be of
marriageable age—say, eighteen years hence. That
bridge no longer existed.

She worked through the figures again: eighteen
years of rent at their present lodgings came to, say,
seven hundred twenty pounds. Add to that clothing for
them both and Chastity's education at even the most
inexpensive dame's school. There were other items:
one of them might fall ill and require the services of a
physician.

She took stock of her jewelry and other valuables,
which were now her all, the remaining fragments of
the bridge that must span eighteen years. They lay on
the table before her: brooches, rings, a diamond-and-
silver hat pin that was reputed to have belonged to
her mother, Mark's sword (no—not that!)—worth,
all told, about one hundred fifty pounds.

Panic seized her. If Chastity were to fall ill, badly
ill, so that she needed constant and protracted medical care, would Purity be able to bring herself to beg
from the Finch-Landlesses? She thought she would.
And what if she herself fell ill in a like manner, with a
young child to care for? Would she also beg under
those circumstances? It would be more difficult, perhaps impossible.

Long past midnight she arrived at a conclusion:
she must find work, and in the meantime she must
economize.

The first economy was easily effected. She informed Mrs. Whipple the following morning that she
would no longer be requiring breakfast and supper,
though Charity would continue to do so. Also, would

she kindly make the requisite reduction in the rent? When the good woman expressed some surprise, Purity explained that she was taking up employment that would keep her out most of the day, and she went on to ask if Susan would be able to care for Chastity on a permanent basis? This was agreed upon.

That same morning, with nothing but a sip of cold water within her, Purity Landless went out into the wintry streets to seek work. In doing so, she made the last flourish of a complete cycle of events that had brought her through misery to beatific joy, then back to misery.

Bowing her head against the wind that tore down Holborn Street and sent rubbish from the gutter skittering high above the reeking chimney pots, Purity tried to recall how many years had passed since she had been destitute in London and seeking work, as she was doing again now. Was it likely that things had changed much? Was there honest work for women of no experience? She would soon find out.

Before midday she had learned the sad truth that things in the metropolis were, if anything, worse than they had been the last time. The war over and countless men having been discharged from the colors, the labor market was grossly overcrowded. Everywhere she saw signs of it: in the droves of miserable creatures who stood in the streets, their hungry eyes on the constant lookout for a chance to score pence by opening a carriage door, holding a horse, picking up a fallen parcel, directing some prosperous-looking person along his way. And, as the day advanced, she saw the poor whores—the young and the old—huddled against the walls from St. Paul's to Whitehall, importuning passersby in the sheltered colonnades of Mr. John Nash's fine new quarters on Regent Street.

But of work she saw nothing. As a sign of the hard times, most shops and business premises bore a sign on their doors or in their windows: NO VACANCIES, or, NO WORKPEOPLE NEEDED.

Weary from trudging the cold streets and faint with hunger, she went, at nightfall, to a respectable-looking tavern off the Strand, where she grudgingly bought herself a small tankard of beer and a tiny oyster pie. She ate and drank while watching those around her. There were no women working in the place. Men, and most of them ex-soldiers and sailors by their looks, were waiting at tables and behind the counter. One woman only, a poor old thing with calloused hands, was on her knees slowly scrubbing the floor.

That night, before returning home to Chastity, Purity sold her diamond-and-silver hat pin at a jeweler's shop in Fleet Street. The spry fellow who examined the article told her that the diamond was no diamond, but only cut glass. He was probably lying, but she was too dispirited to haggle over the two guineas that he offered her. She cried herself to sleep that night, and for many after that.

The long days dragged by, with no improvement in her situation. Every morning Susan would come up with Chastity's breakfast tray, and Purity would delight in spoon-feeding the little girl, thankful that she was at least still able to provide for the child, not begrudging her one scrap of the food, though she was suffering the pangs of extreme hunger. After she had washed and dressed Chastity, she would carry her down to Susan's care in the kitchen. Then it was out on the depressing rounds of trying to find employment.

One evening, less than a week after, she collapsed and fainted on the staircase upon returning home.

"Sip it down, love. 'Twill do you a world o' good."

She was lying slumped in an armchair, her head supported by cushions. A young woman with frizzed-out hair was stooping over her, but the shadow of the candlelight made it impossible to distinguish her face. There was a cup in her hand and she was holding it to Purity's lips.

"What is it?" whispered Purity, sipping.

"Beef tea, love," said the other. "Very nourishing, it is."

Purity took another sip. She choked on a swallow of spirits.

"There's a drop of gin in it and all," said the woman with a chuckle in her voice. "That'll not do you any harm, either."

She came around the side of the armchair, and Purity saw her profile in the candlelight. It was the young woman from the apartment below.

"I . . . I was taken ill on the stairs," faltered Purity.

"I heard the clatter and came running," said the other. "How long since you had a square meal, love?"

The unexpectedness of the question took Purity unaware. She answered with a transparent prevarication. "I . . . I wasn't very hungry at luncheon."

"Oh, yeah?" Her companion regarded her, hands on hips. She was wearing a peignoir that looked none too clean. Her hair was curled up in rags, and her pleasant, pretty face was scrubbed and free of makeup. "And what, pray, did 'er ladyship have for luncheon yesterday and the day before?" There was no malice in the light note of mockery.

"Not much," murmured Purity, chastened.

"And cheap fare into the bargain, I'll be bound," the woman replied. "Penny pies or a plate of oysters at a street stall—I know the game. Looking for work, love?"

"Yes."

"What's your name?"

"Purity Landless . . . Mrs. Landless—I'm a widow."

"I'm Hortense de Courcy."

"Are you French? *Etes-vous française?*"

Her companion laughed, showing white, even teeth.

"Bless you, no," she said. "That's my professional name. You'd hardly credit it after a war with the Frenchies, but there's nothing that goes down so well in my game as a French name."

Purity forbore from inquiring what Hortense's "game" might be. Instead, she said, "It was very kind of you to take me in. And the beef tea with gin has greatly revived me. Now I must go to my little girl." She went to get up, but she was assailed by weakness and sank back in the chair.

"Rest where you are, Purity," said her new friend. "I have fixed everything. Young Susan is sleeping up in your room and taking care of that little treasure. You shall sleep here for the night, free of all worries."

"But . . . I couldn't trouble you," faltered Purity.

"You'll be no trouble to me, lass," Hortense reassured her. "In half an hour I'll be away, and I'll not be back till morning. I'll accept no arguments. Lie back, and you may watch me getting ready."

So saying, she flashed Purity a bright smile and, seating herself before a looking glass, proceeded to take her hair out of the rags and comb it into a Greek chignon, with corkscrew curls falling becomingly over her ears and cheeks. This done, she applied a copious amount of eye shadow to her eyes and rice powder and rouge to her cheeks. Then, quite unselfconsciously, she shrugged out of her peignoir, revealing herself, save for lavender-colored silk stockings and ribboned garters, to be nude. She was slender, small-breasted, and pink with good health. Purity watched

as Hortense stooped again to the mirror and painted
her lips, and then, with a wink in her companion's
direction, she carefully painted the nipples of her
breasts with the same color.

"I like to be got up to the nines," she offered by
way of explanation, "even where it doesn't show."

Her high-waisted evening gown was hanging on the
back of the door. She put it over her head and wriggled
it over her bosom, then buttoned the bodice, tugging
it down so that the upper slopes of her breasts showed
to their best advantage.

"Well, I'm ready," she declared. "Never wear any
jewelry—not that I own any." She took up the fur-
trimmed velvet cloak in which Purity had first seen
her. "Give me your hand, Purity," she said, "and I'll
help you to the bed, where you may sleep till morning and not be disturbed."

She helped Purity lie down on the coverlet of her
own bed and then covered her with a quilt. Purity
saw her profile briefly as she stooped over the candle
and blew it out. Then she was gone.

Probably due to the unaccustomed gin, Purity slept
soundly till daylight, and she had just essayed to rise
when Hortense let herself in. She looked tired, but in
good spirits. She asked if Purity had slept well, then
proceeded to make them both breakfast of tea and
oatcakes.

"You'll not be going out to look for work today,
Purity, will you?" she asked, her shrewd gray eyes
watchful over the rim of her teacup. "Not on such a
morn as this, with snow falling, not after what happened to you last eve."

Purity assured her she was not. Nor did she stir
from her apartment all that day. She spent the time
enjoying Chastity's company, reading aloud to the
child, playing with her, building with her toy bricks,

and relishing her dark loveliness. At noon a knock on the door announced Hortense, who had brought food for the three of them: hot beef, potatoes done in their jackets, a jug of ale, and a bottle of milk for Chastity. Nor would she accept payment in whole or in part.

After one day's brief idyll, Purity was back in the uncharitable streets the following morning. Fearful of a repetition of her fainting episode, she ate a light breakfast in an inexpensive chophouse before starting the dreary round of looking for employment. In the middle of the afternoon, she came upon a sign in a shop window that read: ASSISTANT WANTED—GOOD WAGES. Her heart leaped. But as she reached out her hand to open the door, the card was removed by a stout tradesman who had the grace to shake his head sadly at her.

Too sick at heart to try further, she went into a jeweler's shop and offered one of her precious, small collection of rings for sale. A haughty assistant informed her that they had secondhand rings aplenty in stock, that there was no money around, and scarcely any call for such merchandise. Defeated, she went back to Holborn Street.

Hortense came out onto the landing when she heard Purity's footsteps on the stairs. She had not yet dressed to go out, and her hair was still in curling rags, her face unpainted. One look at Purity's haunted eyes told her all she needed to know. She took her by the arm and drew her into her apartment and closed the door behind them.

"Love, you'll never find honest work in this city," she said evenly. "There's nothing left for you but to try your hand at my game!"

Chapter Eight

"It's not whoring! I'm no strumpet!"

Hortense turned on Purity, her bosom heaving with passionate indignation, her gray eyes flecked with angry green.

"I . . . I'm sorry, Hortense," said Purity. "I didn't mean to insult you. But, if it isn't whoring, what is it?"

"Well . . . " Faced with the direct question, Hortense's fury faded. She put her forefinger to her cheek and looked pensive, reminding Purity of a schoolgirl who has been asked a riddle beyond her comprehension. "Well, 'tis a matter of pleasuring gentlemen," she declared.

"And what is that, but whoring?" asked Purity mildly. "And where do you go every night to offer this pleasure?"

" 'Tis a gentlemen's club off the Haymarket," said Hortense. "Very high class and respectable, it is. There's gentlemen of title, Lord This and Sir That, who're members. I never did see a gel ill used there."

"And what function do you perform, Hortense?" asked Purity.

"Well, if the gentlemen aren't playing cards, they generally like a gel to talk to," explained Hortense. "They'll buy her a glass of brandy, or maybe take her into the supper room. There's a ballroom set aside for dancing, with a very fine fiddler and a feller whose touch upon the pianoforte is a wonder to hear."

"And what wages are you paid for accompanying these gentlemen at supper or into the ballroom?" asked Purity.

"No wages," replied Hortense. "But a gel may take as much as she pleases, by way of a present, from the gentlemen she pleasures."

"I see," said Purity flatly.

"You see! You see!" Hortense's hot temper flared up again, like a sullen fire assaulted by a bellows' breath. "How much do you really see, my fine lady? Do you see what lies ahead for you in this city? I will tell you. A year of the life you are living now, and you'll not know yourself in a looking glass. Starvation will take its toll. You've seen the women out there in the streets, the women looking for work. Every bit of money they scrape together goes to feed their brats—them or some idle husband. Women like that lose their looks while they're still in their twenties. And their teeth fall out, too. They're bags of bones with sagging breasts before they're thirty. My mother was one such, rest her soul, an aged crone before her time—till despair drove her to throw herself off London Bridge. I was reared in a parish orphanage, my fine lady. While still a child of ten, I took the fancy of the master of the orphanage, who favored me greatly. He saw to it that I was always the one who had the second helpings at the table, and I was never beaten for being disobedient or made to work the treadmill. Oh, but what I was made to do to him in return, in his room, behind a locked door. . . . "

"Hortense!" Purity reached out to embrace the other woman, tears of compassion welling in her eyes. But Hortense pushed her away.

"If you've no thought for your own fate," she said, "have some regard for the fate of that sweet babe upstairs. There's no hope of you getting honest work in this city. You're doomed, and the child along with you."

"Hortense, please!" Purity pressed her hands to her ears to shut out the clamor of her companion's voice.

"Would you condemn that sweet babe to a parish orphanage and mayhap to the care of a pious hypocrite like the one who mauled my young body, whose stinking carcass I was made to pleasure?"

"No!" cried Purity. "Please don't torture me anymore, Hortense!"

Then the other's arms were around her. "I tried you hard, love," said Hortense, "but it had to be done to bring you face to face with the truth of it. Get you away upstairs now. Fetch your prettiest evening gown. Tonight, Purity, you'll have the time of your life, and no harm will be done. You'll mayhap meet a fine gentleman who'll take a fancy to you and press a few guineas into your bodice at the end of the evening. What do you say, then?"

"Well, I . . . "

"Come now, love, why are you afeared? There's no one there who will know you, for everyone, gentlemen and gels alike, wears a mask, and no gel may remove her mask, except at the request of her beau for the night."

"Very well, Hortense," said Purity. "I'll come—just this once, just to try. But if I hate it, I shall never go again."

"Spoken like a true Amazon!" declared Hortense, hugging her. "Now, off with you."

Purity had reached the door when her mentor fired a somewhat alarming parting shot: "One thing, love . . ."

"Yes?"

"You're not one of those women who wear the new-fangled drawers, are you?"

"No, Hortense. Why do you ask?"

Hortense had the grace to blush with embarrassment. "It's just that . . . well, the gentlemen at the club . . . though gentlemen through and through, and many of 'em titled, as I've told you, they are sometimes a bit free with their hands. And it vexes them to find that a gel's wearing drawers."

"I see," said Purity coldly.

By the time she reached her apartment, she had changed her mind about accompanying Hortense, and she had again revised her decision. That her new friend was engaged in something very like whoring, she had no doubt. The men's clubs of the kind that were frequented by young blades about town had a certain notoriety. The worst of them were little better than brothels, but others were conducted with a degree of gentility. The fact that masks were the rule at Hortense's establishment was reassuring, for the Venetian custom of mask-wearing, and the anonymity conferred by the mask, suggested that the club was frequented by men who were careful of their reputations. Such men, in Purity's experience, did not take outrageous liberties with women—even with women whose favors they repaid with "presents." Nevertheless, it was disturbing to hear that the wearing of drawers (a new fashion that had begun as a necessity for dancers of the ballet and that was gaining a small following among women of deeply religious persuasion) was frowned upon at the club.

By the time she had dressed her hair, Purity was quite firm in her resolve to pursue the night's adventure. Susan was giving Chastity her supper down in the kitchen, and she had agreed to sleep in the apartment and look after the child. The evidence of Chastity's presence—toys, wooden-top doll, alphabet book, tiny shoes—served to heighten the misery of the day's events. Hortense was right: it was certain that Purity would never get honest work, and without it she and the child were doomed.

She looked at her reflection. Was there not the slightest hint of crow's-feet at the corners of her eyes? A certain hollowness of the cheeks? A coarsening of the mouth? Were despair, weariness, and a frugal diet already making their marks upon her?

Hastily, she stripped to the skin and examined herself in the looking glass. She had lost a little weight, but her breasts were as firm and upstanding as ever, and her belly, unmarked by childbirth (oh, Mark, if only I had borne you an heir!), was flat and taut.

There was no cause yet to fear the loss of her youth and beauty, the qualities which, she now had to admit to herself, were her sole assets on earth—all that lay between them and starvation.

Among the clothes that she had brought from Clumber was an evening gown of *tissu d'or,* in the current Grecian mode. It was high-waisted, with a tiny, low-cut bodice, short sleeves, and a straight skirt. It was of a material so fine that the most vestigial of undergarments would have shown clearly; indeed, she found it necessary to dispose of her garters and trust to the curve of her calves to hold up her pink silk stockings.

An imp of prudence directed her to wrap a silk scarf around her head in the manner of a turban,

which, apart from being in the height of fashion, would
serve to hide her distinctive blonde hair. It was entirely possible, indeed, probable, that there would be
men at the club whom she had met in society. With
her face masked and her hair concealed, she stood
an excellent chance of retaining her anonymity.

Later, scented, discreetly made up, breathtaking in
the *tissu d'or,* she kissed Chastity good night and
left her in Susan's good care. The young girl watched
her go, wistful envy expressed upon her countenance.
The little child was already asleep.

The club was housed in a quiet area off the Haymarket and bore no outward sign of its true nature.
The two women arrived by hackney cab, and upon
knocking they were instantly admitted by a deferential
lackey in powdered wig and knee breeches who
handed them into the charge of another, who brought
them to a room on the ground floor that was a bustle
of feminine chatter, heady with many scents and dazzling with colors of every description. They were immediately descended upon by a large and handsome
woman of middle age who was dressed in voluminous
black.

"Ah, Hortense, my dear!" she cried. "I knew I
could rely on you tonight. And you have brought a
friend, and such a friend." Her dark, boot-button eyes
took in Purity from head to foot.

"This is Suzanne," said Hortense, giving the name
they had decided upon during the drive from Holborn
Street. "Suzanne, meet Mrs. Lamb."

"How do you do, Suzanne?" said Mrs. Lamb. "I
am sure dear Hortense will have told you the few
and simple rules that all my gels must adhere to. You
must speak to no gentleman unless he first addresses
you. Drunkenness will bar you from ever entering this

establishment again, likewise if any gentleman makes a complaint against you for any reason whatever. Within those limitations, you may do exactly as you please. This is a club for gentlemen, not a nunnery."

Her closing sally brought a ripple of laughter from the women already assembled, some of whom were still in a state of undress or attending to their hair and *maquillage* in front of pier glasses set all around the walls. They were all young, ranging from no more than sixteen to their mid-twenties. And all were beautiful, with good bodies that were amply exposed in the near-scandalous fashion of the day. Purity and Hortense took off their cloaks and reassured themselves in a looking glass, while Purity listened with interest and mounting concern to scraps of conversation all about her.

"Mrs. Lamb ain't letting on, but 'tis my belief that [here the informant whispered a name in her companion's ear] is coming tonight!"

"Ah! You don't say!"

"Did you hear that the Coldstream Guards are back from France?"

"Then it's a fig for your maidenhead if the Honorable Bertie and his subalterns descend upon us!"

"Her maidenhead! She bequeathed that to the nation on hearing the news of Waterloo!"

"Bitch!"

"Mare!"

"Who is to do the *poses plastiques* tonight?"

"He thrust five guineas upon me. He said I reminded him of his mother."

"She was stricken with the pox, and 'tis my opinion she got it from the duke."

"The duke had gotten it from his wife, who got it from [another name was whispered]. Would you believe it?"

"Gels, gels!" Mrs. Lamb bustled back into the room bearing a hatbox full of masks, which she proceeded to distribute to the women present. "Get you to the salon, for the gentlemen will be arriving at any time now."

The masks were of a Venetian style, commonly worn by ladies in London society, called the *moretta*: of black velvet, with a fringe of lace that was drawn across the lower jaw, entirely concealing the face. Purity put hers on, confirming, by a glance in the looking glass, that, together with her turban, the gimmick rendered her completely anonymous. She looked around her, to Hortense, to the others, all assuming their disguises. In the space of moments, the chattering throng of individuals had been turned into a group of mystery figures, scented and pampered womanflesh, lightly clad in silks and satins, redolent of sensual promise.

"This way, Purity," whispered Hortense, taking her companion by the hand and leading her out of the dressing room, across the marble-tiled hall, to a large chamber in the rear of the house. It was a place of shadows and discreet lighting, with wall hangings of deep plum-colored velvet, and furnished with sofas and divans of the same color. Beneath a large looking glass that entirely covered one end wall was a table laden with bottles and decanters of every wine and spirit imaginable, together with an army of glasses standing, rank upon rank, ready for use.

The masked women—there were about twenty of them in all—took their places upon the sofas and divans at the opposite end of the room from the drink table. And they waited.

The gentlemen began to arrive soon after. Upon admission to the club they had been handed masks. These were of the Venetian sort called *larva*, which, made of white velvet and reaching down as far as the upper lip, gave the wearer the appearance of a beak-nosed phantom. One by one, or in twos and threes, they entered the salon and congregated by the drink table, where they were served by liveried lackeys. Purity was intrigued to see that the newcomers pretended to take not the slightest notice of her and her companions, but simply quaffed their drinks and conversed with each other in the loud, assured manner of the English upper class.

" 'Tis my opinion the price of wheat will remain at eighty shillings in our lifetime."

"Mayhap, but there will be rioting in the streets, as there was in 1815."

"A whiff of grapeshot will silence the damned mob."

"Do you know that Prinny had a stone hurled through the window of his carriage on his way back from opening Parliament today?"

"Do I not? I was riding escort with my troop. Fellow, give me more brandy."

Hortense nudged Purity.

"Don't think for one moment that we're being ignored, love," she whispered. "See how they cast sidelong glances in the looking glass at us? We're being sized up, never fear. What was that you said, dear? Like slaves on the block, did you say? Now, that's a fine way to talk." She looked offended.

"It just occurred to me," said Purity contritely.

Yes, the men were watching, and in a sly and underhanded manner. They were darting swift glances into the mirrored surface as they brayed loudly to each other. In such a half-shamefaced manner had the salacious idlers of the Algiers slave market scrutinized the young women offered up for sale; in such a way had she been judged, and was now being judged again.

"You've been noticed, Purity," whispered Hortense, "and by more than one of 'em, which means you'll not have to wait long for your beau, for there'll be some competition to get you. Lawks! Here he comes now. Look to yourself, love."

One of the men had detached himself from the group by the table and was sauntering toward the sofa where Purity sat with her companion. The eyes behind the grotesque white mask glittered for her. He was tall, lean, and stooping—not a young man by any means, for his hair was thickly streaked with gray. He wore the ubiquitous evening tailcoat and pantaloons of scrupulously tailored black and the crisply folded white neckcloth—a costume that was Beau Brummell's prime contribution to the Englishman's sartorial eminence.

He halted in front of her and greeted her with a bow that was too elaborate to be sincere.

"Good evening to you, m'lady," he drawled.

"And to you, sir," replied Purity.

"I'll move away and make room for the gentleman," said Hortense, hastily rising and making herself scarce.

He sat down beside her.

"And what do we call you tonight, hmm?" he asked.

"Suzanne," she replied.

"Another Frenchie," he said sneeringly. "Mark you, I detect a quite genuine-sounding Frenchie accent in your speech, little Suzanne."

"I was born, and spent my early years, in France, sir," she replied.

"Were you, now, eh?" His glittering eyes probed at the cleft of her bosom and, below the velvet mask, his tongue emerged to moisten a thin gash of a mouth. "A Frenchie born and bred, eh?"

"Yes, sir," said Purity.

"I have been told that wenches of your country have some confoundedly original notions," he said. Taking from his pocket a golden guinea, he tossed it into the air and caught it in his palm. "I will have a little wager with you, Frenchie."

"And what is that, sir?"

"I'll wager a guinea that you ain't wearin a stitch under that gown."

She took a deep breath. "You have won your wager, sir, and I owe you a guinea."

He laughed, then tucked the coin into her bodice, between her breasts. "It would be a shame to take your money, Frenchie," he declared, "for 'twas obvious at a glance. Tell me some of your original notions. For instance, do you . . . ?"

He leaned forward and, without greatly troubling to lower his voice, uttered into her ear a suggestion that was breath-robbing in its lewdness.

So that was it, she thought. For a man to address a woman so, he would have to regard her as no more than a cheap plaything. And it was for that purpose that they came to Mrs. Lamb's club. The creature at her side—who, without bothering to wait for her reply, was now pouring a stream of obscenities into her ear —was a typical product of the Regency upper class. He was no doubt titled: his signet ring was engraved with a most elaborate crest surmounted by a coronet. His speech was a drawling accent overlaid with an affectation of the way his grooms and jockeys spoke— Eton mixed with the Newmarket racecourse. She had met scores of his type—perhaps even he, himself—in upper-class society. He would not be without his virtues: doubtless brave in war, scrupulously honorable

in his dealings with his equals, kind to horses and
dogs, charitable to the poor of the deserving sort, and
an indulgent father, but a dubious sort of husband.

And the girls he met at places like Mrs. Lamb's—
girls of Hortense's sort, the sort he imagined his present companion to be—were to him no more than toys.

More masked men had come in, a large group of
them in one party, all very young and noisy. By the
sound of them, they had come from some sort of celebration dinner, and it soon became clear that one of
their number was to be married tomorrow morning.
Purity, to shut her mind against the torrent of debauchery that her companion was pouring over her,
directed her attention to the revelers. They were toast-
ing the bridegroom-to-be, a hulking young man with a
riot of golden curls, like a prize bull. They were
commending his past prowess in the boudoirs and
bedchambers of Mayfair and Chelsea, to which scandalous accounts he listened with equanimity. Nor did
he appear put out when they speculated upon his
coming performance in the marriage bed, and all with
the most specific detail as to words and gestures.

Presently, heated up by drink and bawdy talk, the
party looked around them for sport, and they began
to take some interest in the women at the other end of
the room. One of them produced a hunting horn
upon which he commenced to blow the riotous calls
of the chase. Someone shouted "Tally-ho!" and
dragged from one of the sofas a young, dark-haired
lass, declaring her to be a fox, a veritable little vixen
whom they were going to hunt to her death.

It began in high good humor. The girl accepted the
game in good spirits. She was slightly built and nimble
of foot, and she led the whooping "huntsmen" on a
merry chase, weaving around the sofas and divans,
urged on by the excited screams of the other women

and the shrill blasts of the horn. Later, when the men grew hot and weary from trying to catch her, the game took a rougher turn. When one of them managed to seize her by one wrist, he whirled her around and threw her violently toward the wall, against which she struck with sickening force, screaming with shock and pain.

From that moment, good humor was dissipated, and in its place ruled lust of a not very different sort from the bloodlust engendered by a dangerous gallop across hard country after a fleeing fox. When, upon seeing the mad light in their eyes, the girl ducked and ran, one of them tried to snatch her. His hand closed with the shoulder of her gown. A howl of glee went up, and the horn blasted "Gone away!" when the flimsy fabric tore and left the fleeing girl nude to the hips.

The next time they caught her, it was by her flowing black hair. Still holding her, screaming as she was in blind terror, they ripped away the rags of her dress.

"Throw the vixen to the hounds!" shouted one.

"Bring a tablecloth!"

The found a large embroidered tablecloth and rolled the naked, frightened girl in it.

"Toss her! Toss her!"

"No!"

It was Hortense who tried to intervene. She pleaded with them. "Not the tossing, gents, not the tossing! A gel was half-killed by the tossing last year when you dropped her. Now she's crippled and begs her living in the gutter!"

"Step aside, wench!"

They sent Hortense reeling, for they were not to be cheated of their self-indulgence. The screaming bit of a girl was no more than a plaything. Worse, she was a *disposable* plaything, to be handled, mauled, abused, violated, and—as the spirit now moved them—broken,

like one of the discarded nursery toys of their so recent childhood.

"You shall not hurt her!"

They fell back a pace when Purity intervened because of her height, the imperious set of her head, the
flash of the eyes behind the black velvet mask, and
the stunning splendor of her figure. For a moment they
were overawed—but only for a moment. Impressive
though she might be—typical of the sort of woman
whom, by the ethics and mores of their class, they
instantly recognized as a "lady"—her manner must be
a counterfeit of the real thing, mere play-acting. Why,
she was only one of old Mother Lamb's strumpets,
though much better than most.

"By heaven, you're right, wench!" cried one of them.
"Nor shall the little blackie be tossed!"

"Hey! We'll not be cheated out of a tossing!" protested someone. "We caught the little vixen out in the
open, fair and square!"

"Nor shall you. We'll toss this Juno, this proud
beauty with the divine boobs!"

"Yoicks!"

"Tally-ho!"

The raucous horn blared again as they seized Purity and threw her upon the tablecloth that the little
dark girl had hastily vacated during their heated exchanges. Then they gathered it up, with one man holding each corner and four more taking the sides.

"One . . . two . . . three . . . *toss her!*"

A concerted upward jerk ensued, and Purity was
hurled into the air like a rag doll, turning over and
over, finally to return to the extended tablecloth.

"And again! One . . . two . . . "

The next time she rose, screaming, a licentious hand
retained a hold on the hem of her gown, tearing the
skirt from the bodice.

"E-gad! She's a blonde!"

The object of the ancient sport of tossing—an accomplishment nurtured since time immemorial in the ancient educational foundations of England—was so to increase the height of the victim's ascent, and so carefully to contrive it, that he—or, in this case, she—was stunned to unconsciousness by contact with the ceiling. For a victim to be killed, either by being smashed against the ceiling or by missing the table-cloth or blanket and crashing to the floor, was considered unsporting.

Purity, after her initial panic, quietened her screams and addressed herself to the business of staying alive. She postured her hurtling, spinning body so as to avoid striking the ceiling with her head. They had her at the full height. At every toss, some part of her body came in jarring contact with the plasterwork, which she contrived to fend off with her hands and elbows. In every plummeting drop, in which her stomach turned sickeningly, it seemed that she must miss the absurdly small square of colored silk and be dashed against the parquet floor.

"Toss her, toss her!"

Again and again. Up, down, up, down.

Her brain reeled from the vertigo. She lost her sense of balance and, spinning upward and out of control, struck the back of her head against the ceiling. When she fell, it was in the manner of a broken doll —awkwardly. The whooping tormentors shifted position to adjust their catch, fumbled, and missed her. Purity fell squarely upon one of the well-stuffed sofas, narrowly missing a screaming girl who occupied part of it. She rolled onto the floor, more or less unhurt, and clawed her way to her feet, clutching the rags of her gown to her.

It is probable that some of them—the more de-

praved and bloodlusting—might have seized her and
sent her tossing again. But her turban had come unfastened in the fall, and her glory of blonde tresses
was cascading around her bare shoulders. Moreover,
her mask had fallen off, and the arresting loveliness of
her countenance was revealed for all to see.

"By God! What a filly!"

"Look at the mane on her!"

"Damned if I haven't seen her somewhere before!"

Purity's gaze swept around the ring of watching
faces. As her equilibrium returned, a savage fury
burned coldly in her mind. All her aristocratic Latin
blood surged into a wild and all-devouring tidal wave
of passion that had to find a destructive outlet.

"Hey! I know who she is!"

Purity silenced the speaker with one flaring glance.
Then, in a ringing voice, she said, "Once, years ago,
on a previous occasion of suffering the loss of all my
possessions, I was obliged to find work in a common
alehouse. I have to tell you that, amongst the porters
of the Billingsgate fish wharves and common bargees
of the Thames River, I found no worse civility than I
have witnessed here this night."

"Now, see here, whoever you are . . . " someone
began, trying to interrupt her.

"Shut up, Binkie! Let's hear what she's got to say!"
admonished a companion.

Purity tossed her splendid mane, then pulled the
tattered gown more closely around her nakedness.

"Like you, gentlemen, those fish porters and bargees
were coarse of mouth and filthy of mind. Women—
any women—were for them merely objects to be
mauled and mocked. They had no respect for either a
woman's body or for her sensibilities. But there was
this difference—those coarse wretches took what they
wanted with cheerful disregard, but, having pleasured

themselves, they did not then deem it necessary to spoil, to hurt, to destroy!"

They hung their heads at that, and they parted to let her pass as she strode to the door, where she paused and looked back on them all—a half-naked barbarian queen declaring herself.

"As to who I am," she said, "I am doubtless known to some of you as the Honorable Mrs. Landless, widow of Colonel Mark Landless, one time of the Life Guards Cavalry."

Then she was gone from them, leaving an awed silence. Mrs. Lamb was waiting for her in the hallway, and she draped her cloak around her shoulders as deferentially as if she had been in attendance upon a duchess.

There was a hackney carriage passing the corner by the Haymarket. She hailed it and got in. Throughout the journey back to Holborn Street, she sat huddled, trembling with the aftermath of her overwhelming emotions. Reaching Mrs. Whipple's, she was obliged to ask the driver to wait while she collected some money from her apartment, having left her reticule back at the club.

At the top of the stairs, on the third floor, outside her door, stood the tall figure of a man in a top hat and caped coat. He came forward out of the shadows as she approached. She gave a start to see his face presented in a shaft of moonlight from the landing window.

"Robbie!"

"I searched everywhere for you," said Robert Gladwyn, "high and low. It was only when I had the notion of traveling to Norfolk to see Miss Julia Landless that I was able to track you down. Oh, Purity, why did you not send me word of what had happened to you?" He looked around him, at the genteel squalor of the clean but uncarpeted stairs, at the flaking paintwork. "To think that you should have to come to this!"

"Robbie, I'll not accept charity," said Purity, "neither from the Finch-Landlesses, nor from loving friends. I am glad—glad beyond belief—to see you, but . . . "

"I am not offering you charity, my dear," said Robert Gladwyn gravely, his candid eyes fixed upon hers. "I am offering you myself, for what I'm worth—that, and a whole lifetime of devotion to you and to little Chastity."

They were married in the snow, at the little village church of St. Peter's-by-Wymondham, close to Norwich, in the county of Norfolk. Both had rejected the options of either Wiltshire or London in favor of an offer from Aunt Julia to hold the wedding from her rambling old house in windswept Norfolk, and for her sole surviving male relation, Admiral Sir Percy Hobbs, to give Purity away. Moreover, she also provided the loan of her own mother's bridal gown of Brussels lace, in which Mama had been married to one of the most handsome gentleman farmers in East Anglia. The old lady greatly admired Robert, and she heartily approved of Purity's remarrying.

The village church was tiny, and the pot-bellied stove had been stoked overnight so that it threw a red glow over the congregation, though the wintry wind roared from out of the fens beyond the ancient walls. The choir sang and the organ was played. Even Aunt Julia, who was strict "chapel," joined in, though with a sniff of disapproval in the direction of the rector, whom she suspected of being in the pay of the Jesuits.

Purity, her cheeks glowing from the Norfolk air, came down the aisle on the arm of the admiral, and that elderly, retired seadog had put on his full-dress, gold-laced coat, knee breeches and stockings, and had tied his sparse white hair back in a ponytail, in the style of Nelson's old navy.

Robert was waiting for her at the altar rail, and his estate manager, Wainwright, was standing with him as best man. Robert smiled to see Purity, esteem and admiration written large upon his pleasant countenance. She smiled fondly in return, offered him her hand, and was happy to feel his strength close to her. She then turned and blew a kiss to little Chastity, who was sitting on her new nursemaid's lap in the front pew with Aunt Julia.

The rector was not a good speaker. He droned tonelessly through the preliminaries of the service, and Purity's mind wandered to the man by her side. Robert's offer of marriage had been unconditional in the sense that he had made no emotional demands upon her. One chaste kiss upon the cheek had sealed their bargain, and he had not repeated the embrace in the four weeks during the calling of the banns. For her own part, Purity had accepted his offer in complete honesty, telling him that, though she would only love one man in all her life—her dead husband—she esteemed Robert now above all others and would try to be a true and devoted wife.

Tonight they would share a marriage bed at the coach inn at the nearby market town of Wymondham, where, out of consideration for Aunt Julia's straitened domestic arrangements, Robert had secured a suite of rooms for the night.

Tonight, in the dark hours, there would begin another adventure with the passions and the body of a man. Well, for Purity there had been many such—and only one that had lifted her to the realms of supreme ecstasy. It was to be hoped that, however inadequate her own responses were to his passion, she would be able to point Robert toward those blessed realms.

"Purity, wilt thou have this man to be thy wedded husband?"

She then spoke the words that joined them as one. The service drew to a close with an anthem. A dozen shrill treble voices were raised to the ancient rafters while, outside, the white blanket of winter descended upon the earth.

It was all over.

"Mrs. Gladwyn, I think that my office carries with it the perquisite of a kiss," Wainwright said. The first utterance of her new, unaccustomed name confused her for a moment, but she gracefully acceded to the man's request. He was young and rather full of himself, and his eyes were set a bit too close together. The admiral also claimed a kiss; he smelled strongly of mothballs. Then Chastity was rushing to be picked up and embraced. As Purity held the child close to her, she found herself half-laughing, half-crying with something between relief and joy.

"Lace is all well and good for a bride," said Aunt Julia from the front pew in a stage whisper that carried the length of the aisle, "but for a clergyman to have lace trimming on his surplice smacks mightily of popery!"

They held the wedding breakfast in the long hall of Aunt Julia's old barn of a house. Logs the size of strong men blazed and crackled in an open fireplace, in front of which they feasted on roast venison, pheasant and pigeon pies, boar's head, lobster, galantine of veal, larded capon, and ham. Herself a strict abstainer, Aunt Julia had provided numerous temperance beverages in large enamel jugs to be passed around the long refectory table. Her admirable tolerance of other people's inclinations led her also to provide wines and brandies, but, to preserve the proprieties, they were also served, to those who required them, in the anonymous enamel jugs.

Upon Aunt Julia's urging, the admiral rose and delivered a lengthy peroration upon the excellence of the married state in general, the extreme desirability of the present nuptials, and the many virtues of both partners. At the conclusion of his speech, he resumed his seat and then slipped slowly to the floor, having partaken freely from every enamel jug on offer.

The wedding breakfast, which began at one o'clock in the afternoon, was over at five, by which time the night lay over the white fields and thatched rooftops. The wedding party lit flaming torches to cheer the departure of the bride and groom. An old shoe was tied to the axle of the coach, and much rice was flung at the couple. The nursemaid held up Chastity for the two of them to kiss good night. The coachman cracked his whip, and then the vehicle lumbered off through the snow-covered lanes in the direction of the town.

"It went well," said Robert.

Purity reached out her hand in the darkness of the coach interior and took hold of his, squeezing it companionably. They journeyed in silence till the lights of Wymondham came out of the swirling snowflakes ahead, and they presently saw the inn sign and the dark archway of the coach yard.

"Are you tired after a busy day?" asked Robert.

"A little, but not excessively," she replied.

"I will have a nightcap in the taproom before I retire," he said.

"Of course," she said mildly, adding, "but don't be too long."

Their suite of rooms was the pride of the inn. Everything had been arranged with great care and foresight. Their light baggage had been sent on ahead in the care of Aunt Julia's maid, who had unpacked Purity's things in the bedroom and had tactfully left Robert's trunk unopened in the dressing room to make use of as he pleased. There was a cheery fire burning in the grate, and the handles of two warming pans were to be seen protruding from under the sheets of a most commodious tester bed, whose canopy of royal-blue plush was held in the chubby hands of gilded cherubs. It was very obviously a wedding suite, and Purity smiled.

It was not a matter, she told herself, of giving herself to Robert out of any sense of duty. She was truly fond of him, and he was a most attractive and amiable man. She would give herself freely and without hesitation. This resolved, she proceeded to prepare herself for her groom.

There was a nightshift among her wedding attire that had brought a blush to the cheeks of the little *vendeuse* of the smart French haberdasher's in Bond Street when she had held it up to offer it. Of the most diaphanous black silk, it resembled the current Grecian mode, but it was carried to the point where scandal becomes glowing intimacy. Washed, scented, Purity put it on. Her hair she left unbound to spread itself across her pillow in a shower of blonde softness.

Between the snug, warm sheets, she lay and waited for her bridegroom.

An hour passed.

Puzzlement having given way to a real anxiety, she was toying with the notion of getting dressed and going down to look for him in the taproom (some of the male guests from the wedding might have followed after Robert, and they might be importuning him to stay for that never-ending "just one more drink"). Finally, she heard the outer door open and his footfalls crossing and recrossing the dressing room. Next came the thud of his boot upon the floor. Pause, and then the second boot followed. Now he would be undressing, unwinding his neckcloth and folding it carefully, at least she supposed he would fold it carefully, for she had always considered him to be a tidy and methodical, perhaps even a persnickety, man (remarkable, considering the warmth of friendship that had existed between them before their marriage, how little she really *knew* about Robert). Now there was silence. He must soon be undressed. She shrank down lower in the bed and, despite the cosseting warmth, felt her skin prickle.

The silence continued. He was certainly making a most elaborate preparation for bed.

"Robbie!" she called out. "Are you still there?"

No reply.

She waited a while, then said jocularly, "Robbie, my dear, you haven't fallen asleep, I hope!"

He made no reply. She slipped out of bed and went out into the dressing room. His highly polished half-Wellington boots stood side by side, like guardsmen, in their boot trees. His neckcloth, as she had anticipated, lay upon the dressing table, neatly folded. And that was not all. . . .

"Oh, Robbie," she whispered.

There was a small divan, a sort of daybed, in the dressing room, and Robert Gladwyn lay face downward upon it, wearing his shirt, pantaloons, and in his stockinged feet. He was fast asleep and breathing with the force of a man who had swallowed far too much of his favorite spirits. The small room reeked of brandy.

"Robbie, my dear," she murmured, "what a fool I was not to have *realized*. . . . "

His caped coat hung on the back of the door. She spread it carefully over the sleeping form. Then, stooping in her wisp of scandalous black silk, she kissed him gently on the cheek.

Back in the large and lonely bed, she lay a long time and stared up at the reflection of lazy flames flickering on the blackened oak ceiling.

How little, indeed, she knew of the man she had married. Who would have thought that a man so outwardly commonplace and ordinary in manner should have turned out to be so perceptive? He had seen through her own shallowness, her own lack of sensibility. And she was ashamed.

She had resolved to give herself to him. How condescending of her! She had blithely assumed that he— who had never done more prior to their wedding day than present her with a chaste kiss on the occasion of their engagement—would force his attentions upon her on their wedding night and demand his nuptial rights, and she had dutifully awaited his importunity. How gracious of her. How unutterably priggish!

No such man as that was he—to demand what was not freely given . . . no, nor given eagerly and without reservation. A man such as that has his pride, plus a sense of honor toward a weak and helpless woman.

So be it. Gradually, in time, and with loving care, she would learn to give herself eagerly and without condescension to the man to whom she had that day vowed to devote the rest of her life. They were both still young. There was plenty of time in which to build upon what they already possessed: a loving friendship. She would indicate to him, in the innumerable ways that lay within a woman's scope, that she welcomed his amorous approaches. Responding, he would begin to woo her, and she would respond in return. The wooing and wedding that had begun on the staircase of a seedy London apartment house would be played again, but to a new and more lively melody, upon well-tuned instruments, in the hands of better-instructed performers.

She relaxed and let herself glide toward slumber, well content with her new resolution. And her last, consoling thought before she drifted away: her bridegroom's honorable feelings toward the woman he had taken into his care were not so powerful that he had not been constrained to drink himself into a stupor before forswearing her bed and company.

They returned to London, to Robert's house on Cheyne Walk, Chelsea, overlooking the tree-lined edge of the river and the pleasant meadows of Battersea on the Surrey shore beyond. It was a narrow-fronted terrace house of extremely elegant proportions, with a tiled hallway leading to a delicate spiral staircase at the end. Smaller than her former town house on Half Moon Street, Purity nevertheless found it to be more to her taste. There was a warmth and homeliness that had been forever absent from austerely aristocratic Mayfair. By comparison, Cheyne Walk was positively countrified, and little Chastity and her nursemaid were able to gather early aconites in the nearby meadows.

As spring colored the walnut trees in their tiny garden, Purity and Robert soberly planned their future life. His interests lay in the running of his considerable estates in England and Ireland, interests that had taken him on the protracted tour of northern Europe and parts of Russia, from which he had returned to hear the tragic news of Purity's bereavement. They would travel together, he told her. She must voyage down the Rhine from the North Sea to the Alps, see the domes and towers of St. Petersburg shimmering in the frozen distance while crossing Lake

Ladoga by sleigh, and gaze upon the awesome sights
of the Norwegian fjords.

No mention had ever been made by either of them
of their wedding night. Upon their arrival at Cheyne
Walk, Robert had blandly shown Purity her delightful
pink-and-white bedchamber overlooking the river.
Then, with the same imperturbable calm, he had
shown her his own room on the floor above.

The spring advanced, and they never shared a bed.
Purity tried hard to carry out her resolution. She
could not have been more attentive to Robert, more
mindful of his needs, or quicker to anticipate every
shift of his mood. His response to her attentions was
always immediate and gratifying. "What would I do
without you, my dear Purity?" and "How did I ever
manage my life before I married you, my dear?" were
remarks that amply demonstrated his feelings for her.
But in matters physical they remained as far apart
as the night on which he had given her the chaste kiss
that sealed their betrothal.

With Robert frequently absent for days at a time,
visiting his estates in Wiltshire and Essex, Purity gave
herself to the task of managing the house, to certain
charitable works in the parish, and, of course, to the
delights of rearing Chastity. Only one echo of her
recent past arrived to stir the placid backwater of
Cheyne Walk, and it came in the form of a note from
Hortense in response to a small gift of money that
Purity had sent to her at Mrs. Whipple's along with
an account of her wedding. The note, brief and poorly
spelled, put her mind at ease on one score:

Dear Purity,

You need not of sent the ten pound. I am grateful for yr kindness. Glad to here the wedding

went wel. I bet my litle Chastity looked lovly.
Give her a kiss for me, do. No need to worry
about the gents at the club blabbing yr name all
over London. Theyd be too ashamed. Mrs.
Lambs has never been the same since that night.
Youd think theyd all taken up religion.

All love from Hortense.

Purity had confided in Robert about her adventure
in Mrs. Lamb's club, expressing fears that the scandalous story would quickly spread throughout London
society to the detriment of his own reputation. He
shrugged it off, saying that he had no interest in what
London society made of his reputation and that every
man present at the club on the occasion of her magnificent tongue-lashing would certainly not wish to tar-
nish his own good name by associating himself with
the scandal. Hortense's note seemed to confirm this
view.

She had earlier confided in Robert about her experiences in Algiers, mentioning El Diablo and
Azizza by name, but shrinking from telling him the
details of the outrages that had been wrought upon
her body. He had listened, had nodded, and had
reached out his hand and laid it comfortingly upon
hers.

And so, comforted and in tranquility, Purity saw
spring go past, and summer came and turned the water meadows of Chelsea and Fulham into waving seas
of buttercups and parsley where fat cattle roamed. If
deprived of the passions of the flesh, she lived in contentment. The wound of her bereavement began to
heal, and, drawing upon the great fund of inner re-
sources that she possessed, she became her old self
again, strong and self-reliant, capable of dealing with
shock and disaster.

Robert seemed to sense the improvement in her. One morning at breakfast together, he told her that it was high time she spread her wings again and saw something of the life beyond the rustic calm of the Chelsea riverside. For a start, he said, he had tickets for the ballet at the Theatre Royal, Drury Lane.

They drove to Drury Lane in their smart new town phaeton, with Robert at the reins and Purity beside him. Their two matched grays high-stepped through the lamplit streets. Reaching the theater and leaving the phaeton in charge of a groom who had gone on ahead, they joined the smartly dressed throng that wended its way up the red-carpeted steps, under the glittering chandeliers, to the great staircase.

Their box was in the first tier, and close to the stage. Upon their entry, monocles were raised on all sides to regard the statuesque beauty with the ravishing figure and the dramatic blonde hair that was drawn up into a chignon and enhanced by a spray of diamonds. Purity took her seat, serenely accepting the fact that her entry had caused a hum of excited interest.

The vast auditorium was filling rapidly, for everyone wanted to be in place to witness the arrival of the prince regent, who was gracing the occasion with his presence. Not that "Prinny" inspired any great affection among the people of London, who knew far too much about his debts, his disastrous marriage, and his love affairs with Mrs. Fitzherbert, Lady Jersey, and others. Purity borrowed Robert's monocle and peered down upon the sea of powdered bosoms and shoulders, uniformed coats, and white cravats. She saw heads with hair curled and pomaded, bewigged, balding, piled high with confections of jewels and feathers. Her glances were returned from all sides, but she saw no one she knew.

A solitary figure in the opposite box caught her attention. The candles within that particular box had not been lit, which in itself was intriguing, because all the other boxes were ablaze with candlelight. Moreover, the solitary occupant was seated well to the rear, shadowed from the lights of the auditorium by a partly drawn curtain. A single hand and arm emerged into the light, resting upon the edge of the box. Clad in a black velvet glove, the slender wrist was banded with three bracelets that shimmered with pinpoints of diamonds.

"Who could she be?" whispered Purity. "The dark lady in the unlit box."

"Clearly, a lady who wants to remain incognito," murmured Robert.

"Mrs. Fitzherbert, perhaps?"

"It could very well be. Not even Prinny would dare to flaunt her with him in the royal box."

Their speculations were cut short by the tapping of the conductor's baton, which was immediately followed by a drum roll. At the opening chords of the national anthem, the entire audience rose to its feet, for the prince regent now stood up in the royal box, flanked by a group of pretty women and distinguished-looking gentlemen. It was Purity's first sight of the prince, who was showing signs of the dissipation that marked his life. The close of the anthem was followed by some desultory clapping, mixed with the distinct sound of booing from the upper tiers. The prince looked displeased and made an angry aside to one of his companions. The orchestra struck up the prim cadences of a minuet. Then the performance began.

The dancers were from the Paris Opéra, and the ballets were in the convention of the previous century, before the holocaust of the French Revolution swept away the tinsel and cardboard splendor of the royal court. Bright in the flickering candlelight, gods and goddesses, nymphs and fauns, and shepherds and shepherdesses mimed and pirouetted to the music of Glück and Mozart. It was as if the guillotine had never been.

Purity enjoyed the spectacle, the costumes, and the sense of times past never to return. She cast a sidelong glance at Robert and was amused to see that his head had fallen forward on his chest. It occurred to her that his motive for obtaining tickets for the night's performance could certainly not have been for his own enjoyment. No lover of the ballet, he. He had arranged the evening purely for her delight, which she considered very typical of the kindly and considerate man she had married.

A clash of cymbals marked the end of the last ballet before the intermission. Robert woke up with a guilty start and met Purity's eyes with a shamefaced grin.

" 'Pon my word!" he exclaimed. "I must have dropped off for an instant. Delightful, wasn't it? Would you care for some refreshment, my dear? I believe there's a buffet in the entrance hall."

They descended the staircase, arm in arm. Many eyes were upon them, the women with envy, the men with desire. There was a press of people at the buffet tables, and Robert left her in a quiet corner by a marble pillar while he went to fetch two glasses of wine. Purity's attention was immediately, and horrifyingly, drawn to a remark delivered by a voice from the other side of the pillar.

A man's voice said, "There goes that damned swine Gladwyn!"

And another voice said, "You'd think he'd leave the country!"

"Or blow his damned brains out!"

Shocked into rigidity, Purity could only stand and stare. The two men were partly hidden by the pillar. They were not looking in her direction, but toward the tall figure approaching the buffet table. Numbly, she observed that they were officers in scarlet regimentals, and of Robert's age. And they seemed unaware of her presence.

What followed was like the playing out of some hideous mime, to which she was the disquietened observer. The two officers continued to eye Robert's back, muttering to each other all the while. When he turned and retraced his steps, a wineglass in each hand, they were still looking at him. It was not till he was nearly abreast of them that—doubtless because the splash of scarlet tunics attracted his eyes—he glanced in their direction. Instantly, his step faltered and his face expressed recognition, and something else. Was it alarm? Purity held her breath, fearful of the outcome of the encounter. It seemed to her that Robert was about to open his mouth and address the two officers. But in that same instant they pointedly turned their backs on him in the classic "cut direct." As a snub, it had all the brutality of a smack across the mouth.

Robert's hand was steady when he handed her a glass of wine, but his eyes were troubled. Nevertheless, he summoned up a smile.

"It is an iced Bordeaux," he said, referring to the wine, "very suitable for a summer's night. Did you find it too unbearably hot in the auditorium?"

"Not unpleasantly so," she murmured, glancing over the rim of the glass to see that the two officers had stalked away without a backward glance.

"Prinny has put on some weight, don't you think?"

"I have never seen him before," she replied. "And I had no idea that he was so fat, almost as fat as he appeared in the Gillray caricatures."

What can it mean? She tried to assemble her racing mind. What are those men to him, or he to them? "That damned swine Gladwyn": How could such a term be applied to the gentle, kindly man whom she had married? She searched the face before her and saw only blandness. And yet, and yet . . . the candid eyes were still clouded by the encounter.

She realized with a start that he was addressing her.

"Purity, my dear, you are miles away." He smiled. "I was saying that two of the gentlemen in Prinny's box are Foreign Secretary Lord Castlereagh and the lord chancellor."

"Indeed?" she said. "I must quiz them after the intermission."

Do I ask him outright? she wondered. "Robbie, who were those two officers who cut you dead just now?" Or, more pointedly: "Why do they think you should either quit the country or blow your brains out?"

"Another glass of wine, dear?"

"No, thank you, Robbie."

She would not ask him now, not in public, for fear of what it might do to him. Later, perhaps, in the privacy of their drawing room in Cheyne Walk, while he was having his nightcap. Yes, that was the way to do it. She would offer her help and sympathy in whatever trouble, past or present, was signified by the behavior of those two officers. She would help him in the same way he had always rendered help and sympathy to her.

"There goes the intermission bell," said Robert.

They joined the throng of people returning to their seats.

When they reached the box, the orchestra was tuning up, and the conductor was glancing anxiously toward the royal box, awaiting the return of the prince regent and his party. Purity fiddled nervously with her fan, her mind still engaged upon the disturbing scene that she had just witnessed. Her gaze was drawn to the darkened box opposite theirs. The solitary woman was still deep in the shadows, with her jeweled hand and arm resting upon the velvet-covered balustrade, the forefinger tap-tapping a staccato rhythm. This slight movement held Purity's attention, and she was still watching when the mysterious occupant shifted her posture and leaned forward slightly, so that the nearest chandelier cast its blaze of candlelight down one side of her face.

Purity caught her breath, snatched at Robert's arm, and clutched it tightly so that he glanced toward her in alarm.

"My dear, what ails you?"

"That woman . . ."

"Which woman, my dear?"

There was no mistaking her. The hair that fell in ringlets upon the magnificently bared shoulders was no longer flame-colored, but as black as a raven's wings. She wore a Paris gown of the same sable hue, scandalously *décolleté*, that bore no resemblance to her habitual barbarous raiment. But the she-cat's eyes that were fixed upon Purity and the sensuous, full-lipped mouth that smiled mockingly across at her were the eyes and the lips of Azizza the Corsair!

The mummers were acting out an obscure classical legend that called for hideous pantomime masks. By some contrivance, the candles along the edge of the stage had been made to throw green light upon the scene, rendering the capering figures as the characters in a nightmare.

Purity was living a nightmare. The figure in the opposite box had retreated back into total darkness, hand and all. But Purity knew—as clearly as if she could see those green cat's eyes—that the woman was still watching her. She continued to cling tightly to Robert's arm. He was offering her whispered reassurances.

"My dear, it can't be her. It's all your imagination. Let me take you home."

"No! I must stay!" snapped Purity. "It *is* her —Azizza!"

The stage lights had turned from green to red, the color of hellfire, the lurid glare of the Casbah under the nightmare bombardment, so that Purity seemed to hear the screams of the tormented and the dying and see the scarlet galley roll over and sink in the shot-flecked water of the harbor.

"Listen, my dear," whispered Robert, "I will go around to her box on the pretext that my wife believes that she may have made her acquaintance in the distant past."

"No!"

"You will see, I promise you, that the lady is a complete stranger. From her proximity to the royal box, I don't doubt that she's one of Prinny's latest prostitutes."

"She is Azizza!" reiterated Purity. *"I know!"*

The nightmare dragged on, dominated in her mind by the shadowed figure opposite her. The nightmare was given a hideous edge of fantasy by the capering, masked figures on the stage below and by the eerie music of flute and tambour. It ended suddenly with a blare of a trumpet and a roll of drums. And then the mummers had taken off their masks and were advancing toward the footlights, hands joined, bowing to the applause.

"In any event," said Robert in her ear, "we may never know now, for the woman has gone."

Purity looked. In a brief moment when her attention had been distracted by the dramatic finale, she—Azizza—had departed. The door at the rear of her box was open, with light streaming in from the corridor beyond.

They stood through the national anthem. The prince regent was scowling, bored. He was a tubby figure in the all-black evening dress that had been dictated by his former friend and arbiter, Brummell, with the star of the Garter glittering on the left breast.

"Come, Purity," murmured Robert, holding her gently by the arm. "You have had an unpleasant shock, and I am going to take you home and give you a nice cup of China tea."

They left the box and joined the slow-moving stream of people. Purity searched every face around her when they reached the head of the stairs, and she won admiring glances from all sides. Monocles were raised to regard her. One smirking buck was so bold as to bow in her direction, but he looked away hastily when he saw that she was accompanied.

"Here comes Prinny," murmured Robert. "We'll see him go down the stairs."

The prince regent of England was more than a little drunk—he all but stumbled on the top step—and would have fallen but for the helping hand of one of his aides. As he passed below them, they were able to look down upon the grossly bloated figure and observe that his rich chestnut hair owed much to the dyer's art and the hot kiss of curling tongs. The stairs were lined on both sides for his passing: the women dropping deep curtsies, the men bowing, and some of them without much enthusiasm. Tottering down unsteadily on his high heels, the prince acknowledged the salutations of his insane father's dutiful subjects with curt nods to the left and right.

"Oh, my God!"

Purity clutched at Robert's arm.

"What is it?" he asked.

"Look! Down there—at the bottom of the stairs!"

She was at the foot of the curved staircase, almost immediately below them, so positioned that her breasts were half-bared above the low bodice of her sable gown. As the prince regent descended toward her, she swept her skirts wide in a deep obeisance. The tubby figure paused, fumbled for the jeweled monocle that hung over the protrusion of his great belly, lifted it to his eye, and regarded the splendid figure prostrated before him: the glitter of diamonds upon jet black; upturned green eyes regarding him sensuously; moist lips; a hint of bared nipple.

" 'Pon my word, Madame Avanti," said His Highness, "you present a delightful picture to the eye. I declared that it is always a pleasure to encounter you. Shall you be in Brighton next week, I wonder?"

The prince's loud and fruity voice boomed quite clearly up the staircase well, and Purity strained her ears to catch the reply. But even the gross figure to whom it was addressed was obliged to stoop in order to hear the murmured words—words that manifestly afforded him some considerable pleasure, for as the royal libertine went on his way, his florid countenance was smilingly cherubic, whereas it had formerly been petulant and sullen.

"There, my dear," said Robert. "Her name is Madame Avanti, and she's well known to Prinny. That's no guarantee of her virtue, I grant you, but it goes a long way toward dismissing the likelihood of her being a woman pirate of the Barbary Coast."

Purity was not listening to him. Her entire attention was upon the woman in black, who, upon the departure of the prince, received the attention of a liveried coachman bearing a full-length cloak of sable fur, which he laid with reverence upon her bare shoulders, then bowed deeply and proceeded to make way for her to the door, shepherding aside the throng of people who might have impeded her passage, so that they fell back in awe and stared at the magnificent creature as she made her dramatic exit.

Upon reaching the door, she paused in the center of the red carpet that reached down to the carriageway, turned, and directed her green-eyed gaze to the top of the staircase—to Purity.

One look—one brief, enigmatic smile—and she was gone.

"That was Azizza!" insisted Purity.

Chapter Nine

Gone was the tranquility of her quiet house in rural Chelsea. Gone was the peace of mind that she had so carefully assembled, piece by piece, with her own fortitude and Robert's unfailing patience. Azizza was in London, perhaps near at hand. Should Purity flee, or should she stay? Was all England large enough to hide from those terrible eyes? And, if to stay, was it not her duty to denounce the self-styled Madame Avanti for what she really was—pirate, enslaver, murderess? How would one go about such a thing? Swear out a warrant before a Bow Street magistrate? She had heard of such a procedure.

To go . . . or to stay? . . .

The roundelay began all over again. It occupied Purity the whole livelong night. In the early hours of dawn, she arose from her tangled bed and went into the nursery to gaze upon the sleeping child, smooth back the dark curls, and place a gentle kiss upon the soft brow.

The house was silent. Down in the kitchen, she

poured herself a glass of lemonade and, opening the glass doors of the conservatory at the rear of the building, went out into the shadowed garden, under the walnut trees. The sky was lit in the east, and birds were stirring in the leaves above her head. From somewhere over the rooftops of the awakening city came the chimes of a steeple bell marking the half hour.

Purity sat down on a wrought-iron garden seat and sipped her lemonade, holding the glass in both hands as a child would, huddled in her nightshift and shawl in the summer dawn, with the terrible speculation teeming in her brain.

Robert had persisted that she was mistaken about the identity of Madame Avanti, basing his belief upon the fact of her encounter with the prince regent. Was it feasible, he argued, that a woman with such a background could come to England and, in so short a space of time, find her way into the royal circle? Why, even Prinny did not pick up his mistresses in the street, and, from his allusion to Brighton, one inferred that Madame Avanti had been a guest at the royal pavilion there. Such an invitation could only be received by someone with the highest social credentials. Where would Azizza obtain such credentials? That had been Robert's argument.

The greater shock had driven out the lesser: Purity had not even remembered to ask Robert about the two officers who had cut him dead and uttered such scathing comments. With hindsight, and judged against the horror of encountering Azizza, the matter seemed to shrink in importance. After all, she told herself, people often wish each other dead for the slightest of reasons. Men quarrel among themselves as readily as do women—more so, from her experience. The incident most likely stemmed from a dispute in some army mess during the war.

Was there a chance, the remotest possibility, that she might be mistaken about Madame Avanti? The question kept returning, and the outcome was always the same: If she was not Azizza, why, then, had the woman tossed that enigmatic backward look when she had swept out of the theater door? Why the carefull contrived manner in which she had first shown herself: the darkened box, the leaning forward into the light, with eyes directed straight toward the woman opposite, for whom the revelation had been contrived?

The woman opposite!

Purity stiffened with the shock of a sudden realization. The half-empty glass fell from her fingers and shattered on the flagstones, showering her bare feet with its contents.

She had to confirm the notion that had come to her from out of nowhere, and it had to be done instantly. Leaping to her feet, she ran into the house, through the conservatory, across the hall, and up the stairs to the top floor to Robert's room.

She tapped on the door and drew forth a mumbled reply that whoever it was at that confounded hour had better come in. He was lighting his bedside candle when she entered. The shutters were still closed and the room was in darkness.

"Purity, it's you!" He sat up in bed and eyed her in surprise. "What's the matter, my dear?"

"Robbie, from where did you get those tickets for the box at Drury Lane?"

He wrinkled his brow, still half-asleep.

"Why, from my club," he said.

"From your club? What do you mean?" Her voice

took on an edge of sharpness, bordering on hysteria. "Who in your club provided you with the tickets?"

He frowned and said, "That's the strange part about it, Purity—I don't know."

"You don't *know?*"

He said, "Well, you see, in the porter's lodge there are pigeonholes, one for each member, with his name written on it. The other day I found in my pigeonhole an envelope containing these tickets for a box at Drury Lane."

"And you don't know who left them there?" She almost shouted the words. "Isn't that rather odd?"

"I . . . I didn't think so at the time," he replied evenly. "They're a very assorted lot, the members of my club: naval and military men, politicians, lawyers, country gentlemen. We even have a few actors. I naturally assumed the tickets had been left there for me by one of the actors of my acquaintance. I've no taste for the ballet, but seeing that you are French by birth, and that the company was from the Paris Opéra . . . " His eyes widened. "Purity, you don't think . . . "

"The box was immediately opposite hers," said Purity. "It was all very cleverly arranged. She even knew about your club. Don't you see, Robbie? She wanted to show me that she was alive, and here in London. She wanted to savor the perverse, twisted pleasure of seeing the horror written on my face and in my eyes!"

Robert comforted her as best as he was able to. He even persuaded her later to put on one of her pretty flowered peignoirs and join him for breakfast in the conservatory, since he was leaving that morning for the East Anglia estate and would not be returning for a week. They sat facing each other in the early sunlight, Purity silent and obsessed by a thousand fears, Robert voluble and full of strategems. She must do

nothing about the so-called Mrs. Avanti, he told her.
That might be indiscreet, perhaps even dangerous.
When he returned next week, he would set in motion
the most exhaustive inquiries concerning the woman:
investigate her background down to the most minute
detail; discover from where she came and when; find
out her source of income; and if there was a Monsieur Avanti, he, too, would be investigated. Robert
had friends in Whitehall and in both Lords and Commons. There was no secret concerning the mysterious
Madame Avanti that could possibly escape his net.

The sound of the doorbell announced that his estate
manager, Wainwright, had arrived with the traveling
coach. It was time for him to leave. They exchanged
chaste kisses on the cheeks, the nearest they ever
came in their marriage to physical intimacy. She saw
him to the door and watched him get into the coach
beside Wainwright, who doffed his hat and wished her
a good morning. She reflected how strange it was that,
for all the estate manager's civility, she had never
liked the man from the beginning.

She watched the coach draw out of sight around the
bend, and then she went back indoors to bathe and
dress. It was while she was occupied with the former
that her lady's maid brought into the bathroom a letter
which, she informed her mistress, had just been delivered by hand by a liveried coachman.

Purity broke the seal and opened the letter. It was,
in fact, an invitation—and such an invitation!

Madame Avanti
will be at home to ladies
of the Circle for Aid to
Returning Soldiers and Sailors
at 3:30
next Thursday at
199 Sloane Square.

There was never any doubt in Purity's mind that she would accept the challenge—for a challenge it undoubtedly was—and attend the lioness in her den. The Circle for Aid to Returning Soldiers and Sailors was a well-known and perfectly respectable charity organization widely patronized by society ladies, and it offered the mysterious Madame Avanti a bland pretext for inviting Purity to her home without recourse to formal card-leaving or introduction by a third party. Purity supposed that Robert would have advised against going, but Robert was far away in East Anglia and would not be returning till after the weekend.

She dressed herself with scrupulous care that Thursday afternoon, for one goes to more trouble over an enemy than one would dream of taking for a lover's sake. She chose a high-waisted day gown of sprigged muslin, with a short velvet jacket, a bonnet trimmed in the same velvet as the jacket, and a parasol covered in the same muslin as the gown. Her hair she had dressed very simply in a chignon, plus side curls. And she wore the merest hint of eye liner on her upper eyelids. Thus attired, she set off on what she could not bring herself to think of as anything other than an appointment with her destiny.

She was driven to Sloane Square in the town phaeton, and she would have arrived there some minutes before the appointed hour if the traffic had not been held up near the Royal Hospital by a Guards' band and procession. The chimes of the half hour hung in the air as she knocked and was admitted into 199 Sloane Square.

"Your name, ma'am?" The butler was of the lordly sort, who did not soil his fingers with work, but motioned to a footman to take Purity's parasol.

"Mrs. Gladwyn," announced Purity, adding as an afterthought, "The *Honorable* Mrs. Gladwyn." The designation was hers by entitlement from her first marriage, but she seldom used it.

"This way, ma'am." The butler did not unbend one scrap; it would have taken a duchess to ruffle his sepulchral calm.

He preceded her down a long corridor that led to the rear of the large house. Purity was immediately aware—it had struck her upon entering the front door —of the indefinable air of extreme wealth and cultured taste that graced the establishment. It was not merely the priceless Persian rugs laid end to end down the corridor, nor the Italian old masters that lined the walls, nor yet the pieces of exquisite *vertu,* such as Chinese vases, porcelains, glassware, and silver set out in cabinets and upon occasional tables—she was well used to such richness. The house of the mysterious Madame Avanti possessed something extra, and that thing was *style.* And such style was hardly in accordance with the tastes of a barbaric woman pirate.

The butler opened double doors at the end of the corridor.

"The Honorable Mrs. Gladwyn, ma'am," he announced.

There were six women in the room. Purity's eyes went straight to the dark-haired beauty who was sitting immediately opposite the door, with the window behind her and the sunlight casting her face in shadow.

There was a chorus of good afternoons, in which her hostess doubtless joined, but Purity was not able to distinguish hers from the rest, nor did she recognize the characteristic intonation of Azizza's voice.

A large lady in an osprey-feathered bonnet grandly assumed charge of the situation.

"Mrs. Gladwyn, I have been appointed Lady Chairman for this meeting, so it is in order for me to introduce you. Please sit down. Your hostess you know.

On my right is Lady Peter Whatten-Findley; on my
left is the Countess of Lawme. This is Mrs. Maunders,
and this Mrs. Dalgliesh. I am Moira Clonmel. How do
you do?"

"How do you do?" said Purity, taking the proffered
seat, which placed her directly in front of her hostess
at the opposite side of the circle of women. The dark
hair was haloed in light from the window, and the
olive-complexioned face was in deep shadow. It occurred to Purity that the seating arrangements could
have been planned with this in mind.

The Lady Chairman looked around her command-
ingly. Purity knew her by sight: she was Moira,
Duchess of Clonmel, a veritable pillar of high society.
In the days before George III finally went insane, she
had been one of the king's closest friends, which spoke
well for her virtue and respectability. It was not likely
that she was a member of the prince regent's Brighton
set.

"Time is a little pressing," said the duchess, "which
is why we commenced the meeting without you, Mrs.
Gladwyn. We had proceeded to the question of holding a charity ball in aid of the Circle. Estelle Lawme
had offered the use of Lawme House in Piccadilly.
Would you elaborate on that, please, Estelle, dear?"

The Countess of Lawme was a highly complexioned
young woman with a very flat chest. She spoke with
the clipped accents of the hunting field. "Delighted.
The ballroom will hold four hundred at a pinch. We'll
have a buffet in the drawing room and fiddlers in the
minstrel gallery. It would be a spanking fine evening,
I'm sure."

"Thank you, Estelle, dear," said the lady chairman.
"Next items on the agenda: Who'll take charge of the
buffet arrangements? And do you think we dare lower
the tone of the affair by inviting the prince?"

The meeting continued, and Purity speedily lost track of the proceedings. Though half-inarticulate, the upper-class English women around her were used to this kind of thing and dispatched the business in swift order. Tea was brought in by a file of footmen at four o'clock. By four-thirty the charity ball was arranged down to the last detail, and Purity discovered, somewhat to her surprise, that she had agreed to supervise the floral decorations.

Their hostess—the enigmatic figure who sat with her back to the light—had not spoken throughout the entire meeting. Purity had never taken her eyes off the shadowed countenance.

"I must fly," declared the duchess, "for I am due at the palace!"

"Tell me, Duchess," said one of the ladies, "how is His Majesty faring?"

"Very poorly," said the other, rising. "And he scarcely knows anyone. I fear that his time must be near at hand, and we shall see a coronation. His hair and beard are quite white, and they don't shave him, poor, dear man. Don't get up, my dear Madame Avanti, I will see myself out."

"I will share your carriage, Moira," said the countess.

"Please do, my dear."

"Good-bye, Madame Avanti."

"Thank you for tea."

They were drifting out, first crossing over to shake hands with the woman by the window. Purity could not have moved if her life had depended upon it.

One by one they left. The butler looked in and saw his mistress and the beautiful blonde woman facing each other across the wide room. He quietly shut the doors.

They were alone together.

Now Purity saw the impossibility of her task. It was as Robert had said. One simply could not go bald-headed at the outrageous proposition, one could not come straight out and say, "See here, Madame Whatever-You-Call-Yourself, the world may know you for what you claim to be, but I challenge you that you are . . . "

This simply could not be done at 199 Sloane Square —not with a string of Titians, Tintorettos, Duccios, and Tiepolos out there in the corridor, not to mention the lingering scent of the Duchess of Clonmel, who had just left to go see the dying king.

Purity stared against the afternoon sun that blanked out the other woman's face, willing herself to speak, determined above all that she would not retreat, would not rise and go.

Suddenly, the object of her attention made a swift move. She lowered her head in her hands and appeared to go into a paroxysm of coughing—shoulders heaving, chest racked with uncontrollable spasms, rocking back and forth in her chair, and almost falling to the floor. Purity watched her, dismayed, for it seemed to her that the woman was likely to collapse and perish before her very eyes. Presently, the crisis passed. She who called herself Madame Avanti rose to her feet, one hand still pressed to her mouth, and crossed over to a table upon which stood a decanter of red wine, from which she poured herself an ample amount and tossed it down in one swallow. Another paroxysm, of considerably lesser intensity, racked her frame. Purity, who now saw her more clearly away from the glare of the window, was shocked to realize that the other woman had not been coughing at all. . . .

She had been consumed by uncontrollable laughter!

Brimming with tears of mirth, the tawny green eyes met hers. Just as Purity framed the hated name, the other reached up, took hold of a handful of the blue-black tresses, and drew them away to reveal her own flame-red hair underneath.

"Azizza! I knew it was you! I *knew!*"

"You milk-white whore! What a dance I have led you on, haven't I?" said Azizza. "Will you have some wine?"

Purity ignored the question.

"What do you want of me?" she cried. "Why have you come back into my life?"

Azizza poured herself another glass of wine and carried it with swaggering, hip-swinging steps to a sofa on which she lay down, first drawing up her skirts to reveal shapely, stockinged legs to the thigh. She laughed throatily, self-indulgently.

"We left Algiers in a hurry," she said. "Ugo was sent to fetch you, but he never returned. What happened to him? Do you know?"

"I shot him dead," said Purity flatly.

The green eyes flared widely. "Did you, now?" said Azizza. "How very . . . enterprising . . . of you, my dear. Really, you continue to furnish me with surprises."

A carriage rattled past outside, and iron wheels reverberated loudly on the cobbled surface of Sloane Square. Azizza took another swallow of her wine and smiled at Purity over the rim of her glass.

"I repeat," said Purity, "what do you want of me?"

"The question, my dear," countered Azizza, "is, rather: What do *you* want of me?"

"What should I want of you?" blazed Purity, rising in fury. "You brought my husband to his death, you and your foul accomplice! What more can you do to ruin my life?"

Azizza smiled. "I have in mind to take you into my employ," she said.

"*Your* employ?"

"That is so. I have had excellent reports on you, my dear. There was Ugo, who babbled in his incoherent, barbaric way about your delights. My friend—my associate, the one whom you know as El Diablo—spoke very highly of your ardor, your delicious perversity."

"What are you trying to say?" Purity felt her lower lip tremble, and some of her assurance slipped from her.

"I need you for my whore," said Azizza bluntly. "And I possess the means to secure you to my service."

"You are insane!" blazed Purity.

"Not so," replied Azizza. Reaching into her bodice, she took from the cleft of her breasts a piece of folded paper, which she tossed to Purity. It fell onto the carpet between them. "Read that," she said.

After a moment's hesitation, Purity reached down and picked up the paper, unfolded it, and stared down at the brief message written thereon.

There was a date—the previous day's date—written in an elegant Italic script that she knew as well as her own dashing scrawl:

Wednesday, May 14, 1817

Under it was a neat signature that removed the last vestige of doubt from her suddenly assaulted, totally bewildered, mind:

Mark Landless, Colonel, British Army (Retired)

"He's alive? Mark's alive?"

Azizza nodded. She was clearly enjoying herself. She had said nothing, adding not a bit to the slight but totally conclusive evidence that she had offered. She had merely contented herself in watching the effect upon the woman before her.

"He is alive, as you see."

"And well? Tell me that he's well!" pleaded Purity.

"Well enough," said Azizza. "Better than when you last saw him in Algiers."

"But, how?" asked Purity. *"How?"*

"How did he escape the holocaust? Quite simple, my dear. My friend and I were at sea in my *xebec* on the eve of the assault upon the port. We sighted the approaching allied fleet and escaped from it to Algiers. To facilitate our own escape, we did not break the news to the rest of the brotherhood. It would have been useless, you see. The Corsair fleet, Algiers, in fact, everything was clearly doomed, and a general panic would only have impeded our own departure. We had your husband brought ashore from the red galley."

"I saw it sink," whispered Purity awesomely. "In all the months since then, I have carried the sight before my eyes. And to think he was not aboard that galley!"

"You would have been taken, also," continued Azizza. "We dispatched Ugo to fetch you—and with what fatal result you have just informed me. Together, the four of us—myself, El Diablo, your dear husband, and a trusted Bashi-bazouk from my *xebec*—sailed along the coast to Tripoli, from where, by easy stages, we journeyed to England."

"Where is he?" cried Purity. "Bring him to me, or take me to him, and I will do anything—*anything!"*

Azizza smiled her sharp-toothed, cat-like smile.

"Not yet," she said sweetly, "not quite yet, my dear."

"But is he near at hand?" persisted Purity. "In London? In this house, perhaps?"

"Not here," said Azizza, "not in London, but within a day's ride."

"Within a day's ride," echoed Purity, glorying in the wonder of the thought.

Azizza preened herself; she ran her fingers through her flame-red hair, stretched out her shapely legs, and settled herself more comfortably on the sofa.

"Can we now discuss business, my dear?" she purred.

"What business?" retorted Purity.

"The matter of your husband's safe release," said Azizza, "which I anticipate will take place—all things being equal—in, say, December of this year."

"All things being equal?" queried Purity. "What do you mean by that?"

Again came the hateful, cat-like smile.

"Come, come, my dear," she said. "Don't be obtuse. What were we discussing a while back?"

"You want me to play the whore for the release of my husband," said Purity flatly.

"As you have done before," responded the other. "As you did with El Diablo. As, I have no doubt, you did with the wicked and dashing Omar Manzur, alas, no longer with us. Surely, at this juncture, you are not developing scruples?"

"To secure Mark's release," said Purity simply, "I would give my body to any man on earth. I think that to win his freedom I would sell my soul to Satan."

Azizza laughed. "You really must not say things like that, my dear," she said, "or we will presently find ourselves honored by a visitation from the devil himself, with fire and brimstone and a strong reek of hell. No, it will not be necessary to part with your soul, merely to part with your scruples—as on previous occasions."

Silence.

"With whom?" questioned Purity.

"With five men," said Azizza, "not, I hasten to add, all at once."

"Who are these men?"

Azizza ticked off on her fingers. "Lord Peter Whatten-Findley, General Gordon Maunders, Nathan Dalgliesh, M.P., the Earl of Lawme, and the Duke of Clonmel."

Purity stared at her in dawning realization.

"The . . . the husbands of the women who were here this afternoon," she sighed.

"Precisely," said Azizza. "The nonsense over the Circle for Aid to Returning Soldiers and Sailors provides an excellent pretext to conceal our true intent."

"And your true intent is?"

Azizza shook her head. "That is our business, my dear," she said. "Suffice it to say that the Brotherhood of the Corsairs having been broken up, we—that is, El Diablo and I—have perforce been obliged to direct our not inconsiderable talents to other outlets. In the furtherance of our interest, we need the support of rich, powerful, and influential men in this country. The five I have mentioned are just such men."

"And I am to . . . pleasure them . . . to further your interests?" asked Purity."

"And your own interests, my dear," said Azizza. "Don't overlook your own interests."

"When?" asked Purity. "When do I . . . ?"

"You will attend the Duke of Clonmel this evening," said Azizza briskly. "He is a gentleman of somewhat—how to put it?—*advanced* tastes. He maintains a discreet little *pied-à-terre* in Maida Vale, where he regularly entertains young actresses and others of the *demi-monde*. The duchess knows nothing of this arrangement, for she is . . . well, you have met the duchess. My coachman will pick you up at your house in Cheyne Walk at seven o'clock and return you there after your . . . little adventure."

"Very well," said Purity in a small, defeated voice. "And after that?"

"You will receive a message from me from time to time," said Azizza, "as to when your services are required."

"And when I have . . . when I have given myself to these men, you will set Mark free?"

"When you have pleasured those five, and possibly others," said Azizza, "you will have put yourself on good terms with us. In December, or thereabouts, when our enterprise is brought to a satisfactory conclusion, your husband will be released."

"You say there will possibly be others!" cried Purity bitterly. "My God, you will have your pound of flesh, will you not? I am to be your whore, and no mistake!"

The green eyes opened wide. "Do not think for one moment that you are carrying the entire burden of this enterprise, my dear," she said. With a sudden smile, she stroked her rounded thigh. "The list is quite long, and I am sharing the work with you."

"May I go now?" asked Purity.

"You had better. I am expecting a visitor."

"One thing more—one question."

"Ask on. I will not guarantee an answer, nor yet a truthful answer."

"You told me when we first met," said Purity, "that you had lain with my husband. It was a lie, was it not?"

Azizza shrugged. "You saw the state he was in

at Algiers," she said. "His body was still beautiful, but his mind . . . well, my dear, what profit is there in lying with a man who has forgotten all he ever knew about the secrets of pleasuring a woman? I lied to you for my own amusement and to test your temper. Does that answer your question?"

"It does," said Purity. "But I never doubted for one moment that you lied."

She crossed to the door, paused there, and looked back when her name was called by the sensuous figure curled up on the sofa.

"Purity, my dear, I scarcely have to tell you that, if one word of what has passed between us goes beyond these walls, you will never see your husband alive again. Do you understand that?"

"Yes."

"That also precludes you from confiding in the excellent and virtuous Mr. Gladwyn, to whom, as you will now appreciate, you are only joined by the tenuous bonds of bigamy." She laughed.

Purity did not reply to the jibe. She went out, closing the door behind her. Reaching the hallway at the end of the corridor, she saw that the haughty butler had sufficiently unbent as to be taking a gentleman caller's hat and cane. When the latter turned upon hearing her approach, Purity saw a heavily jowled face and a pair of pouched, blue eyes that probed her figure with swift expertise. His chestnut hair was crimped and pomaded, and a diamond star glinted on his left breast pocket. Azizza's long list included the very highest in the land!

A footman brought her parasol for her. She did not at first recognize his swarthy countenance above the snowy-white neckcloth. Only when the fellow grinned to show broken teeth did she place him as the selfsame brute—Ugo's Bashi-bazouk henchman—across whose sweat-streaked back she had been spread, naked, during her flogging.

He was still grinning to himself when he preceded her out into Sloane Square and whistled for her coachman, who had parked the phaeton under the cool shade of the lime trees opposite the house.

Mark was alive—nothing else mattered. Purity unfolded the piece of paper and read again the two brief lines that constituted proof positive, kissed them, and placed the paper carefully in her reticule.

Mark lived. What did it matter that she would have to debase herself to win him back? As Azizza had cynically pointed out, she had done it before and could therefore do it again.

Her only regret was for Robert. It was a cruel irony that Robert, so upright and respectable, should have become a bigamist overnight, a partner to an illicit union which, because of his own sensibility and his consideration for her feelings, had never been consummated. And the tragedy was that, till Mark was safely returned, she would be unable to tell Robert that they were living a lie. She would have to play out the masquerade of their false marriage in the long weeks that lay ahead, while he, who had had to drink himself into a stupor on his wedding night, would be living with a woman who was playing the whore to half of London's high society.

The thought lay heavily upon her conscience and soured the joy of knowing that her husband lived, for the human mind is a fickle instrument, and the watershed that separates laughter and tears has never been charted in all the wisdom of the ages.

It was a small wonder, then, that six o'clock found her in a pent-up and nervous state. It was the hour at which the nursemaid habitually brought little Chastity

to her to enjoy a brief playtime before going to bed.
On this occasion, Purity found that she could not
bring herself to see the child, and she made some
lame excuse to the nursemaid, who looked put out.
No sooner had the girl departed, however, than she
ran after her to the nursery and, taking little Chastity
in her arms, pressed the child to her breast and rained
abandoned kisses upon the soft face and lips, so
that the little one was frightened and burst into heart-
rending sobs. Tearful, stricken, numb with misery,
Purity had to ask the nursemaid to take and comfort
the small, frightened bit of humanity.

It seemed important that she bathe, as if a ritual
cleansing would go some way toward lessening the
defilement to which she was about to submit herself. Once bathed and scented, she took the practical
course of choosing a costume that she could remove,
or have removed, without much difficulty: a simple
day dress with a buttoned-up bodice. She wore it with
nothing underneath. Finally ready, bonneted, para-
soled, with a clean handkerchief tucked into her sleeve,
and her heart in her mouth, she sat in the hallway
and awaited her conveyance.

As a vile joke, Azizza sent the Bashi-bazouk with
her carriage. It was his grinning face that greeted
Purity when the door was opened in answer to his
knock: top-hatted, cockaded, liveried in gray and
black—her former flogging post. He helped her into
the carriage and, climbing up onto the box, sent the
horses off in a brisk pace through the pleasant summer's evening, across Chelsea, the park, and northward to the quiet suburb of Maida Vale, with its
high-walled gardens and discreet villas.

The Duke of Clonmel's *pied-à-terre* was a white-
painted villa in the classical mode, with a bijou pedi-
ment in front and a cupola over all. Her coachman

knocked upon the door and it was answered by a middle-aged woman in black bombazine who had the appearance of a housekeeper. She avoided Purity's eyes and asked her to accompany her upstairs. The interior of the villa smelled of beeswaxed furniture and lavender, and it was scrupulously clean and polished. Purity followed her guide up a carpeted staircase to a room overlooking a sunlit garden. It was a gentleman's dressing room, with an armchair, chest of drawers, pier glass, daybed, and commode. Through a partly open door, she could see a four-poster bed in the room beyond. The woman mumbled something that Purity did not hear, curtsied, and left her. She was not alone for long.

"Is that you, dearie?" a woman's voice called from the bedchamber. It was a young voice, and it carried the unmistakable overtones of one who was a Cockney.

Purity went in. Seated before a looking glass and brushing her mane of long chestnut hair was a girl in a peignoir. She met Purity's reflection in the glass and flashed her a quick, ready smile.

"Oh, 'tis you, is it?" she said. "I heard as how a new lady was expected today. Howdy-do. I'm Cora."

"Hello," said Purity, staring bemusedly at the girl, whose face, though young—she could not have been more than eighteen or nineteen—had the look of worldly experience lightly borne, with a pair of shrewd eyes that looked at Purity down a tip-tilted nose, and a humorous mouth that was surely capable of framing a ripe and ribald expletive. Her body was generously mature; that much was apparent because she was wearing nothing beneath the peignoir, which was unbuttoned. When she got up, she made no attempt to mask her nakedness from the newcomer, but unconcernedly dabbed rice powder over her full breasts, her belly, and thighs.

"Are you in the profession, dearie?" she asked, taking from a jewelry box a tiny black velvet star, which, after a moment's consideration, she licked and stuck on the upper slope of her right breast.

"Profession?" repeated Purity.

"The acting profession, silly. Are you on the boards?" asked her companion. Without waiting for a reply, she added, "Me, I've been at it since I was old enough to be carried onto the stage. Dancing's my line, though I've a good voice. But it's my weakness that holds me back in the profession."

"Weakness?" said Purity. "I'm afraid I don't understand."

" 'Tis gin that's my weakness, dearie," said the girl, "the old mother's ruin. 'Twill be my downfall, like so many others, if my rolls in the hay don't get me first." She picked up a bottle from among her array of paints and powders, placed it to her full lips, and took a long swallow, afterward offering it to her companion.

"No, thank you," said Purity.

"Please yourself," said Cora good-naturedly. "Speaking of a roll in the hay, have you seen his nibs yet?"

"His nibs?"

"Lawks! You're a slow 'un, and no mistake," declared the girl. "Have you been living in a field all your life?" She scratched her dimpled belly. "I mean the duke, silly. Have you seen the duke? Is he ready for his sex games?"

"I'm sorry to seem rather stupid," said Purity, "but I have an appointment with the duke, and . . . "

"For some fun and sex," said Cora, nodding. "That's right, dearie, same as me."

Purity had a very clear sensation of getting further and further out of her league—a feeling that had be-

gun from the moment she had stepped into the room
and set eyes upon this sprightly young Cockney spar-
row. She strove to reach out and make some contact
with reality.

"I think you may have made some mistake . . . er
. . . Cora," she said. "Today is Thursday, and *I* have
an appointment with the duke."

"That's right," responded Cora. "Thursday it is.
Thursday's my day with his nibs, and seven-thirty is
my time. Aren't you going to get undressed?"

"Undressed? But . . . " Purity could do nothing else
but gesture toward the other's nakedness.

Cora seemed about to deliver another exasperated
rebuke, but realization intervened. Her bright, common little face broke into a mischievous grin.

"My, you're in for a surprise, and no mistake," she
said. " 'Tis plain you were never told of the bargain
you've struck. There's no more of in bed with a girl
for his nibs, he's well past all that. Come every Thursday at seven-thirty and he takes his pleasure by sitting and watching me perform with some other wench.
And today 'tis you." With a curiously tender smile, the
girl reached out and offered a light caress to Purity's
bosom. "And from what I see of you, that'll be very
nice."

Shame!

Would Purity ever be able to kiss little Chastity
again? In her shame, could she bring herself to defile
that innocent flesh with lips that had pleasured a brazen young trollop in a bedroom in Maida Vale? Could
her hands—the hands that had caressed Cora's sinful
body—ever again be allowed to stroke the sweet brow
of her adopted child?

Alone in her own bedchamber, restored once more
to her life in rural Cheyne Walk, she regarded herself

nude in a looking glass. She had bathed herself. Bathing would never wash away the shame, nor would perfumes mask the musky odor of the other woman's body that remained imprinted upon her senses.

In her mind, she was back again in that room in Maida Vale, with Cora embracing her, breast to breast, and Cora's mouth doing moist and unbelievable things to hers, with the gray-haired old man watching their every move from a chair set close to the bed, never speaking a word, but occasionally taking a pinch of snuff from a silver box and blowing his nose into a red-spotted handkerchief.

The ceiling above the bed was decorated with plasterwork in the form of nymphs and cherubs, all entwined, voluptuous. She saw it very clearly over Cora's bare shoulder and through the haze of Cora's cascading chestnut hair.

It was important not to look at the old man. When Cora gave a small moan of pleasure and began to rain kisses on Purity's breasts and belly, she was left open to the gaze of those rheumy old eyes, so she turned her head and looked in the other direction, to a picture that hung upon the wall. It depicted two nymphs embracing on a grassy bank in a forest, nude and entwined like Cora and her. She closed her eyes.

The recollection became less distinct. Was it shortly after that, she wondered, that a sense of aloneness crept in on her? Aloneness—with Cora. It was as if the old man was banished, and the two of them, like the nymphs in the picture, were together in the forest wilderness, with warm sunlight upon their bare flesh and the scent of a million wildflowers sweetening the air. Was it then that the sweet pleasure drove itself into her senses, and she was lost to all restraints, all shame? Try as she might, she could not remember the moment when she crossed the barrier between hesitancy and acceptance, between modesty and passion. All she knew was that Cora's hands and Cora's soft lips had beguiled her into a world of sunlight and abandonment, so that she was returning kiss for kiss, caress for caress, so that they rode together into the infinite blueness of the summer sky, flesh to flesh, shouting their joy to each other.

Nothing else mattered. When it was all over, when they had slaked their mutual passion and lay, breasts heaving, still entwined, the old man got up and shuffled to the door without so much as a backward glance at the two nude women upon the bed, and she had been able to watch his departure without shame. He had not intruded upon the secret world to which she had journeyed with the Cockney girl. Likewise, when she was dressed and ready to leave, when Cora laughed and planted a hearty, hoydenish kiss upon her cheek, she was able to meet the other's eyes, for the fires of their passion had burned out, and come next Thursday at seven-thirty Cora would be journeying to ecstasy with another woman upon the selfsame bed, and every Thursday thereafter. Let a week go by, or less, and she would have forgotten Purity, with the beautiful, soft blonde hair.

But she, Purity, would never forget. She watched her reflection in the mirror, watched her hand explore her own body from neck to thighs, slowly, caressingly, as Cora's hand had explored. And that was her shame: not that she had allowed herself to be pleasured by another woman for the delectation of a perverted old aristocrat, and not that she had allowed herself to be seduced, for all flesh is weak—but that, to her shame, she had found a unique gratification in Cora's arms, a once-and-for-all-time of an unrepeatable rapture.

Robert returned on the following Monday. Purity had spent the weekend trying to compose herself to receive him. She had made up a most elaborate network of lies and half-truths to account for her doings during his absence; they all flew from her mind, to be replaced by a helpless panic, when his tall figure bounded up the steps to the front door and he greeted her with his familiar, quirky grin.

"Hello, my dear," he said, kissing her cheek. "Have you been busy while I've been away?"

"Quite . . . quite busy," she faltered, avoiding his gaze and looking over his shoulder. Wainwright was lifting baggage down from the traveling coach. He paused and raised his hat when he saw her gaze upon him.

"By the way, I asked Wainwright to join us for luncheon," said Robert. "Will that be all right, my dear?"

"Of course, Robbie," she murmured.

He followed her into the drawing room. She pressed her hands together till the knuckles showed white. Her face in the looking glass over the mantelpiece looked pale and strained, and surely he must notice her state. Now was the time when she must begin the string of fabrications she had contrived, for to delay would be to betray her deception. Truth, unlike falsehood, comes tumbling out, and it is easy and pleasant to communicate.

She must begin immediately—now.

Blessedly, he provided her with an opening. "Have you given any more thought to the mysterious Madame Avanti, my dear?"

"Why, yes," she said. "I was just about to tell you. Would you believe, just after you left, that I received this?" And she showed him Azizza's invitation.

He glanced at it and exclaimed. When he looked

up, she had directed her gaze to the looking glass and was patting her chignon in place with hands that were visibly trembling.

"You went to this meeting, Purity?"

"Yes."

"And?"

She took a deep breath and said, "Robbie, you were right. I was entirely mistaken. Madame Avanti bears a superficial resemblance to Azizza, that's all." She laughed; surely he noticed the false note in the laugh. "Azizza was quite uncivilized, a barbarian. Madame Avanti is cultured, with a most remarkable collection of paintings and *objets d'art.*"

He beamed at her, head on one side, admiringly. "Now, I'm very glad to hear that," he said.

The entry of Wainwright interrupted their conversation, and he and Robert discussed matters relating to the East Anglian estates till luncheon. Purity, grateful for the respite from her lying, was content to sit and watch the two men. Wainwright was holding forth volubly, his whole attention upon Robert, notwithstanding which, Purity's intuition told her that his words and gestures, the way he held his head, and the way he smiled were all directed to her alone. The young estate manager was good looking in a pink-cheeked, boyish sort of way, with a head of crisp brown curls that made her think of Hugo Sheriffs, the former captain of the *Minerva.* Why, he even crinkled the corners of his rather close-set eyes when he smiled, and he positively preened himself. Handsome, and he knows it, she thought. At that moment, the butler entered to announce luncheon.

She sat between the two men, willing them to keep up their conversation and spare her the necessity for more deceits. It was not to be. At the conclusion of the soup and fish course, Robert reintroduced the topic she dreaded.

"A very odd thing happened, Wainwright," he said. "My wife recently experienced a most alarming case of mistaken identity."

"Indeed, sir," said Wainwright, looking straight at Purity and treating her to a boyish smile. "I trust that the incident brought you no embarrassment, ma'am."

"Indeed, it could very well have done so, could it not, my dear?" said Robert. "You see, Wainwright, the person my wife had in mind was a lady of very dubious, not to say appalling, reputation, whereas the lady in question turns out to be a person of impregnable virtue, and a member of the Circle for Aid to Returning Soldiers and Sailors."

"What more impeccable credential than that, sir?" smirked Wainwright.

Turning to Purity, Robert said, "By the way, my dear, shall you regularly be attending Madame Avanti's meetings of the Circle?"

Wainwright looked up sharply from his plate. "Avanti, sir?" he asked. "Did I hear right? Was that Avanti you said—Madame Avanti? I beg your pardon for interrupting you."

"That is so," said Robert. "Do you know the lady?"

Wainwright's eyes were directed to Purity, who felt a cold finger of dread course slowly down the length of her spine. What was he thinking? Surely there was something very curious about the way he was looking at her—curious and . . . dangerous?

"I have heard of Madame Avanti," said Wainwright, "but, of course, I have not had the pleasure of meeting the lady." He looked very hard at Purity. "I do not aspire to the elevated social circles in which she moves," he concluded.

He *knows,* thought Purity, horrified. For someone

with the ears to hear, there was a note of sarcasm in
the last remark. And if he doesn't know that she is
Azizza, he has heard something about Madame Avanti
that makes him dangerous to me—here and now.

"Is there a Monsieur Avanti, my dear?" asked
Robert.

"I . . . " She faltered, seeing Wainwright's eyes
narrow in her direction. "Do you know, I really have
no idea," she concluded lamely.

"Do you think we should invite her to dinner?"
asked Robert. "And her spouse—if any?"

"No!"

The vehemence of her reply made both men stare
at her in surprise. Wainwright gave a discreet cough
and readdressed himself to his plate. Robert smiled.

"But I thought you must have got on famously together, you two," he said, "since you have decided to
remain in her Circle. By the way, my dear, when do
you go again?"

"I . . . I don't know," said Purity. She was trembling
so noticeably that she was obliged to put down her
fork and hide her hands on her lap. "She . . . she will
send a message when the next meeting is to take place.
And she will also provide a carriage to pick me up
and bring me back here." Purity delivered the last
statement in a breathless rush, then looked down at
her hands.

"That's very civil of her," said Robert. "Yet, despite which, you don't wish to cultivate her friendship
socially? And you have so few friends, my dear. I'm
surprised that . . . "

*"I don't like her, do you hear? Why do you keep
badgering me? Why can't you leave me alone?"*

The hasty words were past her lips before she could
put a rein upon her emotions. Robert's candid eyes
filled with sudden concern. Wainwright was watching

her, but with what expression she did not dare to find out.

"I'm so sorry, my dear," said Robert mildly. "I promise you I had no intention of badgering you."

"I . . . I didn't mean that," she said. "It's just . . . well . . . I don't particularly take to Madame Avanti as a person, though I greatly approve of her good work for the Circle. And it's for that reason that I shall continue to attend the meetings."

"If I may interpose an observation, sir," said Wainwright. He was looking directly at Purity as he spoke. "I can appreciate Mrs. Gladwyn's sentiments, for I have heard that the lady in question is a somewhat— how shall I say?—domineering sort of lady. But my informants, those who have met her, attest that Madame Avanti's labors for the Circle for Aid to Returning Soldiers and Sailors are an inspiration to London society." He smiled winningly at Purity, who realized to her alarm that she was staring at him with all the fascinated horror of a rabbit confronted by a weasel. "And, ma'am, on a point of information, there *is* a Monsieur Avanti, though he resides at the mansion in Sloane Square but infrequently."

Robert shrugged, opined that there was no accounting for folks, and signaled the attending footman to refill their wineglasses.

Purity, feeling that her emotions had been taken out, stripped, and flogged, took refuge—and silence —in Wainwright's placating pronouncement. The conceited young man had provided a smooth explanation that had plastered over the inconsistencies of her lies and half-truths. He had also let slip what, for her, was a most disquieting piece of information: the fact that Azizza, the raven-haired beauty who reigned at 199 Sloane Square, who was "a domineering sort of lady," and whose charitable labors were "an inspiration to London society," was supposed to be married to a man who resided there "infrequently."

Like a cat approaching an unfamiliar saucer of cream, slowly and with infinite caution, she allowed herself to speculate upon the probable identity of the infrequent "Monsieur Avanti," and she could only conclude that it was he, and not the former and semi-barbarian woman Corsair, whose impeccable taste had furnished the mansion in Sloane Square.

The inescapable conclusion: as "Madame Avanti" was an alias for Azizza, so the pseudonym of "Monsieur Avanti" served as a concealment—somewhat like the dark blue winding cloth veil of the desert Tuaregs —for the sinister and elusive creature to whom, under the influence of opium and with what depravity she could not begin to imagine, she had given herself on two occasions in far-off Algiers.

Purity lived in awful dread of Azizza's next summons. Robert departed for Wiltshire that same evening, and the following morning she was shocked to sudden awareness at the sight of a sealed piece of folded paper lying upon the breakfast tray that her maid delivered to her in bed. The girl informed her that it had been delivered by a liveried coachman. Prudently waiting till the maid's footfalls had died away down the corridor outside her room, Purity gingerly took up the note and opened it. The message within was brief and to the point of explicit brutality:

> The carriage will pick you up
> at nine o'clock tonight. Be
> ready. You will pleasure Lord
> Peter Whatten-Findley.

As on the first occasion, she speedily progressed, in her tormented mind, from firm resolve to total panic. Her day was spent stalking around the house and garden; in making the most elaborate excuses for not having luncheon in the nursery with little Chastity, a custom she had adopted at times when Robert was absent; in bathing herself not once, but twice; in trying on every suitable, and many a totally unsuitable, garment in her wardrobe; in picking her way through a solitary dinner at seven o'clock, pushing food around her plate and finally drinking two large glasses of brandy to steady her nerves. At eight o'clock, when the butler announced the arrival of Madame Azizza's carriage, she was dressed in virginal white, with a bonnet trimmed with swansdown, plus a white feather boa. She was also more drunk than she had been for many a year.

She saw the Bashi-bazouk's grin in the light of the footman's torch and the winking carriage lamps. She was past caring. He drove her straight along the riverbank to Westminster, under an awning of a full moon and the Milky Way. The night breeze cooled her brow and imparted a lightness of spirit that was in no way connected with the brandy she had imbibed. Alighting from the carriage in a discreet mews behind Smith Square, she was conducted to what—did she but know it—was a house of assignation, rented by the day or by the week by men-about-town for the entertainment of the *demi-monde,* with a staff of servants whose silence was a marketable commodity, a supply of rich provender, and a cellar of fine wines. Purity was admitted by a bewigged flunky and ushered into a candlelit drawing room where not one, but two young men were drinking, smoking, and playing cards.

"Ma'am, we have been waiting for you."

The speaker rose from his seat at the card table.

She knew him to be Lord Peter Whatten-Findley, heir
to a marquisate and one of the prince regent's Brighton
set. Purity also knew him as the husband of the
pale and articulate young woman whom she had seen,
but not spoken to, at the Circle meeting. Lord Peter
was also pale, and foppishly handsome, with sensual,
brooding eyes. His portrait, painted by the prince regent's protégé, Sir Thomas Lawrence, had been the
scandal of the season, since it depicted the dissolute
young aristocrat nude, save for a fortuitously positioned sword and buckler. The portrait was entitled:
Lord Peter Whatten-Findley as Mars, God of War,
and it was a top seller in every print shop in the king-
dom. It was from the prints that Purity recognized
him.

"Good evening," she said demurely.

"Allow me, ma'am, to present . . . well, a friend,"
said Lord Peter, indicating his companion. "Let us address him as Mr. Arthur."

"Ma'am, I deem it an honor." The companion rose
and implanted a kiss upon her proffered hand. Drawl-
ingly aristocratic, like the other, his florid face had
the same porcine look that she had discerned in the
prince regent. He—the friend, "Mr. Arthur"—was
reeking of brandy and was none too steady on his
feet.

"Will you have a drink, ma'am?" asked Lord Peter.

"I thank you, sir, yes," murmured Purity. What
does it matter, she thought, if I do not know whether
I'm my head or my heels? I wish to God I had
some of poor Nancy's opium draft. Not the two of
them, please, not the two of them together. . . .

He poured her a shot-glass of liquor, and they both
toasted her, eyeing her covertly over the rims of their
glasses, their eyes probing her wonderful hair, her figure, and her moist lips.

"Do you play cards, ma'am?" asked he who was to be addressed as Mr. Arthur. "Whist, perhaps, or *quinze?*"

"I have played *quinze,*" replied Purity, "but not recently."

"Quinze, I think, is very smart," observed Lord Peter.

"Exceedingly smart," said Mr. Arthur, stifling a belch.

Lord Peter shuffled the cards and winked at his friend—a communication that was not lost to Purity.

"May I propose a game of chance?" he drawled. "I am of the opinion that one should not over-tax one's intelligence after a heavy dinner. My dear Arthur, I will stake you on the turn of a card. Aces high, and, shall we say, a hundred guineas?"

Mr. Arthur's reply came pat: "Zounds! I will raise the stake, Peter, for I'm no pinch-penny."

"That you are not, Arthur, that you are not," declared his friend. "What is your stake?"

"Against your hundred guineas," said Mr. Arthur, with a sly, sidelong glance at Purity, "I will stake a thing of inestimable beauty. I will stake . . . the lady's bonnet."

Purity's fingers tensed on the brandy glass.

"By jove! You are a devilish gambler when aroused, Arthur," said his friend. "With your permission, ma'am, I accept the wager. And may the best man win." Whereupon he dealt a card across the table and Mr. Arthur picked it up, turning it over with a cry of triumph.

"Aha! The king of hearts! The hundred guineas is as good as mine, my dear Peter."

"We shall see, we shall see," said Lord Peter. And smiling broadly at Purity, he dealt himself a card from the bottom of the deck and flicked it across the table so that it landed close to her glass. The ace of hearts.

"This is unbelievable!" declared Mr. Arthur, choking on a laugh and taking a deep swallow of brandy. "I am afraid, ma'am, that my confounded bad turn of luck has condemned that mighty handsome bonnet of yours—with your permission, that is."

Purity, marveling at her own coolness, raised her hands, unpinned the bonnet, unfastened the white silk ribbon from under her chin, and laid the piece of milliner's work upon the card table.

Both men exhaled loudly, shifted in their seats, and grinned at each other.

"Shall we play again, my dear fellow?" asked Lord Peter. "Perhaps you will have better luck this time" —he smiled sidelong at Purity—"though I have a clear impression that Lady Luck is sitting upon my shoulder this night."

"You will not cheat?" demanded his friend.

"Would I cheat you?"

"Indeed, not. What is your stake?"

"This time I will wager two hundred guineas. And you?"

The sly, porcine eyes slid toward Purity, crawling down her body from neck to thighs.

"Against your two hundred, I will stake . . . the lady's gown. Do I have her permission?"

The question hung in the air.

Purity reviewed her options. There was coquettishness, which did not seem to be her style. She could shrink away from them and bring down upon herself more brutal methods. It was their intent to outrage her in a manner that was a mockery of the drawing-room veneer of high society. Well, then, she would give them a Roland for their Oliver.

"By all means," she said coolly. "I am not one to deny a gentleman a brief flutter at the cards. Proceed,

by all means. My gown against two hundred guineas—
and may the best man win."

The grinning Bashi-bazouk dropped her off at the
gate of her house in silent Cheyne Walk. It was past
three o'clock. In mid-river, a loaded barge was creep-
ing slowly downstream with the flood tide, one winking
light in its stern. The dawn chorus of starlings would
soon begin from the lime trees down the walk.

She waited till the clop-clop of the carriage horses
had faded away, and then she walked slowly down to
the water's edge and sank to her knees on the dusty
earth. A slow tear coursed its way down her cheek
and splashed onto her hand.

"Sales bêtes!" she whispered. *"Dégénerés! Sales
aristocrats!"*

Herself an aristocrat by birth and upbringing, wife
of aristocrats, her earliest memory, back in pre-
Revolutionary France, was of the overwhelming
power of the old aristocracy. A child of six, she had
been present at a village wedding of a pretty milkmaid and her brash, ruddy-faced swain. Dressed up
in their poor finery, with nosegays of flowers and
bright ribbons, they had stood at the church gate to
receive the kisses and good wishes of their relations
and friends. Purity had been an enchanted onlooker.

She had never forgotten the arrival of the marquis'
coach and outriders; they had come like a flock of
carrion crows among a field of doves, darkening the
scene with a sudden horror. The peasants had un-
capped, curtsied, and some of them knelt.

The marquis had looked out of his coach window.
His was a face as old as evil: raddled with disease
and debauchery, painted and patched under the snowy-
white court wig and befeathered tricorne.

She could still hear the question. It was more than a command: "What is this?"

"A wedding, and it please *monseigneur.*"

"Who is that?"

"*Monseigneur,* that is the new bride, my daughter Eloise."

"Bring her forward."

The trembling, frightened girl had been pushed toward the coach, to be quizzed by Monsieur le Marquis. She screamed when, at a motion from the painted old man, lackeys seized her and bundled her into the coach, ribbons, nosegays, and all. The wedding guests had to restrain the frenzied groom by force, for he was a big, strong fellow, with lust in his loins and love in his heart for the girl-bride who was being taken from him in the gilded and crested coach of Monsieur le Marquis. He would have struck the marquis if he had been able to, or hit the marquis' lackeys, but he would have been hanged immediately on the nearest tree, so his friends held him back.

Purity had been horrified, puzzled.

"Why did the marquis take away Eloise, and on her wedding day?"

They gave her evasions, half-truths, lies. Not for years after did she hear the truth of it: the ancient, half-legendary law of *droit de seigneur,* or, *jus primae noctis*—the Right of the First Night, which was by no means half-legendary in the remote corner of northern France where Monsieur le Marquis held sway of life and death over his peasantry, and over the nubile bodies of their children.

Purity had known violation. The brute Ugo had taken her, and others of his kind had also known her beautiful body. Curiously, it was creatures of that sort —half-animal, half-human—that had made the least impression upon her sensibilities, for were they not incapable of knowing the havoc that their lusts could wreak upon the mind and spirit of a woman? But for a man of gentle birth, of education, for a man who was capable of appreciating fine painting, knew the niceties of architecture in the Grecian style, enjoyed the chamber music of Mozart, Handel, and Scarlatti—for such a man to outrage a woman, in the certain knowledge of the horror he was visiting upon her, was, to Purity, an obscenity against civilization. It was a conviction that hardened in her mind every time she remembered the tragic little Eloise, who had been returned to her agonized groom on the day after her wedding, distraught, deflowered. It was a conviction that returned to her that night, by the dark banks of the Thames River.

"Filthy aristocrats!" she whispered.

She dipped her hands in the cool water, a ritual cleansing. She touched her flushed cheeks with her hands, washing away the bitter tears. She touched her body and felt the puckered skin under the thin silk of her gown.

They had won her gown. More precisely, the porcine Mr. Arthur had "lost" her gown when Lord Peter had openly dealt himself another ace from beneath the deck. After that, they had played a protracted game of whist for her two stockings, while she sat there nude, except for the stockings. After that, they drank a lot more brandy, and when their minds were sufficiently inflamed that they were able to forget about fine painting, Grecian architecture, Mozart, and civilization, they threw themselves upon the beautiful, poised woman with the stunning blonde hair and breasts that were a revelation. Not content with her calm acquiescence, they dragged her to a sofa by her hair and brutally took her one by one, while the other licked spilled brandy from her breasts.

"Mark, Mark, my darling," she intoned, "if it were not for our too perfect love, it would have to stop here. If your life were not at stake, I could not answer another summons from Azizza!"

A footfall made her turn. Someone was walking slowly along the riverbank toward her. It occurred to her that he—it was a man in a tall hat—must have been lurking by one of the lime trees, or she would have heard his approach from afar. And that meant that he must have been there since she had arrived home in the carriage. Indeed, he must have been watching her all the time she had been down by the water's edge.

She rose to her feet, her heart beating quickly. She, however, was not over-frightened, for she was a stone's throw from her own front door, and a staff of servants were within calling distance, though doubtless asleep.

"Who is that?" she called out in a steady voice.

"Ma'am, it is I—Wainwright."

"Wainwright? But what are you doing here?"

"One might ask the same question of yourself, ma'am," came the answer.

The estate manager came close to her. His manner was strange. It was strange, also, that he did not have the courtesy to remove his hat. And he was smiling too much.

"Sir," she said, "you are impertinent."

"That I am, ma'am," he replied coolly. "And as time advances this night, I shall become progressively more impertinent—as you will discover."

"You are drunk!" she exclaimed.

"I had a little brandy," he admitted. "It was surprisingly chilly here waiting for you."

She took a sharp intake of breath. "Waiting for me?" she cried. "Why should you be here at this hour waiting for me?"

"I was not here all the time," he said. "I retraced my steps here just ahead of you. You see, I waited all those hours in the mews behind Smith Square."

"Behind Smith Square?"

He nodded.

"You have been following me?"

"I have been following you," he said.

And then the unbelievable was happening. His hand was advancing to encircle her waist, pulling her close to him. Smiling with the crinkles in the corners of his eyes, he looked down at her quizzically, as if offering a challenge to her to prevent him. She was too astounded, too appalled by the implications of his pronouncement, to do anything but stare back at him.

"Why have you been following me, why?" she whispered.

"Because, Mrs. Gladwyn—beautiful Mrs. Gladwyn—I know the game you're playing," he replied. "You gave yourself away at luncheon the other day when you gave your husband that cock-and-bull story about Madame Avanti."

"What do you know about Madame Avanti?"

"Enough," he said. "Oh, I don't know the lady intimately, and all I know is servants' gossip. I, too, am a servant, you see—although I am occasionally permitted to dine at the table with my betters."

He hates us, she thought, hates both Robbie and me. And now what is he going to do?"

"What is this . . . servants' gossip?" she asked tremulously.

"That Madame Avanti is the highest-paid whore in London," he replied, "perhaps the highest paid in all England. She beds with royalty and the nobility, so I'm told. And that isn't all. . . ."

"What else?" She had to hear him to the end.

"The lady's not only a strumpet, but also a bawd.

She procures other women. And tonight, Mrs. Glad-wyn—beautiful, chaste Mrs. Gladwyn—tonight she procured *you!*"

"No!" She threw the lie into his face, then saw it fly wide of its mark. His smile only broadened.

"The house where you went," he said, "the house where Madame Avanti's coachman took you, is a notorious place of rendezvous for the gentlemen and their high-priced whores. You see, I know it all, Mrs. Gladwyn. I know how long you were there and who you were with. His coach was standing at the end of the mews all night, with his coat of arms emblazoned on the door. I make it my business to know the arms and quarterings of the nobility, Mrs. Gladwyn. 'Tis a useful accomplishment for a servant."

"What do you want?" she demanded. "I'll get money for you—plenty of money—if you'll go away, leave my husband's employ."

"Money's a thing we can discuss later, Mrs. Gladwyn," he said. "Here and now, after a tedious night of waiting, I've a fancy to sleep between satin sheets with a toothsome wench, and later—say, about noon—to wake up and stretch out my hand for her . . . so . . . "

Slowly, still holding her around the waist, he raised his other hand and deliberately slipped his forefinger into the neck of her bodice, into the warm cleft of her bosom.

"No-o-o!" she howled.

"Oh, yes," he said, "or there'll be a written report awaiting your husband on his return: date, times, place, and a name—Lord Peter Whatten-Findley. I have it right, the name, don't I?"

A distant steeple bell chimed the half hour. Purity shuddered, as if it had been tolling for her death.

"Please . . . " she whispered.

"You lead the way," he said, "in through the door and straight up to your bedchamber, Mrs. Gladwyn. I've a fancy to take you there, between your satin sheets, all smelling of French scent and soft woman. Why do you tarry?"

"The servants . . . " She sketched a helpless gesture.

"The servants will never know. You'll lie in bed tomorrow as if you were taken with a headache. Don't tell me that fine ladies of leisure like yourself have to beg leave of their servants before they can spend the day in bed upon the slightest pretext."

"My maid!" she cried desperately. "My maid awakens me with a cup of chocolate . . . "

"Lock your door," he said. "When she knocks, tell her to go away and drink the chocolate herself. Why do you tarry, Mrs. Gladwyn?"

"But . . . you . . . how shall you . . . ?"

"How shall I leave undetected? Simplicity itself, Mrs. Gladwyn. I shall depart from your bed tomorrow night when the rest of the household is asleep. We have a long day ahead of us, Mrs. Gladwyn. Let's get what sleep we can before noon, when the notion takes me to reach out and . . . "

She broke away from his grasp and ran with stumbling steps up the riverbank, across the wheel-rutted, sandy road and through the gates of her house. Taking the key from her reticule, she slipped it into the lock, then gave a sharp intake of breath as, when doing so, his hand caressed her buttocks.

They crossed the darkened hallway, she leading. They went up the curved staircase to the upper floor where her bedchamber was. No sound was to be heard but the strident ticking of the long-cased clock in the hallway below. Her door had a slight creak, which she had long intended to have rectified; it sounded like the portals of hell being flung wide open.

She took as long as she could to strike a match and light a candle by the bedside. He was watching her from the other side of the room when she turned to face him. He had taken off his coat and waistcoat, and he stood regarding her in his shirtsleeves, arms folded.

She said, "And now?"

"And now," he said, "I have a fancy for you to divest me of my shirt and breeches. After that, I will lie in bed and watch you disrobe, Mrs. Gladwyn. 'Twill inspire me to sweet dreams and strengthen my ardor for noontime, when we begin our long day of pleasuring."

Chapter Ten

She did not dare to open her eyes for fear that her slightest movement might arouse the man lying by her side.

He had taken her in the dawn—carelessly, self-indulgently, as the young so often do (she supposed him to be three years her junior, or more—but he seemed of a different generation), but without the questing tenderness that the young and the inexperienced bring to their lovemaking. But, of course, Wainwright was by no means inexperienced; that much had been obvious from his antics—learned, no doubt, from casual coupling with tavern wenches and whores. She shuddered at the insults her body had been compelled to suffer, and she yearned to bathe herself. She would have done so gladly—if only she could have crept out of the bed and into the dressing room, where there stood a tin washbasin and a pitcher of cool water.

A distant clock in Westminster chimed noon. Twelve hours to go, at least that; she could not pos-

342

sibly risk letting him leave till the butler had locked
up for the night and had gone to bed.

Twelve hours . . .

"That husband of yours—he's a scoundrel. Do you
know that, Mrs. Gladwyn?"

His voice—his sneering voice—close to her ear
made her start, plainly betraying that she had been
wide awake and lying with her eyes closed, feigning
sleep.

"What do you mean?" She looked straight into his
face. It seemed strange to be regarding her husband's
servant across the distance of a pillow.

"I mean what I say," replied Wainwright. "Gladwyn's a scoundrel. Ask anyone in the know. He's been
blackballed from every club in London except the one
he now belongs to. And *they'll* even accept actors and
the like."

"You're lying!" She snapped the words, and she
instantly would have recalled them when she saw the
truculent look come into his face: the look of a spoiled
boy grown up, the boy who hates to be contradicted.

"I'll make you swallow that remark, Mrs. Gladwyn," he said.

She stiffened as his hand came out and, encircling
her waist, pulled her close to him, hard against his
bare flesh. Face to face, mouth to mouth, eye to eye,
they stayed for a full minute.

"You're hurting me," she whispered.

He laughed. Skirting her cheek with his lips, he
murmured an obscenity in her ear.

"No!" she exclaimed.

"Yes," he said. "And now—right this minute."

"I won't do it! You can't make me do it!"

"Very well, then. I shall take my leave, Mrs. Gladwyn." With that, he threw aside the sheets and, vault-
ing out of her bed, picked up his tumbled clothes and

went toward the door. He was tall, upright, grinning, and nude.

"No . . . please . . . " she pleaded.

He paused with his hand on the door handle and turned. The grown-up spoiled little boy's face was creased in a smug smile.

"Don't you want me to go? I shan't hurry away. I'm sure your butler will give me luncheon, and maybe even arrange for one of the footmen to shave me and help me dress."

"Please . . . "

"You want me to come back to bed?"

She nodded.

The intolerable smile broadened. "Then say so."

"Come to bed," she said, then remembered to add, "please."

"And what else? What will you do if I come back to bed?"

For all that I have, she thought, for Chastity, for all my hope of future happiness, for the sake of poor Robbie, who never should have been reduced to marrying a creature who bears the burdens I carry. But —most of all—for my darling Mark. . . .

"I'm waiting," he prompted her, reaching again for the door handle.

"I will pleasure you in the manner you ask," she whispered, praying that he would spare her from mouthing the shameful words.

Fortunately, he made no such demand. Throwing aside his pile of clothes, he instantly rejoined her in the bed and proceeded to extract from her the promise of total abandonment and the slaking of his most base desires.

Much later, she still imprisoned in his arms in the tumbled bed linen, both slippery with sweat, he gave a low chuckle.

"Heh, 'twould be a fine thing to see my excellent employer walking in at this moment to observe how I am enjoying the pleasures that are so sternly denied him. Oh, don't bother to deny it, my dear Mrs. Gladwyn. We servants talk, you know. 'Tis the gossip of your household that you forbid him to come to your bed."

"My God, you people know everything about us, don't you?" she said wearily. "Or you think you do."

She choked on a scream when he pinched her buttock hard.

"Less of your lip, my lady," he said. "Yes, all in all, we know a great deal about you, and I know more than most—more than you know yourself. For instance, were you aware that your excellent, upright husband, of whom so many think so highly—except from those few in the know who have blackballed him from all the best clubs in London—is not only a scoundred, but an impostor?"

A heated rebuke rose to her lips, but, remembering the humiliating punishment he had visited upon her on the previous occasion, she contented herself by giving a shrug.

"Oh, yes," resumed Wainwright, "an impostor. He claims to be a veteran of the Peninsula war. He has never been to Spain and Portugal in his life, save as a civilian traveler."

"He served with my"—she choked on the phrase —"with my late husband."

"In Spain? Where in Spain?"

"I . . . I don't know. Salamanca, perhaps. Badajoz . . . "

"In what capacity? Did your late husband ever speak of him and of the times when they were together in Spain and Portugal? What regiment was he in? What rank did he hold? Answer me, lady."

She shook her head frantically so that her wealth of blonde hair lashed Wainwright's breast.

"I don't know! I don't know!" she cried. "I have never thought to question him on these matters. What reason have I to suppose that he is an impostor? What possible proof have *you* that he is an impostor?"

"The proof's there for you to find," he said. "You may find it easily enough, Mrs. Gladwyn, just as I did."

"Where?" The question was out before she could stop herself.

He laughed. "Ah! I can see that I've whetted the lady's curiosity," he said. "But that's as far as I intend to go this day, my lady, for we have far to travel along the road to bliss, you and I. Tell me now, you're not without a few guineas to rub together. You've taken up high-class whoring in Madame Avanti's stable, and 'tis surely not for gain. For what, then?"

She saw the trap and evaded it instantly.

"For pleasure," she whispered against the thick pelt of hair that spanned his chest.

"Louder—I didn't hear you."

"For pleasure!"

"Well, now, since 'tis to pleasure the upper classes that brings you to whoring, let me see your wares, my lady—unless, that is, you are such a confounded snob that you only delight in tumbling with gentlemen of title. Are you a snob, then?"

There was no escape for her. To deny him anything, to give the overgrown, spoiled boy the impression that he was less desirable to her than any other man, would only bring worse humiliations upon her. Steeling herself, she allowed her hand to approach his loins, her lips to close upon his mouth.

"How could *you* think such a thing?" she asked.

Summoned to sudden desire, he took her rapturously, neither offering her humiliation nor caring if she joined him in the enterprise, but using her as an indifferent craftsman will use a beautifully fashioned tool: coarsely and against the grain, hastily, savoring neither the pleasure of the handling nor the ease of performance, but laboring only for the end.

Withdrawn from the creature who vented himself upon her, heedless of his gasping breath in her ear, Purity addressed her thoughts to the new and alarming proposition that Wainwright had put to her.

Robert a scoundrel? That was out of the question, of course. Anyone who had known Robert for any time at all (how long had she known him? . . . really a surprisingly short while, only since the end of the war, when she and Mark had returned to Clumber) would dismiss that accusation out of hand. He was the kindest, most faithful, most considerate . . .

But . . . an impostor?

Her mind went back to the conversation—almost forgotten by her—that she had overheard at the theater. The two officers had known Robert well by sight and had spoken of him with flat contempt. He had known them, also; she had seen it in his face. Might there be some connection between that incident in the theater and Wainwright's claim that Robert had lied about his army service? It was a disquieting thought.

Wainwright was clawing at her in his frenzy, kneading at her breasts with his strong fingers so that she was constrained to cry out and beg him to desist. The painful intrusion upon her thoughts only served to remind her of the misery of her situation.

She was caught between two fires: on the one hand, Azizza's demands upon her body, for the sake of Mark's life and freedom; on the other hand, the spoiled, demanding creature who was at that moment

spending himself upon her. And there was no person
on earth to whom she could turn for help.

It was possible, she conceded, that, sooner or later,
she might have turned to Robert. Wainwright had
been aware of the situation, and that, doubtlessly, had
been his reason for dropping the poisoned words into
her ear. However, not knowing the true reason behind
her nocturnal foray in Azizza's carriage (she had told
him that she did it for pleasure—ye gods!), he could
have no idea how effectively his poison had worked
upon her.

To place Mark's life and liberty in the slightest
jeopardy by confiding her agonies in another would
call for her unquestioning trust in that other person.

It had to be admitted to herself: Robert Gladwyn no
longer rated that degree of trust in her mind.

He left her shortly after midnight, after a long day
of unremitting humiliations, when even in sleep he
held her bare body to him, and awoke only to despoil
it again.

They ate nothing, for no food could be brought up
without arousing the suspicions of the staff, already
puzzled, it was certain, by her brusque dismissal of the
maid who had brought her early morning chocolate.
A few swallows of water from the pitcher in the dressing room had sufficed them. Wainwright had laughed
and said she was all the meat and drink he required.

He left her with the instructions that she was to visit
him, at his apartment in the Barbican, thrice weekly
at the hour of seven. Excuses to give her husband?
That he left to her silken tongue, he said. If she could
contrive to play sexual games in Madame Avanti's stable, well, then, she could do the same with him.

The following afternoon, after a long night of deep,
dream-haunted sleep, she received word from Azizza

that she was to be ready for the carriage at six o'clock. Azizza did not specify who was to be the recipient of Purity's favors. Robert Gladwyn arrived home from Wiltshire just as the Bashi-bazouk was remounting his driving seat after having delivered the message.

Purity saw it all from the open window of her drawing room, which fronted Cheyne Walk. She was so close that she could hear every word in the still summer afternoon. She saw Robert alight from his traveling coach and, noticing the carriage drawn up outside his own front door, turn to address the dark-skinned coachman in the cockaded hat. The fellow answered in broken English, then immediately reverted to his own language.

Robert Gladwyn answered him in the same guttural tongue.

It was some few minutes before she heard the carriage drive off down the rutted road toward Westminster. During this time, she had stood regarding herself in the looking glass over the mantelpiece and attempting, with no notable success, to compose herself. She turned at Robert's entry.

"My dear, how radiant you look—as ever," he said, crossing the room and kissing her on both cheeks.

"How was Wiltshire?" she asked.

"Well enough. And how is our darling Chastity?"

"She has a slight cold. It's nothing."

"I will go up and see her," he said. "By the way, I see we have had a visitation from Madame Avanti's carriage. What news of Madame Avanti?"

Purity said, "She has called a meeting of the Circle this evening at six."

He frowned. "What a shame. I had so looked forward to an evening with you, my dear. Cannot Madame Avanti manage without you for once? I see the answer in your eyes: she cannot. *Tant pis. Madame's* gain is my incomparable loss. I will go up to the nursery and kiss Chastity."

She watched him walk to the door: tall, in his gray riding coat and Hessian boots, going a little gray over the ears, not so young as he was.

"Robbie . . . " she began.

He turned and smiled. It was the quirky, lopsided smile—more of a grin—that had always disarmed her. The eyes: candid, and surely without any guile. Twenty-four hours ago, she would have trusted him with her life, with Mark's life. But now?

"I had no idea you spoke Arabic," she said as evenly as she was able to.

"Did you not, my dear?" he replied without so much as a flicker of an eyebrow.

"Where did you gain this accomplishment, Robbie?" she asked.

"In Constantinople."

"During the war, perhaps?"

"I was not in Constantinople during the war, Purity," he said. "I am speaking of my youth, before the war, when my doting uncle, who was my guardian, sent me on a grand tour to broaden my mind. I visited Paris, of course, then Avignon, to see the papal palace and the famous bridge *sur qui l'on y danse*. For artistic and intellectual refreshment, my tutor, who accompanied me, then directed our path to Florence, Rome, Siena, Padua, and Venice. I found Venice enchanting. And then we went to Constantinople."

"Where you learned Arabic—just like that?"

He chuckled. "You do me more than justice, my dear. I picked up a few phrases in both Turkish and Arabic. It would be putting it too high to say that I am on more than nodding terms with either language. With Madame Avanti's coachman just now, I exchanged a few commonplace pleasantries in his native

tongue, which is, in fact, not Arabic, but Turkish. By
the way, what a most disagreeable-looking fellow,
don't you think? I declare, I should not like to meet
him in a dark alleyway unless I had my pocket pistol.
Capable of anything, wouldn't you say?"

"Capable of anything," repeated Purity dully.

In her mind, that instant, she was again aboard
Azizza's *xebec* and spreadeagled across the bare back
of the Bashi-bazouk, breasts and belly slimy with his
sweat, waiting in screaming terror for the next kiss of
the dampened silk.

And mingled with that memory was another image,
another terror, which had suddenly and all unbidden
come very close to her once more: the image of a man
in the dark blue veiling of a desert Tuareg.

Nathan Dalgliesh, member of Parliament for the
constituency of Crumble-with-Croyne, married to another of the ladies present at the fateful meeting of the
Circle for Aid to Returning Soldiers and Sailors that
Purity had attended, was a thrusting and ruthless
young man who had wed an ugly girl for her fortune
and for her father's patronage over the constituency of
Crumble-with-Croyne. It was a happy combination of
circumstances that had elevated Mr. Dalgliesh, son
of a Wapping fish merchant, to the ownership of his
wife's fortune, a fine town house in Grosvenor Square,
a mansion and a thousand acres in Middlesex, and a
seat in the Commons. All these things having been
achieved, Dalgliesh then used his Parliamentary connections to further his career in diplomacy. And he
used his wife's money to purchase for him the curious
pleasures that alone satisfied his appetites. The ugly
little wife he abandoned to her own devices.

Upon arrival at the Dalgliesh establishment in
Grosvenor Square, Purity was shown to a sumptu-

ously appointed study, where the M.P. for Crumble-with-Croyne was dictating a letter to two clerks from the Foreign Office. Peering at the newcomer over the top of his severe spectacles, he asked her in polite tones to be seated while he finished the letter, adding that he would afterward be able to devote half an hour of his time to hearing her business. Purity took a seat, wonderingly, and watched and listened while Dalgliesh concluded his dictation, whereupon the clerks gathered up their writing tables, their pens, inks, and papers, bowed to the distinguished M.P. and to his lady visitor, and departed.

A long silence: only the ticking of a marble clock on a giltwood console table by the window.

Dalgliesh cleared his throat, peered at his visitor over his spectacles, and cracked his knuckles noisily.

"Er . . . would you care for tea, ma'am?" he asked.

"Thank you, no, sir," replied Purity.

"A glass of sherry, perhaps?"

"No, thank you."

His eyes were small, pale, and shifty. They swam around the room desperately, but they always returned to the beautiful blonde woman in the chair—and always nervously. It soon became clear to Purity that Dalgliesh's reputation for thrusting ruthlessness —which was the talk of London society—did not extend to his activities in the Courts of Hymen.

"Ahem!" He cleared his throat again.

Purity said, "Sir, touching upon my reason for coming here . . . "

He jumped. "The matter of your coming here—yes!"

"Can we not begin, sir?" asked Purity mildly.

"Begin? yes, by all means!" cried Dalgliesh. "Let us, by all means."

Silence. . . .

"What do you wish of me, sir?" asked Purity.

He had very large hands, very strong. Red-faced, with pale eyes seeking every corner of the room save the spot where Purity sat, he wrung his hands together in a torment of indecision.

"I . . . that is . . . " he faltered.

"Yes, sir?" asked Purity.

It came in a whisper: "I would like you to . . . that is . . . "

"Yes?"

"Madame, I would be obliged if you would . . . if you would lower your bodice to the waist!" The last part came out in a rush of expelled breath.

"My bodice?" asked Purity. "Is that all, sir?"

He nodded vigorously. "That is all, ma'am."

Amused despite herself, Purity rose, deposited her reticule and gloves upon the chair, and, unbuttoning the front of her bodice, slipped it from her shoulders and down to her waist. She was wearing nothing underneath. She turned to face the M.P. for Crumble-with-Croyne, who had also risen to his feet and was staring at her in slack-mouthed awe.

"Well, sir?" asked Purity. "Anything else?" . .

He swallowed hard, and his prominent Adam's apple jounced up and down.

"Madame," he said hoarsely, "would you be so kind as to . . . to walk across to the fireplace?"

"Of course," said Purity.

This she did, conscious of his eyes upon her. Reaching the fireplace, she turned to regard him. He had seated himself again, overcome, perhaps, by excess of emotion.

"Madame," he whispered, "I should be obliged if you would continue doing that"—he glanced across at the long-cased clock that stood by the door—"I

should be obliged if you would continue for half an hour."

If Dalgliesh was a pitiable impotent, and the experience merely an embarrassment, Purity's first visit to Wainwright's apartment in the Barbican the following evening—she was summoned there by a note that he thrust into her hand when he called to see Robert Gladwyn that day—was a far worse ordeal, demanding all her courage and all her fortitude. To begin with, the apartment was on the top floor of a tenement that was inhabited by impecunious young men making their own ways in the world: students, newly practicing lawyers, clerks, and estate managers, bachelors all. The apartment was looked after by a caretaker who scanned all arrivals through a window set by the street door. Purity, who had had the foresight to wear a veil with her bonnet, which concealed most of her face, was nevertheless conscious that the prying eyes took in every detail of her appearance. Moreover, in the ascent of three rickety flights of uncarpeted stairs to Wainwright's rooms, she was passed by three men going the other way. All gave her curious glances, and one of them doffed his tall hat and inquired if she would like to tarry a while.

Wainwright was awaiting her in his dressing gown. He laughed when she told him that she could not possibly being herself again to run the gauntlet of so many prying eyes, and that, if he insisted upon making his lustful demands upon her, they must rendezvous elsewhere. He thrust aside the notion, telling her that he enjoyed the pleasure of taking her under his own roof, upon his own bachelor bed. It was then clear to her that he delighted having it known—as soon it must be known—among the hard-up young gentlemen in the tenement that Mr. Wainwright, on the third floor rear, was regularly entertaining a lady, a richly dressed lady, a beauty with stunning hair and breasts that would knock out your eyes. Not only was she being obliged to give herself to this wretch, but she was also being used to puff up his self-importance.

She stayed an hour, no more. He would have kept her all night, but she protested, telling him that she had offered the excuse to Robert that she was attending a meeting of the Circle. Having learned, through the interminable hours as captive and concubine in her own bedchamber, that it profited her nothing to withhold her favors from him, Purity swallowed her revulsion and deliberately dictated the pace of their amours. She it was who, after having disrobed herself before him, slowly, languorously, and in such a manner as to inflame his passions, then divested him with her own hands of his dressing gown and led him by the hand to his bed. He, in a sense, cheated of the opportunity to amuse himself with salacious preliminaries, threw himself upon her with frenzied vigor, to bring about a rapid release from the inferno that she had lit within his brain and his loins. Knowingly or unwittingly, Purity had played one of the oldest tricks in the harlot's game—but she paid for it dearly in pride and self-respect.

She left him after the hour, with the assurance, reluctantly given under duress, that she would attend him again two nights later at the same hour. Then she retraced her steps down the dingy stairwell, past the door below Wainwright's, behind which someone was practicing on a violin, and on down to the street door and the searching gaze of the old man behind the Judas window. She went back home to peaceful, rural Cheyne Walk in a hackney cab, back to the husband —no husband—for whom she was slowly assembling in her tormented mind a most disturbing skein of

tangled doubts and suspicions to which she could
scarcely give a coherent name.

Luckily, Robert Gladwyn saved her from the next
assignation with Wainwright by taking him with him
on a visit to the estates in East Anglia again. Purity
enjoyed a blessed five days of freedom from violation,
days that she spent in the company of her beloved
adopted daughter. The weather being so splendid,
they were able to go on the river. Purity hired a sailing
gig and a two-man crew of Thames watermen to manage it, and she, the nursemaid, and the child made
pleasant forays downriver as far as Richmond and
Staines, picnicking in the old deer park and playing
innocent children's games of pat-ball and blind man's
buff—a far cry from the tumbled, narrow bed under
the eaves of a tenement in the Barbican, or from the
duke's perfumed boudoir in the villa in Maida Vale.

All things must have an end. The end of Purity's
brief respite came with a summons from Azizza on
the sixth day after Robert's departure. But before the
carriage came for her, she had an unexpected visitor.

It was about three in the afternoon. She had been
instructed to be ready by seven, and, as usual when
she was under notice to play Azizza's whore, she was
in a distracted frame of mind, had dismissed Chastity
to play in the garden with the nursemaid, and was
alone and fretful in her sitting room. The butler entered.

"A Mr. Harker-Marlowe has called, ma'am," intoned the butler from the sitting room door, "Mr.
Hubert Harker-Marlowe, from Wiltshire. Are you at
home, ma'am?"

Unaccountably, Purity's spirits brightened at the
mention of a name from the recent past, a past from

which she was separated by a deep gulf of grief and misfortune.

"I am at home to Mr. Harker-Marlowe," she said. "Ask him to come in, please."

The squire of Clumber Parish was the same as ever: still in his tailcoat of hunting scarlet, stupidly handsome and boyish looking, though he must have been well over forty. In an unguarded instant, Purity was whisked back to the dinner party that she had given on the night that Chastity had fallen down the stairs, the night when, later, she had dreamed of Mark's capture.

"Howdy-do, Mrs. Landless, ma'am. I . . . " Harker-Marlowe's pleasant, guileless face blushed alarmingly. "Damn it, ma'am, I'm very sorry for the blunder. It's Mrs. Gladwyn now, isn't it? You're looking as fine as ever, ma'am."

"Hello, Squire," she said, holding out her hand. "How nice to see you. And how are your mother and your brother, pray?"

"Well enough, ma'am," said he. "Mama still suffers most dreadfully with the wind, but she is determined to make a hundred. And, by George, I have wagers all around the county that she will so do. It is because of Mama that I have called to see you upon my passing through London."

"Indeed, sir?" said Purity. "And how is that?"

"Why, you will recall that dinner party you gave before the colonel was . . . I mean, before you had news of . . . "

"Do not embarrass yourself, Squire," said Purity mildly. "I have been through the worst of my grieving and have come to accept my loss."

"Mightily glad to hear it, ma'am," said Harker-Marlowe. "And may I belatedly express my sorrow and the sorrow of Mama and my brother Roger for your sad loss."

"Thank you, sir," murmured Purity, lowering her gaze. Oh, my God, she thought, why must he go on? I received him with so much pleasure. . . .

"To return to the dinner party," resumed Harker-Marlowe. "You will recall, perhaps, that Mama promised you a case of the Irish whiskey from our estate in County Wicklow?"

"Why, yes, I remember it well," said Purity. "It was very kind of her, very thoughtful."

"Well, I brought some back with me from Ireland," said Harker-Marlowe, "but by the time I had returned, you were away in foreign parts. There the matter languished till now, when, recalling Mama's promise, I have brought a dozen bottles with me in my coach, ma'am, and will hand them over to your butler on my departure." He sat back in his chair and beamed across at her.

"Thank you, Squire," said Purity. "Will you have tea?"

"Thank you, no, ma'am. Never drink it. Find it gives me the colic."

"Chocolate, perhaps?"

"Never touch chocolate for fear of the gout, ma'am. Gout runs in the family. My father suffered with it from my age till the day he broke his neck riding to the hounds, the Lord rest his soul."

Purity glanced covertly toward the clock.

"Perhaps you would prefer a brandy," she said. "Or, indeed, would you like some of your excellent Irish whiskey?"

His pleasant face brightened. "Brandy will be capital, ma'am," he said, "for I would never broach a whole case of spirits for the sake of a single nip. Brandy it is, if you please."

Purity crossed the room and pulled the bell rope to summon the butler. Hubert Harker-Marlowe stretched his booted legs before him and yawned with contentment. Then he gave a short laugh.

"Ha! Oh, yes."

"Did you speak, sir?" said Purity.

"I was recalling in my own mind," said Harker-Marlowe, "an incident—a highly indelicate incident that I'm not so sure I should mention—that took place during that dinner party of yours, ma'am."

Purity's hand froze on the bell rope. She seemed to see a face—a plump, pretty face—looking out at her in its death agony. And she shuddered despite the heat of the summer's afternoon.

"You mean . . . the nursemaid," she said slowly.

"How you caught her in the act of being tumbled by the damned footman!" chuckled Harker-Marlowe. Then, recovering his sense of propriety, he added, "Damned appalling way to carry on. But, then, ma'am, what can one expect of today's servants? Give 'em an inch, and they'll take a mile. I blame it on the French Revolution. Damned country's never been the same since." He looked anxiously to Purity to see if he had given her offense. "However, you gave the trollop her discharge," he added, "and good riddance."

"Yes, I discharged her," said Purity, "and without a reference. Poor Nancy."

"Well, it's all over now, ma'am!" declared Harker-Marlowe. "You need have no conscience qualms about that abandoned young minx. Why, she had not gotten a yard outside your gate before she had found herself a rich beau."

Purity, whose mind had been far away, reliving memories of times and places and people that had seared her forever, was dragged back to the there-and-then by his remark—heard and comprehended imperfectly though it was.

"What . . . *what* did you say just then, sir?" she murmured.

"Why, the trollop—the nursemaid—found a protector immediately upon leaving," said Harker-Marlowe. "Waiting for her in a coach outside the gates of Clumber, he was. He called to her and took her in. They were driven off into the night. No need for you to repine, ma'am. She tumbled straight from one bed into another, if you'll pardon the expression."

The door opened. Someone in a powdered wig was standing in front of Purity, bowing at her, waiting for instructions.

"You rang, ma'am?"

She caught her breath. "Oh, yes. Will you give . . . er . . . Mr. Harker-Marlowe a glass of brandy, please?"

The butler crossed to the closet, opened the door, took out a brandy glass, unstoppered a decanter, and poured a generous measure into the crystal container. She watched it all, her mind racing, willing the fellow to hurry about his menial task and then be gone.

"Will that be all, ma'am?"

"Yes, thank you."

The door closed again.

She turned swiftly to face Harker-Marlowe.

"How do you know that?" she cried.

"Ma'am?" The bland squire of Clumber Parish gagged on his first swallow.

"You said that Nancy had someone waiting for her in a coach outside Clumber's gates. How do you know that? Tell me, man! Tell me!"

"In truth, ma'am," said Harker-Marlowe, "I know because I was witness. I was standing there, ma'am, having walked down the driveway after the minx, Mama having gone off—as you might recall—in our carriage. I saw it all plainly, as I see you now. There was this wench, Nancy, with her baggage. On reaching the gate, she saw a coach waiting by the edge of the road, close by. I was near enough to hear the fellow in the coach—it was certainly not the driver—call out to her. It was some such summons as: 'Come here, lass,' or 'Ho, there, girl.' I heard him clearly."

Purity waited till she was sure she had complete control over herself before she dared to essay the next question. "Mr. Harker-Marlowe, did you have any idea of the identity of the man in the coach?"

The guileless eyes widened. "Why, no, ma'am," he said. " 'Twas obvious that he was one of your guests at the dinner party. That much was certain."

"One of my guests?" She stared at him in horror.

"Who else, ma'am? A string of coaches and carriages passed me by as I traipsed down your driveway. As they passed me, so did they pass the wench up ahead of me. All of 'em saw her struggling along with her baggage. One of 'em—and I've no idea who—drew to a halt at the gate to await her. 'Tis obvious."

The enormity of his conclusion bore down upon Purity's tormented mind. Of course, Harker-Marlowe was right. One of the guests had picked up the homeless girl. Having seen her nude and judged her to be to his taste, having witnessed that she was handy with her favors, any man with a roving eye might have done the same. It was highly likely that Harker-Marlowe himself was in pursuit of Nancy and planning the same thing before he was forestalled.

Forestalled—by whom?

"It could have been any one of a dozen fellows," said Harker-Marlowe, "but what's the odds? A lot of water has passed under a lot of bridges since then, and I for one don't begrudge a fellow his bit of sport. Lucky devil!"

Yes, any one of a dozen, as this brandy-swilling

dunderhead had remarked. There had been . . . oh
. . . thirty or so guests that night (it was unlikely that
she still had the seating list somewhere), and a fair
proportion of them had been single, unattached males.
Any one of them might have been . . .

"Another brandy, Squire?" she asked absently,
crossing to the window and looking out across the
river. She must get rid of him. She needed to be alone
to think.

"Thank you, no, ma'am," replied Harker-Marlowe.
" 'Pon my word, 'tis nearly half-past three, and I have
an appointment at my club at four o'clock. Great
pleasure to have seen you again, ma'am. You are
greatly missed. The Finch-Landlesses . . . well, I won't
go into that . . ."

"The Finch-Landlesses?"

What were the Finch-Landlesses to her any longer?

"Scandal of the county, ma'am. The wife's trying
to buy her way into local society. The husband's made
so many serving wenches pregnant that there's not a
mother in the parish who'll let her daughter work up
at Clumber. And that brat of theirs shot a game-
keeper. Ma'am, I am tiring you with my prattle and
had best be gone."

"Please, Squire, forgive me if I appear preoccupied
today," said Purity. "You have been very welcome,
and I greatly appreciate your gift." Heavens, she must
be distraught if even Harker-Marlowe noticed it.

He took her hand and bowed.

"Good day to you, ma'am," he said. "And if ever
you are in the county, I beg you to call on us. You
are greatly missed. It's a poor exchange, we all say,
to have the Finch-Landlesses up at Clumber."

At four o'clock Purity put down her pen and examined the list of names that she had written in one

column down a sheet of paper. They were the names of all the single, unattached males—or as many of them as she could recall—who had been present at the dinner party.

One name, only, she had omitted. Taking up her pen once more, she steeled herself to write in capital letters at the end of the list:

ROBERT GLADWYN

With a harsh intake of breath, she crumpled up the paper, threw it into the empty fireplace, and watched it lying there. Then she found that her hands were trembling. Heavens! She must not leave the list lying about, for that would be a folly, and possibly a dangerous folly at that. She knelt and picked it up, cramming it between the cleft of her breasts.

What next? What was to be done?

Wainwright's words came back to her: "The proof's there for you to find . . . you may find it, as I did."

Find proof—where? Where else but upstairs, in the bedchamber above hers? The idea having taken shape, a strange calmness came upon her, stilling her fears, steadying her nerves, quietening her trembling limbs. She took one last glance at herself in the looking glass (she looked pale, wild-eyed, and guilt-ridden) and then she swept out of the room, across the hallway, and up the stairs, not pausing a moment for fear that an instant's reflection for second thoughts might destroy her resolve. She went past her own room door and up again, till she came to the door of Robert Gladwyn's bedchamber and let herself in.

It smelled of him: a mixture of cologne, Macassar oil, polished leather—pleasant, manly odors. Symbols of his life lay all about: prints and paintings of the

English countryside; places he had visited, like Venice, Paris, the Rhineland, the Golden Horn of Constantinople; his books. She picked one up—*An Inquiry into the Principles and Practice of Animal Husbandry*—and another—*The English Shire Horse*. By his books is a man known.

He slept in a military-style bed with a canvas canopy; very austere. The military theme was taken up by a portrait of his late father over the mantelpiece. Colonel Gladwyn had taken his regiment to the Americas to fight the French and had led them in the storming of Quebec, being the youngest commander in the field. The son, as she well knew, was inordinately proud of his father's glory. She studied the face in the painting. The family resemblance was very striking: Gladwyn *père* had the same sandy hair, candid-looking eyes, and humorous mouth. Only by the sterner and more rugged set of the jaw did another character emerge—a character more ruthless than the son, more the soldier, perhaps less the human being. But it was a good face.

There was Colonel Gladwyn's military chest under the window. It was made of Indian teak and was brass-bound at all the edges and corners—a piece of furniture that had seen service wherever the British flag had been carried. It was unlocked, and it creaked open to her touch.

Lying upon the top was a scarlet uniform coatee. Purity took it up and examined the braiding and facings, which were very similar to those worn by Colonel Gladwyn in the painting. There was a tailor's name tag at the neck, and hand-written on it was the name: LIEUTENANT R. J. GLADWYN. She put it aside. One thing at least she had proved to herself: he had served in the army at one time in his career. If an imposter, he was not a total imposter.

She delved deeper into the chest, laying aside other items of military uniform: pantaloons, boots, hats in tin boxes, a sword, a horse pistol in a case. At the very bottom of the chest, her hand came into contact with a leather briefcase. She took it out.

His initials—R. J. G.—were on the front. With trembling fingers, Purity opened the latch and lifted the flap. She took out a sheaf of letters, packets, prints, and engravings. There was an etched copy of his father's portrait and a steel engraving representing the storming of Quebec. Another engraving depicted the burial of General Wolfe after the victory. And there was a further portrait of Colonel Gladwyn. She put them aside and turned to the letters.

> Poona, India
> March 14, 1787

My dear Robert,

Be assured that there will be a place for you in the old regiment when your time comes. Meanwhile, I request and require you to address yourself diligently to your studies at Eton. . . .

They were all from the father, and all in the same vein: the record of a stern man's relationship with an adoring and hero-worshipping son. There was little of affection in the stilted lines, and not much in the way of praise for the son's efforts at school and later at the military academy, only unremitting injunctions to strive harder, to be worthy of king, country, and—later—of regiment. Not a word of fatherly love.

The last item in the briefcase was a document wrapped in an oilcloth. Purity had no sooner touched it than some sixth sense told her that she had reached the heart of the matter, the proof of which Wainwright had spoken.

It provd to be a single sheet of writing paper, the ink—like the ink in the letters—faded by the passing of time, and the paper smelling musty.

> Aboard the Transport *Scarborough,*
> Out from Bombay, India,
> February 12, 1809

Whereas the Undersigned, officers of the Duke of Loamshire's Own Light Dragoons, having tried Lieutenant Robert Justin Gladwyn by summary Court Martial in private, do find the said Lieutenant Gladwyn guilty as charged. *Viz:* he did bring, by his infamous conduct, disgrace and dishonor upon his regiment.

In view of our desire to save the good name of the regiment, and also out of regard for the honor of the late Colonel F. J. Gladwyn, father of the above, we are resolved that the matter shall end here—provided that Lieutenant Gladwyn will immediately resign his commission and never again take up arms for the country he has dishonored.

Witness our hands this day. . . .

There followed a string of scrawled signatures.

Slowly, her mind teeming with a nightmare maze of speculations, Purity folded up the paper in its oilcloth cover and replaced it, along with everything else, in the briefcase.

So that was Robert Gladwyn's secret: he was a disgraced officer, condemned by his fellows to abandon the career for which he had striven since boyhood, urged on by his stern and unbending father, whose memory he still cherished above all.

What had been the "infamous conduct" that had brought the punishment upon him? It could be a crime great or small. From her knowledge of regimental life, it could have been something as trivial as cheating at cards. Men, particularly men of the officer class, set great store by the code of honor that forbade cheating under any circumstances; many a promising career had been broken by a misdealt card in a game of *quinze*.

On the other hand, Robert Gladwyn's crime might have been grave. Not murder, certainly—even to save the good name of their regiment and to protect the honor of their late, revered colonel, the officers would not condone murder and be parties to allowing the murderer to go free. But it could have been something equally vile, though sometimes countenanced in war: rape, perhaps, or pillage. Did that sound like the man whom she had taken for her husband?

Whatever his crime, Robert Gladwyn stood guilty as accused by Wainwright: he was an impostor. He had not served in the army throughout the war, as he had always implied, but had been elsewhere, doing other things, in the years between resigning his commission in 1809 and the end of hostilities after the defeat of Napoleon at Waterloo in 1815.

But where? And doing what?

Her mind racing along tortuous paths, and recoiling time and again from appalling visions of a Robert Gladwyn whom she had never known, Purity placed everything back in the military chest and lowered the lid. She had no idea of the time; she seemed to have spent a lifetime delving among the relics of Gladwyn's past. It would soon be seven o'clock, surely, and she would have the agonies of humiliation to add to the fresh, living nightmare that had been visited upon her.

One last look around to make sure that she had left no evidence of her passing, and she opened the door.

Robert Gladwyn was standing at the head of the stairs, facing her!

"My dear, I have been looking everywhere for you." His voice was quite calm, his manner unruffled. He merely gazed at her in mild surprise, as well he might, for she had never before set foot in his room during his absence from it.

"I . . . " Her brain revolved wildly around possible explanations.

"Yes, my dear? You were about to say?"

The words came out in a torrent. "I'm looking for our marriage license, Robbie. I . . . I've a notion to start a family album, you know, and I thought it might be amusing to have our marriage license on the first page, only . . . I can't seem to lay my hands on it," she concluded lamely.

"And you were looking for it in my room?" he said. "Well, you will have looked in vain, as you now know. I never had the document."

"Yes, I recall now that I had taken it after the ceremony," she said. "It must be somewhere among my papers, after all. No matter. Did . . . did you have a successful journey to East Anglia? And did you have an opportunity to call upon Aunt Julia?"

"That I did, and the dear soul sends you and Chastity her dearest love. And how have you been amusing yourself these past days, my dear?"

He took her by the arm. Together, they descended the stairs, like any happily married, upper-class couple living in an exquisite house, with servants galore, ample means, and not a trouble in the world.

Alexander, Ninth Earl of Lawme, to whose country mansion in Chiswick Purity was delivered that summer's evening, was a statesman who stood high in the councils of the victorious allies. He was due to represent Regency England in the forthcoming congress to be held at Aix-la-Chapelle. His lordship, a man of thirty-five or so, was a keen rider to the hounds—like his wife, the flat-chested young woman who had offered their town house for the charity ball in aid of the Circle. Fox-hunting was the only activity that the earl and countess shared in common, for they lived apart: her ladyship in Lawme House, Piccadilly; her spouse at the Chiswick mansion. It was whispered in society that the earl's tastes were somewhat—how to put it? —gamey. . . .

Lawme received Purity in one of the sumptuous state apartments that had been designed for his father, the eighth earl, by Robert Adam. The chamber was set about with columns and entablature of the Doric order, and the ceiling contained fine plasterwork bearing the same motifs of anthemion, dentils, and metopes. The vast floor was tiled in marble squares of black and white, arranged in convoluted patterns that dazzled the eye. A nude, life-sized statue of Venus Anadyomene rising from the sea graced the center of the chamber, and the trickling of the fountain that lapped the goddess's feet sounded pleasantly to the ear.

The earl kissed Purity's hand, guided her to a seat upon a Louis XV sofa, and summoned two bewigged footmen, who were standing by, to pour champagne for them both. Having toasted to her health with the rare wine, his lordship threw the glass the length of the chamber and nodded to the footmen. This was a signal for them to seize Purity and strip her naked. Once done, they tied her hand and foot, spreadeagled, upon the sofa. Watched by their noble master—and he proffering them encouragement and advice from time to time—they set about playing with the helpless Purity in the most licentious ways imaginable: fingering her nipples to erection and toying with her thighs; stroking her yielding, soft flesh caressingly, as if to summon forth her desires, the way a lover will. And, when she remained obdurate to their blandishments, they turned her over upon her face, still bound, and spanked her upon her taut behind with a whipping cane and also with their hands. Finally, when his lordship considered that the victim was in a proper state of subjugation, he ordered his lackeys to desist. Then they disrobed their master, assisting him from his over-tight pantaloons, his cambric shirt, and his silk stockings. The lackeys stood by, like sentinels, holding the items of his clothing, as the earl outraged the helpless, inert Purity while she lay with eyes closed, a slow, bitter tear upon her perfect cheek. And when he had finished with her, he strode away down the long chamber, nude as he had left her, with one footman padding after him, bearing his clothes. The lackey who remained behind, after a longing glance at the beautiful, bound figure, untied her bonds and set her free. He watched in silence as she struggled back into her gown, and then he saw her to the door and to her waiting carriage, with the Bashi-bazouk at the reins. Of all the humiliations she had suffered as Azizza's "whore," her experiences at the hands of the Earl of Lawme were by far the most searing, and they left their mark upon her for a long time after.

That night, bathed and somewhat recovered from her ordeal, Purity lay on her scented sheets and watched the ceiling while the moonlight made its passage from one end to the other, and was followed by the rosy glow of dawn. And all the livelong night her thoughts were upon the man she had joined in bigamous marriage. How had Robert Gladwyn employed himself in the six years prior to the war's end, when he claimed to have been serving in the army in the Peninsula and France? Where had he spent that time?

Other questions followed. Was it mere coincidence that he had been traveling abroad during the time that she, Purity, had been in Algeria? And that he had returned not long after she had?

There was another, larger, and more searing question that lay just outside her immediate speculations. She could not bring herself to ask it—even in her mind.

Wainwright took the opportunity to slip her a note the day after, demanding her attendance at his apartment on the following evening. Oddly enough, she welcomed the chance to be alone with him, for she had a question to ask: one of the unanswered questions that had teemed into her mind in the night of sleeplessness.

Wainwright let her into his apartment and gave her a possessive kiss upon her lips, from which she forced herself not to recoil. There was a heavy stench of brandy and tobacco on his breath, and the hand that fumbled at her bodice was unsteady. She submitted herself to his kisses and his maulings, assisted his clumsy attempts to undress her, helped him out of his own clothes, and followed him docilely to the bed. There, he contented himself to lie atop her, his face pillowed between her breasts, and was soon asleep and snoring loudly. Her unwanted swain had drunk too much to tilt a lance at Venus.

"Wake up, wake up!" she said, pulling his ear.

"Eh? Wassit . . . what d'you want? Oh, 'tis you."

"Listen, I want to ask you something."

"Ask? What do you want to ask?"

Purity said, "I want you to tell me about Madame Avanti's husband."

"What about Madame Avanti's husband?"

"Have you ever seen him? Do you know him by sight?"

"No," he said, "never set eyes on him."

"I see," said Purity. His answer closed one avenue of speculation, but it left another wide open.

Wainwright, partly awakened, had recalled the business they were supposed to be about, and he began kneading her thighs.

"Enough of the questions," he muttered thickly. "Let's to the pleasure part of the evening, Mrs. Gladwyn."

"You're hurting me," said Purity. "Be patient for a few moments, do. Listen, you told me that you knew of Madame Avanti through servants' gossip. Who among her servants gossips with *you?*"

"One of the footmen," he said. "He frequents an alehouse in Charing Cross where I sometimes drink of an evening. 'Twas he who told me that his mistress was no more than a high-priced whore for the gentry."

"And that her husband resided on the premises, but only infrequently?"

"Yes. And now can we . . . ?"

She brushed aside his questing hand. "I promise you all you ask if you will just be patient for a few moments. Does your friend—this footman—know the husband by sight, though he comes but infrequently?"

"I should think so," said Wainwright. "Mark you, he gave me to understand that this Avanti fellow's an eccentric, to say the least. 'A strange sort of person' were his words. He has quarters of his own at the top of the house, where only one manservant is allowed to enter, and he's a black fellow—the same one who drives her carriage."

"I know the man you mean," said Purity. "One

thing more: Will you ask your informant if he will give you a brief description of Monsieur Avanti?"

Wainwright sniggered. "What, Mrs. Gladwyn, don't tell me you've a fancy for the husband of your own procuress!"

"The thought may have crossed my mind," said Purity, insinuating a note of coquettishness into her voice. "Does it concern you greatly?"

"I'm not one to be jealous," said Wainwright, "provided he doesn't receive any special favors that you'd deny to me."

"What have I ever denied you?" said Purity in truth.

"Then you'll not deny me"—he breathed the licentious suggestion into her ear—"if I take the trouble to seek that fellow out again and quiz him about his master's appearance?"

"You will do it tomorrow?"

"That I will. And if you come here the following evening, you shall hear it from my own lips. I promise. And now . . . ?"

Steeling herself, she submitted her superb body to his callow and unfeeling lusts; serving with the most exquisite taste and delicacy his most outrageous demands; transcending, by the very grace of her actions, the base servitude thrust upon her. Thus, all unknowing and uncaring, the panting and half-drunken estate manager was the recipient of the most unselfish homage that a woman may render to a man.

When he was spent and snoring again, she crept out of the bed and, hastily dressing herself, left him to his drunken sleep. She carefully descended the stairs so as to make as little sound as possible. She flipped past the ever-seeing eye of the caretaker and went out into the summer night.

It was in doing so, while crossing the street in search of a hackney cab, that she saw a tall figure in a

caped coat and high-crowned hat watching from under
a lantern at the far end of the tenement building.
Even as she espied him, the unknown watcher turned
on his heel and strode swiftly down the street away
from her and was swallowed up in the gloaming.

In her dream, she was riding through the night,
bareback, upon the white palfrey that Omar Manzur had lent her. She was nude, save for the thinnest
of shifts, her hair unbound and streaming in the night
air, her bare thighs in close contact with the taut muscles of the hurtling mount, shoulders bowed over its
flowing mane, hands light as gossamer upon the rein,
thundering over the sand and broken rock under the
desert moon.

Ahead was Omar Manzur, who was also Mark—as
he had always been when they had lain together, save
on that one occasion when her body had received the
Corsair as himself. Alone together in the wilderness
of sand and rock, they were chasing the moon to the
edge of the world, he in the lead, and she slowly gaining on him.

Faster, faster, she urged the tireless palfrey, calling to the steed to render everything it had in order to
draw abreast of the black stallion and the man in the
flowing burnous so that she could claim her prize, so
that he would dismount and, snatching her from the
palfrey's back, would bear her to the yielding sand
and take her to himself.

How her loins yearned for him. The touch of the
palfrey's smooth back was like fire upon her. The
mount's every movement translated into promises
of ecstasies unimaginable and bliss beyond endurance.
She had only to catch her love—and she would be his.

Faster, faster. . . .

And now, surely, the black stallion was flagging.

With every flying stride the palfrey was lessening the gap between them. And now the desire within her had opened up like a burgeoning flower—a scarlet rose blessed by an eternal sun, now become her own body. And she cried out in her blissful agony, calling his name and telling him she was close and about to claim her prize.

Three more strides, and she was almost abreast. His face was averted from her, staring ahead of him, shadowed by the *haik* that covered his head.

Another stride brought them side by side.

"Mark, my darling—Mark!"

He turned to regard her, and she saw only a pair of gleaming eyes peering through a slit in a mass of dark blue veiling that entirely covered the face. And she knew a great fear.

Purity awoke screaming. The clamor in her ears increased her terror all the more, so that she screamed again, then choked it off abruptly, clasping her hands across her mouth.

She sobbed an indrawn breath.

Surely *he* must have heard the screams in his room above!

She crouched, listening, fearful. Her skin crept as she heard movements above her head: the grating of a chairleg on the wooden floor, as if someone had bumped against it in the dark; the opening of a door, its hinge creaking slightly.

Footsteps on the stairs, then in the corridor outside.

And then came a gentle tap on the panel of the door, not loud enough to awaken a sleeping person, but sufficient to signal his presence if she was awake.

She held her breath and willed her heart to quieten its beating, lest the sound be carried to the listening man outside her door.

An eternity dragged past. The door was unlocked. She knew beyond all doubt that she would scream again if his fingers so much as touched the handle to open it. The sight of his eyes, peering out at her through the gloom, would have driven her out of her mind.

Silence. . . .

And then she heard his retreating footsteps up the staircase, followed by the closing of the door above.

She lay back against her pillows, trembling like an old woman with the ague.

Purity had avoided Robert Gladwyn the previous night. Upon her return from the Barbican, she had gone straight to her room. Similarly, she kept out of his way the next morning, remaining at the window till she saw him drive away to the city in the phaeton. His business—whatever that was—kept him absent the whole day, but, short of pleading illness, she had no option but to join him at dinner.

Robert was solicitude itself over dinner, inquiring about her well-being, observing that she looked rather tired and pale, but—blessedly—making no allusion to her screams in the night. She needed a change and a rest, he told her. She was working too hard for the Circle, and she must be more firm with Madame Avanti and not allow herself to be taken advantage of and put upon. Toward the end of the summer, he said, when he had assured himself that the estates were in sound order, he would take her to Paris for a month or so. How did the notion strike her?

Purity answered with as much enthusiasm as she could bring herself to simulate, and he appeared to notice nothing amiss with her reaction. He went on to explain that it was imperative for him to remain with his hand on the helm of the estates till the harvests were well advanced, because he could not trust Wainwright to deal with everything on his own.

"I'm not pleased with that young fellow," he said. "His work has always been indifferent. These last few weeks it's been downright shoddy. He's gotten himself entangled with some woman, I shouldn't doubt."

Purity averted her eyes to her plate and said nothing.

The long day through, she had moved restlessly about the house, her eyes straying constantly to the clock. It was at six that she had decided Wainwright must have finished work at his city office and was possibly taking a hackney cab to Charing Cross, to the alehouse where his garrulous friend the footman was a habitué. Between six and seven, she had play-acted in her mind the likely outcome of their conversation. Would the footman be able to give a clear description of his master?

Would Wainwright recognize, from that description, anyone of his own acquaintance?

She cast a covert glance across the table to the man seated opposite her.

Purity had hoped that Wainwright might call upon his employer the following morning, as was often his habit, and she was ready, dressed, and busying herself quite uselessly in the hallway and within sight and sound of the front door when the time came for Robert to leave for the city, or for Wainwright to call upon him. Neither option offered itself that particular morning; the servant did not put in an appearance, and the master stayed late in bed. It also rained, a driving, thunderous downpour that turned the dust of Cheyne Walk to a quagmire of mud in which coaches, carts, and carriages slipped and slithered. The rain lashed

the surface of old Father Thames to a veritable maelstrom of white water, in which the topsail barges
pitched and tossed like frigates in a Biscay squall.

There was no comfort for her, then, that morning,
and no reassuring nod and beck from her fellow conspirator that might indicate that he had received a fair
description of the elusive and mysterious Monsieur
Avanti. Nor, yet, was there a wide-eyed stare that
might tell her that Wainwright had divined a connection between the footman's description of his master
and a person of his own acquaintance.

There remained only the matter of living through
the day till the hour of seven, which was her time for
presenting herself at Wainwright's apartment in the
Barbican. Characteristically, she was unable to spend
it in the manner that would best have solaced her—in
the company of little Chastity. Instead, she avoided
the child's company and went for a long walk along
the river front, missing luncheon. She was glad upon
her return to be told by the butler that Mr. Gladwyn
had gone out and would not be back for dinner.

At six o'clock she dressed very carefully in a simple
gown of black-and-white-striped gingham, with a bonnet of dyed black straw, and a white mohair shawl.
She found herself to be trembling with nameless emotions as she set off down Cheyne Walk to where, at a
discreet distance from the house, she hailed a passing
hackney cab and directed the driver to take her to the
Barbican.

Disturbing thoughts of her last visit to Wainwright
troubled her during the journey: thoughts of the tall
watcher under the street lantern who had been witness
to her departure. It had been of no consequence, and it
had no possible connection with her doings, surely, but
the guilty mind will seize upon the slightest hints of

its transgressions being uncovered. The watcher in the high-crowned hat may have been no other than a street-corner loafer. In Purity's guilt and shame, she had been seen leaving an assignation with someone who, for want of a better term, could be called her lover, and she was still warm from his bed, with the memory of his touch still imprinted upon her skin and his male smell still haunting her nostrils.

There was no sign of the watcher when she alighted from the cab close to the tenement. She took a handful of loose change from her reticule and paid the driver. She waited till the hackney cab's harness bells had faded away into the distance, then walked swiftly toward the street door of the tenement, past the piles of refuse lying there, past the questing glance of the caretaker, and up the narrow stairs.

The violinist on the second floor rear was scraping his way through a hesitant jig, and a scruffy-looking black cat eyed her tentatively through the banisters above as she tapped gently upon Wainwright's door. Upon receiving no reply, she knocked again; still no response. On the previous occasions, she would have rejoiced at the opportunity of him seeming to be out; she would have run from that hateful place. Tonight was different.

She tried the door handle, and it opened. Quickly entering, she closed the door behind her. The room smelled of spirits and stale tobacco, and Wainwright's tall hat stood on the small table in the room's center, among an array of dirty supper plates, a glass, and a half-empty brandy decanter. At the far end of the room, his bed lay as it had been when he climbed out that morning: tousled, and the sheets none too clean. These were the grubby surroundings in which she had repeatedly given her body to a man she despised. She shuddered at the thought.

There seemed no option for her but to wait for his return, for she was determined to see him that night, no matter how late, and learn how he had fared with his informant. Accordingly, she laid her gloves and reticule upon the table and sat down. The violin in the apartment below continued its hesitant progress through the jig. A door slammed in the distance.

The brandy decanter enticed her eyes. Purity was no drinker, but the temptation to lessen her nervousness with a nip of the neat spirit was very strong. She reached for the decanter and was taking up the glass when she saw that it still contained some liquid. Unable to bring herself to drink from a receptacle that had been soiled by Wainwright's lips (and to think of the shameful intimacies she had been obliged to endure from those same lips!), she went to fetch another.

A curtained alcove contained all that the apartment had in the way of a kitchen and bathroom, together with a few shelves for utensils. She drew back the curtain and set one foot within the alcove.

And then she saw—*him*.

At first—after the immediate shock—it occurred to her that he had contrived to frighten her by remaining silently behind the curtain. He was sitting on the floor, the upper part of his body leaning against the wall, head back, eyes wide and staring at her.

Next, she saw what appeared to be some kind of brooch attached to his shirtfront, above the heart. On second glance, with a scream rising to her lips, which she immediately quenched with the knuckles of her hand, biting down hard, she saw that the thing on his chest was the pearl-and-filigree handle of a woman's hat pin, and that the steel bodkin was driven hard into him, and that there was a carmine stain upon the none-too-clean shirt.

While she stood and stared in uncomprehending horror, there came the sound of slow footsteps ascending the staircase outside.

Chapter Eleven

There was a bang on the door.

"Be you there, Mr. Wainwright? I want to talk with ye. 'Tis about the rent."

Somewhere Purity found the unbidden resource to dart swiftly and silently across the room and slide the bolt of the door. She stood there, her heart hammering. Trapped.

"I know you're in there, Wainwright. Aye, and you're not alone, either, that I know, too." Clearly, it was the old caretaker from downstairs.

What to do? If the old man was after Wainwright for his rent, surely the best course was for her to thrust him some money under the door without comment. But how much? And how much did she have in her reticule? She tiptoed to the table to fetch it.

"I can hear you moving about, Wainwright," called her tormentor. "Open up, there, and let's be seein' the color o' your money."

The door handle rattled and turned, but the bolt resisted the old man's pressure, causing him to growl with a fresh outburst of fury. Purity delved into her reticule to see what money she had, and she realized that she had brought out only the few shillings needed to pay her cab fare.

"You're a week in arrears, an' there's this week that was due yesterday. Eight shillings I want from you, Wainwright, and I ain't a-leavin' this spot till I've had that eight shillings from ye."

She counted the loose change in her hand: five shillings and six pence. It was grotesque, a living nightmare—to be trapped in a locked room with a stabbed corpse, held to ransom in hell for the sake of a few shillings, the sort of sum she might give to a beggar in the street.

There was another bang on the door. "Open up, Wainwright, and hand over that money. If ye don't have it, why, then, borrow it from yon fine lady you've got in there with ye. Do ye hear me, lady? There'll be none o' the handie-dandie for ye this night unless ye help 'im out—not unless ye fancy takin' your pleasures with me hammerin' on the door all night."

A door slammed. Someone called up the stairwell: "What in the deuce is going on, Perkins? How the hell can a fellow study when you're making that confounded racket?"

"Mind your business, Mr. Evans-Jones!" retorted the furious old man, and he gave another hammer on the door.

Purity knelt. Fortunately, there was a generous gap at the bottom of the door. She slid the five silver coins under it, then the coppers.

"Oh, ho!" came the response from the other side. "So the fine lady's coughed it up, oh? What have we here? Five bob? Five and six? That ain't enough. Not by two and sixpence, it ain't. What's wrong, Wainwright? Didn't your fine lady do any trade in the streets tonight?"

Purity closed her eyes and pressed her throbbing temple to the door panel. Please, God, make him go. Make him leave me alone.

"Oh, well, I s'pose it'll have to do for now," growled the old man, "for it covers the arrears and part o' this week. But I'll be after ye on the morrow, Wainwright. Oh, yes. I'll be back again."

He stomped off down the stairs, and Purity heard him exchange a coarse word or two with Mr. Evans-Jones in passing. His footfalls faded away into silence. She breathed her thanks.

What to do next? Clearly, she must get away: from the death room, from the building, from the district. To be found alone with a murdered man—she had not the slightest doubt that Wainwright had been murdered—would bring her into grave suspicion, particularly since the victim was, had been—for want of a better term—her lover. They would say that she had killed him out of jealousy, because he had ill-used her, or because he had tired of her. Twelve good and true men would declare her guilty, and the bewigged judge, on his high bench, would place the black cap on his head and declare the sentence. She would be hanged before a roystering crowd outside the Newgate jail, and Mark would see her no more in this life.

But not yet—she could not possibly leave the tenement in broad daylight, for, given the incident that had just taken place, it was certain that the caretaker would bestow more than his usual attention upon her passing. He might even—horrors!—come out of his quarters and address some comment to her.

She must wait till it was dark. How long? Two hours? Three? Better still to wait until it was likely that the caretaker had gone to bed. But did he lock the outside door and take away the key? Better to risk a quick dash past his window just after dark.

Averting her gaze from the thing that lay within, she drew the curtain back across the alcove. It made no difference; the dead presence continued to fill the room. With trembling hands, she poured a measure of brandy into the dirty glass and tossed it back, retching on the raw spirits.

Huddled in a chair, she waited for the darkness to come.

The bells of St. Paul's chimed the half hour, coming to her over the dark rooftops, as she slid the bolt and stepped out into the shadowy passage, closing the door upon the room of death.

It seemed to her that every stair creaked in protest at her passing, and that she would be challenged by a flung-open door and an angry demand to know what she was doing. No such challenge came, and all was silent behind the closed doors. Reaching the foot of the stairwell, she saw that there was no light behind the caretaker's window, and she suffered a stab of anguish that was only allayed when the street door opened to her touch. The next moment, she was running pell-mell down the high-walled street with rain lashing her face and plucking with a thousand tiny fingers at her clothing. Nor did she stop till she had put a safe distance between herself and the Barbican. Then she leaned against a wall to recover her breath and to still her pounding heart.

And then came the shocking realization that she had left her gloves behind on the table in Wainwright's room!

There was no question of returning to retrieve them. Rather than mount that staircase again, she would have thrust her hand into a fire. Rather than reenter that darkened room, with the staring-eyed corpse awaiting her, she would gladly have died.

The gloves would be found: another piece of evidence that might well lead back to her and condemn her to the gallows. So be it; she would rather hang than go back into that room.

With not a bit of money with her, Purity was faced with the prospect of a long, wet, and possibly dangerous walk home through some of the roughest districts in the city—unless she could find a hackney cab driver who could be persuaded to take her as far as Cheyne Walk and wait while she fetched his fare. As she quickly discovered, vacant cabs were at a premium on such a wet night; several went past her, ignoring her wave, splashing her with muddy water from the streaming cobblestones.

Rounding a corner not far from the grim, black walls of Newgate, she came across two figures huddled in a doorway.

"Oy! This is our pitch, you lousy mare!"

"The brazen hussy! I'll have 'er eyes out!"

They came at her, hands clawing: two viragoes, the cheapest possible women of the night, creatures of the sort who, by reason of dissolution and disease, plied their ancient profession only in dark corners and for the pleasure of wretches as corrupted as themselves. Screeching obscenities, they snatched at Purity's shawl and ripped it from her shoulders and knocked off her bonnet. They would have taken her reticule if she had not held tightly to the drawstring. She fought them off, one-handed, backing away down the street.

"Rip the clothes off the bitch!"

"We'll teach you to walk our pitch, Miss Fancy-Boobs!"

They clawed at her clothing. A raddled face was pressed close to hers, reeking of stale beer. The other

was stooping to seize hold of her ankle and topple her
to the cobblestones.

"What goes on, then? Who've you got there? Stand
aside!"

A bulky figure loomed out of the rain-soaked darkness. He wore a battered tall hat of enormous size, a
greatcoat that reached to his ankles, and he carried a
knobby cudgel. Purity could not make out his face.

"Sam! See what we've . . . " began one of the
women.

"Shut your face!" retorted the newcomer. "Can't I
turn me back for a minute without you startin' a fight?
I tell you two mares that you'd best make a round ten
shillin' between you afore morn, or there's a beatin'
for the both o' you. 'Ello, 'ello, what've we got 'ere,
then?"

He drew close, and Purity could see a brutish
countenance, a black eye patch, stubbled chin, and
blackened teeth. The man saw her, also, and he bared
his fangs in a grin.

"The hussy was a-walking our beat, Sam!" cried
one of the whores.

"Was she, now?" came the retort. "Then you ain't
got a chance in 'ell of makin' that ten shillin', that you
ain't—not with this choice morsel a-walkin' your beat.
I declare I ain't seen a finer piece o' womanflesh in
many a long year. Mark that boobie on her. Come
here, sweetheart. Come to Sammy."

He advanced toward her, his hand outstretched.
Purity backed away in alarm, and, noticing the direction in which his eyes and hand were inclined, she
glanced down to see that she was exposing a breast.
Hastily covering it with her torn bodice, she looked
around her for the best avenue of escape. The one-
eyed brute seized upon her moment's inattention to
leap forward and grasp her around the waist.

"Let me go!" she cried, beating impotently against his massive chest. He only laughed.

"Sammy likes 'em with a bit o' spirit, so you may squawk and struggle as much as you please, sweetheart," he said. "Squawkin' and a-strugglin's to the handie-dandie what mustard is to roast beef. And it's you for the handie-dandie, my gal. Up against the wall with you."

Unbelievably, this brute was thrusting her back against the streaming, wet wall. With one hand he was dragging up her skirts, and with the other he was fumbling with the flap of his breeches. He had thrown aside his cudgel.

"No-o-o!" she cried.

"Squawk on, love," he said good-humoredly. " 'Tis music to Sammy's ears."

He had her skirts almost to her waist, exposing her bare thighs and buttocks to his questing hands. That done, he went to uncover her breasts. It was as he shifted his grip to do this that she was relieved of the pressure of his massive body, and she had room to bring up her right knee sharply. She felt it jar against flesh and bone. He screamed and let go of her. Purity ducked clear of him, evaded the clutching hands of the two viragoes, and fled into the concealing night, not checking her headlong pace till sheer fatigue brought her reeling to a halt within sight of the rain-lashed river.

She had escaped rape, but her situation was greatly worsened. Without her bonnet or shawl, her gown torn, soaked to the skin and with her hair in rats' tails, what chance was there of persuading a cab driver that she was Mrs. Robert Gladwyn, chatelaine of an elegant residence in exclusive Cheyne Walk? None whatsoever.

With a shrug, she pulled her ripped bodice more

closely around her, she bowed her head against the torrent, and she turned her footsteps toward distant Chelsea.

She escaped further molestation. The lateness of the hour, in conjunction with the sheer fury of the rain, had swept the streets of all life. From the Strand to Westminster, from Westminster to Chelsea, she saw not a soul in all the streaming darkness.

It was nearly dawn when, having let herself in the side door of her house, she stripped off her wringing-wet gown and slid between the smooth sheets, too weary, even, to dream of the horrors of the night.

Morning brought a swift, shocked recollection on awakening, followed by a piling of fear upon fear as fresh aspects of her terrible position presented themselves to her.

It was inevitable that, as Wainwright's employer, Robert Gladwyn would be among the first to be informed by the authorities of his employee's murder. It was inevitable that he—and possibly she—would be questioned about the dead man's antecedents by the magistrates' constabulary, the so-called Bow Street Runners. How would she answer? Deny all knowledge of the murder, of course. For Mark's sake, for Chastity's, she must keep her own head out of the noose. She was not responsible for Wainwright's death.

Or was she?

By prompting him to question the footman-informant about his master's appearance, had she not unwittingly steered Wainwright toward his awful fate? For it was certain that the bodkin must have been driven into his heart by, or at the orders of, either Azizza, her mysterious "husband," or both. It strained coincidence too far to suppose that a humble estate manager could have put his life in jeopardy from two

sources in one day. No, it had to be faced: she had been
the unwitting agent of his death, and, despite his
vile treatment of her, she would not have wished
him such a wretched end.

Which brought her thoughts, inevitably, to Robert
Gladwyn. And she did not even want to speculate
about the part he might, or might not, have played in
the tragedy.

Though Purity took elaborate pains to avoid Gladwyn, they had an early encounter: he caught her on
her way up to the nursery to see Chastity. He was
irritated. He told her that he had instructed Wainwright to meet with him immediately after breakfast,
for they were to journey down to Wiltshire that day
and return the day after. And the wretched fellow had
not turned up.

"The fellow's got some wench in tow, Purity," he
said. "That's what's behind it all. He'll have to go, yes,
he'll have to go."

Purity said nothing, but her flesh crept with the
sudden vision of a stiffened corpse lying propped up
against a wall in a curtained alcove.

Gladwyn, without troubling to send a messenger to inquire of Wainwright at his apartment in the
Barbican, set off later that morning for Wiltshire on
his own, leaving Purity to exist through the interminable hours of suspense, waiting for the knock upon
the door that would herald the arrival of the Bow
Street Runners with news of the murder.

By the middle of the afternoon, she had sufficiently
calmed her nerves as to be able to take up her embroidery frame, and was engaged upon a quite elaborate piece of petit point when the sound of the front
door knocker sent the frame flying from her instantly
tensed fingers and bowling across the sitting room and
clattering against the wainscot. She waited, not daring

to breathe, as one or another of the servants crossed the hallway, opened the front door, and had some conversation with the caller. The door then closed, and the footfalls approached the sitting room. There was a discreet tap on the panel, and one of the footmen entered. He was alone.

"A message has just been delivered, ma'am."

She flew to the window in time to see the Bashi-bazouk walking toward his carriage. His leering face turned to look back over his massive shoulder. Seeing the white-faced woman in the window, he raised his cockaded hat in a mocking salutation. Purity drew back, affronted.

"Thank you, Andrews," she whispered, taking the folded paper from the silver salver that the footman held out.

"Thank you, ma'am. Will that be all?"

"Yes, you may go."

Another summons from Azizza! As if she had not enough to torment her. Who was it to be now? Who was left upon the hateful list of men she must pleasure? Or was it to be someone for the second time? With nervous fingers, she broke open the seal and spread open the sheet of paper.

General Gordon Maunders has suffered a most unfortunate accident and will not be requiring your services. However, you will hold yourself in readiness for pleasuring a certain party at the charity ball on September 13.

A blessed release. General Maunders, as she then remembered, was the last of the creatures to whom she had agreed to play the whore to save Mark's life, and he, like the rest, was husband to a member of the Circle. Thank God that Purity was to be spared that, for *Mrs.* Gordon Maunders, as she recalled the lady, was well into her sixties.

But there was the matter of another assignation at the charity ball. And with whom?

Purity had all but forgotten the ball—which had ostensibly been the reason for the meeting she had attended—and how she had taken on the chore of supervising the floral decorations. She supposed that both she and Robert Gladwyn would have to attend, and how she was going to keep an enforced assignation when accompanied by a man whom the world supposed to be her husband was beyond all conjecture. And that was not to mention the suspicions she entertained about that man—suspicions that, day by day, were hardening into certainties.

The day wore on. Night fell. After a light supper, which she pushed around the plate, Purity told herself that fate had granted her a short reprieve, and that the authority of the law would not be descending upon Cheyne Walk that night. She went to bed, but she slept little.

Over breakfast in the conservatory next morning, she anxiously scanned the day's copy of the *Times* for possible news of Wainwright's death. There was no mention of his body having been discovered, but one item caught her eye:

FATAL STREET ACCIDENT
DISTINGUISHED OFFICER
KILLED

A fatal accident occurred yesterday at noon in Pall Mall, in which General G. C. Gordon Maunders was struck by a passing carriage while leaving his club and fatally injured. The carriage did not stop, and pass-

ersby have not been able to give good
descriptions of either the vehicle or its passengers.

General Gordon, who had a distinguished
career in the army from . . .

Though the sun streamed in through the plate-glass
windows of the conservatory, warm upon her hands,
face, and arms, Purity shuddered to read the cold
print: struck by a passing carriage that did not stop.
And then the chilling appendage from Azizza: "General Gordon Maunders has suffered a most unfortunate accident."

Was it not likely that here was yet another victim of
the foul conspiracy that had fled from the maelstrom
of Algiers and was now spreading its tentacles over
London society? What transgression had the gallant
general committed against Azzize and her "friend" to
be cut off so brutally—and he a man who surely had
been one of Azizza's specially hand-picked gentlemen,
elected to enjoy the favors of beautiful Mrs. Robert
Gladwyn, and his wife a member of the magic Circle
for whom Azizza had been a hostess.

The latter thought sent her skimming through the
rest of the paragraph, till, near the end, she came to a
name that stood out:

. . . condolences to the bereaved Mrs. Gor-
don Maunders have also been received from
Madame Avanti on behalf of the Circle for
Aid to Returning Soldiers and Sailors. . . .

Purity lived through all that day, and the night following, in a state of agonized apprehension. She retired early to bed and shortly heard Robert Gladwyn's
return. She froze, breathless, as his footfalls ascended

the stairs. It seemed to her overheated imagination that he paused an instant by her door, then continued on up.

She did not go down to breakfast the following morning, but kept an eye at her bedroom window, which gave a view out onto Cheyne Walk, so that she would see him if he went out. She was standing there, struck with a sudden horror of realization, when *they* came. . . .

They arrived in a hackney cab, which the taller of the two solemnly paid for with coins that he carefully extracted from a large pocket purse. They both wore dark, caped coats and very large, tall hats. They walked purposefully together up to the front door. Their knock echoed through the house.

Purity shrank back against the wall and covered her face in her hands. She was never in an instant's doubt about who they were and what their business was.

She had plenty of time to compose herself, for it was Robert who received them, of course. She had time to splash her face with cool water, to pinch her cheeks and bring out some color, to slip into her most modest gown, and—for additional prudence—to tie a *fichu* around the bodice and mask the cleft of her breasts. Then, holding a clean lace handkerchief upon which she had dabbed a few drops of cologne, she stood ready to be summoned. They did not keep her waiting long.

A tap came on the door.

"Mr. Gladwyn presents his compliments, ma'am, and will ma'am please be so kind as to attend him as soon as is convenient in the drawing room?"

"Tell Mr. Gladwyn I will be down at once," she replied in a voice that sounded, to her ears, like someone else's.

The descent to the drawing room was like a walk

to the guillotine. In such a manner—as slowly as the circumstances permitted, keeping rein upon the emotions, looking neither left nor right, and remembering above all to keep the head erect—must her kinsmen, the condemned aristocrats of the old regime, have gone to their deaths upon the guillotine before the howling mob.

No howling mob for her—only Robert Gladwyn, looking rather distressedly in her direction, and two other figures, leaping to their feet and bobbing awkward bows.

She said coolly, "Good morning, gentlemen." And she looked questioningly toward Gladwyn, raising one eyebrow.

"Good morning, my dear," replied Gladwyn. "These gentlemen, who are from the office of the Bow Street magistrates, have some very disagreeable news to impart. Wainwright is dead."

By not so much of a flicker of an eyelid did she betray herself—in her opinion. Instead, she gave a sharp intake of breath, a look of shocked disbelief.

"How awful!" she cried. "How did . . . ?"

"It was murder, ma'am," said the taller of the two Bow Street Runners. "Permit me to introduce myself. I am Sergeant Piper, and my colleague is Constable Hackforth. The man, ma'am, was foully done to death with this."

She took a backward pace as he produced from his pocket a glittering point of steel, topped with a twist of filigree and a pearl, and held it toward her, point down.

"A . . . a hatpin," she intoned.

"Otherwise known as a bodkin," said Sergeant Piper. "It was thrust into his heart."

"Horrible!"

"Yes, ma'am." One of Sergeant Piper's eyes was

slightly darker than the other, which gave him a curiously lopsided appearance. He gazed very steadily at her. "What would you say concerning same hatpin, ma'am?"

"I?" She gazed in dismay at Robert Gladwyn.

"My dear," he said, responding to her silent plea, "the good sergeant is seeking your expert opinion as a lady. Is it a good, bad, or indifferent hatpin? Fashionable or unfashionable? Cheap or inexpensive? Do I have your meaning correctly, Sergeant?"

"That is so, sir," replied the man of the law, "though, to presume upon Mrs. Gladwyn, we have already elucidated that it is an expensive item. The pearl is real, and the filigree work is of real silver and gold, with not a touch of cheap metal."

They were all looking at her, the sergeant with the bodkin still held out. Surely he did not expect her to take hold of the thing, nor did she. She took a pace nearer and looked at it closely, and she was disturbed to see that the bright shaft was discolored in places.

"It is not a fashionable pin," she said, "insofar as hats that have been fashionable since the war, being mostly tied with a bow under the chin, have not required hatpins."

"By jove! That's a good point, my dear," said Robert Gladwyn.

"Indeed, it is, sir," declared the sergeant. Turning to his assistant, he said, "Note that down, Hackforth —has not been fashionable since the war."

Constable Hackforth was seated at a writing table with a portable pen-and-ink set and a notebook in which he proceeded to write as instructed. He wrote slowly, laboriously, with a very scratchy quill. The pause gave Purity time to collect her thoughts, and it seemed to her that she should be displaying more curiosity.

"Have you any idea of the identity of the murderer, Sergeant?" she asked.

"That we have, ma'am," replied the other. "'Twas a woman who knocked him off."

"Did I not tell you, my dear?" said Gladwyn. "I said he was mixed up with a woman, and I was right —and a married woman to boot, I shouldn't doubt."

"She was seen, several times, by people entering and leaving the building," said Piper.

"What manner of woman was she?" asked Gladwyn. "Did they give a good description?"

Purity clenched her hands tightly behind her back, then realized that Constable Hackforth, having finished his writing, was looking at her with pale, reflective eyes from behind thick spectacles.

"A lady," said Piper, "fashionably dressed and of good—by several accounts, excellent—appearance. Whether fair or dark cannot be said, for she was always bonneted and veiled."

"A married lady," persisted Robert Gladwyn. "Why else the subterfuge? For a lady to visit a man's apartment unaccompanied, she would need to be without shame or sensibility. Only a married woman, for the sake of prudence, would feel the need to conceal her features."

"Another good point, sir," said Sergeant Piper. "I say, we are proceeding excellently well. Mark that down, Hackforth: the woman stooped to concealment because she was married."

The scratchy pen moved slowly across the paper.

"Are you acquainted with the dead man's apartment in the Barbican?" asked Piper of no one in particular.

"No, we are not," replied Gladwyn firmly as Purity looked toward him. "My wife and I had no social dealings with Wainwright, save that on a couple of occasions, out of civility, we invited him to join us at luncheon."

"I see, sir," said Piper.

Without any prompting from his superior, the constable made another small entry. This being done, he took off his spectacles and carefully cleaned them on a handkerchief.

"Is there anything further, Sergeant?" asked Gladwyn. "Be assured, I shall be glad to be of any assistance to your inquiries, but, as I have said, I simply have no knowledge of Wainwright's antecedents. He has worked for me eighteen months. He was not without ability, but idle and feckless. He was just the sort of fellow, one would think, who might get himself entangled with a married woman, who, no doubt, killed him in a fit of jealous fury. Did you say the woman was *seen* there on the night of the murder?"

"The body was not discovered till this morning, sir," said the sergeant. "As far as can be reckoned, it had lain there since Tuesday night, when the woman was last seen entering. The caretaker it was who, after repeated attempts to Wainwright for the balance of his rent owed, finally broke open the door this morning."

And found the thing sitting there on the floor behind the curtain, thought Purity. But what else did he find?

"I think we need trouble you no further, sir," said the sergeant. "I thank you for your help. I thank you, also, ma'am, for your . . . ah . . . expert opinion upon the bodkin."

"I am glad to have been of service, Sergeant," replied Purity. Her mind was racing. It was highly likely that the caretaker, finding a quite expensive pair of almost new ladies' kid gloves, would pocket them without a second thought, then sell them later in the nearest pawnshop for the price of a quart of gin. No danger there.

"Just one other thing," said Sergeant Piper, turning on his way toward the door. "I'm sorry, I quite forgot."

Constable Hackforth, who had folded up his portable pen-and-ink set and pocketed his notebook, replaced both upon the writing table and addressed his short-sighted gaze toward his chief.

Purity felt fear encompass all her body, beginning with a prickling in the crown of her head that descended to her feet.

"And what was that, Sergeant?" asked Robert Gladwyn.

"It concerns your wife, sir," said Piper. His oddly dissimilar eyes were upon her, humorlessly, the mouth unsmiling. "I have the need for more of her ... expert opinion."

"I am sure my wife will be only too happy to oblige," said Gladwyn. He smiled at Purity. "My dear?"

"Of course," said Purity.

From the corner of her eye, she saw that Constable Hackforth had uncovered his inkwell and was dipping the tip of his quill into the ink.

"I wonder, ma'am," said Piper, delving into the capacious side pocket of his caped coat, "if you would be so kind as to give me your expert opinion on these?"

They lay in the palm of his big hand, looking curiously small. The caretaker had not, after all, pawned them to buy a quart of gin.

"Gloves," said Robert Gladwyn. "Ladies' gloves, hey?"

"Found in Wainwright's room, sir," said Piper.

"Belonging to the woman in question, you think?"

"Oh, undoubtedly, sir."

"My dear," said Robert Gladwyn, "can you give an opinion on them?"

She supposed they were all looking at her: the constable, with his scratchy pen poised and ready; odd-eyed Sergeant Piper, with the suddenly hard and humorless look that he displayed for her; she could not begin to imagine the expression on Robert Gladwyn's face.

She said, "They're exquisitely fashioned—from Paris, I would say. The English glovers never seem to get this fine stitching quite right; consequently, their work is so much more bulky, not so refined, not so flattering to the hands."

"From Paris, Hackforth," said Piper in a flat voice. "Write that down. Anything else upon which you could advise us, ma'am?"

"Expensive," she said.

"They'd have to be, ma'am, wouldn't they? I mean, from Paris and all. As to size: Would they fit a lady of large, medium, or small size of hand? I am puzzled, for, you see, I have not had much experience with such matters."

Gladwyn was peering over her shoulder at the gloves, which she had taken in her hands and was turning over and over.

"They look somewhat on the small side to me, wouldn't you say, my dear?" he commented.

"They are . . . quite small," murmured Purity.

Somewhere out of the range of her vision, a quill pen scraped and spluttered her reply.

"Ah, but *how* small, ma'am?" asked Piper. "That's the question."

"My dear, you have a small hand," said Gladwyn.

"Why do you not try them on, by way of a demonstration?"

"A demonstration, that's it," said Piper.

With a dull feeling of inevitability, Purity drew one of the gloves over her hand, smoothed down the fingers, fastened the small buttons at the wrist, and held out her hand for their inspection.

"Fits perfectly," said Gladwyn with the air of a man introducing a paragon.

"Could have been made for you, ma'am," said the Bow Street magistrate. "Indeed, as I have said before, we are proceeding exceedingly well today. Listen to me, Hackforth."

"I am listening, Sergeant," responded his obedient aide.

"Mark this down, Hackforth," said Piper. "The glove is of a very small size. For reference, we may say that it is of a size to fit Mrs. Gladwyn."

Avoiding the sergeant's eyes, Purity took off the glove and meekly handed both back to him.

"I thank you again, ma'am," said he, "and you, also, sir. Now we must indeed be on our way. Good day to you both. Come, Hackforth."

"I trust you will be fortunate and speedily apprehend the murderer, Sergeant," said Robert Gladwyn.

The Bow Street Runner's answer was in direct reply to Gladwyn's remark, but Purity knew it was all for her: "Not speedily, perhaps, sir," said he, "but we shall have her in the end, never fear. Like the famous mills of God, we of the Bow Street magistrates' office grind slowly—yet we grind exceeding small."

They knew, of course. They had known even before coming to Cheyne Walk—that much was plain. The caretaker, or, more likely, one of the men she had encountered on the stairs, had given a better description of her than Piper had admitted. Perhaps someone had spoken of the telltale blonde hair that he had espied under the concealing bonnet and veil. She had been trapped into putting on the glove, and that had confirmed Piper in his opinion. Of course it fitted her perfectly. She was very fastidious about gloves, and the one in question was one of half a dozen pairs that she had bought in Paris on her way back to England with Mark after the war.

And he, Robert, did he know? Did he guess? Had he recognized the gloves? She tried to remember the occasions upon which she had worn them in his company, but she could not remember.

Perhaps he knew; she had no idea. The complexity of her opinions concerning the man she had bigamously married had become tangled past all reckoning.

That night her dreams were all of hangings.

There was M. le Marquis—he who had taken the peasant child-bride on the first night of her marriage. Purity, still only a child and dumb with horror and disbelief, had seen the selfsame marquis hanging by his neck from the massive cut-glass chandelier suspended from the ceiling of his great hall. He was slowly revolving, like a marionette on a string, with a look of pained surprise on his contused, painted old face. She dreamed of him.

In the park of M. le Marquis' château, on that same occasion, there had been a hanging tree. Upon that tree, the revolutionaries had strung up by their necks men, women, and children so that they looked like grapes upon a vine. Purity had attended the village school with some of the little ones who had stirred up there in the night wind, turning, turning in a dance of death. She dreamed of them.

There was a handsome, wicked highwayman to

whom, for the wrong reasons and entirely in innocence, she had once given herself. She had, by a tragic mischance, been present when they hanged him at Newgate amidst the plaudits of an adoring London crowd, who cheered him as if he had been the great Mr. David Garrick himself. She had not been able to bring herself to watch his death agonies, she who had seen so many hang. She dreamed of him.

And when they brought her out of the doors of the jail, in solemn procession with the city officers in their regalia and the mace-bearer up in front, and brought her to the scaffold, where the hangman and his assistants stood ready with hood and noose, she broke away from them and ran screaming. She was still screaming when, awake, she found herself standing in her nightshift outside the door of her bedchamber.

In the weeks that followed, Purity found herself more and more distanced from Robert Gladwyn. It was as if the gentle, kindly man who had been her loving friend might never have been. There was a constraint between them that neither the bonds of proximity nor the necessities of civility could bridge. They ate together, but rarely, and when they did their conversation seemed, to her, largely designed for the ears of the footmen who stood behind their chairs. Chastity, who might have served as a link between them, passed through one of the many and varied phases of infancy during those weeks: she developed a temporary aversion to Mama and Papa Robert that was compensated by a blind adoration for her nursemaid.

Purity's suspicions regarding Gladwyn—suspicions that were starving for want of fresh evidence—began to lessen. She knew he was one of the handful of men who could have picked up Nancy Shaw on the fateful night of the dinner party, and she did not flinch from facing up to the implications that must follow such a conclusion. On the other hand, she had always liked Gladwyn, and she had gratefully entrusted her adopted child and herself to his care and protection. For all her suspicions, it would have required a very considerable proof for her completely to believe that he was other than he appeared to be.

But she no longer trusted him.

In the last week of August, she received a visit from an extremely elegant gentleman who was, notwithstanding his manner and appearance, a mere tradesman: a florist from Covent Garden. He had called upon Purity, he informed her, upon instructions from Lady Lawme, since she, Mrs. Gladwyn, had undertaken to supervise the floral decorations for the forthcoming ball at Lawme House, Piccadilly. Mrs. Gladwyn was not to worry about a thing, he assured her, for he could see, from the furnishings of her beautiful house, that they were two minds that thought as one, two sensibilities that vibrated in the same key. As to the floral arrangements on the night of the ball, he saw roses and chrysanthemums. Did she not agree? September was such a splendid time of the year for the floral *artiste,* was it not? They would have banks and banks of roses, fresh from Kew, likewise, chrysanthemums. One simply had to be extravagant to the point of absurdity, did one not? He looked very carefully at Purity for a reply to the latter declaration, and, having received an affirmative, he speedily took his leave.

Somewhat to her amusement, Purity realized that, so far as supervising the floral decorations was concerned, her only role in the proceedings would be to foot the bill.

Shortly after, a numbered invitation card arrived

for Mr. and Mrs. Robert Gladwyn to attend the ball in aid of the Circle for Aid to Returning Soldiers and Sailors, to be held at Lawme House, Piccadilly, by gracious permission of the Earl and Countess of Lawme, on Saturday, September 13, at eight o'clock. Fancy dress and masks were to be worn. Purity was the one who opened the invitation at breakfast time, and she passed it across the table to Gladwyn, who read it without comment.

Knowing that the forthcoming event would be yet another occasion on which she would be whoring for Azizza, Purity viewed it with considerable apprehension, which was only relieved by the devout hope that the man she would be obliged to pleasure at Lawme House on the thirteenth—whoever he was—might be the last.

As she regarded her costume, she could summon up no more enthusiasm than to dispatch a note to her Bond Street dressmaker, a Madame Dupuis, to whom she had been going for years, in good times and in bad. Briefly, and writing in French, she asked *madame* to concoct for her a fancy dress and mask in good time for the ball. She would not trouble to come for a fitting; *madame* had her measurements. As to the subject of the costume, she had no very good preference, she wrote. And then, remembering that she was supposed to be the floral supervisor, she suggested that a floral theme might be suitable.

In less than a week, a smart equipage, consisting of a box cart and a pair of horses, with driver and footman, pulled up outside the house in Cheyne Walk, and a diminutive youth in an over-large cocked hat delivered a package: it contained Purity's costume. Intrigued despite herself, she opened the package and liked what she saw there, whereupon she hastened to try it on.

Madame Dupuis had outdone herself in the concept and execution of the floral costume, which consisted of a gown that subtly followed the line of the then current Grecian mode—that is to say, it was high waisted, sleeveless, and with a bodice cut just short of scandal. There the resemblance ended, for the gown was entirely composed of thousands of flower petals, cut from silk and sewn upon a net base. *Madame* had chosen autumnal colors: russet browns, bright reds, shades of ocher, greens, misty grays, and touches of blue. The creation, which fit Purity perfectly, had an uneven, raggedy hem at mid-calf. With the gown, *madame* had supplied a pair of silk stockings, one of russet brown, the other pale gray, to be worn with silk slippers that laced at the ankle like buskins. The ensemble was completed by a headdress and mask combined: a skullcap of petals that entirely covered the head and extended to the mouth, with slanting slits for the eyes, which gave the wearer a bewitchingly feline appearance. Purity examined herself critically in the mirror and approved. The costume had one tremendous advantage—in it she would be unrecognized by all but her intimates.

A mere three days before the ball, Gladwyn made his intentions known. He would be unable to accompany her, he informed Purity. Having as yet found no replacement for Wainwright, he was perforce obliged to act both as landowner and estate manager, and it was essential for him to supervise the harvest in East Anglia. He would leave tomorrow, he said, and he added that he trusted Purity would enjoy the ball.

Purity bowed her head and kept her own counsel.

The morning of Saturday, September 13, showed the Thames valley in the trappings of autumn, with the distant hills of Surrey sharp in the clear air and the lime trees of Cheyne Walk all turned a golden yellow. Purity took little Chastity for a walk down to the river's edge to feed the swans, and she returned in time to be greeted at her own gate by a lad carrying a large parcel. He doffed his cap civilly enough and inquired if this was the Gladwyn residence.

"Yes, and I am Mrs. Gladwyn," said Purity. "Can I help you, son?"

"I'm from Meek and Hawkes, theatrical costumiers of Drury Lane, ma'am," piped the youth in a shrill treble. "I have a fancy dress costume for Mr. Gladwyn, as ordered."

Purity shook her head. "There must be some mistake," she said. "My husband could not have ordered a fancy dress costume. There is a ball this evening, yes, but Mr. Gladwyn is not attending."

The lad was not one bit put out, but, producing a piece of paper from his pocket, he read aloud from his instructions contained thereon: "'Costume for Mr. R. G. Gladwyn, to be delivered to his home in Cheyne Walk if completed before the twelfth of the month, or to the Wanderers' Club, St. James's Street, if completed after the twelfth.' Them's my instructions, ma'am," he said.

"But today is the thirteenth," murmured Purity, trying to come to grips with a suddenly disturbing notion that had sprung to her mind.

The youth blinked and wrinkled his forehead.

"'Swelp me, ma'am, the thirteenth it is!" he exclaimed. "And here's me, come all the way to Cheyne Walk when I could have saved myself an hour's traipse by delivering properly at St. James's Street. Well, it's back there I go. Good day to you, ma'am."

He set off back toward Westminster at a brisk pace, with Purity staring after him, and he was soon out of sight beyond the bend in the road.

"What did the big boy thay, Mama?" lisped little Chastity, tugging at Purity's hand.

Still staring the way the boy had gone, Purity replied slowly, "Darling, he told me that Papa Robert is going to the ball, after all."

"Where ith Papa Robert now, Mama?"

"Staying at his club, my darling."

"Why, Mama?"

"I think, darling," said Purity, "that it's his intention to give me a surprise at the ball tonight."

Too late, she cursed herself for not having inquired of the delivery boy about the nature of the fancy dress costume that Robert Gladwyn had secretly had made for himself at Meek and Hawkes, theatrical costumiers of Drury Lane. It was too late to go after him, encumbered as she was by the child.

William Kent, architect most versatile, was responsible for the noble Palladian-style mansion in Piccadilly that was commissioned of him by the Seventh Earl of Lawme, grandfather of the present incumbent, in 1734. Restrictions of site in the teeming metropolis did not easily permit the extended treatment that landed nabobs called for in their country houses, but Kent made cunning use of the area available to him. Lawme House was not only the biggest private residence in London, but it also *looked* like the biggest.

To Lawme House, Piccadilly, on the balmy, fresh-scented evening of September 13 came the rich, the powerful, the beautiful, and the aristocratically splendid people of Regency England, an England that, as senior member of the European alliance that had defeated Napoleon and possessor of a fleet that—the most unfortunate American War of 1812 excepted—had been unchallenged since Trafalgar, was set fair for a hundred years of world supremacy.

The area surrounding and approaching the mansion
had been crowded since early morning by Londoners
(and others from farther afield) enticed by the oppor-
unity of viewing their betters at close range. It was ru-
mored that "Old Nosy" was attending. The Duke of
Wellington, indisputably the most popular man in England, if not in Europe, was worth twelve hours' wait of
anyone's time. It was also said—without enthusiasm
—that Prinny would be there.

The idle unemployed—and there were plenty of
that sort in London, with thousands of men having recently been discharged from the colors at the termi-
nation of a long war—formed a large proportion of
the crowds around Lawme House that evening. Ex-
soldiers who had stormed Badajoz under Old Nosy,
veteran Jack Tars of Nelson's day—some of them
limbless, some blinded, some raving lunatics—and the
whores—all of the cheapest kind and doing a busy
trade quite openly—sprawled in the gutters to cheer
their betters, for this was a charity occasion, was it
not? The profit of the evening would go to the returned soldiers and sailors, would it not?

(The most elementary arithmetic could have demonstrated that a noble lady who had bought a two-
guinea ticket for the ball and spent thirty guineas on
a gown to grace the occasion displayed a very curious
attitude to the ancient virtue of charity.)

As darkness fell and the lamplighters went about
their business, and all the wide windows of Lawme
House glittered with the brightness of crystal chandeliers, the crowds grew restive with anticipation.
Throughout the long day, pie vendors had moved
among them, together with oyster sellers, purveyors of
jellied eels, hawkers of lime juice, lemonade, and gin-
ger ale, and tapmen from local taverns bearing foam-
ing pitchers of beer, cider, and jugs of gin at a penny

a glass. Most people present, even the poorest, were gorged with abundant food. Many were drunk; some were very drunk. A holiday mood was upon them, and they were, after the manner of Londoners, grimly determined to enjoy themselves.

The arrival of the first carriage drew a roar of appreciation. The descent of the attendant lackeys, the opening of the carriage door, the lowering of the steps, the handing down of the passengers—all were greeted with an awesome silence. The recipient of this homage —a minor government official with his wife and daughters—could never again in all his life have hoped to be the cynosure of so much devoted attention. After him and his brood, the guests arrived thick and fast: peers and peeresses, admirals and politicians, the rich and the famous—and most of them in fancy dress, and many masked.

Presently, the murmur went up: "Tis the duke! Nosy's come!" An ordinary hackney cab drew up and disgorged the hero of Waterloo. Wellington had scorned to don fancy dress or to mask his famous countenance. He paused on the top step of the mansion for a moment and acknowledged the plaudits of the crowd with a brief wave, then went in. A great sigh of contentment went up: the long wait had not been in vain.

And then, like a comet blazing across the dark firmament, came the goddess in the gown of petals. A most profound silence greeted her arrival. Jaws ceased to chomp, and bottles raised halfway to mouths remained frozen there. Whores who were plying their trade in nearby doorways and dark corners came out to see what was amiss. Who was she? Who was this apparition?

Purity alighted from her phaeton in a swirl of autumnal petals, the feline slant of her masked eyes

sweeping over the sea of watching faces. Her figure
was all, for of her face and hair there was nothing to
be seen, save the perfection of mouth and jaw. Men
lusted and felt their loins stir at the revelation of waist
and thigh, of half-bared bosom; women ached with
jealousy to mark the way she climbed the steps. Long-
legged, proud, queen of the evening, she entered the
hallway of the mansion, leaving a desolation of desire
and envy in her wake.

Lawme and his countess received their guests at the
head of a sweeping curve of wide staircase that ascended from the hallway. Names were not announced,
this out of consideration for those who, by wearing
masks and keeping their anonymity, hoped to enjoy
adventures of amorous dalliance that night. Purity
handed her numbered invitation card to an obsequious
lackey, who discreetly checked it against a list in his
gloved hand, then motioned her to the stairs.

All eyes were upon her as she ascended. Lawme
was dressed as a faun, with horns, appropriately
enough. His close-set eyes narrowed lasciviously behind his mask as he regarded Purity's approach. She
curtsied to him and his countess. Lady Lawme, her
bucolic complexion only slightly quenched by a thick
layer of rice powder, and her rudimentary bosom
forced upward beyond all imagining in the tight stays
of the previous century, was essaying to impersonate
Queen Marie Antoinette. Purity gained the impression
that neither of them recognized her, and she was relieved.

The great salon on the upper floor, with its painted
ceiling and pillared minstrel gallery, was crowded with
color and the glitter of jewelry. There was a cacoph-
ony of parakeet chatter, above which the string
orchestra of the Grenadier Guards was manfully bowing its way through Mozart up in the gallery. Purity

looked around her for someone she knew—someone
to whom she might, without embarrassment, reveal
her identity. She saw Wellington leaving a group, and
she went toward him before he became involved with
another. The opportunity of addressing him never
came, for at that moment the orchestra stopped in
mid-bar and struck up the national anthem, to the
strains of which the prince regent waddled into the
salon with an assortment of cronies, both male and female, at his heels.

The prince espied Wellington and went toward him.
The duke regarded the regent with some surprise, as
well he might have, for the royal voluptuary, together
with his followers, had chosen the theme of *chinoiserie*
for his attire. He wore a mandarin's robe of lime-
green, embroidered with yellow dragons, and a curious
hat that trailed a peacock feather. The bloated royal
features were quite unmistakable under a golden
domino mask, and, as if to remove all traces of doubt
about the wearer's identity, the star of the Order of
the Garter glittered upon his breast.

"My dear duke, I must say I am surprised to see
you here," declared the prince. "Not at all your style,
I should have thought, correct?"

"Sir, I had just as well come as stay away," replied Wellington dryly, "for, my house being only a
few yards farther down Piccadilly, I should get
no sleep from the clatter here this night."

The duke's sally brought a laugh from the regent,
in which his cronies dutifully joined.

"But since you have come, Duke, you should at
least have masked yourself," said the prince.

"Sir," replied Wellington, "it would be an irrelevance. This nose of mine would outstrip any disguise
devised by man."

Purity turned her back on the laughter and passed

on through the crowds. Wellington would have been a useful ally on this night of all nights, and she told herself that she would make another attempt to identify herself to him when the opportunity arose. Meanwhile, she was alone, alone in an anonymous crowd. And somewhere in the crowd were her enemies.

Somewhere in the crowd, also, was Robert Gladwyn. . . .

A hand took her elbow. Would she care to dance? No, she would not. The would-be swain was too short to be Gladwyn, and the figure was too scrawny beneath the harlequin's suit, the voice nothing like Robert's. She walked on.

For the most part, the menfolk—doubtless in the interests of pursuing adventure—appeared to have concentrated upon disguise in their choice of costume. The women—most of them, both young and not so young—had seized upon the opportunities for voluptuousness. In an age which, in imitation of classical Greek and Roman sculpture, idealized the female breast, the bodice had become merely a temporary place of concealment, from which—as could be seen in the contemporary prints and caricatures—one's nipples could, with perfect propriety, be permitted to make an occasional appearance under stress of movement. Purity's own display was quite considerable, but she was far outstripped by many around her.

But there was no woman in the room who came within a mile of the voluptuous creature who had just put in an appearance at the salon entrance. Every gaze swept toward her. The chattering was hushed. Somewhere up in the minstrel gallery, a fiddler misbowed a note. And Purity felt all her courage, all her resolve, drain away at the sight.

No longer was it Madame Avanti, doyenne of the

Circle for Aid to Returning Soldiers and Sailors; it was Azizza the Corsair *reis* who stalked, cat-like, an uncaged leopardess, across the wide sweep of floor toward Purity, and the crowd fell back to let her pass.

She was dressed as Purity had seen her in the torture chamber beneath El Diablo's palace—in the barbaric silver armor and scarlet turban with the osprey plume, in the breastplate that enhanced every nuance of her upper torso, and scandalously. She was masked in a silver visor that concealed her face to the nostrils, and she wore her own flame-red hair flying free. No one in all that gathering, save one, recognized her as Madame Avanti.

And she was walking straight toward that one person who would have given the world to have been far away.

"Purity, my dear, I would have known you anywhere. But, then, though there are men present here tonight who have known your body as intimately as I have, it takes a woman to detect a woman, and the more so when there is the bond of hatred and rivalry, don't you think?"

Purity said, "Tell me what it is that you want of me tonight. Give me your orders. Let it happen now— straight away. Then give me permission to go."

The sensuous mouth parted in a malicious smile.

"You wish to run away? So unflattering, my dear. And after all the trouble we took to rid you of that lout Wainwright."

Purity drew breath sharply. "So it *was* you! I thought so. I knew you must have had a hand in it. Was it because he questioned your footman?"

Azizza shrugged. "The footman hardly came into it. Wainwright was doomed long before he made that clumsy attempt. I have had you watched, my dear, and I knew that he was having his way with you. I must say I am surprised. I credited you with more . . . discrimination." She laughed.

"He forced me into it," snapped Purity.

"Of course, of course," said Azizza. "It was obvious that he was blackmailing you, so he had to be killed. There is too much at stake for us to have our plans put in jeopardy by the Wainwrights of this world."

"So you killed him," said Purity in distaste, "the way a child will squash a fly. But how . . . who . . . ?"

"The old fool of a caretaker was lured away on a pretext," said Azizza, "whereupon my Bashi-bazouk went upstairs and killed him with one of my hatpins. That neat touch, my dear, was an attempt to point the finger of suspicion at the mysterious woman who visited him occasionally. I must say you somewhat overdid it by leaving your gloves behind for the Bow Street men to find. You are under strong suspicion, you know. They believe you are the murderess."

"How did you know that?" queried Purity angrily.

The she-Corsair preened herself, hand on hip, well aware that almost every eye in the salon was upon either her or the equally breathtaking creature at her side.

"Nothing is hidden from us, my dear," she murmured, "nothing. I will tell you, furthermore, that they would arrest you—would have done so weeks ago—if it had not been for a certain *influence* that I invoked."

"You have the power to do that?" asked Purity. "To obstruct the workings of the law?"

"We are our own law," declared Azizza, "just as we were in Algiers. We judge. We condemn. We execute."

"As you also executed General Gordon Maunders?" interjected Purity.

The green, she-cat's eyes flared dangerously, and Purity knew in the instant that her remark had struck a sore spot.

"Maunders was an old fool," hissed Azizza. "He could have had the whole world, but the prospect of the whole world was too much for him. In his cowardice, he suddenly remembered that he had scruples. An old man's scruples could not be permitted to stand in the way of our great enterprise. And, so . . . " She snapped together her slender finger and thumb.

The string orchestra came to the finish of a long and convoluted coda while Purity was weighing a question in her mind. There was a mild splattering of applause.

"What *is* your great enterprise, Azizza?" she whispered.

Azizza gazed at her archly.

"Can you not guess?" she asked. "Surely, you of all people!"

Purity recoiled a pace from her in horror.

"Not . . . *the slave trade!*" she cried.

"What else?" Azizza smiled. "What other enterprise in the whole wide world would better suit a Corsair?"

"You're lying!" said Purity. "The Corsairs are finished—you have said as much yourself. Your fleet is destroyed, and Algiers is no longer your stronghold."

"There will be other fleets," said Azizza, "and new strongholds."

"You're lying, you're lying!" cried Purity wildly. "The allies will never permit it. The congress at Aix-la-Chapelle will outlaw your filthy trade forever. They will . . . "

"They will do no such thing," said Azizza flatly. "They will talk. Oh, there will be talk aplenty. Noble resolutions will be aired. Fine resolves will be brought out, dusted, and then put away till next time. Nothing will be done. We have given our instructions."

"You have given . . . *instructions?*" Purity stared at the barbaric figure in blank disbelief. "And by what power have *you* given these instructions?"

"By the power of greed, ambition, and lust," said Azizza. "Every man has his price. We have been the paymasters. Some we have paid in bright gold; some we have paid with titles, decorations, or the trappings of ambition; some—the lustful—we have rewarded with the voluptuous bodies of beautiful women." She made the last remark while regarding Purity meaningfully.

For an instant, Purity thought she was going to strike the creature before her; instead, there came into her mind a vision of the toiling wretches she had known: the frightened little concubines; poor Meg O'Grady, with the hot iron being burned into her nakedness; the young Greek sailor whose profile could have been carved by Praxiteles. And the tears came.

"You made me play the whore to those men," she said brokenly. "You put my husband's life at stake and made me give my body for the slave trade—to help reestablish that hideous, hateful traffic in human misery."

"Nor have you finished, my dear," responded Azizza, her green eyes coolly sweeping Purity from head to foot. "This night you will play the whore again, or not only will your husband die, but I shall withdraw the protection that is saving you from the gallows for the murder of your lover."

"Who is this man?" asked Purity dully, past all caring.

"El Diablo!"

"El Diablo?" echoed Purity, appalled.

"He has possessed you before," said Azizza, "but

it was obvious to him that—though abandoned beyond
all belief and squandering your favors, as if it were
your last night on earth—you were drugged at the
time. True?"

"Yes," confessed Purity.

"Tonight," said Azizza, "he wishes to enjoy you
with your mind in a clear state. It is his great desire.
I will not conceal from you my jealousy, for you, a
woman, will see it written plainly. He, that man, is
the only lover for whom Azizza has ever made an
exception to her rule that no man knows her twice.
He is all fire and air, Purity. There is a terrible bewitchment in his loins. You will never, never know a
lover such as he."

"When?" whispered Purity.

"At midnight," said Azizza. "You will be summoned to him at midnight. The Bashi-bazouk will
fetch you."

The charity ball, everyone agreed, was turning out
to be a most tremendous success. The prince regent
was enjoying himself. After a token gavotte with his
hostess, whose scrawny charms were not to the royal
voluptuary's taste, His Highness did the rounds of the
prettiest and best-endowed women on offer. He
danced till the sweat made rivulets down his painted
face, breathing brandy-scented compliments and flow-
ery obscenities into every bewitched ear. He would
greatly have wished to dance with the two stunning
creatures whom he had observed conversing together
earlier, the red-maned temptress with the silver-plated
breasts and the bewitching morsel in the flower petals.
But, even though he sent his fawning minions far and
wide to search them out, neither was anywhere to be
found.

Azizza had disappeared immediately after giving

Purity her instructions. Purity had gone herself to the powder room, where, to the sound of a stout dowager snoring quietly on a sofa next to hers, she turned the thoughts over in her teeming mind and waited for the hands of the clock to crawl inexorably to midnight.

She was a slaver's whore!

The cries of tortured thousands—men and women laboring like animals in the broiling sun, raped girls and gelded boys—condemned her for what she was. It was useless to excuse herself by pleading ignorance. She now knew the truth, and nothing on earth would prevent her from answering El Diablo's summons when it came. For the love of one man, for his life and liberty, she would turn her back on the tortured thousands and shut her ears to their cries. Oh, Mark, Mark, forgive me, for I shall never be able to forgive myself.

As the hour grew later, her thoughts became wilder. Only one course seemed to commend itself, and that was to find some means of killing El Diablo and then—since this was England and she must inevitably pay for the crime upon the gallows—to destroy herself. But she had no weapon at hand, not even a bodkin to drive home into an unsuspecting heart.

Eleven-thirty. . . .

The dowager rose up, nodded to Purity, and opined that it was damnably hot down in the salon. Did she not think that Prinny's antics would disgrace a farmyard billy goat? The old lady replaced a tall court wig upon her near-bald pate, picked up her walking stick, and hobbled out to view the revels. Save for a young girl lying asleep at the other side of the room, her face white with fatigue and too much champagne, Purity was alone.

Killing El Diablo would serve her nothing, for

Azizza could still take her revenge and destroy Mark
There was no other course open to her but to submit
—as she had so often submitted in the odyssey that
could only end when she was once more enfolded in
Mark's arms. She ran her trembling fingers over her
body, so firmly rounded beneath the flimsy silks, the
body that, within the half hour, would be the plaything of he who must surely be the most dangerous
man alive in England. And it would not be for the
first time; he had known her on two previous occasions, though, mercifully, the remembrance was denied her. She had no recollection of having enjoyed
the "terrible bewitchment in his loins." In tomorrow's
dawn, she would be looking back on the night—and
would it be in self-loathing? Purity knew that her
intent was firm, that her love was boundless and un-
shakable. She also knew, to her constant dismay, that
her warm and passionate Latin nature was capable of
being tempted and lured to surrender, and her body
—that perfect instrument of lovemaking—the more
so.

It was five minutes to the hour. . . .

She rose, and, crossing to a pier glass, she regarded
herself, unmasked as she was, her hair bound in a
plait around her head, her lissome form plainly
etched through the thin gown by the light from the
candelabrum behind her. She replaced the mask and
headdress and turned to go.

Her path to the door passed the sofa where the
young girl lay asleep. One abandoned curl from a
domino headdress brushed a satin cheek with every
breath. A dried tear lay upon that cheek. One child-
like breast had fallen free of its bodice. She could
have been Chastity grown to seventeen or eighteen
and Purity's heart melted toward her. The child had
made herself very drunk. Was it for love of a boy

who had failed to notice her, or that of an older man who, having pleasured himself with that young body and then tiring of her immature eagerness, had cast her off?

Purity paused and touched the soft forehead with her fingertips, as if in a blessing. Sleep on, little one. No one will hurt you in your dreams, and tomorrow your hurt may not seem so grave, after all.

Summoning up her courage, she went out into the hall and closed the door behind her. The Bashi-bazouk was lolling against the opposite wall, picking his teeth. He straightened up and leered to see her. Without a word, he set off down the passage, beckoning her to follow.

Beyond the great salon, from which came the prim strains of a minuet, her guide led her through a maze of staircases and galleries till they came, at length, to a large, colonnaded chamber in the center of which was a low-sided circular pool, with the statue of a small boy holding a dolphin, from whose open jaws cascaded a stream of clear water. Skirting the pool, her guide approached a door set in the marbled wall, knocked on it, and ushered her inside.

A fragment of distorted memory came to her: of another occasion, another such room, lit by a single hanging lamp, another dark-veiled figure reclining upon a divan by the far wall.

He rose as the door was quietly shut behind her. He was dressed in black robes, with a black *haik* covering his head, and the dark blue veil of the desert Tuaregs covering all but the eyes.

She licked her dry lips.

"Hello . . . Robbie," she whispered. "So you came to the ball after all."

He laughed.

Chapter Twelve

He was striding to and fro, up and down the confines of the small chamber, in and out of the lamplight, his shadow cast grotesquely large upon the tiled walls. He talked and gesticulated as he went.

She watched his every move in awful fascination, as a cornered mouse watches the antics of the adder that is moving to strike and devour it.

It may have been his costume, or the surroundings, but he had taken on a stature that was quite unlike his own. His voice, also, had a hard edge of authority that she had never detected in him. Where there had been gentleness, there now was power. And something else—a brutal masculinity emanated from him in an almost physical force.

He was talking about . . . her.

"I wanted you from the first, my Purity," he said. "How was I to know that I would encounter a creature like you in the depths of rural Wiltshire? We knew of Landless's appointment, you see. Nothing escaped the brotherhood in those days. We had our spies and our friends in high places. I was in England at the time, nothing easier than for me to come to live in the district and to introduce myself to the Landlesses. I went with the purpose of discovering how and when the gallant Colonel Landless was going to make his move against the Corsairs. I stayed to worship his ravishing, most exquisite, and lewdly licentious wife."

"That isn't me!" she cried. "You're speaking of someone else!"

He paused in his stride, then pointed to her.

"I will hold up the mirror and show you to yourself before this night is done," he told her. "In my arms this night, you will discover your own self—the self that, released by the power of the drug you imbibed in Algiers, spent itself for my delight and for yours."

"No!" she cried. "Never! It isn't true!"

He took a swift stride toward her. Seizing her by the wrist with one hand, with the other he ripped her bodice to the waist, baring her splendid breasts and the dimpled mound of her firm belly. And he laughed when she tried to cover herself.

"I will tell you of those nights when you pleasured me, my Purity," he said. "I will tell you how, unprompted and unasked, you devoured my body with your soft lips, how your slender fingers enticed me to perform the most delicious and supremely immodest acts upon your own. It is all within you, my Purity. There is no hiding from your true nature—which is that of a libertine."

She shook her head, numb with horror, staring up into the unmasked face of he whom she had otherwise known as the Reverend Honorable Mr. Bevis Mauleverer. She willed him to cease with the obscenities that poured from those pale, once ascetic lips.

He had outraged her mind. Her body, though still

half-bared to his gaze, was as yet undefiled by his touch. And now he was continuing his frenzied pacing up and down the chamber while she watched and listened.

He was talking about himself. . . .

"I was born the third son of a viscount. Third son —ha! You, who have yourself had experience with the English laws of primogeniture, will know what that means: the firstborn takes all. There is no escaping one's fate. The law that governs the offspring of the English aristocracy is as immutable as the law of the jungle. My first brother took the title and the estates, my second brother went into the army, and I was destined for the Church. I could have starved, of course, but I chose not to.

"I was a brilliant scholar, and without any effort. My entire effort was devoted to more *amusing* pursuits. I was debauched by an older boy for whom I drudged at Eton. The same fellow, when we were up at Oxford together, persuaded me to be a founding member of a secret society he was forming at the university. An excellent, lusty society it was, based on the precepts of the Hellfire Club, famed in song and story. On Mondays we held black mass with a nude virgin for sacrifice. To tell the truth, as often as not she was a strumpet from an Oxford alehouse passing for a virgin. On Tuesdays and Wednesdays we played a sex-and-pleasure version of ring-of-roses with a strumpet for every Jack. Thursdays were free. On Fridays we'd snatch a girl, any girl, from off the streets, take her back to our rooms, and rape her. It cost us a pretty penny, always, to placate her afterward. But one learns cynicism in the raping game; one learns that every woman has her price. That brings me to Saturdays. Now, when I tell you what we did on Saturdays . . . "

"You disgust me!" cried Purity. "And you posing as a man of the cloth!"

"I *am* a man of the cloth!" he cried. "Taught. Examined. Ordained. That was what my noble family demanded of me, and it was a simple matter to oblige them. I left Oxford with a fellowship and every cash prize that could be won. With the money, I went to North Africa, but not, I hasten to add, to spread light among the heathens there."

"You went into the slave trade!" She could scarcely bring herself to utter the hateful words.

His eyes flashed. How could she have ever thought that he was a mild and gentle person?

"You should have known those days, my Purity!" he cried. "The fortunes we made—all of us! All through the war years! Even the Royal Navy was pleased to come to terms with us, the Corsairs. In the war, it saved their patrolling frigates a lot of hard work if they paid protection money against our molesting their merchantmen, but always on condition that we continued to harass the French—which we were pleased to do. Within the first year, the single galley that I had bought with my prize monies became one of a fleet of three. I had everything I had ever wanted in my life: power, riches, women—any woman I desired . . . even you, my Purity."

"By force of blackmail," she whispered.

"At first," he conceded. "You came here, as you came to Algiers, to save Mark Landless. Tonight, when I have finished with you, you will not care if Mark Landless lives or dies. You will be all mine."

"You are insane!" she cried. "Insane!"

He shook his head. "Not so, my Purity," he said mildly. "These are not the empty ravings of a madman. I will explain. While in Cairo, during my early days as a Corsair, I was brought to see an incredibly ancient man—an adept of a cult that was descended from the days of the Ptolemies, who embraced the decadent cults of old Greece, the worshippers of Aphrodite, goddess of carnal love. Before my astonished eyes, this man—he must have been going on a hundred—pleasured no less than three women in turn. They were young and vigorous women, with bodies made for pleasuring. I saw them writhing with ecstasy under the assault of that incredible old man, saw them moaning with contentment and sweet pleasure when he had finished with them. I resolved to discover the old man's secret and, if possible, to have it for myself. Accordingly, I paid the price—and it was considerable—to become his pupil in the ancient arts of Aphrodite. The way to truth was long and thorny, the disciplines so grueling as to be sometimes too hard to bear, so that I would resolve to abandon the attempt. But always I had a vision of a woman, a woman of impossible beauty, lying in my arms, writhing with the fire of wild ecstasy. So I persisted in the disciplines, and I became an adept."

Purity regarded him with apprehension. She felt her skin prickle and her nipples pucker and harden. She seemed to hear, as from afar, poor Nancy Shaw's often repeated declarations about the man known as El Diablo. Nancy had feared him, hated him, even, but she had not swerved from her fixed devotion to the lover who came first in her desires.

She recalled the words of Azizza, she who never permitted any man save he to know her a second time.

"I am afraid of you," she whispered.

"Cast out all fear," he said. "You are the vision come to life—the woman of impossible beauty who inspired me when my footsteps wavered along the long and thorny path to the truth. I will set you free from the love that keeps you shackled to the earth. I will carry you on the wings of passion to the outer stars."

He reached out for her. Purity retreated from him till her bare back came in contact with the cold tiles of the wall.

"No-o-o-o!" she pleaded.

"The whole world will be yours, my Purity," he said. "Listen, my Purity, after this night, the Corsairs will be reborn. The matter is all but completed and needs only a final agreement of the parties involved. Next year there will be a fresh Corsair fleet in Egypt, in Alexandria. Have you heard of Mohammed Ali? Appointed as viceroy of Egypt by the Turks, he has risen to be the ruler of that country. Mohammed Ali needs one thing above all: he needs a navy. He will not mind if that navy engages itself in the slave trade in times of peace. He will not withhold his protection just because the ships are captained by Corsairs and paid for by a small group of influential and wealthy Englishmen."

His hands were upon her, doing unbelievably beguiling things to her yielding flesh.

"Please, please!" she moaned.

"A year, two years, and the riches of the Orient will be mine, my Purity. I shall be made a pasha, a prince of that country, rich beyond the dreams of avarice. You shall be my princess."

The last of her flimsy garment was falling from her hips. His hands encircled her smooth flanks, drawing her close to him. His robe had come open, and he was naked beneath. Her mind was reeling. Her thoughts reached desperately for something—anything—on which to anchor herself to reality. She tried to assemble the image of Mark's face, but nothing would materialize.

In the meantime, the seductive voice was mouthing

in her ear: "Surrender to me, my Purity. Surrender, and I will show you all the glories of creation. I will draw aside the veil and reveal to you the mysteries of the outer world. In my arms, I will transport you to paradise. The power that lies within my loins will carry you beyond madness to the supreme truths of life and death."

"No!" she protested. "No!"

But her resolve was slipping away, and the power of his body was overwhelming her. His hands—surely the most practiced and beguiling hands ever to touch her nakedness—were destroying her will.

By his next words, he sensed his coming victory: "As the lotus opens to the sun, so shall you open to me, my Purity. I will take you and make you whole, and when that is done you will be free.

"When you have known me, when you have drunk of my power, you will never find pleasure in any other living man. *If I were to tell you to take a knife and plunge it into the breast of Mark Landless, you would do it gladly!*"

"*No!*"

It was like a great tree falling upon a frozen lake, shattering the vast carpet of ice into uncounted fragments and freeing the life within it. Starkly into her mind came the vision she had striven to conjure up: the image of Mark's face.

With a cry, she twisted herself free of him, fighting her way from his questing fingers, his demanding maleness.

"Never!" she screamed in his suddenly astonished face. "I will never surrender to you! Rape me if you will, but you will never have me by reason of persuasion! And you will never drive out the love I bear for Mark Landless! Never!"

"I have need of you!" he cried. "Tonight is destined to be the climax of all my plans. To prepare myself, I must drink deeply of a woman's body. I must drink of yours!"

She leaned back against the wall, her arms spread wide, helpless, yet defiant.

"Then you must take me," she said calmly. "My body you may possess. My soul and my love are my own."

A fire of fury blazed in his pale eyes. "In the devil's name, that I will do!" he cried. He tore the robe from his shoulders, rendering himself as nude as she.

"Leave her be!"

The command came from the doorway. Purity turned to behold the tall figure of Robert Gladwyn, dressed in medieval costume of jerkin, hood, and hose. He was unmasked, and there was a sword at his hip.

"Robbie!"

Uncaring about his nakedness before the other man, the creature who called himself The Devil folded his arms and gazed sneeringly at the newcomer.

"So, it's the knight in shining armor," he drawled, "the gentle, perfect Mr. Gladwyn, without fear and without reproach. What, are you going to prevent me having my way with your so-called wife, do you think?"

"I will prevent you, Mauleverer," said Gladwyn evenly.

"You—a coward?"

"Even I—a coward—will prevent you."

With a laugh, Mauleverer darted across the room to where, above the mantelpiece, there were crossed sabers and a Moorish shield. He snatched down one of the swords. The lamplight winked from its polished blade as he flourished it.

"I should tell you, Gladwyn," he said, "that I

learned my swordsmanship from the finest masters in
Toledo. Are you still determined to die?"

"Robbie, no!" cried Purity.

Gladwyn smiled across at her, nude as she stood
against the wall. He drew his own blade from its
scabbard.

"I am ready for you, Mauleverer," he said. "On
guard!"

The naked man took swift strides across the room,
his point advanced. Purity gave an involuntary intake
of breath as he made a vicious cut to Gladwyn's head.
Their blades met with a clash.

"I am not entirely untutored, Mauleverer," murmured Robert Gladwyn.

The meeting of steel on steel had the tune of bells,
the labored breathing of the two men providing a
counterpoint, the shuffling of their feet as they advanced and retired being a continuous descant. Purity watched, sick with horror and apprehension. It
seemed to her that Robert, being the taller, had
a distinct advantage over his opponent, but that
Mauleverer, shorter and more lithe, was able to move
more quickly. Moreover, being naked, he was unencumbered.

Back and forth they battled, cutting and thrusting.
Gladwyn made a vigorous assault, driving the other
before him, out of the doorway, and into the colonnaded chamber beyond. There, with ample room in
which to maneuver, the fighters' movements became
broader, more perilous looking to the eyes of the distraught onlooker. Purity followed their progress down
the long chamber and back again, circling the dolphin
fountain, dodging in and out of the tall columns . . .
cut, slash, advance, riposte. And now Mauleverer was
visibly tiring. A rivulet of sweat descended the cleft
of his bare chest. He it was who took the first cut—

a badly deflected feint to the right shoulder caused Robert Gladwyn's blade to nick his forearm, and a splash of crimson fell upon the tiled floor.

He's winning, Robbie's winning, Purity told herself as she pressed herself against a stone column to allow the two men to move past her, blade ringing against blade.

And then, looking to one side as a movement caught her eye, she saw Azizza. . . .

The she-Corsair had entered the chamber unnoticed by the duelists and their onlooker. Purity, hidden from the newcomer by the column, was not more than three paces from her. Azizza had a pistol, which she was aiming at Robert Gladwyn's back.

"Robbie! Look out!" Purity screamed the warning.

Gladwyn half-turned, failed to parry a thrust, then seemed to flinch and cry out. Purity was already leaping forward, hands extended, as Azizza's finger tightened on the trigger. The pistol discharged an instant after Purity collided with the other woman. It was a shocking blossoming of terrible sound that shut out everything else.

Purity reeled back. Azizza was screaming, pointing in horror at the nude figure of the man who spun like a discarded doll and toppled headlong into the pool.

"My God, I've killed him! I've killed El Diablo!"

The waters were still. There was only the gentle sprinkling of the fountain that spewed from the open mouth of the dolphin. The nude figure was floating, face down. From it issued a thick jet of crimson that spread quickly in the clear water.

There was the madness of despair in the cat-green eyes of the woman Corsair. She was unmasked, and her too-perfect countenance was suffused with hatred. She pointed a finger at Purity.

"It was you who killed him—*you!*" she mouthed.

"From first to last, you have brought nothing but disaster upon us. Well, now you will pay—and in coin that will destroy you, also!"

Turning, she ran the length of the chamber.

Purity looked to Robert Gladwyn for help and counsel, and she was shocked to see him leaning back against one of the columns, his sword arm hanging limply, his left hand pressed to his side. There was blood welling between his fingers.

"Robbie! You're hurt!"

"Go after her!" called Gladwyn. "Follow her, Purity! Quickly!"

"But your wound!"

"Go!"

His urgency communicated itself to her. With one last glance at his white, pain-racked face, she went in pursuit of the woman Corsair.

Beyond the chamber was a staircase leading down. She could see Azizza's hand upon the railing as the other woman descended, still running. She was not far behind.

Pursuer and pursued, the one in silver armor, the other nude to the skin, they raced through the echoing rooms of the mansion while, from afar, there came the continuous sounds of revelry, the lilt of strings and drum, the rhythm of dancing feet.

Azizza had led them to the ground floor. Through a long line of windows, Purity could see a dark garden with overhanging trees, a hint of starlight above. They had come to a long, empty chamber with a door at the far end. And it was there that Azizza halted and faced her pursuer, hatred and defiance in her eyes. And something else: Was it triumph?

"A life for a life," she said. "Yours was the hand that guided the bullet that killed the only man who ever touched the heart of Azizza. Now I will kill *your* man!"

"What are you saying?" shouted Purity.

For answer, Azizza took from between her silver-covered breasts a key on the end of a ribbon. She then indicated the door behind her.

"He is in there," she said.

"You mean *Mark?*"

Azizza nodded. Replacing the key, she unwound from her slender waist a silk scarf of the same silvery sheen as her breastplate. She wound it between her two hands, stretching it wide.

"He is bound and helpless," she said. "Have you ever throttled a man, my dear? Of course you haven't. It is really quite simple. One encircles the throat, draws tight the scarf, chokes off the breath, then watches the victim fighting vainly for his life. I have done it many times. I never saw a man die well of the throttling. Your Mark will die badly, I promise you."

"No, you shall not!" cried Purity. "You shall not harm him, you she-devil!"

Azizza bared her white teeth in a grin of savagery. "You are going to try and prevent me," she hissed. "Nothing would give me greater pleasure." Reaching to her shoulder, she unfastened a latch that held together the two parts of her armored corselet, back and breast; she let them fall to the floor. Unencumbered, her splendid bosom jounced free, a fleshly replica of the silvered armor. "Now I am ready for you, my dear," she said, advancing on Purity, with the silken scarf held before her, stretched between her hands.

They fought, flank to flank, belly to belly, finger-nails and teeth. Purity, evading Azizza's early attempt to wind the throttling scarf around her neck, snatched at the ribbon that secured the key that hung between her opponent's breasts. The ribbon snapped, and the key tinkled away against the wainscoting.

They fought standing, till the lithesome Corsair, winding one leg around Purity's, tripped her headlong and fell with her. Flesh against flesh, slippery with their mingled sweat, they rolled together on the floor, fighting for supremacy, fighting for life, for love, for hatred.

As if in a dream, far off, Purity was translated back to another time, another place, where she had wrestled with another woman's nude body, in passion. She tasted Cora's sweat as she was tasting Azizza's, felt the weight, the roundness, the fullness of Cora, as she was now feeling the body of Azizza upon her. But in place of gentleness, there was now violence; fingernails now raked at her breasts, where Cora had rained kisses. . . .

She screamed.

Her cry was answered from afar: "Mrs. Gladwyn! Is that you, ma'am?"

The weight of Azizza's nudity was lifted from Purity. Snatching up a rag of her nether clothing, the she-Corsair raced across the chamber.

"Mrs. Gladwyn!" The call was repeated—nearer.

Purity rolled over on one elbow and looked across to where Azizza was flinging open a French window that let out upon the dark garden. She saw her pose there, nude, breathless, hate-filled, vengeful. Defeat had not quenched Azizza's spirit, nor had it tamed the leopardess that lived within her olive-skinned body.

"Never forget me, Purity!" she hissed. "Waking or sleeping, I shall never forget you, that I promise! And one day I shall come back into your life! Remember me!"

Then she was gone.

The clatter of running footsteps came close, and a stream of men issued into the chamber. Wellington's tall figure was well to the fore. Seeing the naked figure sprawled on the floor, he stripped off his tailcoat and advanced toward Purity with it held out before him.

"Mrs. Gladwyn, ma'am, thank heaven we have found you," he said, "and unharmed, I pray. There has been bad business afoot this night—bad business, indeed."

There was a dark bruise upon his lordship's brow.

"Are you badly hurt, Your Grace?" asked one of his companions.

"I had my progress checked by a dark-faced devil with a cudgel," replied Wellington, "but a straight left to the jaw cut *his* strength."

Two men were carrying in the Bashi-bazouk, whose head lolled.

"The devil's still unconscious, my lord," said someone.

"He will recover in time to hang at the Newgate gallows," retorted Wellington dryly. "Ma'am, might one inquire for what you are searching down there on the floor?"

Purity was on her knees, scrabbling with her fingers along the dark wainscoting till they closed around the key. All her being, her life, her reason, and her awareness hung in a limbo as she put the key in the lock of the door, turned it, flung open the door, and stepped into a darkened room.

A figure was slumped in an armchair by the fireplace, head back, eyes closed. Heavy ropes were lashed around his chest, wrists, and ankles. He was not gagged. There was no need for it—the stench of common ether hung heavily in the room.

Purity ran to him and fell on her knees beside him,

her frantic hands already fighting with the tightly bound knots that held him fast, looking up as she did so into the drugged face, her whole being melting with love and compassion to see the cruel scar that still marred his forehead.

"Mark, my darling, Mark!" Purity whispered.

He stirred. She, standing on the edge of eternity, watched and wondered as his eyelids flickered open and his eyes lit upon her—not with the bemused gaze of the insane, but with the light of intelligence.

"Purity, my dearest, my wife," whispered Mark Landless in return.

They had carried Robert Gladwyn to a quiet room on the upper floor, laid him on a bed, and made some attempt at caring for his wound. There was a surgeon with him when Purity entered. She looked questioningly at the man, who was white haired, gray faced, and had the air of one whose constant companion was death. He shook his head and walked out of the room, leaving her alone with the figure on the bed.

She drew close to him. His eyes were open, and she smiled to see her, his hand seeking hers. His hand was very cold.

"I have been such a fool," he said, "Such a very bad conspirator. Will you ever forgive me, Purity?"

"You came here to protect me," she said. "You dressed in that absurd costume, put on a mask, and came here to watch over me and make sure no harm came to me. Oh, my dearest, dearest Robbie."

"I am such a fool," he said. "I knew nothing, suspected nothing, till I recognized that glove upon your hand. After that, I decided that Madame Avanti must have been Azizza, after all. You know, Purity, I really thought at one time that she had blackmailed you into killing young Wainwright."

"I might have done as much to save Mark," she said. "Robbie, he's still alive. Mark's alive—and well."

"I'm so very glad," said Gladwyn, "so glad for you both, Purity."

The talking seemed to have tired him, for he closed his eyes and was silent for a while.

Then he opened his eyes and spoke again. "You know my secret," he said. "I think you went to my father's old military chest that day and unearthed my dreadful secret."

"It was Wainwright who prompted me," said Purity. "My dear, I am so sorry. Poor Robbie. You never even bothered to lock the chest, never suspected that an unscrupulous servant and a faithless wife would so betray your trust as to pry into your past."

"It was cowardice," he said. "Mauleverer learned it from somewhere, did he not? The secret was not well kept, despite the document my fellow officers so carefully concocted. One man talked. I was mysteriously blackballed from several clubs. It scarcely matters now. . . ." His voice trailed away.

"You are no coward, Robbie," she whispered. "You proved that tonight."

"It was in India," he said "near Seringapatam. The Marathas were in revolt and our regiment was ordered to the attack. We were ambushed. They came out of the dawn, their swords swinging. I saw one of them take off the head of one of my men. I never saw a man beheaded before. It was not so much fear as it was astonishment. I needed time to think, to comprehend the awfulness of it. They said that I ran. I think I must have run. . . ."

"Shh!" said Purity gently. "It doesn't matter now.

All that is in the past, forgotten. Tonight you were a
hero. The boy who ran away was part of another lifetime."

His hand was very limp within hers, and his voice
was fading.

"I have loved you from the first," he said. "And I
was glad and happy to be your friend and protector.
Knowing you still loved Mark's memory, I could not
bring myself to make any demands . . . " He broke
off as a racking cough brought a thin trickle of blood
from the corner of his mouth.

"If you had come to me, I would have given myself gladly," said Purity. "For you are what you have
always been—my loving, giving, undemanding friend."

"Purity, are you still there?" he whispered.

"Yes, Robbie, yes!" She felt her throat contract, and
his face was lost in the sudden blindness of her tears.

She was still holding his hand in the thin, chill
dawn when some of Wellington's aides came and
sought her out and led her away, offering her what
solace they were able to. And someone had the good
sense to cover Robert Gladwyn's serene, dead face.

The prince regent's birthday fell on August 12, and
it was on that date of the following year that Colonel
Mark Landless and his wife were invited to attend a
reception at the Royal Pavilion, Brighton. It was an
invitation of which they availed themselves, traveling
from Clumber to Sussex in company with little
Chastity and her nurse, and residing for a week in
Brighton at a small house that Landless had lately
purchased in the Steyne for use during vacations at
the vastly popular seaside resort. (Upon Mark's return
to life, his mental faculties fully restored, all his lands
and properties had reverted to him, and the abomi-

nable Finch-Landlesses had returned to whatever limbo they had come from.)

The Royal Pavilion, built for His Highness by John Nash at the close of the Napoleonic wars, was a tasteless confection of varied architectural styles, which, by its very ostentation and vulgarity, transcended mere taste and was a delight to the eye. On that August afternoon, Purity and Mark, together with Chastity and her nursemaid, walked the mere hundred yards from their house to the princely pleasure dome, all in the glorious sunshine. They received by liveried majordomos, gentlemen-in-attendance, Guards officers, and the like. They were ushered into the Chinese interior, with its lacquer and bamboo furniture, its Oriental wallpaper, columns designed to look like palm trees, most fantastical chandeliers. Then they were deposited in the care of the Duke of Wellington. Old Nosy was in the full dress uniform of a British field marshal and looking distinctly jaundiced with the proceedings. Nevertheless, he greeted his former aide and his wife with considerable warmth.

"Wonderful to see you, ma'am, and you, too, my dear Landless. There's bad business here today, bad business. But we must suffer it in silence, I fear." His lordship looked about him. The famous yellow drawing room was packed with the highest in the land—or with such of the highest who were in the regent's favor. Purity experienced a chill to see the debauched countenance of the Earl of Lawme among those waiting for Prinny's appearance. Her glance and her reaction were not lost on Wellington.

"They are all here," he said, "every last one—a true gathering of the rascals. But, as I have said, since there's nothing to be done about it, we must suffer in silence."

"Were they *really* involved in the slave trade?" asked Purity.

"Undoubtedly," replied Wellington. "General Gordon Maunders, before they killed him, told me all he knew. They were all in it together: Lawme, Clonmel, Whatten-Findley, and the rest. There was to have been a meeting that night, you know, the night of the ball. The conspiracy would have been signed, sealed, and delivered to back a new Corsair fleet in Egypt with ten million in English gold. Mauleverer had 'em all in the palm of his hand. Would you credit it—that a country parson could have made such a clatter? Makes one think one should examine the credentials of every damned parson in the land. Here comes the prince regent."

A string ensemble of the prince's own Hussars regiment struck up the lively cords of the national anthem, and the royal lecher waddled into the yellow drawing room with a group of courtiers in his wake. He bowed right and left to the obeisances of his insane father's subjects, progressing the length of the room till he came to a throne and footstool set at the far end. A splattering of heralds in bright tabards stood there, one of them bearing a sheathed sword, another a scroll of parchment from which he read in a sonorous voice.

"The Right Honorable Earl of Lawme," he mouthed, "for services to the Crown."

"For services to the regent's reputation," muttered Wellington, *sotto voce*, in Purity's ear. "He gets a knighthood for suppressing the fact that Prinny himself had shares in the Corsair conspiracy."

Lawme stepped forward, knelt before the stout figure by the footstool, and was tapped on each shoulder by the drawn sword, to arise with another not inconsiderable title to add to those he already owned. Next came the Duke of Clonmel, and after him Lord Peter

Whatten-Findley—all the major conspirators in the affair that had ended with Mauleverer's death and Azizza's disappearance. All knighted.

"Colonel Mark Landless!" declared the herald.

"The only honor deserved here today," declared the Duke of Wellington, scarcely troubling to keep his voice down. "Well done, Landless."

Purity's eyes brimmed with tears of pride and little Chastity jumped up and down with pure delight as Mark Landless strode forward and faced the regent.

"Colonel Mark Landless, for services rendered in Algeria during the late troubles," intoned the herald.

The royal voluptuary tapped Mark on each shoulder with the bright blade.

"Arise, Sir Mark Landless," he commanded.

The reception and bestowing of honors had gone on till six, at which time the assembled company sat down to a dinner of ten courses, a notable feast that lasted till ten o'clock and was terminated by the prince regent being reduced to such a state of inebriation that he had to be carried out by a pair of footmen and put to bed. Afterward, the string ensemble played music for dancing in the blue drawing room. There were long lines of ladies and gentlemen, glittering in their splendid jewelry and silks, orders and uniforms.

Mark and Purity advanced to each other, joined hands, bowed and curtsied, then whispered to each other.

"I want you."

"I want you."

"When?"

"Now. Why wait?"

Sedately, hand in hand, they left the ballroom and went out into the soft-scented night. Little Chastity had long since been taken home by her nursemaid.

The lights burned in the windows of their house in the Steyne. But it was toward the seafront that their footsteps were turned, down to the pebbled Brighton beach and the long lines of breakers, phosphorescent in the moonlight.

They embraced down by the water's edge, their mouths joined in passion, his hands already slipping the silken gown from her shoulders, baring her milk-white orbs for his delighted kisses, while, with hands that trembled with radiant anticipation, she was already stripping the shirt from his back, then fumbling with the waistband of his breeches. Nude at last, they kissed through a lifetime of bliss, and then, gathering her up into his arms, he bore her into the sea, carrying her, breast deep, into the clean, cool foam.

"Tonight I shall conceive, my Mark," she whispered close against his ear above the roar of the breakers. "Tonight you will give me a son. I know it."

"And we shall call him Robert."

"Yes, oh, yes—Robert he shall be."

The joined in the deep water, and Purity was gathered up by his hands, into the ecstasy that lies beyond comprehension and into worlds unimaginable and delights that known no ending.